The Tycoons

Every woman's fantasy!

The Greek Tycoons

THE SECRET WIFE
by
Lynne Graham

NO GENTLE SEDUCTION
by
Helen Bianchin

PASSION BECOMES YOU
by
Michelle Reid

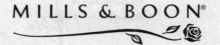

MILLS & BOON®

*MILLS & BOON and MILLS & BOON with the Rose Device
are registered trademarks of the publisher.
Harlequin Mills & Boon Limited,
Eton House, 18-24 Paradise Road, Richmond, Surrey, TW9 1SR*

THE GREEK TYCOONS
© by Harlequin Enterprises II B.V., 2001

The Secret Wife, No Gentle Seduction and *Passion Becomes You* were
first published in Great Britain by Harlequin Mills & Boon Limited in
separate, single volumes.

The Secret Wife © Lynne Graham 1997
No Gentle Seduction © Helen Bianchin 1991
Passion Becomes You © Michelle Reid 1994

ISBN 0 263 82771 2

05-0104

*Printed and bound in Spain
by Litografia Rosés S.A., Barcelona*

Lynne Graham was born in Northern Ireland and has been a keen Mills & Boon® reader since her teens. She is very happily married with an understanding husband, who has learned to cook since she started to write! Her five children keep her on her toes. She has a very large dog, which knocks everything over, a very small terrier which barks a lot and two cats. When time allows, Lynne is a keen gardener.

Look out for
THE BANKER'S CONVENIENT WIFE
by Lynne Graham
coming soon from
Mills & Boon Modern Romance™.

THE SECRET WIFE
by
LYNNE GRAHAM

CHAPTER ONE

HER heart beating like a drum, Rosie crept into the church when the rush was over, sliding into a pew near the back to listen to the memorial service from a safe distance. Anton Estrada had been well-known in the city of London. The dim interior was crammed to capacity with those who wished to pay their last respects.

A black gold-embroidered scarf covering her bowed head, Rosie shivered, lost in the dark well of her grief. As far back as she could remember she had been alone, but for a few agonisingly brief months she had had Anton. And now he was gone, that warm, laughing man, who had called her the joy he had waited for all his life and the greatest love of his existence. Tears shimmering in her shadowed green eyes, she stared down at the huge ornate emerald on her finger until it blurred out of focus. Well, who would love her now? she thought painfully. Who indeed would ever love her like that again?

The silence and the soft murmur of voices finally penetrated. In a daze, she glanced up and realised that the service was over and the church was almost empty again. Disconcerted by her loss of concentration, she flew upright and headed for the exit. A corner of her scarf caught on the end of a pew, jerking her head back, making her stumble.

She would have fallen but for the strong, masculine hand that came out of nowhere to close round her slender forearm and steady her. 'Are you all right?' a dark, honey-rich drawl enquired and her lush dark lashes fluttered in momentary bemusement as the fleeting familiarity of accented English washed over her and filled her with unbelievable pain. 'Perhaps you should sit down again—'

'No…' Riven with tension, Rosie straightened and broke free of that male grasp. Forgetting that her scarf was caught, she barely felt the pull as it trailed off and freed the wild, tumbling mass of her Titian hair from confinement. Involuntarily, she glanced up and froze in stark horror, her breath snarled up in her throat, her beautiful face stiffening like pale, tear-streaked marble into stricken stillness. Sheer shock slowed her heartbeat to a numbing thud that echoed sickly in her eardrums.

Constantine Voulos stared down at her, apparently entrapped by the same immobility that paralysed her. He *was* gorgeous, even more gorgeous than he had looked in Anton's photographs, Rosie registered helplessly. Luxuriant black hair, stunning bone structure and a wide, wickedly sensual mouth. A wave of dizziness engulfed her as she collided with mesmeric dark deep-set eyes. Her bemused gaze locked with compulsive intensity to his. It was as terrifying as walking off a cliff-edge and falling…and falling…and falling. She couldn't breathe and she couldn't speak. It panicked her.

'Who are you?' he murmured thickly, in one fluid movement drawing closer again as he tugged her scarf free and extended it to her.

Rosie turned white as death and backed off on legs that were ready to buckle, a dark, ferocious wave of violent and confused emotion consuming her. Constantine Voulos, the child whom Anton and his Greek wife, Thespina, had raised as their own.

'Your scarf…'

Jerkily, reluctantly, she reached out to the child who had become a man. It was a mistake. He caught her thin, trembling fingers in his.

'*Please…*' Rosie gasped, attempting to break the connection, her slim body already twisting on the brink of flight, panic currenting through her.

'*Christos!*' Constantine vented in raw disbelief as he recognised the antique emerald adorning her hand. 'Where did you get that ring?'

Astonished recognition had made him temporarily loosen his grip. Rosie snatched her fingers back and raced down the steps. The wintry breeze caught her curling torrent of hair and the long, loose black coat, making them flow out behind her like wings as she broke through the lingering groups of people outside and flew across the busy road, indifferent to the screeching brakes and honking horns that accompanied her dangerous passage.

Rosie wandered one last time round the silent rooms. Without Anton's larger-than-life presence the pretty little house was an empty shell. Having eradicated every scrap of evidence that she had ever lived within these walls, she would slam the door behind her and walk back into her own world. It couldn't have lasted much longer anyway, she told herself.

She cherished her freedom, yet she had allowed Anton to clip her wings. He had stubbornly persuaded and pressurised and finally pleaded until she'd surrendered and moved in, willing to compromise, wanting to be what he wanted her to be if that pleased him…but always knowing that sooner or later she would be forced to rebel.

'I am an independent spirit,' she had said to him gently once.

'Your independence was forced on you and it was a most unnatural responsibility for a young girl to carry,' Anton had countered with staunch disapproval. 'You no longer need to bear that responsibility now that I am here.'

And she had laughed and argued but not very hard, wryly aware that he could not begin to understand the life she had led or the background she came from any more than she could really comprehend *his* and that it would upset him if she were too honest. So they had built a bridge across the great divide of wealth and culture by making careful allowances on both sides, and ironically it had been remarkably easy for right from the beginning there had been this amazing sense of mutual recognition.

She had been lucky to have that much, she reflected painfully. Four months of perfect happiness was more than some people achieved in a lifetime. Four months of being loved passionately, unconditionally, selflessly. Good memories had taken the edge off the bad ones. She swallowed the thickness of tears in her throat and smiled with sudden brilliance. Nobody could take those memories away. Or the ring that had been in the Estrada family for two centuries, the single surviving heirloom which Anton had slid onto her finger with unashamed tears in his dark eyes.

'Now it will be worn again for only now is it where it truly belongs.'

Rosie recalled Constantine's outraged incredulity when he had recognised that ring and a humourless laugh escaped her. So I accepted one little memento; think yourself lucky, Constantine Voulos, for had I been greedy I could have taken far more! Because Anton had wanted to lay the world at her feet. His joy and pride in her had dangerously overwhelmed every other loyalty. That was the only thing they had ever argued about.

And Rosie was guiltily conscious that it had been a struggle to keep her conscience in control. It hadn't been his wealth that had made her feel like that; she simply couldn't imagine *having* that kind of money. No, it had been the squirming attacks of resentment which she had fought to conceal, knowing just how much those feelings would have distressed him. But she was human, fallible, as capable as anyone else of thinking self-pitying thoughts and experiencing envy.

At the age of nine, Constantine Voulos had lost his parents in a car accident. Anton and Thespina had taken Constantine into their home and brought him up as if he were their own child. It had never occurred to Anton that Rosie might resent his constant references to his substitute son's innumerable virtues and talents, only to despise herself for the unreasoning injustice of such childish promptings.

The silence began to get to Rosie. She shivered at the echo of her own footsteps. She *should* have cleared out the day Anton had died but she had been in such shock she had simply stopped functioning. Only six weeks earlier, a mild heart attack had put him into hospital. She had been first at his bedside, reluctantly torn from him only when she'd realised that Thespina and Constantine were already on their way from the airport.

'Stay…to hell with them all!' Anton had grated recklessly, already inflamed by the nurse who had attempted to prevent her visit to his private room.

'You know you don't mean that. You can't do that to your wife,' Rosie had muttered tightly, her better self talking, her worse self bitter that she, who had more right than anyone, should have to fight her way in and then sneak her way out.

'You never use her name,' Anton had sighed heavily.

And she had flushed hotly, avoiding his gaze, too many complex emotions swirling about inside her, too much guilt, too much pain. Thespina had been his wife for over thirty years. A wonderfully loyal and loving wife, who had nonetheless been cruelly betrayed. And the simple fact that Thespina was unaware of that betrayal and indeed must be carefully protected from that

knowledge did not make the brick-wall barrier of her
very existence any more easy for Rosie to accept.

Rosie had slunk in and out of that hospital for an
entire week, her natural buoyance soon reasserting itself
to soothe her initially frantic fears about Anton's health.
He was only fifty-five. He had been working too hard.
Oh, they had talked endlessly about all the sensible
things he would have to do in the future! It had occurred
to neither of them that that future might be measured
only in weeks.

He had taken a convalescent cruise round the Greek
islands but on the same day that he'd flown back to
London again Anton had had a massive heart attack.
'Gone within minutes!' his secretary had sobbed down
the phone, still in shock. 'Who am I speaking to?' she
had asked then for Rosie had never rung his office before, but when Anton had failed to meet her for lunch
she had been worried sick.

Rosie had replaced the receiver in silence. Naturally
she could not attend his funeral in Greece. Sick to the
heart at her cruel exclusion, she had gone to the memorial service instead, only to run slap-bang into
Constantine Voulos through her own clumsy lack of attention. That encounter yesterday had appalled Rosie.
She should have packed her bags long ago and gone
home! But she had wanted privacy in which to come to
terms with the loss of the father she had known for so
painfully short a time.

'Rosalie...?'

Her heart lurched sickly against her breastbone, the
oxygen locking at the foot of her convulsed throat. She
jerked round in horror.

Constantine Voulos was standing on the landing outside her bedroom. He was breathing fast, his hard, strik-
ingly handsome features set in a dark mask of fury as
he moved towards her. 'That *is* your name, is it not?'

'What are you doing here?' Rosie gasped, her entire body turning cold and damp with instinctive fear. 'How did you get in?'

'You evil little vixen,' Constantine grated, his six-foot-three-inch all-male bulk blocking the doorway that was her only avenue of escape. He couldn't take his shimmering dark eyes off her. It was like being pinned to a wall by knives.

With enormous effort, Rosie straightened her slim shoulders and stood her ground but she was deathly pale. 'I don't know who you are or what you want—'

'You know exactly who I am!' Constantine slung at her, unimpressed, taking a frightening step closer.

'Stay away from me!' Rigid with tension, Rosie wondered frantically how he had found out about her and how much he knew.

'I wish I could...I really do wish that I could,' Constantine bit out with clenched fists, the explosive anger that emanated from him screaming along her nerve-endings like a violent storm warning.

Rosie retreated until the backs of her knees hit the divan bed. 'What do you w-want?'

'I want to wipe you off the face of this earth but I *cannot*...that is what inflames me! How did you persuade Anton to do something so insane?'

'Do...what?' she whispered blankly, too scared to be capable of rational thought.

'How did you persuade one of the most decent men I ever knew to sacrifice all honour and family loyalty?' Constantine seethed back at her.

'I don't know what you're talking about—'

'Don't you know what Anton did only days before his death?' Constantine demanded rawly, scanning the suitcase on the bed with a contemptuously curled lip. 'Have you any idea what his final words were before he died in my arms?'

Numbly, sickly, Rosie shook her head, a dense cloud of spiralling curls the colour of flames rippling round her rigid shoulders. She hadn't known that Constantine had been with her father when he died. Ironically that new knowledge brought a lump to her throat and warmed that cold place inside her as she thought of that dreadful day. Anton had not been alone but for his secretary. Constantine had been there, Constantine had been with him, and whether she liked it or not she knew just how much that would have meant to her father.

Constantine gave a great shout of raucous laughter that chilled her. Eyes black as night dug into her with unhidden repulsion. 'Every word which he struggled to speak related to *you!*'

'Oh…' Her stifled response barely broke the smouldering silence. And she heard his pain and didn't want to recognise it for what it was because she did not wish to admit that she could share *anything* with Constantine Voulos.

'He made me swear on my honour that I would protect you and respect his last wishes. But I didn't even know of your existence! I didn't understand who or even what he was referring to…nor did I know until last night *what* those last wishes were!' Constantine vented on another surge of barely contained rage that visibly tremored through his long, muscular length. 'He wrote a new will, and were it not for the fact that the publicity would destroy Thespina I would trail you through every court in Europe and crucify you for the greedy, calculating little vixen that you are before I would allow you to profit by a single drachma!'

'A *new* will?' Her teeth gritted as she withstood the lash of his insults. Hot, angry colour drove away her previous pallor. But at least she now understood what Constantine Voulos was doing here and why he was forcing such a confrontation. Evidently Anton had been

foolish enough to leave her something in his will in spite
of her fierce assurances that she wanted and needed
nothing.

His nostrils flared as he surveyed her with dark fury.
'Months ago, Thespina suspected that there was another
woman in his life. *Christos*…I actually laughed when
she shared her fears with me! I convinced her that it was
only the excitement of a new business venture which
was making Anton spend so much time in London. I
was naïve indeed. I underestimated the lure of youth and
beauty on even the most honourable of men. Anton was
obsessed with you…he died with your name on his lips!'

'He loved me,' Rosie mumbled helplessly, the acid
sting of tears burning behind her stricken eyes as she
turned defensively away.

'And I would lay my life on the line before I would
allow Thespina to endure that knowledge!' Constantine
growled rawly.

She understood then. Evidently Constantine Voulos
did *not* know who she was. He assumed that she was
the other woman, Anton's mistress cosily set up in the
proverbial love-nest. It was laughable but she couldn't
laugh. Her tremulous mouth compressed into a bloodless
line. Anton had kept their secret to protect his wife. A
twenty-one-year-old betrayal had gone to the grave with
him. She owed it to her father to keep faith with him.
The truth would only cause greater pain and distress and
for what gain?

She didn't need whatever Anton had left her. She had
her own life to lead and she had no desire to take possession of anything which more rightfully belonged to
her father's widow. That would be wrong, morally
wrong, she felt. The ring was different. It was her only
tangible link to a heritage and a background she had
lived all her life without.

'As you can see…I'm leaving.' Rosie lifted her bright

head high and surveyed the intimidatingly tall, dark Greek with bitter antipathy. 'You have nothing to worry about. I wasn't planning to hang around and embarrass anyone—'

'If it were that simple, we would not be having this distasteful meeting,' Constantine incised fiercely. 'I would be forcibly ejecting you from this house!'

Rosie vented a scornful laugh, her own hot temper steadily rising. 'Really?' she challenged.

He glanced at the open suitcase, his hard mouth twisting. 'You weren't leaving. Possibly you were planning a brief trip somewhere but nothing will convince me that you were about to make a final departure.'

Rosie dealt him a withering glance. 'My, aren't we self-important? What gives you the idea that I would waste my breath trying to convince you of anything?'

A dark surge of blood accentuated the savage slant of his dramatic cheekbones. Naked derision fired his dark eyes. 'I will not lower myself to the level of trading insults with a whore.'

Rosie had a sharp tongue which few attempted to match. She hadn't expected a provocative response. Thwarted fury stormed through her. 'Get out!' she launched at him abruptly. 'Just get out and leave me alone, you ignorant swine!'

'Not before you answer one question,' Constantine asserted in a sudden hiss as he stared broodingly back at her. 'Are you pregnant?'

Rosie stilled in shock, glancing down at the flowing swing blouse she was wearing and then intercepting his narrowed glance travelling in exactly the same direction. Her cheeks crimsoned.

'If you are pregnant...then and *only* then could I understand Anton's motivation,' Constantine conceded grudgingly, and yet he was perceptibly devastated by what his own imagination had suggested.

And only now had that possibility even occurred to him, Rosie registered, and boy, did the idea make him sick! That naturally golden skin had assumed an unhealthy pallor as presumably the implications of such a development sank in. This was how Constantine Voulos would have looked had she revealed her true relationship to Anton, Rosie realised with a sudden stab of satisfaction.

Few would deny that Anton's child, illegitimate or otherwise, might have some sort of claim on his estate. Had she chosen to tell the truth, Constantine would not have *dared* to insult her. She was Anton's daughter, his only child, the very last of the Estrada bloodline…and certainly not some calculating little gold-digger!

'You don't answer me.' Abruptly Constantine swung away and then he spun just as swiftly back, his strong features clenched and taut. 'If I have stumbled on the truth, my opinion of you is unchanged, but I should apologise for having approached you in such anger.'

Morbid amusement touched Rosie. He was backtracking fast on his offensive. Was he afraid of her now, afraid of the power she might have to disturb the smoothly planned future he no doubt envisaged for himself as sole controller of Anton's various business enterprises? The idea that she might be carrying Anton's child was a threat that shattered Constantine Voulos.

'But be assured,' he drawled flatly. 'Should there be a child, every possible test would be required to prove your claim.'

Rosie was helplessly entertained by the knots he was tying round himself. Having come up with his own worst-case scenario, he was forgetting the boundary lines he had mentioned earlier. 'But wouldn't that be terribly upsetting for Thespina?'

His breath escaped in a startled hiss, his eyes flashing ferocious gold. 'Your malice is indefensible…'

The instant Rosie had voiced the words she had wished to retrieve them, had realised too late how she would sound. For a moment she had longed to strike back at Thespina and Constantine and now she was bitterly ashamed of that spiteful prompting. She dropped her head, closed the case and tugged it down off the bed. 'I'm not pregnant. Go in peace, Constantine. I am not a threat to either you or Thespina,' she muttered heavily.

Downstairs the doorbell shrilled, breaking the pulsing tension within the bedroom.

'That'll be my cab.' Rosie moved past him with relief. Her knees felt wobbly but she was bolstered by a feeling of innate superiority. Her father had been wrong about Constantine, his ward and son in all but name. Constantine was not, after all, Mr Perfect—well, that was hardly a surprise, was it?

Anton had been naïve to imagine that Constantine would generously open his arms to his own natural child. Rosie had never paid much heed to her father's oft-repeated assurances that if Constantine was ever given the chance he would fall over himself to be welcoming to the sudden advent of a little sister…not that Anton had ever referred to her and Constantine in such gruesome terms as brother and sister!

No, instead Anton had talked with immense warmth and approval about 'family obligations…family support…family honour', blithely ignoring the fact that Rosie would sooner have put an end to her existence than become anyone's obligation! Furthermore she had been born a dyed-in-the-wool cynic.

Constantine had reacted exactly as she had expected to the idea that Anton might have fathered a child—with shock, horror and dismay as he foresaw what an expensive dent such a child might conceivably make in his own financial expectations. Feeling that she was a better person than Constantine Voulos because monetary greed had no hold on her, Rosie held her head high.

'Don't open that door!' Constantine suddenly bit out from behind her.

Rosie's head spun. He was halfway down the stairs, his diamond-bright gaze centred on her with ferocious intensity. 'What the—?'

'Quiet!' he whispered rawly, slashing an overpoweringly arrogant brown hand through the air in emphatic command.

With an exasperation she did not even seek to conceal, Rosie simply ignored his demand and yanked open the front door. Disorientatingly, however, it was not a cab driver who stood on the doorstep. Rosie blinked, gulped and froze.

A small, slim woman in a black suit stared at her in wide-eyed distress, every scrap of colour slowly fading from her olive skin. She took a hesitant step back and then stilled, a look of complete bewilderment drawing her brows together as Constantine's large dark frame appeared behind Rosie.

Faced with her late father's wife in the flesh, Rosie had stopped breathing. Not a muscle moved on her paralysed face as she struggled not to let her horror show. A heavy hand came down on her shoulder like an imprisoning chain of restraint. Constantine said something soft in Greek but Rosie could feel the savage tension holding his big, powerful body in tautly unnatural proximity to hers.

Without warning the older woman lifted her hand and gently caught Rosie's fingers, raising them to study the emerald which trapped the sunlight in its opulent green depths. 'The Estrada betrothal ring,' she whispered unevenly, and then she slowly shook her head in comprehension. 'Of course...Anton gave you the ring for *her!*

Constantine, how foolish I have been; I should have guessed…but why didn't you tell me?'

In receipt of that bemused appeal, Constantine inhaled sharply and Rosie felt his rigidity. 'It did not seem an appropriate time to make an announcement—'

'Only a man could believe that…as if the news that you are to marry would not bring me joy at *any* time!' Her face wreathed in a delighted smile, all her uncertainty and anxiety vanished, Thespina beamed appreciatively at Rosie. 'Exactly how long have you been engaged to my son?'

'Engaged?' Rosie echoed in a daze of disbelief, the pink tip of her tongue snaking out to moisten her dry lower lip.

'It is very recent,' Constantine drawled flatly.

'But you should have told me,' Thespina scolded in a troubled but tender undertone. 'How could you have believed that I would be distressed by your happiness? If you only knew what madness was in my thoughts as I came to this door—'

A taxi filtered noisily into the driveway. 'My cab,' Rosie muttered in stricken relief.

'You are leaving? But I have only just met you,' the older woman protested in surprise and disappointment.

'I'm afraid that Rosalie has a plane to catch and she's already running late,' Constantine slotted in inventively, closing a lean hand round Rosie's case before she could reach for it again and carrying it swiftly from the house, presumably to enable her to make a faster exit.

'Rosalie…that is a very…a very pretty name,' Thespina mused after an odd moment of hesitation, her eyes swiftly veiling before she glanced up again and continued with apparent warmth. 'Forgive me for arriving without an invitation but I shall look forward to spending time with you very soon.'

'I'm sorry I have to rush off like this,' Rosie mumbled

in a stifled voice, quite unable to meet the older woman's
eyes, twin spots of high colour highlighting her cheekbones.

Constantine already had the door of the cab open. She
sensed that if he had had access to supernatural forces a
smoking crater would have been all that survived of her
presence. But as she began to slide into the cab he
caught her with a powerful hand and lowered his arrogant dark head, diamond-hard eyes raking over her with
cold menace. 'We have business to discuss. When will
you be back?'

'Never.'

'You'll come back for the money all right,'
Constantine forecast between gritted teeth, the necessity
of keeping his voice down lest he be overheard by
Thespina clearly a major challenge to his self-control.
'Now I must force myself to bid you goodbye as a lover
would.'

'If you want a knee where it will really hurt, go
ahead,' Rosie invited with a venomous little smile and
scorching green eyes full of threat.

'*Theos...*' Constantine breathed rawly, his hard fingers
biting into her elbow. Bending down with a grim reluctance she could feel, he dropped a fleeting kiss on her
brow. One blink and she would have missed it.

Until he touched her, Rosie was as stiff as a little tin
soldier, and then she shivered, backed away and scram-
bled at speed into the cab. It drove off and she could
not even make herself look back or wave to add a re-
alistic note to his masquerade. Her heart was racing so
fast, she felt physically sick.

Her fingers clenched together tightly on her lap. She
felt the ring and she was furious with herself, for hadn't
she asked for what she had got and the trouble she had
caused? She should have moved out of the house the
instant she'd learnt of Anton's death! She should not
have openly worn the emerald either.

Her stomach cramped up. She saw Thespina's face as she had first seen it and repressed a shudder. At first Anton's widow had looked devastated. The older woman had somehow found out about the house and she had valiantly come to face whatever or whoever she found there. And, like Constantine, her intelligence had supplied only one possible explanation for Anton's surprising use of a second residence in London...that the husband she had loved and so recently lost had been keeping another woman.

Rosie felt horribly guilty. If Constantine hadn't been the sleek, sneaky type of male who thought fast on his expensively shod feet, what would have happened? If he hadn't pretended that he had given her the Estrada ring because they were engaged, what on earth would Anton's wife have thought?

The sheer intensity of Thespina's relief when she had believed she could lay both house and youthful redhead at Constantine's door rather than at her late husband's had been painful to behold. And her resulting sincere friendship had mortified Rosie. The art of deception was not one of her talents, even if in this case it had been a kindness to protect a woman who had never done anyone the smallest harm and who had already had more than her fair share of disappointment in life.

After all, Thespina had *not* been able to give Anton the child they had both so desperately wanted. One miscarriage after another had dashed their hopes. Only once had Thespina managed to carry a baby to term but the result had been a stillborn son, a shatteringly cruel and final blow to them after so many years of childlessness.

When Thespina had then sunk into deep depression, leaving Anton to struggle alone with his grief, their once strong marriage had begun to crumble. It had been during that period that Anton had been unfaithful with Rosie's mother, Beth... Rosie crushed that discomfiting awareness out. But it was, she discovered, difficult to forget Thespina again. Had they really managed to set the older woman's fears to rest? Had she been convinced?

Before she got on the train that would take her back to Yorkshire, Rosie found herself queuing for a public phone. She dialled the number of the house, praying that Constantine was still there. As soon as she heard his voice, she sucked in a deep breath and said stiffly, 'It's Rosie. Look, I meant what I said earlier. You can keep the money…OK?'

'What sort of a game are you playing?' Constantine launched back wrathfully down the line. 'You think I am impressed by this nonsense? Thespina's gone and we *have* to talk. If she hadn't arrived, I wouldn't have allowed you to leave. I want you back here right now!'

Rosie's teeth ground together. It wasn't as if she had even wanted to speak to Constantine Voulos again and she honestly didn't give two hoots about the money. That had only been her opening salvo, calculated to soothe. Her conscience had driven her to the phone. She felt bad about Thespina. She wanted reassurance that her father's widow hadn't smelled a rat in their performance and had her worst suspicions reawakened. 'I—'

'You think I have got all day to waste on a trashy little tart like you?' Constantine lashed in roaringly offensive contempt.

'Just *who* do you think you are talking to?' Rosie raked back at him, losing her own temper with a speed that left her dizzy. 'Some brain-dead bimbo you can abuse? Well, let me tell you, you overgrown creep, it takes more than a big loud mouth and a flashy suit to impress me and this is one trashy little tart who has no plans *ever* to cross your path again!'

Shaking with temper and mortification, Rosie crashed the phone back down on the cradle and grabbed up her case again, furious that she had put herself out to phone him. Talk about wasting the price of a call! She had got too soft. Anton had done that to her. He had mown down her prickly defences and challenged her to meet his trusting generosity with her own.

But now that her father was gone she could not afford that kind of weakness. This was the *real* world she was back in, not that sentimental, forever sunny place which Anton had cheerfully and somewhat naïvely inhabited. And being soft was only an open invitation to getting kicked in the teeth...

CHAPTER TWO

MAURICE strolled wearily into the kitchen. Well over six feet in height, he had shoulders like axe handles and a massive chest, but hard physical work had taxed even his impressive resources. His thick mane of long blond hair hung in a limp damp tangle round his rough-hewn features. 'Any chance you bought some beer while you were out shopping?'

Barely lifting her head from the grimy cooker she was scrubbing, Rosie threw him an incredulous glance. 'You've just got to be joking!'

'You can't *still* be mad at me.' Maurice treated her to a look of pained male incomprehension. 'You should have phoned. If I'd had some warning that you were coming back, I'd have brought Lorna in to clean up—'

Scorn flashed in Rosie's eyes. 'Your sister has a full-time job of her own. You should be ashamed of yourself, Maurice. When we moved in here, you promised you'd pull your weight. And the minute my back's turned, what do you do?' she demanded with fiery resentment. 'You turn the cottage into a dirty, messy hovel and my garden into a junkyard!'

Maurice shifted his size thirteen feet uncomfortably. 'I didn't clean up because I wasn't *expecting* you—'

'Stop trying to shift the blame. Put those bulging muscles into shifting those hideous old baths off the lawn and into the barn!'

Maurice grimaced. 'The barn's full.'

'Then sell them on and get rid of them! They make this place look like a rubbish tip!'

'Sell them on? Are you nuts? They're worth a packet!'

23

Maurice was openly appalled by the suggestion. 'I make more flogging one bath than you make in a week of selling knick-knacks on your market stall!'

Involuntary amusement filled Rosie, defusing her exasperation. Her conscience stabbed her too. Maurice had been her best friend since she was thirteen. She sighed. 'Look...why don't you go and have a shower? I'll help you clear the garden later.'

But Maurice hovered and cleared his throat. 'I should have said it yesterday but I couldn't find the words... I'm really sorry you lost your dad so soon after him finding you.'

A lump ballooned in Rosie's tight throat. 'He was a nice bloke,' she mumbled, and swallowed hard. 'I was lucky I had the chance to get to know him.'

'Yeah...' A frown darkening his brow, Maurice hesitated before plunging in with two big feet. 'But why leave London in such a rush when he seems to have left you a share of his worldly goods?'

'I *don't* want to talk about that—'

'Rosie...you can't keep on running away from people and situations that upset you.'

A fierce flush lit her cheeks. In self-defence she turned her head away. The reminder that that had been a habit of hers when she was younger was not welcome.

'And you can't leave a legacy hanging in legal limbo either. The executor will be forced to track you down. That's his job.'

'He'll find it difficult. I left no forwarding address.'

'Collect what's coming to you and I bet you could say goodbye to market trading and start up an antique shop here, just the way you always planned,' Maurice pointed out levelly. 'Then between us we could make an offer to buy this place from my uncle instead of renting it.'

Maurice's fatal flaw, Rosie reflected wryly. A complete inability to miss out on any opportunity to make or attract money. And because of it he would probably be a millionaire by the time he was twenty-five. His architectural salvage business was booming.

'You could make a better life for yourself. That's obviously what your father wanted,' Maurice continued with conviction. 'And why do you act so flippin' guilty about his widow? I'm quite sure he hasn't left *her* destitute!'

Rosie spun round, pale and furious, but, having said his piece, Maurice took himself safely upstairs before she even reached the hall. Baulked of the chance to tell him to mind his own business, she scowled on the threshold of the tiny lounge, surveying the all-male debris of abandoned take-aways, squashed beer cans and car magazines. Her nose wrinkled. It was going to take her days to restore the cottage to its former cleanliness. With a rebellious groan, she rubbed at her aching back with a grimy hand and wandered out into the pale spring sunshine.

A silver limousine was in the act of turning in off the road. The impressive vehicle drew to a purring halt behind Maurice's lorry. As Rosie watched with raised brows, a uniformed chauffeur climbed out and opened the rear passenger door. She started to walk towards the barn. It might be the one day of the week that Maurice didn't open for business but he never turned away a customer. However, when a very tall, dark male sheathed in a breathtakingly elegant dove-grey suit emerged from the limo, Rosie stopped dead in her tracks, shock and dismay freezing her fragile features.

Sunlight arrowed over Constantine Voulos's blue-black hair, gilding his tanned skin to gold and accentuating the hard-boned hawk-like masculinity of his superb bone structure. He strode across the yard towards her, his long, powerful legs eating up the distance with a natural grace of movement as eye-catching as that of a lion on the prowl. Rosie connected with glittering dark golden eyes set between dense black lashes. Her stomach clenched, her heart hammering thunderously against her breastbone.

''All women find Constantine irresistible,'' Anton had told her ruefully. ''I don't think he's ever met with a refusal. Unfortunately that has made him rather cynical about your sex.''

Rosie surfaced abruptly from that irrelevant memory to find herself being regarded much as she herself might have regarded a cockroach. She flushed, suddenly embarrassingly aware of the soiled sweatshirt and worn jeans she wore and then as quickly infuriated that she should even consider *his* opinion as being of any importance!

'We'll talk inside,' Constantine informed her grimly.

'How the heck did you find me?'

He elevated a sardonic winged ebony brow. 'It wasn't difficult. Anton's desk diary contained this address.'

'Well, I don't want you here,' Rosie retorted with angry heat. 'So you can just take yourself off again!'

'I'm not leaving until we have reached an agreement.' Constantine stared down at her, his arrogant jawline hardening, his nostrils flaring as a black frown built between his brows. 'What age are you?' he demanded abruptly.

'Twenty...not that that's any of your—'

'Twenty?' Constantine shot her an appalled look, his sensual mouth twisting with flagrant distaste. '*Christos*...what was Anton thinking of?'

'Not what you're thinking of, anyway!' Rosie scorned.

'But then it takes a male of my experience to understand how the mind of a rapacious little tramp works,' Constantine returned without skipping a beat. 'And you must have put Anton through hell the last weeks of his life!'

Rosie went white with shock. 'What are you talking about?'

Constantine strode past her into the cottage. 'We'll discuss it indoors.'

'I asked you what you were talking about,' Rosie reminded him shakily.

Constantine stood poised on the threshold of the messy, cluttered lounge, his hard-cut profile set in lines of derision. 'You live like a pig!' he breathed in disgust as he swung round again. 'Unwashed...your home filthy. My skin would crawl if I entered that room. You need pest control.'

Stunned into rare silence, Rosie gasped at him as he sidestepped her and swiftly strode back outside again.

'We will stay out here in the fresh air.'

Her cheeks burning with outrage and mortification, Rosie charged out after him again. *'How dare you?'*

'Keep quiet.' Constantine treated her to a chilling look of cold menace. 'Keep quiet and listen well. Anton was one of nature's gentlemen but I'm not and I've already worked out what your game was. I now understand *why* Anton wrote that new will. He drew it up without legal advice, had it witnessed by the servants and then he placed it in his desk the day he returned to London. He was afraid that he would have another heart attack and was seriously worried about your future...and *why* was that?'

Her breath tripped in her throat. 'I—I—'

Icily judgmental dark eyes raked her flustered face. 'Before Anton went on his convalescent cruise, you told him that you were carrying his child...*didn't you*?'

'Don't be ridiculous!' Rosie gasped.

'Your object was to try and force him into divorcing Thespina. You put him under intolerable pressure but you were lying. You weren't pregnant. If you had been, you'd have thrown the news in my face with pleasure yesterday!'

Rosie blinked up at him, her lashes fluttering in bemusement. Even though his suspicions were wildly off beam, she was shattered by the depth of calculation he laid at her door.

Constantine studied her with seething contempt. 'And I'm afraid that Anton chose to deal with a problem that he could not cope with by tipping the whole bloody mess into *my* lap!'

'I don't understand—'

'Of course you don't,' Constantine asserted, his hard mouth curling. 'No doubt you think that he left you a fortune and that all you have to do is sit back and wait for the money to come pouring in. But, sadly for you, your sordid little game-plan backfired... Anton did not leave you *anything* in his will!'

Rosie's brow furrowed as she struggled to comprehend what he was telling her. 'But you said—'

'Anton left his estate to me just as he had done in his original will. But in the new version he added a condition to that inheritance. I still inherit...but *only* if I marry you!'

'M-marry me?' Her tongue felt too big for her dry mouth and her green eyes were huge with disbelief. '*You*...marry...*me*?'

'Clearly Anton believed that you *were* pregnant!' Constantine loosed a harsh, embittered laugh as he swung away from her, broad shoulders fiercely taut beneath the fine fabric of his jacket. 'Anton panicked and scribbled out that new will without any reasoned forethought whatsoever. Why did he do that? Because if anything happened to him he wanted his fictional child to be protected and legitimised and he could not face the idea of Thespina finding out the truth.'

'You've got it all wrong,' Rosie protested in a shaken rush. 'My relationship with Anton was strictly platonic. I didn't tell him any lies. I—'

'What sort of a fool do you take me for?' Constantine interrupted with raw contempt. 'You were having an affair. He was living with you in that house and he was besotted with you!'

Her knees giving way, Rosie sank slowly down on the weathered bench at the edge of the overgrown lawn. Even presented with Constantine's twisted interpretation of the facts, she now saw the complete picture and she finally understood. *Anton, how could you do this to me?* she almost screamed, and inside herself she cringed. Unable to freely and publicly acknowledge her as his daughter, her father had nonetheless been determined that her future security should be safeguarded.

And in a moment of madness, in a moment of desperate anxiety about his health, Anton had come up with what only a madman could have seen as a solution! No, not a madman, she immediately adjusted with a suppressed groan, merely an old-fashioned man who honestly believed that all young women were pitifully vulnerable little creatures, helpless without the support and guidance of some big, strong, domineering man.

'It can't be legal…' she whispered tautly.

'It is perfectly legal but it would have been better had that will never seen the light of day,' Constantine acknowledged harshly. 'It *could* be challenged and it might well be overturned in court, because Anton made no provision for what was to happen to his estate in the event of no marriage taking place. As a result his business holdings and accounts are now frozen. But it is impossible to take legal action without exposing Thespina to considerable distress.'

Rosie was finding it very hard to think with clarity. 'Surely she must already know about all this?'

'She does not. Acquainted as she was with the terms of the original will, she has no suspicion of the existence of a later one. It was only discovered when Anton's secretary cleared out his desk two days ago—'

'But what about her? I mean, for heaven's sake, Anton *must* have made some provision for his widow.'

'Thespina is a very wealthy woman in her own right. Anton had no other living relatives. She shared his wish that I should be his heir.' Constantine's shrewd dark gaze skimmed her strained white face and a grim smile clenched his lips. 'And it is not in your own best interests to invite publicity. Open that trashy little mouth and I won't give you a penny!'

Rosie's legs suddenly regained the power of movement. She surged upright, her eyes alight with raw antagonism. 'I don't *want* anything!'

Constantine Voulos studied her with cold, reflective eyes. 'If you think you can drive the price up, you're making a major error of judgement. You will go through a ceremony of marriage…and in return you will receive a big, fat cheque and a divorce as soon as I can arrange it.'

'Are you out of your mind?' Rosie demanded incredulously. 'You really think I would go through with a marriage just so that you can get your greedy hands on Anton's estate?'

A sash window above them was noisily opened. 'Rosie? What did you do with all the towels?' Maurice shouted down.

Constantine stiffened and took a step back, the better to get a view of the half-naked young man leaning out of the window. Rosie looked up too, absently conceding that from that angle Maurice looked rather like a blond version of King Kong.

'Sorry…' Maurice muttered, belatedly taking in the male with her and withdrawing his tattooed biceps and extremely hairy chest from view. 'I didn't know you had company—'

'Who the hell is he?' Constantine Voulos raked at Rosie, a rise of dark blood emphasising the savage line of his cheekbones.

'Do you want me to come down and handle this, Rosie?' Maurice enquired.

'When I need you to fight my battles for me, I'll be six feet under!' Rosie bawled back, mortally offended by the offer.

The sash window slid reluctantly down again.

'Anton is scarcely cold in his grave and already you have another man in your bed!' Naked outrage had turned those brilliant black Greek eyes to seething gold.

Rosie's hand flew up and connected with one hard masculine cheekbone with such force that her fingers went numb. Stunned by the blow, Constantine Voulos stared down at her with blatant incredulity.

The thunderous silence chilled her to the marrow.

'I'm sick of you insulting me,' she muttered through chattering teeth, almost as stunned as he was by the violent response he had drawn from her. 'And if you touch me Maurice will pulverise you!'

'He didn't pulverise Anton...did he?'

Even hot with shame at having used Maurice as a threat to hide behind, Rosie registered the oddly roughened quality of Constantine Voulos's deep, dark drawl and the indefinable change in the charged atmosphere.

The tall Greek stared broodingly down at her, smouldering golden eyes alarmingly intent. Involuntarily she met that molten gaze and her heartbeat thundered, her throat closing over, heat igniting in the pit of her stomach. She pressed her thighs together in sudden murderous unease.

'That...that was d-different,' she stammered, utterly powerless in the hold of that entrapping stare which was somehow making her feel things she had never felt before. Sexual things, sexual feelings which filled her not only with astonishment but also with appallingly gauche confusion. Why…how…she didn't understand because she couldn't think straight any more.

Constantine Voulos took a fluid step back, his lean, powerful length emitting an electric tension. Inky black lashes dipped, closing her out again, severing her from the power source that had made every pulse in her treacherous body leap and leaving her disorientated and trembling.

'I haven't got time to play games, Miss Waring. I'll give you twelve hours to think over your position…and then I'll put the pressure on where it hurts most,' Constantine warned in a soft drawl that sent a shiver down her rigid spine. 'With a little help from me, life could become exceedingly difficult. This property is rented. What happens to the junkyard business if the lease isn't renewed?'

Dawning perception filled Rosie's shocked eyes. 'You can't be serious.'

A cold half-smile briefly slanted his hard mouth. 'If I was free to follow my natural inclinations, you'd be begging on the street for your next meal. I'll call again tomorrow morning.'

'How did you know we rented this place?' Rosie prompted helplessly as he walked away from her.

Constantine spun gracefully back. 'And may I put in a special request?' he murmured silkily, ignoring the question. 'You strike me as a woman who knows how to please a man. So have a bath before I show up again.'

Rosie's breasts swelled as she sucked in a heady gush of air. 'Why, *you*—!'

The door of the limousine shut with a soft, expensive clunk. Her head whirling, Rosie stalked into the cottage and threw herself down at the kitchen table. Frustrated fury was hurtling about inside her. For an instant she genuinely thought she might explode. He had actually dared to try and threaten her! But then the stakes he was playing for sounded very high…

What had Anton been worth in terms of cold, hard cash? She shuddered with revulsion. Anton had owned a boatyard, a hotel and a chain of shops in Greece. His business dealings within the UK had been tied up in various speculative property ventures. That nonsensical will! But how very like her father…impulsive and over-protective as he had been.

Her eyes smarted with stinging tears and she gulped. Anton had talked so much about Constantine and always with pride, affection and more than a hint of awe. Wealthy Greek parents expected to have a healthy say in their children's choice of a life partner…he had told her that too.

"Just as well you're Spanish!" she had teased.

"Mallorquin," her father had reproved, still proud as punch of his birth in Majorca even after forty years of living in Greece.

Dear heaven, but she despised Constantine Voulos! Her small hands curled into fists on the table-top. Tramp, whore, trash, tart. And, most unforgivably of all, he had accused her of subjecting Anton to such anxiety that she had shortened his life. Her stomach heaved. Well, he could sling his very worst threats and he would find her immovable. Rosie smiled a little to herself then, her smile slowly growing into a decided smirk. Their land-lord *was*, after all, Maurice's uncle. No way was she going through some disgusting charade of marriage just to help Constantine Voulos circumvent her father's will and profit from it!

'That was the brother from hell…am I right?' Maurice dropped down opposite her and ruefully appraised her hotly flushed face and over-bright eyes. 'Who else do we know rich enough to travel around in a stretch limousine? Not only your dad's substitute son but also large enough and verbal enough to make you so mad you are spitting tacks—'

'Yes, he *was* Anton's favourite, wasn't he? But then I only had four months, not twenty years to make an impression!' Rosie condemned painfully, and then she crammed an unsteady hand against her wobbling mouth, ashamed of the bitter envy she could hear splintering from her words.

'Did you tell him who you were this time?' Maurice enquired gently.

'Why should I? Why should I tell that hateful creep anything? If Anton couldn't trust him with the news, I certainly couldn't!'

Maurice sighed. 'Presumably Voulos came up here to sort out this inheritance of yours.'

A choked laugh was dredged from Rosie. 'I haven't inherited anything! Anton left *me* to Constantine instead!'

Maurice frowned. 'Excuse me?'

'In fact my father tried to *force* me on him…as if I were some brainless little wimp in need of care and protection!' Registering Maurice's still blank scrutiny, Rosie thrust up her chin and the words of explanation came spilling out of her.

'Holy Moses…' Maurice breathed at one stage, but it was his sole interruption. From that point, he listened intently.

'Can you imagine that ignorant, arrogant louse even thinking that I might agree?' Rosie pressed, in a furious appeal for sympathetic accord.

Maurice leant back in his chair, looking very thoughtful. 'Your father has left him in one hell of a fix.'

'I beg your pardon?'

Maurice slowly shook his head. 'Have you any idea

how fast a business can go down with its cash flow cut off? No money going in, no money going out—'

'I know next to nothing about Anton's business ventures and I don't much care either,' Rosie said huffily.

'Get your brain into gear, Rosie. Voulos is in a very tight corner. No wonder the guy's furious—'

'Exactly whose side are you on?'

'As always, on the side of common sense and profit,' Maurice told her without apology. 'Do you like the idea of your father's business concerns going bust on a legal technicality? And naturally Voulos doesn't want to drag this whole sorry affair into an open court.'

Rosie reddened uncomfortably, not having considered the situation from either of those angles.

'Voulos came here to bargain with the enemy because he had no other choice. The fastest, easiest solution *is* to meet the terms of your father's will.'

'I can't believe I'm hearing this—'

'And Voulos is offering to compensate you for your time and trouble. I wonder how much he's prepared to put down on the table?' Maurice mused with a slow grin, unaffected by Rosie's look of appalled reproach. 'The trouble with you, Rosie, is that you're an idealist. Voulos isn't and neither am I. You'd cut off your nose to spite your face.'

'Then why don't *you* deal with him when he comes back tomorrow?' Rosie snapped, rising angrily to her feet.

'Do you want me to? I'll willingly stay around and keep an eye on the negotiations. If his temper is anything like yours…well, we don't want bloodshed, do we? What would we do with his body?' Maurice asked cheerfully. 'And dead men can't write big, fat cheques.'

'I won't be here tomorrow,' Rosie informed him thinly.

'Look, it's a business proposition, nothing more. You

won't have to live with the guy or like him. And if you won't do it for yourself,' Maurice murmured with a shrewd eye on her frozen face, 'think about your father's employees and what's likely to happen to them if his businesses go down. You can't hit back at Voulos without bringing grief to other people.'

'I don't want to hit back at him, I just want him to *leave me alone*!' Rosie slung in frustrated rage, and stalked out of the room.

Hunched within the capacious depths of an old waxed jacket, Rosie stamped her feet to keep warm and watched her breath steam in the icy air. On a cold, frosty morning the market was always quiet. Maurice strolled up and slotted a plastic cup of coffee into her hand. Rosie surveyed him in surprise. 'What are you doing here?'

Maurice shrugged, carefully avoiding her eyes. 'How's trade going?'

Rosie grimaced. 'It's slow.'

Maurice picked up a large green ceramic rabbit and frowned. 'Isn't this part of your own collection?'

It was Rosie's turn to shrug, faint pink spreading over her cheekbones. 'I'll pick up another one.'

'Nobody's ever going to pay that for it,' Maurice told her, studying the price tag and wincing.

'It's already attracted interest—'

'But not a buyer. You're overpricing it because you can't bear to part with it.'

Frowning at that uncomfortably accurate assistance, Rosie sipped at her coffee. 'Did *he* show up?'

'Yeah…' Maurice rearranged the stock on her stall without raising his head. 'I told him where to find you.'

'You did *what*?' Beneath the brim of her black trilby, Rosie's startled brows shot heavenward.

'I'll watch your stall. Here he comes now…'

As Rosie's horrified eyes fell on Constantine Voulos, her heart turned a somersault and lodged somewhere in the region of her working throat. Her nerveless fingers shook and coffee slopped everywhere without her noticing.

The tall Greek stationed himself on the other side of the stall, his vibrantly handsome features taut with sardonic impatience as he spread a derisive glance around the shabby covered market. 'You do like to play childish games, don't you, Miss Waring?'

Maurice uttered an audible groan. Striding forward, he planted the green rabbit into Constantine Voulos's startled hands. 'Can I interest you in an increasingly rare example of Sylvac pottery?'

'It's a piece of junk,' Constantine gritted, and dumped the item back down at speed.

'You wouldn't know any different, would you?' Rosie snapped as she swept round the stall to check that his rough handling hadn't chipped the rabbit.

Constantine Voulos ignored her to study Maurice with icy contempt. 'I get the picture. You want me to *pay* for the lady's time?'

Maurice folded his arms, his pugnacious aspect belied by the ever-ready sense of humour dancing in his bright blue eyes. 'Suit yourself, mate.'

'What the heck is going on here?' In utter disbelief, Rosie gaped as Constantine flipped out a wallet, withdrew a handful of notes and stuffed them into her pocket. 'I don't want *his* money!'

'When a guy expects to pay for every little thing in life, you ought to satisfy him,' Maurice contended cheerfully. 'Take him across to the pub, Rosie.'

'I'm not going anywhere with him...in fact the two of you can go take a running jump together!' Rosie attempted to move past Constantine but a lean, hard hand

snaked out and closed round her forearm. 'Let go of
me!'

'You harm a hair of her head and I'll swing for you,'
Maurice warned with gentle emphasis as he extended a
laden carrier bag. 'Don't forget your purchase, Mr
Voulos, and treat it with respect. Rosie's very fond of
rabbits—'

In a gesture of supreme contempt, Constantine
grasped the bag and dropped it from a height into the
metal litter bin opposite. The sound of shattering pottery
provoked a stricken gasp from Rosie.

Maurice groaned again. 'There is just no telling some
people.'

Wrenching herself violently free of Constantine's
hold, Rosie darted over to the bin and looked inside the
bag. She paled as she viewed the extent of the damage.
It was irreparable. Momentarily her fingertips brushed
the broken pieces and then she rounded on Constantine
like a spitting tigress, green eyes ablaze. 'How could you
do that? How *could* you do that?'

'Why are you shouting?' Incredulous black eyes
clashed with hers.

'You selfish, insensitive, snobbish pig...' Rosie condemned wrathfully. 'I was prepared to sell that rabbit,
but only if it was going to a good home!'

'Are you unhinged or merely determined to cause a
public scene?' Constantine snarled down at her.

'At least I'm not wantonly destructive and spiteful!'

'Spiteful? I wouldn't be caught dead walking around
with that ugly piece of tasteless junk!'

With the greatest of difficulty, Rosie haltered her temper. Well, he needn't think he was getting his money
back *now*. She swallowed hard, dug her hands into her
pockets and walked off. Crossing the pavement, she
stepped into the road—or at least she'd started stepping,

when a powerful hand closed over her shoulder and yanked her back bodily as a car sped past.

'Do you have a death-wish?' Constantine Voulos grated.

'I'm surprised you didn't push me,' Rosie snapped, shaken by the experience but determined not to betray the fact. 'Oh, I forgot, didn't I? I'm only worth something to you as long as I'm alive and kicking!'

Across the road, she headed in the direction of the small bar used by the market traders, but her companion strode towards the luxury hotel twenty yards further on. Rosie's chin came up. She squared her shoulders and then hesitated. The sooner she dealt with the situation, the sooner he would be gone. A wave of exhaustion swept over her then. She had had little sleep the night before and now she found herself thinking guiltily about her father again.

Anton would have been appalled by the animosity between his daughter and his ward. In drawing up that wretched will, her father had clearly expected her to tell Constantine who she was. Left in ignorance of their true relationship, Constantine had assumed that she was Anton's mistress. What other role could he possibly have assigned to her?

So why hadn't she told him the truth? Rosie's strained mouth compressed. In her mind, Constantine Voulos had been the enemy long before she'd even met him and Anton's death had simply increased her bitterness. She resented the fact that Constantine had grown up secure in *her* father's love and affection. Why not admit it? At the same age she had lost her mother and had been put into the care of the local authorities...

Dear heaven, could she really have been that unreasonable? The creeping awareness that she had been unjust and immature filled Rosie with discomfiture.

CHAPTER THREE

Two men in dark suits were waiting in the hotel lobby. They looked tense and sprang forward with a strong suggestion of relief when Constantine appeared. A spate of low-pitched Greek was exchanged. Striding ahead of them into the quiet, almost empty lounge bar, the younger man rushed to pull out a pair of comfortable armchairs beside the log fire.

Fluidly discarding his black cashmere overcoat, Constantine sank indolently down and snapped imperious fingers. While Rosie looked on in fascination, the second man stationed behind him inclined his head to receive instructions. The waitress was summoned and drinks were served at spectacular speed.

'What's with Laurel and Hardy?' Rosie nodded in the direction of the two men.

'Dmitri and Taki are my security men.'

'I won't ask why you need them. Your personality kind of speaks for itself.' Bodyguards, for goodness' sake? To conceal her embarrassment, Rosie whipped off her hat and a mass of wildly colourful spiralling curls cascaded round her shoulders. In a gesture of impatience, she finger-combed her hair back off her face. As she removed her jacket to reveal the ancient guernsey sweater she wore beneath, she intercepted a disturbingly intent stare from her companion.

'What are you looking at?' she demanded aggressively.

An aristocratic ebony brow climbed but rich dark eyes gleamed with grudging amusement and without warning a devastating smile slashed his hard features. That smile blinded Rosie like a floodlight turned on in the dark. Taken by surprise, she squirmed like a truculent puppy unsure of its ground. Her eyes colliding with that night-dark gaze, she experienced the most terrifying lurch of excitement. Her stomach muscles clenched as if she had gone down in a lift too fast.

'Your hair is a very eye-catching colour,' he murmured wryly.

'And usually only rag-dolls have corkscrew curls,' Rosie completed in driven discomfiture, carefully studying the soft drink she had snatched up, her palms damply clutching the glass and her hands far from steady.

In the church she had assumed that it was the shock of meeting him which had shaken her up. But yesterday she had experienced a magnetic and undeniably sexual response that had briefly, mortifyingly reduced her to a positive jelly of juvenile confusion. But it wasn't her fault—no, it definitely wasn't—and there wasn't anything personal about it either, she told herself bracingly. So there was no need for her to be sitting here with her knees locked guiltily together and her cheeks as hot as a furnace.

It was *his* fault that she was uncomfortable. He was staggeringly beautiful to look at, but then that wasn't the true source of the problem. Constantine Voulos had something a whole lot more dangerous. A potent, sexually devastating allure that burned with electrifying heat. Out of the corner of her eye, Rosie watched an older woman across the lounge feasting her attention on Constantine's hard-cut, hawk-like profile and felt thoroughly vindicated in her self-examination.

'Let us concede that we met for the first time in inauspicious circumstances,' Constantine murmured. 'But the time for argument is now past. There is no reason why this unfortunate affair should not be settled quietly and discreetly.'

Rosie sat forward, tense as a drawn bowstring. 'I haven't been honest with you,' she began stiffly. 'I made things worse than they needed to be but then you didn't make things easy either…leaping off on a tangent, making wild assumptions and insulting me—'

'I don't follow.' Impatience edged the interruption.

Pale and tense, Rosie snatched in a ragged breath. 'I'm not who you think I am. I wasn't Anton's mistress…' She coloured as she said that out loud. 'I'm his daughter, born on the wrong side of the blanket…or whatever you want to call it…'

Constantine Voulos dealt her an arrested look and then his gaze flared with raw incredulity. 'What the hell do you hope to achieve by making so grotesque a claim?'

Rosie's brows drew together. 'But it's true… I mean, I suppose you have every reason not to want to believe me, but Anton *was* my father.'

His mouth curled with distaste and impatience. 'You really are a terrible liar. Had Anton been related to you in *any* way, his lawyers would have been well aware of the fact.'

Rosie stared blankly back at him. It had never occurred to her that the truth might be greeted with outright contempt and instant dismissal. 'But he didn't tell anyone—'

'And the proof of this fantastic allegation?'

'Look, it was Anton who traced *me*—'

'Let me relieve your fertile imagination of the belief that the nature of your relationship with Anton has any bearing on the size of the cheque I will write,' Constantine broke in with withering bite. 'And now please stop wasting my time with ridiculous fairy stories!'

Rosie dropped her head, a surge of distress making her stomach churn. Proof? She had *never* had any proof! Anton's name was not on her birth certificate and

Constantine was so full of himself, so convinced that she was an inveterate liar, that he wouldn't even listen to her. For the first time she realised that with Anton's death she had been dispossessed of any means of proving that he had been her father. And even though she had never planned to do anything with that knowledge that reality had a terrible, painful finality for her.

'Let's get down to business,' Constantine suggested drily.

Utterly humiliated by his disbelief, Rosie wanted very badly to simply get up and walk out. Only the grim awareness that he would follow her and fierce pride kept her seated.

'With your agreement, arrangements will be made for the marriage ceremony to take place as soon as possible. The legal firm I use in London will liaise with you. When this matter has been dealt with, you will be most generously compensated,' Constantine assured her smoothly before going on to mention a sum which contained a breathtaking string of noughts. 'All I ask from you is discretion and also the return of the Estrada betrothal ring.'

Rosie looked up, her face drawn and empty of animation. 'No.'

'It is a family heirloom. It must be returned.'

'No,' Rosie said again.

'In spite of its age, the ring has no great financial worth. The stone is flawed.'

Rosie flinched, nausea lying like a leaden weight in her over-sensitive stomach. 'There must be some other way that the will could be sorted out.'

'If there was, do you seriously think that I would be here demanding that you secretly go through such a ceremony with me?'

The harsh, derisive edge to the question made Rosie flush. No, Constantine Voulos had no other choice. His very presence here told her that. Nor could she fail to see how deeply and bitterly he resented the necessity of being forced to ask for *her* co-operation.

'But Thespina seemed to like me,' she began awkwardly. 'And she already thinks we're engaged. Is there any need for all this secrecy?'

'If she knew who you really were, do you think she would like you?' Constantine breathed scathingly. 'She'd be furious. As for the engagement…I'll tell her it was a soon regretted impulse on my part. There is no need for her to know about the marriage. I don't want you meeting her again.'

Rosie's eyes fell uneasily from his. She might not have been Anton's mistress but even as his daughter she would be no more welcome an advent in Thespina's life. And if she agreed to a secret marriage of convenience Constantine would inherit and Anton's business interests *and* presumably his employees would continue to prosper. Thespina would have no reason to become suspicious again…indeed, everything would go back to normal, just as if Rosie herself had never existed.

Rosie lifted her head, green eyes veiled. 'You keep your money, I keep the ring.' Pulling on her jacket, she stood up. 'Now if you don't mind I'd like to leave.'

'I prefer to pay for favours. Have I your agreement?'

'I'm agreeing only out of respect for Anton's memory…just you understand that. But how could you understand it? You only think in terms of financial gain,' she completed in disgust, and spun on her heel.

'I think only in terms of the well-being of Anton's *wife*,' Constantine countered with icy emphasis.

Contempt froze her fragile features as she turned back to him. 'That sounds so impressive coming from a male who sleeps with another man's wife whenever the fancy takes him!'

Taken by surprise, Constantine Voulos sprang upright. '*Christos*…'

Rosie widened her huge green eyes, revitalised by the shock stiffening his darkly handsome features. 'Your long-running secret affair with the actress, Cinzia Borzone. So don't go all pious on me!'

As Rosie walked away, head held high, she heard the ground-out surge of explosive Greek that followed that revelation. The depth of her knowledge about his private life had come as a most unwelcome surprise to Constantine Voulos.

Certainly Anton had lamented long and hard on the topic of that unsuitable relationship. In *his* opinion, Constantine had, at the tender age of twenty-five, fallen live into the paws of a designing married woman with a husband who was perfectly content to turn a blind eye to his wife's infidelity if the financial rewards were great enough.

And although several times over the past four years Anton and Thespina had been encouraged to hope that the affair had run its course Cinzia had ultimately appeared to triumph over every other woman who entered Constantine's life. Maybe that situation had even been on Anton's mind when he'd changed his will, Rosie reflected ruefully.

Anton had had the optimistic hope that marriage would cure Constantine's desire for another man's wife. And long before his death Rosie had known that her father cherished a happy daydream in which *she* and Constantine met, fell madly in love and married, thereby bringing his daughter into the family by the only possible route that would not hurt his wife.

Maurice frowned in surprise when she rejoined him. 'Don't tell me you walked out on Voulos again.'

'No. I agreed…OK? I even told him who I was this

time.' Rosie gave her friend a grim little smile. 'Only he didn't believe me.'

Taken aback, Maurice stared at her. 'Why not?'

'Why should he have? I don't even look like Anton. I don't have any evidence of who I am either. In fact, sitting there with Constantine Voulos, those four months started feeling like a rather embarrassing juvenile fantasy,' Rosie confided thinly, tucking herself back behind her stall. 'So, if you don't mind, I'd rather not discuss it any more—'

'But Anton had all those photos your mother sent him and he must have had other things.'

'If he did he never mentioned them and heaven knows what he did with those photos.' Tired and drained of emotion, Rosie shrugged. 'It doesn't matter much now, does it?'

Late that night, the front door slammed noisily. Half-asleep on the sofa after an evening of exhaustive cleaning, Rosie sat up with a start. Maurice burst into the lounge looking excited and tossed a glossy but somewhat dog-eared magazine down on her lap. 'Lorna had this. She was able to tell me all about Constantine Voulos.'

'What are you talking about?' Rosie mumbled drowsily.

'My sister has a stack of magazines about the rich and famous. The minute I mentioned his name it rang a bell with her and she looked that out for me. Voulos is a genuine Greek tycoon,' Maurice informed her impressively. 'He's loaded! The guy was *born* into a fortune. Your father was only a small-time businessman in comparison.'

'So?' Rosie groaned as she stood up.

'Rosie…you don't want to sign anything away before or after that wedding,' Maurice warned her. 'Voulos doesn't need your father's estate. He's already rich as sin. It's all wrong that you should be cut out just because the guy doesn't want you around!'

'I'm going to bed—'

'I'm trying to look out for you, Rosie. *You* have got rights too,' Maurice told her with stark impatience. 'Your dad would turn in his grave if he knew what Voulos was doing!'

'Maurice, Constantine Voulos has not one thing that I want.'

But was it true that Constantine was wealthier than her father had ever been? Anton certainly hadn't travelled around in a chauffeur-driven limo or hauled bodyguards in his wake. She shrugged. Either way, what did it matter to her? And even if Constantine was filthy rich it didn't mean he couldn't also be disgustingly greedy.

But she still took that magazine to bed with her. There was a picture of Constantine, looking spectacularly dark and smooth and dangerous in a dinner jacket. A beautiful blonde was clutching his arm as if she was afraid he was about to escape. Rosie surveyed the blonde with pity. Constantine was the sort of male animal you kicked hard and walked away from. He would thrive on that kind of brutal treatment and comne back for more. Even *she*, with her limited experience of the male sex, had worked that out at first glance.

As Rosie drove herself to the chosen register office in a nearby town three weeks later, she was struggling to suppress a deep sense of unease. Even if she couldn't condone her father's ill-considered attempt to endow her with the lifestyle she might have had as his legitimate daughter, she knew that he had written that will in sincerity and that made her feel guilty and disloyal.

As she drew her little van to a reluctant halt in the car park, she espied the now familiar limousine and pulled a face. Constantine's bodyguards were outside the register office, on the lookout for her. Neither was dressed for the chill of a late Yorkshire spring. They were blue with cold and the younger man, Taki, was sneezing. Both men fell over themselves in their eagerness to open the door for her and follow her indoors.

'You're late,' Constantine grated, striding forward to intercept her.

'But I'm here,' Rosie pointed out flatly. 'Don't look a gift-horse in the mouth.'

Incredulous dark eyes roved over her waxed jacket and jeans. '*Theos*...didn't Anton buy you any decent clothes?'

Rosie reddened, her mouth tightening as she took in the full effect of his exquisitely cut navy pinstripe suit, white silk shirt and gold tie. 'Surely you didn't think I would get all dolled up for this charade?'

'This is not a charade,' Constantine growled in a repressive undertone. 'We are about to undergo a legal and binding ceremony.'

A split second after a clerk approached them to invite them into the room where the civil marriage service would take place. Rosie froze. 'I don't like this at all,' she whispered frantically. 'I wish I hadn't agreed—'

Impatient long brown fingers enclosed her own and urged her onward. 'You will go through with it for Thespina's sake.'

Rosie paled at that cruel reminder of her father's vulnerable widow. This was a cover-up, she reminded herself, an unpleasant but essential manoeuvre to enable Constantine to inherit Anton's estate without challenging his will. She focused on a rather tired flower arrangement on a nearby table and then minutes later, from somewhere outside herself, she watched in helpless amazement as Constantine lifted her ice-cold hand and slotted a slender gold ring onto her wedding finger.

'I believe you drove yourself here,' Constantine murmured on the pavement outside. 'Give me your car keys.'

Rosie frowned. 'My car keys?' She already had them in her hand. 'Why?'

Without hesitation, Constantine swiped her keyring from between her fingers, tossed it deftly to Taki and said something in Greek.

It happened so fast that Rosie blinked in bemusement as Taki sped off with her keys. 'What on earth do you think you're playing at?' she demanded furiously.

'He will drive your vehicle home. We're spending the night at a hotel.' Constantine closed a restraining hand round her shoulder as his limousine pulled in by the kerb.

'*We*... Say that again?' Rosie shot aghast eyes to his dark, strong face.

'Were we to part immediately after the ceremony, it would look very suspicious.'

'To whom?' Rosie gasped.

'Should this arrangement of ours ever be questioned, I will not lay myself open to a charge of having entered the marriage on false pretences—'

'But that's exactly what you've done!'

'And wouldn't it be very foolish of me to make that obvious?'

'No way am I spending the night with you!' Rosie told him hotly.

'You have no choice. This is part of the deal.'

Rosie folded her arms and stood her ground. 'No way,' she said again. 'I wouldn't trust you as far as the foot of the street!'

'Do you require assistance to get into the car?' Dangerous dark eyes of warning rested on her.

For an instant, Rosie hesitated, and then she climbed into the limousine in one quick, angry movement. 'A man who has to threaten to use brute strength to get his own way is a pathetic apology for a man!'

'Pity me, then,' Constantine advised with silken unconcern, treating her to a long, lingering scrutiny that made her shift and tauten. 'Every time you shout at me I want to slap you down so hard you'll be scared to raise your head again. I can't say that you bring out the best in me and you must have put on one hell of an act for Anton. Anton would have run a mile from that mouth of yours.'

'There's nothing wrong with my mouth—'

'It's an incredibly sexy mouth...until you open it.' Night-dark eyes partially veiled by lush black lashes rested on the full pink lips in question.

Sharply disconcerted, Rosie flushed. 'Don't talk to me like that.'

'Don't tell me what I can and can't say,' Constantine drawled softly. 'Nobody does that.'

Involuntarily, Rosie stiffened, feeling that sudden chill even in the warmth of the luxurious car. 'I'm not prepared to stay at a hotel with you.'

'But you will. It's part of our little arrangement. I will not run the risk that at some future date this marriage could be set aside as null and void. I am merely ensuring that we abide by the law to the letter.'

Silence fell, thick with tension, between them.

'Just how much *did* Anton tell you about me?' Constantine demanded abruptly.

'Much more than I wanted to hear, believe me!'

His sensual mouth hardened and twisted. 'We were close but evidently not close enough,' he mused grimly. 'He was too ashamed to tell me about you—'

'Anton was *not* ashamed of me.'

'Anton was a very happily married man until you came along.'

Rosie bit her lip and made no response. Anton had

spent several years and a lot of money striving to trace his illegitimate daughter. For the first nine years of her life he had received photographs of her on every birthday, but her mother, Beth, had included no return address. Rosie had often wondered why her mother had taken the trouble to secretly post those photos to Anton's London office. Had the exercise simply been an annual embittered reminder of the brief affair which had messed up Beth's life and cost Anton his only child?

Rosie didn't know. By the time she had heard the full story of her parentage, her mother had been dead for many years. But she could still remember her mother struggling to handle the brooding bitterness of a husband who had never been able to forgive her for marrying him when she was pregnant by another man. Beth had been dead only a week when Rosie's stepfather had called in the social services to tell them loudly and aggressively that he had no intention of keeping a child who wasn't his. That had been *his* revenge.

The limousine drew up in front of a country-house hotel. Rosie climbed out and hovered. 'This is ridiculous.'

'It wouldn't look quite so ridiculous if you weren't dressed like some revolting teeny-bopper hitchhiker I happened to pick up on the road here!'

In the intimidatingly elegant foyer and from a distance of almost twenty feet Rosie watched him sign the register. The hotel receptionist was far too well trained to stare but she squinted surreptitiously at Rosie. Rosie went pink and turned her back.

On the first floor, they were shown into a beautifully furnished suite. Seeing the connecting door, Rosie hastened through it to explore. Beyond lay only one bedroom complete with bathroom. He was out of his mind, she thought incredulously.

'If you think I am spending the night in there with you, you are living in a world of fantasy!'

Constantine dealt her a sardonic glance. 'I take the bedroom. You get the couch.'

Momentarily, Rosie couldn't get oxygen into her lungs. Wild-eyed, she stared back at him.

'I'll ruffle the pillows in the morning. Taki also has instructions to collect a change of clothes for you. No doubt Maurice will rise nobly to the occasion,' Constantine continued with smooth derision. 'I think your muscle-bound boyfriend would sell you to cannibals for the right price.'

'Maurice is a friend, not a lover!'

Constantine elevated an unimpressed brow, his expressive mouth curling.

'You have *such* a dirty mind,' Rosie told him fiercely.

Unexpectedly the beginnings of a smile tugged at the corners of his ruthless mouth. Brilliant black eyes rested intently on her furious face. 'So much fire and spirit. That intrigues me. If you hadn't been Anton's woman first, I would be very tempted to take you to my bed.'

Rosie went from fury into deep shock. Her lips moved but no sound came out.

'And I guarantee that within five minutes you would be eating out of my hand like a tame dove trained to please,' Constantine forecast with a feral flash of even white teeth.

Rosie unglued her tongue from the roof of her mouth. She was trembling. 'You have an incredible imagination!'

Constantine spread his elegant brown hands in a gesture of flagrant mockery. 'But how can you try to deny what we both know to be true? The very first time you saw me, you felt the heat rise between us. I felt it too. Raw sexual attraction, nothing more complex—'

Rosie forced a jagged laugh that hurt her throat. 'Your conceit is unbelievable.'

'Never challenge a Greek unless you're prepared to meet fire with fire,' Constantine drawled softly. 'But then perhaps that is exactly what you would like...?'

The atmosphere was so tense that her heartbeat thundered while those black eyes smouldered over her in challenging gold enquiry. A brisk knock sounded on the door and she jumped. Dmitri entered.

On dreadfully wobbly legs, Rosie retreated to the couch. There were goose-bumps all over her skin and she was horribly aware of the dull ache in her breasts and the painful tightness of her nipples. Just by standing there, just by looking at her like that, talking to her like that, *he* had done that to her body. That was scary; that was very scary indeed.

He had attacked on her weakest flank, smiling at her animosity because he could afford to smile while he laid bare the sexual charge between them. 'Raw sexual attraction'—no, that didn't embarrass him. Why should it? Constantine was Greek to the backbone, earthy in his blunt acknowledgement of nature's most driving force. But perhaps Rosie was most shaken by his unashamed admission that what she was feeling *he* was feeling too...

But then he was ninety per cent sexual predator, only ten per cent civilised. Hadn't she got great taste? Bitterly resenting the unfamiliar sense of inadequacy assailing her, Rosie watched Dmitri flip out a sleek portable computer and set it on the desk by the window. A porter entered with a fax machine and hurried to install it. Then a waiter arrived with a tray of coffee...coffee for *one*! Rosie's eyes flared. Seeking guidance, the waiter tried to catch her attention but Rosie ignored him, too proud to indicate a need for anything that would be supplied as a mere afterthought.

Meanwhile Constantine talked in fluent French on a mobile phone, his back turned to her, one large brown hand dug into the pocket of his well-cut, elegant trousers, his silk-lined jacket elbowed back to display a murderously flat stomach, the jut of a lean, taut masculine hip and long, long, powerful thighs. He looked so incredibly good *in* his clothes, she stopped breathing altogether at the thought of what he must look like *out* of them. Then, truly appalled by a kind of curiosity she had never experienced before, Rosie reddened fiercely, lifted the remote control within her reach and switched the television on to a satellite music channel.

'If you want to listen to music, use the set in the bedroom,' Constantine told her, breaking off from his call with a look of extreme irritation and then swinging away again.

Rosie bounced upright, digging angry hands into her pockets. 'I'll go out for a walk.'

His imperious dark head turned. 'No. You stay in the suite. Go and wash your hair or something,' he advised impatiently. 'I have work to do.'

Rosie breathed in so deeply, she was frightened she would burst and scream round the ceiling like a punctured balloon. 'I do what *I* like, Mr Voulos.'

'Not around me, you don't.' Casting aside the mobile phone, Constantine slung her a long, hard look of warning.

Her hands balled into fists inside her pockets. 'And what makes you think that?'

'I should have locked you in the boot of the limo for the night and hired someone else to play the bridal role. What am I getting in return for my money? You look about fifteen in that get-up. The hotel staff must think I'm a pervert...not that anyone in their right mind would credit that we *are* a newly married couple! And when you're not sulking it's yap, yap, yap.' Flashing black eyes raked over her in unconcealed exasperation. 'It's like having a chihuahua, snapping and snarling at my heels!'

Rosie shuddered with incredulous wrath. 'How *dare* you?'

'If you had had *me* in your bed for four months, you would at least know when to shut up and make yourself scarce!'

'You would be dead,' Rosie spelt out in a voice that shook with pure rage.

'You think so?' A slow-burning smile of savage amusement slashed his strong dark features. 'No, I think you would have learnt how to behave around me by the end of the first week. Unlike Anton, I'm low on patience and high on expectation and right now you are scoring zero all the way down the line.'

'Not ten minutes ago you were trying to make a pass at me!' Rosie condemned in outrage. 'But you knew you weren't going to get anywhere, so now you're being deliberately offensive!'

Constantine tilted his arrogant dark head to one side and narrowed his eyes to allow them to wander with slow incredulity over her. '*That* was a *pass*?' he derided in disbelief. 'So that's what's biting you. I'm supposed to be panting with uncontrollable lust, am I? And you call *me* conceited? At this moment you have all the sex appeal of a vagrant—'

'If you say one more word, I'll…I'll…'

A winged ebony brow rose enquiringly. 'You'll what? You'll *bite*?'

Speechless with rage, Rosie could only gasp, green eyes blazing like emeralds in her hotly flushed face.

Constantine dealt her a cold smile of menacing strength. 'Let's get one thing straight, little rag-doll. You bite me, you'll get bitten back to the bone. And if you're cherishing the wild and ambitious hope that I plan to

become your next wealthy meal-ticket you're losing
touch with reality. I felt the heat but I have no intention
of melting—'

'You ignorant, arrogant swine!' Rosie splintered, finding her tongue.

'I have this curious feeling that our minds are finally
meeting in perfect harmony,' Constantine murmured lazily, his lush black lashes lowered over brilliant dark,
incisive eyes. 'And the thought for the day is…better to
be an old man's darling than a young man's fool!'

Rosie shivered with rage and backed away from him.
Never in her life had she felt as if she could kill…until
now. She wanted Maurice's muscles. She wanted to
knock Constantine off his feet, swing him around her
head and then pound him into a pulp.

The mobile phone buzzed again.

Rosie reached the bedroom door on wobbling legs.

'Can you type?' Constantine enquired without warning and it was as if the previous conversation had not
taken place.

'T-type?' Rosie stammered helplessly.

'Take dictation?' he prompted impatiently. 'The fewer
people who are in on this arrangement the better…but
it's bloody inconvenient not to have my personal staff
around.'

'I don't type or take dictation,' Rosie breathed through
rigidly compressed lips.

Constantine angled a scathing, unsurprised glance
over her slight, stiff-as-a-board figure. 'But I bet you'd
be a rousing success at climbing cutely onto any middle-
aged employer's lap.'

CHAPTER FOUR

AN HOUR later, Taki having delivered an embarrassingly unimpressive plastic carrier bag to the bedroom, Rosie turned from her incredulous examination of what Maurice had packed on her behalf and reached immediately for the phone.

'Are the contents of this bag supposed to be a joke, Maurice?' Rosie demanded, threading outraged fingers through the diaphanous nightdress, the silky little raspberry-coloured slip dress and sheer tights. Three-inch-heeled strappy velvet shoes and the box of make-up that had been a Christmas gift from his sister completed the collection of impractical items. Naturally there was neither a change of underwear nor a toothbrush included.

'It's your wedding night. I thought you might want to dress up.'

'Ha, ha,' Rosie gritted, unamused.

'Has Voulos asked you to sign anything yet?' Maurice prompted worriedly.

'Not even the hotel register.'

'I think he knew a pre-nuptial contract mightn't be worth the paper it was written on if it ever came before a British court but he's sure to try and get you to sign something surrendering any financial claim on him. On the other hand,' Maurice mused, 'should the Press get to hear about the marriage, his goose would be fairly cooked.'

'Maurice, I'm very fond of you but right at this minute I am thoroughly ashamed of your greed!' Rosie spelt out angrily, and slammed down the receiver.

She called Room Service and a menu was delivered.

She wasn't very hungry but she put in as much time as possible working her way through a pot of tea and a plate of chicken sandwiches. As a rule she never watched much television and she paced the floor in growing boredom and resentment, an unappreciative audience to the buzz of the fax and the stream of constant phone calls in the next room.

By seven, she was ready to go stir-crazy and wondering why she was allowing *him* to intimidate her into remaining hidden in the suite. What did it matter if anyone saw her downstairs alone? They would hardly be surprised. Her pretend bridegroom was patently a selfish, insensitive workaholic.

An utterly hateful, bad-tempered swine too, Rosie reflected fierily as she freshened up in the bathroom and reached for the sheer tights. The heart-stopping looks of a dark angel crossed with the temperament of a snarling beast. So brutally sarcastic as well. He never missed a chance to put her down.

Lack of physical size had always meant that Rosie's tongue was her first line of defence. She was furiously conscious that for a few minutes in that room next door Constantine had overpowered her with the smooth, ricocheting speed and force of his derisive attacks. She hadn't made a single dent in that tough hide of his! No, she had gone into retreat. And yet here she was, doing him a huge favour for free, and what thanks was she getting for it?

Well, tomorrow morning, when she tore up his precious cheque in front of him, she would be the party holding the moral high ground then, wouldn't she? Rosie tilted her chin as she added a little colour to her lips and experimented with a touch of shadow on her eyelids. When she opened the door a crack, Constantine was talking in cold, quelling tones on the phone.

'Tomorrow isn't good enough,' he was saying with

icy precision. 'When I say move, I expect a sprint, not a soft-shoe shuffle.'

Rosie peeped out, saw him poised with his back to the room, tiptoed along the wall and crept out as quietly as a mouse. In the corridor, she ignored his hovering security men and calmly slipped on her shoes while inwardly wincing at the sound of Taki's harsh cough. However, when she stepped into the lift, the young security man stepped in behind her. And when she strolled into the low-lit, intimate bar on the ground floor he was still tailing her.

Well, at least his presence would save her from the boredom of having to pretend to read the glossy hotel brochure she had brought down with her, she reflected ruefully. She had planned to look occupied lest some cruising predatory male see her solitary state as some kind of invitation.

Every male head in the bar turned to follow her elegant passage. Titian curls rioted round the perfect oval of her face. Shoestring straps curved over smooth white shoulders, the raspberry silk flowing fluidly against slender curves, the hem caressing surprisingly long and shapely legs. Rosie selected a seat. Taki hailed a waiter and then went off into another choking bout of coughing.

'You should be in bed.' Rosie flicked the young Greek a look of grudging sympathy as she noted the feverish flush on his cheekbones. 'But I bet you'd have to go into convulsions and drop dead before Constantine would notice.'

Shivering, he frowned, his grasp of English clearly of the basic variety, and then he started coughing again and spluttering what sounded like a croaking apology. Rosie groaned, 'Oh, for goodness sake, sit down! You need a hot whisky with cloves in it. That should clear your head and help you to sleep.'

He slumped hesitantly down on a chair, regarding her

with bashful, bemused eyes. Rosie ordered a double for him and urged him to drink it all down. He shook his curly dark head uncertainly.

'*Drink it!*' Rosie commanded with force.

He was much more obedient than Constantine. Indeed after that one drink Taki became astonishingly garrulous, but since he was talking in his own language Rosie couldn't understand a word. She suspected that might be just as well. A look of intense admiration now glowed in the young Greek's befuddled stare.

'What the hell do you think you're playing at?' The seething demand penetrated Rosie's introspection at the same time as a big black shadow fell over the table. Her bright head lifted, her hand jerked and wine slopped out of her glass.

Taki shot upright and fell noisily over a chair. Taking in the situation at a glance, Dmitri surged forward to lift and steady the younger man and urge him towards the exit. His superb bone structure a mask of outrage, Constantine stared at Rosie, his eyes molten gold and as hard as diamonds.

'I had no idea you'd left the suite. You will return there immediately,' he ordered in a low-pitched growl of raw intimidation.

There was something about Constantine, something about that outrageous domineering attitude, that brought out the very worst in Rosie even when that same attitude could send an undeniable current of fear shooting through her veins. 'Or what? I get forty lashes before midnight? I'm just sitting here having a quiet drink—'

'*Upstairs,*' Constantine bit out, pale with rage beneath his olive skin.

'You Tarzan, me Jane?' Rosie fed the flames with a flashing little smile of warning. 'I don't think so.'

'We have an agreement,' Constantine thundered in a repressive undertone that shimmied down her taut spine like abrasive sand on silk. 'And you are behaving in an inappropriate manner.'

Rosie tilted her head back, her fiery tresses gleaming as bright as her eyes. 'Frankly, I think I'm behaving very much in character. I'm playing a bimbo,' she told him helpfully. 'Lots of bimbos marry rich older guys who bore the pants off them—'

'Say that again,' Constantine invited, a slow rise of dark colour accentuating the taut slant of his high cheekbones.

'So the neglected little wife gets restless and comes down to the bar to watch life pass her by,' Rosie continued with a sad, soulful aspect.

'People are looking at us.' His expressive mouth hard as iron, eyes blazing, Constantine sank down with controlled animal grace into a seat. But he still reminded her of a ferocious tiger prevented at the very last moment from springing.

'Of course they are...and congratulations—you're adding real veracity to this masquerade. Enter suspicious bridegroom in a seething temper. I shall try to look sufficiently quelled by the display,' Rosie promised, hanging her head and shrinking her shoulders as if she were withstanding the blast of his righteous wrath with suitable humility. 'But I am certainly not going back upstairs to vegetate in that bedroom.'

Constantine breathed in very, very slowly and deeply in the rushing silence.

Rosie grinned. 'You're shrewd, Constantine, I'll give you that. You see, if you tried trailing me out of here by force, someone might feel they had to intervene on my behalf.'

'Tomorrow morning cannot come soon enough for me,' Constantine swore with a feral flash of gritted white teeth.

'I know...we're not exactly a match made in heaven.'

'You are very brave in public places.'

'You're a very big guy.'

'So is Maurice.'

Rosie smiled. 'Maurice is as gentle as a lamb. He *never* loses his temper.'

'But then you wear the pants in that relationship,' Constantine interposed with scathing bite, a look of blatant disgust in his gaze.

'I expect you like women servile and adoring. You were born out of time, Constantine. You should have been an Arab potentate with a harem. Do you know that concubines were trained to crawl across the floor of their master's bedroom and up under the covers from the foot of the bed?' Rosie told him informatively.

Luxuriant black lashes dipped. His sensual mouth twisted. 'I am in the middle of a takeover bid for a company I have been working to acquire for some months.' The lashes shot up to reveal savagely impatient dark eyes. 'I don't trust you. I am not leaving you down here alone to pick up some man on what is supposed to be our wedding night.'

'I am not going to pick up a man. I have *never* picked up a man in my life.'

'I saw how those men at the bar were watching you. Like drooling, sex-starved sailors on shore leave!' Constantine grated, a faint flush highlighting his taut cheekbones. 'You wouldn't need to flex a fingernail. No decent woman would sit in a bar on her own—'

'I had Taki in tow.'

'You got him blind drunk!'

'He's got a bad cold and he was feeling foul and he must have a very low tolerance level for alcohol.' Rosie grimaced. 'But I told him to have a drink—'

'And his miscalculation in doing so will cost him his employment.'

Rosie went white with shock. 'That's not fair, Constantine. I *insisted* that he had that drink—'

'Did you also insist that he made love to you?'

'What the heck are you trying to imply?'

Black eyes glittered, his nostrils flaring. 'I heard what he was saying to you...a member of my staff making romantic advances to my wife—'

'Your wife? I am *not* your wife!' Rosie cut in with incredulous heat and vigour. 'I wouldn't be your wife for a million pounds!'

'Oh, I think you could push yourself for that amount...indeed a great deal less,' Constantine asserted with raw, biting cynicism. 'What price did you put on your body for Anton? He stuck you in a rented house. He didn't even buy you the roof over your head—' As the remainder of the wine in her glass splashed his strong, dark face, he broke off and stared at her with charged, thunderous disbelief.

Rosie stood and returned that look with venomous loathing. 'You make Neanderthal man look like Einstein!'

Constantine made it into the lift before she could get the doors closed on him. Consumed by rage, Rosie kept on stabbing wildly at the button. With a raw growl, he closed his arms round her and the lift doors finally slid shut.

'Let go of me, you caveman!' Rosie splintered breathlessly.

Constantine gazed down at her, blazing golden eyes intent, and splayed hard fingers to the curve of her hip and forced her up against him. That close to that lean, muscular male frame, Rosie froze, bright eyes bewildered as the heat and the scent of him washed over her in a heady, disorientatingly pleasurable tide. A tiny little muscle deep down in her stomach jerked, making her legs feel oddly weak and hollow. Her heart started slamming suffocatingly fast against her ribcage.

'You were trying to flirt with me,' Constantine murmured with a slight frown, his deep, dark drawl sending the most peculiar little shivers travelling down her taut spinal cord. A faint curl of sardonic amusement suddenly quirked his hard mouth.

'Flirt?' Rosie queried in a daze. 'When I threw the wine in your face?'

'You weren't on a winning streak.'

Her bemused gaze connected with molten gold eyes and time seemed to slow down yet move in curious synchronisation with the heavy pounding of the blood in her veins. She struggled to breathe, outrageously conscious of every skin cell in her trembling body, the taut swell of her breasts, the aching sensitivity of her nipples and the straining, melting rush of heat and awareness between her thighs.

No…! she told herself in profound shock. I don't flirt.

As he lowered his arrogant dark head, Constantine smiled lazily, sexily. Rosie was transfixed. His mouth claimed hers with shocking effect. Excitement exploded like a greedy, out-of-control fire inside her, overwhelming her with a voracious passion. She kissed him back in a wild surge of hunger, moaning low in her throat at the stabbing, wickedly erotic intrusion of his tongue. He shifted fluidly against her, making her crave closer contact with a desperation that screamed through every nerve-ending.

He lifted his head to survey her stunned face and drew her out of the lift. Plunged from the breathless heights of unbearable excitement down to the simple business of movement, Rosie met the descent in an agony of disorientation. Inside the suite, he reached for her again with confident hands. The vital energy that flowed from him attracted her like a honey trap. His shimmering golden gaze enveloped her, igniting a floodtide of instinctive heat and response that made her tremble.

'Tell me that you like to make love over and over again,' Constantine invited huskily, his accent roughening the explicit invitation. 'And I will tell you that I will satisfy your every desire.'

Involuntarily, Rosie stiffened and then backed off a shaken step, forcing him to release her again. She felt hideously out of her depth and the shock of that realisation renewed her grasp on reality again. 'I can't sleep with you...' she began shakily.

'Who said anything about sleeping?'

'You said you wouldn't melt,' Rosie reminded him almost accusingly.

'I can melt for one night and repent in the morning...'

'I'm terribly tired...and anyway you have your take-over bid to work at,' Rosie gabbled as it struck her with paralysing force that there was nothing she wanted more, nothing she had *ever* wanted more than she wanted Constantine at that moment, even though every sane sense rebelled and she loathed him with every brain cell she possessed. That was such a devastating truth to face that Rosie was completely floored by it and incapable of retaliating with her usual fire and aggression.

His ebony brows drew together, his soul-destroyingly sensual mouth compressing as a blaze of derision fired his gaze. '*Christos*...I hate women who play sex games! And one night is the only offer I am likely to make,' he delivered with cold clarity. 'I don't pay for sex—'

'And you couldn't *talk* a zombie into it!' Rosie slung at him, feelingly, and stalked into the bedroom, but once she got that door shut her hot face crumpled and her throat convulsed. She leant back weakly while she fought the choking, burning rush of tears dammed up behind her eyelids.

* * *

Hours later, Rosie lay awake in the darkness, filled with self-loathing and rampant insecurity. She was still shattered by the sexual response which Constantine had drawn from her. As a teenager she had been subjected to a frightening assault and although she had mercifully emerged from that attack unharmed the encounter had deprived her of any desire to experiment with physical intimacy.

Indeed, growing up, Rosie had developed a deep and abiding distrust of the opposite sex. Furthermore, every time she'd got into a tight corner or felt unhappy she had run away from whatever council home she had been living in. That habit had got her into a lot of trouble until Maurice had convinced her that turning her back on her problems didn't settle them.

All her energies had gone into building up a viable business which would pay the rent. Her need for independence and security had made her drive herself hard. But Anton had cracked her self-sufficiency by persuading her to come down to London. And that was when she had begun to change, opening herself out to emotions and possibilities she had never allowed herself to explore before.

Anton had even dragged her out shopping, making it painfully obvious that he couldn't understand her dislike of feminine clothing, and once again she had given way, helplessly hooked on gaining her father's approval. Tears burned her eyes. Anton had had a struggle to accept her platonic relationship with Maurice. But he had never been able to comprehend the simple fact that most men left her cold. In fact, she would have said that *all* men left her cold…until Constantine Voulos had appeared in that church.

Constantine—the only male she had ever wanted to rip the clothes off and flatten onto the nearest bed. Her cheeks scorched with embarrassment and she scrubbed furiously at her eyes. So that was the power of sexual desire; well, she didn't need him or anyone else to spell out the obvious to her, but nothing could have prepared her for the raw, terrifying strength of that hunger. One kiss and she had gone to pieces like a starstruck groupie.

Thank heaven that after tomorrow she would never, ever see him again. That encounter had meant nothing to Constantine. In the heat of male lust and without even an ounce of liking or respect for her he had offered her a one-night stand. You couldn't get much more sleazy, she thought painfully. He had been tempted but not so tempted that his better judgement hadn't experienced a certain relief when she had turned him down. She had seen that in those surprisingly expressive eyes of his. She grimaced, exhaustion creeping over her like a heavy fog.

Waking with a start, she found Constantine staring down at her. Blinking in the lamplight, Rosie jerked bolt upright, a cold spasm of fear impelling her.

'Do you usually go to bed with all your clothes on?' Constantine enquired, studying the jeans and T-shirt she had put back on.

Taking in the short black robe he was wearing, shaken eyes widening at the slice of bare hair-roughened brown chest that was visible, Rosie leapt out of the other side of the bed.

'*Christos*…what do you think I was about to do? Attack you?' he demanded, openly taken aback by her reaction.

'The sofa is more my size.'

'We can share the bed. It's three in the morning and I have nothing on my mind but an overwhelming desire for sleep,' Constantine asserted with distinct hauteur.

But Rosie closed the bedroom door without answering, traced her way across the dark room beyond and curled up wearily on the sofa. It felt as if she had only just closed her eyes when a loud, persistent knock started hammering on the door. She pushed her tousled head under a cushion and groaned, snuggling into the warmth of a blanket that hadn't been there when she'd gone to sleep. Only when an impatient burst of Greek sounded did she lift her head again.

By then Constantine, clad in close-fitting charcoal-grey trousers and a white silk shirt, was yanking open the door. Dmitri surged in, waving a newspaper and showing every sign of a man throwing a fit. Constantine took the newspaper, exploded briefly back into Greek and then fell silent. Both men turned almost simultaneously to study Rosie…

Caught up in the drama, Rosie stared in wide, innocent enquiry back at them. Constantine opened the door again and the bodyguard departed with unconcealed eagerness. Then Constantine swung back to face Rosie.

'You conniving, cheating little shrew!' he condemned without warning, crossing the room in one long, powerful stride and raising her off the sofa with an even more powerful hand.

'What's the matter with you?' Rosie gasped, shocked by the rage burning in his black, diamond-cutting eyes.

'*Theos*…you will suffer for this!'

'What am I supposed to have done?'

'I was a fool to trust you even this far… My lawyers warned me…why the hell didn't I listen?' Constantine grated, glowering down at her with such loathing and disgust that Rosie turned pale as milk and began to shake, a sick feeling stirring in the pit of her stomach.

He released his hold on her crushed fingers, drew himself up to his full, thoroughly intimidating height and watched her collapse on trembling legs down into the nearest armchair. He lifted a lean brown hand and spread his fingers, the extraordinary force of that single physical gesture capturing her shocked stare.

'You really want to find out what it is like being married to me?' Constantine bit out with a flash of pure fire in his mesmeric, menacing gaze. 'You will wish every minute of every day that you had stayed in your slum dwelling where you belonged and you will be on your knees begging for a divorce before I am finished with you!'

CHAPTER FIVE

WITH extreme difficulty, Rosie snatched in a ragged breath to steady her jumping nerves. 'I still don't know what you're talking about...'

'Don't you *dare* lie to me!' Constantine thundered.

Rosie squinted with fearful curiosity at the newspaper he had flung on the coffee table. Constantine snatched it up again and displayed it like prosecution evidence. TYCOON'S SECRET WEDDING, ran the headline on the front page. Rosie gulped and then gaped at the familiar photograph of herself standing outside the cottage. The last time she had seen that photo, it had been inside a frame on the lounge mantelpiece. It had been taken the day she'd moved in, proud as punch of her first real home since childhood.

'Maurice...' she whispered with pained comprehension, for surely only Maurice could have given that picture to the Press.

'*Maurice,*' Constantine savoured with seething satisfaction. 'I will break him in two!'

'No, it wasn't Maurice!' Rosie gasped in horror, recognising that satisfaction for what it was and even more appalled by the sight of Constantine's clenching fists and rampant aura of physical violence. She coiled her shaking hands together and her tongue stole out to moisten her dry lips. 'It wasn't Maurice...it was *me.*'

'Why try to protect him? He was your accomplice. You must have phoned him to tell him where we were staying because you didn't know our destination until we arrived.'

'Yes, I phoned him,' Rosie muttered tightly, and bent

70

her fiery head, the appalling tension in the room tensing her muscles so hard that they ached.

'I presume that you realise what you have done.' His accented drawl fell like a whip, the anger reined back to a chilling coldness which made the tiny hairs at the nape of her neck prickle. 'Thespina will soon know that a wedding has taken place. She has friends in London and she will naturally demand an explanation of my strange failure to inform her of my marriage. Did you think of that…did you even *care*?'

Rosie flinched, tears of strain stinging her eyes.

'No, of course you didn't care. You couldn't see beyond your own greed. Anton left you nothing in his will and you resented that, didn't you?' Constantine condemned with raw-edged distaste. 'No doubt you dreamt of great riches. But two weeks before his death Anton took out a crippling loan to buy a mouldering ruin on the island of Majorca. Sentiment drove him to stake everything he possessed against that single, insane purchase and he was far too proud to approach me for either advice or assistance.'

'Majorca?' Rosie repeated unsteadily, her bright head slowly lifting.

'Son Fontanal, the former Estrada home, complete with contents and a thousand stubbly, infertile acres fit only for a mountain goat,' Constantine recited half under his breath, his lingering incredulity at such a move palpable. 'The ruin even comes complete with an embargo on further development because it stands in an environmentally protected area. It was all but worthless to anyone but Anton. The heirs of the late owner saw him coming…'

'Anton bought back Son Fontanal?' Rosie whispered in breathless shock.

'He was always a deeply sentimental man,'

Constantine conceded tautly but with the air of a male striving without success to comprehend such feelings.

But Rosie understood…Rosie understood as if her father had been in the room talking to her. *This* was what Anton had wanted his daughter to have. Son Fontanal, sold out of necessity by his widowed mother when Anton was only fifteen. Her father might have spent the rest of his life in Greece but his deep pain and regret at the loss of his ancestral home had never left him. As a powerless, frustrated teenager, Anton had sworn over his father's grave that if he ever got the chance he would mortgage his soul to bring Son Fontanal back into the family again.

'He loved that house,' Rosie muttered softly. 'No price would have been too high.'

'It was an act of financial suicide. Had he lived…' Constantine's hard mouth clenched, a muscle pulling at the corner of his lips as his deep voice roughened with suppressed emotion. 'Had Anton lived, he would have had a choice between bankruptcy or coming to me. I like to think that he would have overcome his pride and approached me for help—'

'Not his wife?'

Constantine shot her a look of naked disbelief. '*Christos*…what man would want to borrow money from his wife? Why am I discussing these private matters with you?' he grated with sudden ferocity. 'Go and put on that dress you wore last night. We are leaving this hotel.'

'Forget the "we"…I'll call a cab to take me home.'

Constantine loosed a derisive laugh. 'You're coming to Greece with me. That is the only option I have left…and believe me,' he intoned with merciless black eyes, 'if I have to drug you and tie you up to get you there I will do it.'

'G-Greece…?' Rosie stammered incredulously.

'A short meeting with Thespina will be necessary

now.' Constantine dealt her a ferocious look of antipathy. 'That is rather unfortunate when I have already told her that our fake engagement was broken and that we had parted.'

'I don't care how you choose to explain yourself but I am definitely *not* going to Greece,' Rosie assured him flatly as she got up.

'If necessary I will strip you and dress you myself.'

Rosie collided with black eyes of shamelessly steady threat. She went into the bedroom. Constantine strode in after her and detached the phone from its socket. 'From now on you will not be communicating with the rest of the world. Now get dressed,' he instructed.

Haunted eyes looked back at her from the bathroom mirror. How could Maurice have done such a dreadful thing? How could he have contacted the Press? He would know exactly how she would feel about that betrayal. He *knew* that she had been determined to protect Thespina from any further distress. She opened the bathroom door again and peered out.

Constantine was shrugging his broad shoulders into a superbly tailored jacket. Her mouth ran dry as she watched the sleek-toned muscles ripple beneath the fine silk of his shirt and noted the dark, tantalising shadow of the hair-roughened chest she had glimpsed during the night when he'd woken her up.

'Why aren't you changing?' he demanded.

Her cheeks hot as hellfire, Rosie regained her wandering wits and muttered frantically, '*Please* let me phone Maurice...I have to speak to him.'

Densely lashed dark eyes of outrage landed on her. 'No.'

'Please,' Rosie persisted.

'The first rule of a Greek wife is obedience,' Constantine delivered, moving towards her with the predatory grace of a prowling leopard. 'And if you don't jump when I say jump, little rag-doll, I will take action to re-educate you and after a very little while in my undiluted company crawling across the floor of my bedroom like a submissive slave will come entirely naturally!'

Rosie slammed the door and locked it for good measure.

'I *can't* go to Greece,' Rosie told him again in the lift.

'I'll content myself with beating Maurice to a pulp and putting him out of business, shall I?' Constantine smiled down at her shaken face. 'And don't you doubt that it can be done. Discreet enquiries have revealed that much as Maurice's old uncle likes his nephew Maurice got his profiteering instincts from the same source, and for the right price Uncle Dennis would regret the necessity but he would shove the pair of you out into the snow!'

Rosie was shattered that Constantine was already aware of the fact that their landlord was related to Maurice. 'You *knew*—?'

'I never make a threat I can't carry through on. You step out of line, I take action in progressive degrees of unpleasantness. I will make Maurice Carter sorry he was ever born and even sorrier that he once shared a bed with you.'

'You're angry...you don't know what you're saying...'

'Anger sharpens my wits but it would appear to scramble yours.'

'Maurice is a completely innocent party in all this.' If Maurice *had* alerted the Press, it could only have been because he genuinely believed that Constantine was trying to cheat her and that publicising their marriage would somehow strengthen her position. In other words, Maurice could only have done it for *her* benefit, so ultimately the responsibility was hers. 'I can't believe that you would want to injure him.'

'Yet you say that Anton told you so much about me.'

Rosie's troubled mind roamed over Anton's frequent descriptive references to Constantine. A ruthless aggressor in business and temperamentally incapable of accepting defeat. A relentless enemy who never forgot a slight, fiercely loyal only to his family, and a male who didn't know what relaxation was...except in the bedroom, women being his one leisure indulgence. Was that how he kept himself so fit?

Colouring, Rosie frowned at her inexcusable loss of concentration and then felt her stomach sinking at the reality of what she had recalled. Her father had loved and admired Constantine for all the qualities that he himself did not possess, she acknowledged wryly. So what did Constantine's enemies have to say about his character?

'This is an evening outfit...I look really stupid in this,' she objected as the cooler temperature of the foyer assailed her bare arms and shoulders.

'You look exactly as I want you to look...like a bimbo who hasn't a clue how to dress in daylight. You don't need to smile for the paparazzi either,' Constantine added as mortified pink erupted over her cheekbones. 'In fact the more miserable and out of place you appear to feel, the less surprised everyone will be when I ditch you again. You see, these rich older guys who bore the pants off their bimbos have a disastrously short attention span for those same bimbos!'

As he led her in the direction of the exit, Rosie was in an agony of teeth-clenching discomfiture. 'Are you saying that there might be reporters outside?'

A split second later, she was confronted with a frightening sea of faces, snapping cameras and shouted questions. As she shivered violently, Constantine doffed his black cashmere overcoat and, draping it round her shoulders with exaggerated gallantry, banded a controlling arm round her spine. He strode silently through the parting crush to the limousine. Nobody got in their way. Rosie was grudgingly impressed by his cool, commanding presence and relieved to see Taki climbing into the front seat beside the chauffeur.

'Are you still planning to sack Taki?' she asked uncomfortably.

'I am still considering the matter.'

'It really wasn't his fault, it was mine.'

Silence rewarded that assurance.

'I can't go to Greece without a passport or clothes,' Rosie pointed out next. 'I'll have to go home first.'

'Dmitri is taking care of that problem. He'll meet us at the airport.'

'I'm hungry.'

'We'll eat on the plane.'

In frustration, Rosie subsided back into the warmth of his overcoat. The rich fabric harboured the faint, elusive male scent of him. Her nostrils flared and she found herself breathing in deeply. Stiffening, she stole a covert glance at him. He was on his mobile phone again but somehow he immediately sensed her surveillance, his long, spiky lashes lifting to reveal compelling dark golden eyes.

Her heart skipped a startled beat but she couldn't break that involuntary connection. Those eyes were extraordinarily arresting in that lean, hard-boned face. His gaze roamed at an outrageously leisurely pace down over the exposed length of her shapely legs. Her skin burned as if he had touched her, her pulses racing wildly. A bitter-sweet ache stirred inside her. It was an effort to breathe as the tension thrummed ever higher between them.

Constantine smiled with sudden raw, earthy amuse-

ment, challenging her scrutiny with clear knowledge of
the exact effect he was having on her. That awareness
shook Rosie inside out. It gave her a shocking foretaste
of the very sexual male animal she was dealing with and
she was completely unnerved. With a jerk, she turned
her head away and flipped his coat hurriedly over her
legs.

Constantine threw back his head and laughed.

'Shut up!' Rosie snapped without looking at him.

'You have an astonishing air of innocence,' he murmured silkily. 'I am no longer surprised that Anton fell
hook, line and sinker. He was at a dangerous age. It's a
shame that he never had the opportunity to see you in
your true environment. Only then might he have sensed
how false the image was.'

'He had an equally false image of you. He told me
that you had great charm, beautiful manners and fascinating conversational skills.' At that point Rosie
screened a yawn of boredom with her hand, and was
secretly furious and thoroughly disconcerted when
Constantine laughed with even greater amusement.

Less than an hour ago, he had been incandescent with
rage. But now he *exuded* the indolent cool of a male in
supreme control. But he *is* in control, an unwelcome
inner voice reminded her. And all, seemingly, because
of Maurice. Yet Rosie was still stunned by that apparent
betrayal. She had to get her friend on the phone and find
out what had really happened. Maybe the photo had been
stolen. Maybe the Press had already been on
Constantine's trail…

Rosie was deriving precious little pleasure from her first
trip abroad. As the car wove through the heavy Athens
traffic, she sat rigid-backed and tense at the prospect of
having to face Thespina again.

When Dmitri had joined them at the airport with her

one suitcase and shabby backpack, she had tried to question him about Maurice but Constantine had prevented her. Since then, her temper had been further exacerbated. On board the private jet she had at least had the opportunity to change into more appropriate clothing but she had then slept through the whole of the flight, waking up only as they landed. By then, having gone without both breakfast and lunch, she had been so hungry that she had been forced to beg Constantine for the appropriate currency with which to buy a bar of chocolate as he'd dragged her through Athens airport, refusing to let her out of his sight for a second.

'If you don't put that blasted phone down, I will scream!' Rosie's hot temper erupted with startling suddenness.

'What is wrong with you now?' Constantine lowered the mobile with the long-suffering aspect of a male dealing with a very tiresome child.

Rosie's teeth gritted. 'I do not want to be involved in telling any more lies to Thespina.'

'Would it give you a bigger kick to walk in and announce yourself as her late husband's mistress?'

Frustration filled her. 'I was *not* Anton's mistress—'

'The mistress who has now become the offensive equivalent of a daughter-in-law? Thespina deserves neither the pain nor the humiliation of that kind of truth,' Constantine countered with fierce emphasis.

The limousine drew up in front of a large, elegant town house. Rosie climbed out into the heat of mid-afternoon, feeling hot, crumpled and sick with nerves. While Constantine spoke to the manservant who had hurried out to greet them, she hung cravenly back behind him.

He swung round and expelled his breath in a stark hiss of pent-up tension.

'Thespina is not here. She flew out to Brazil this

morning to stay with friends. Apparently she tried to contact me to let me know her plans but she was unable to reach me.'

A simply huge tide of relief engulfed Rosie. She scooted back into the limousine at speed.

'Now what?' she asked almost brightly.

Constantine frowned. 'It is unlikely that she will hear news of our marriage before her return. Her friends live on a coffee plantation in a remote area.'

'You could phone her.'

'I will wait until I see her. One does not make that sort of announcement on the telephone...' His strong face shuttered.

'So what do we do now?'

Constantine ignored the question. He was in a filthy mood again, Rosie registered. It was not the time to share with him her belief that deception only dug deceivers into a deeper hole. She tried to be fair, tried to ask herself what she would have done in his position. Their secret wedding, designed only to meet the terms of Anton's will, was now a matter of public record. And Constantine's response to that hideous unforeseen development was simply to pretend that he had nothing to hide, indeed that their marriage was a *genuine* marriage...

As that belated acknowledgement finally dawned on Rosie, she turned pale. Earlier in the day, Constantine's fury, her distress over that wretched newspaper article and concern for Maurice and Thespina had blinded her to her own predicament. Now she focused on her companion in open shock. 'You're expecting me to pretend to be your wife?' she whispered in shock.

'You *are* my wife,' Constantine reminded her with driven emphasis.

'Legally speaking, I suppose,' Rosie conceded weakly. 'But— '

'The fiction will have to be maintained for a couple of months at least.'

'I'm a rotten actress. We don't even *like* each other. People aren't so stupid that they're not going to see that!' she protested.

Constantine ignored her again. She hated it when he did that. He closed her out as if she weren't there. It made her feel like an irritating fly he couldn't be bothered to swat.

'I couldn't live with you for one week, never mind a couple of months!'

Constantine shot her a look of naked derision. 'Who do you think you're kidding? You're about to enter bimbo paradise! I have no choice but to keep you in the lap of luxury. But the prospect of rewarding you for your treachery and guile disgusts me!'

Hot-cheeked and seething with resentment, Rosie started practising ignoring *him*. If he fondly imagined she intended to hang around eating humble pie and imitating a wall fixture for the next couple of months, he had another thought coming!

But two hours later, a truly enormous and absolutely delicious meal having brought her back from the edge of starvation, Rosie had a remarkably sunny smile on her formerly disgruntled face. She was lying back in the Jacuzzi in the fabulous bathroom attached to her allotted bedroom. Constantine lived in a breathtakingly beautiful walled estate outside the city. His vast palatial villa swarmed with servants, wondrously keen to ensure that she didn't have to lift a finger to help herself. It was like staying in a five-star luxury hotel.

Admittedly, she had been most uncomfortable when Constantine had introduced her as his blushing bride to the domestic staff. But she had been delirious with delight when she had understood the ramifications of his care in explaining the internal phone system to her. He had informed her that if she *had* to speak to him she was to dial a certain number. He would grow old and grey waiting for her to call. And in a house this size she was sure to get hold of a phone with an outside line to contact Maurice soon. Constantine could not be everywhere simultaneously.

She hated him. And he despised her. So how could she possibly be attracted to him? Surely that amount of animosity ought to be a complete turn-off? And why was that extravagantly gorgeous face of his somehow etched behind her eyelids like a burr under a saddle? And why, even though she was frantically glad to finally be free of his company, could she think of very little else *but* Constantine? Rosie frowned over that conundrum. She felt oddly dislocated...as if she had lost something, as if she was missing out on something...what, *another* fight?

But, much as it went against the grain, she had to give him points for some virtues. He clearly adored Thespina. Seemingly there was nothing that Constantine would not do to keep her in happy ignorance of her late husband's last will and testament. And greed had nothing to do with it. Rosie flushed uncomfortably. Constantine was every bit as filthy rich as Maurice had said he was. His private jet, his fantastic home and his lifestyle spoke for themselves.

He had loved her father too, Rosie conceded reluctantly. Yet they had been such different men with diametrically opposed personalities. Anton had always been cracking jokes and grinning, looking on the bright side of every problem and, if possible, cheerfully ignoring the problem altogether.

Was it easier for Constantine to believe that Anton had gone off the rails for a young and pretty face? The truth, she suspected, would be far more damaging. Anton had kept a big, dark secret from his family for over twenty years. But then her father had wanted what he could not have: he had wanted his daughter without hurting his wife.

And although he had often talked about confessing all to Thespina he hadn't been able to grasp that nettle even when he was contemplating his own death. How *could* her father have demanded that Constantine marry her? Rosie shook her head and sighed. Even had Constantine accepted that she was Anton's daughter, her father had had no right to demand such an outrageous sacrifice from his ward.

Wrapped in the towelling robe put there for the purpose, Rosie strolled out of the bathroom, feeling reasonably rested and relaxed. The sensation was short-lived. The bedroom harboured a tall, dark, very masculine intruder.

Rosie tensed, green eyes flying over the Italian-styled double-breasted beige suit Constantine was wearing. It gave him the look of a stunningly sexy and dangerous gangster. For a split second, he quite took her breath away and she was transfixed. That sensation didn't last either.

Constantine frowned at her. 'Did I not make it clear that for the duration of your stay here you were to behave as if this was a normal marriage?'

Uncertainly, Rosie nodded.

'Then why did you insist on dining from a tray instead of joining me downstairs for dinner? And why did you refuse my housekeeper's offer to give you a guided tour of the villa?'

Rosie heaved a stoical sigh. 'Anything else I've done wrong?'

'You're not a guest here. This is supposed to be your home. Act like a newly married woman.'

'I haven't a clue how a newly married woman acts.'

'But you have an incredible imagination. *Use it*,' Constantine suggested with sardonic bite.

It was already being used. In her mind's eye, Constantine had mysteriously become a brooding gangster from a shadowy old black and white movie. And mysteriously sharing that same scene *was*...Rosie, garbed in a fabulous fringed twenties dress, the sole focus of her gangster's seething passions. Emerging in shock from her first experience of erotic fantasy, Rosie drew in a tumultuous, steadying breath and wondered frantically what was going on inside her head.

'What's the matter with you? You're unusually quiet.' Constantine ran suspicious black eyes over her.

'Jet lag,' Rosie said shrilly, embarrassed to death by that sexual daydream.

'I'll see if I can arrange a flight for you *every* day,' Constantine drawled without a flicker of a smile on his way out of the door.

While she had been in the Jacuzzi her luggage had been unpacked but Rosie was surprised to see her little brocade jewel case sitting on the dressing-table. In fact, having already had an unhappy preview of the collection of motley garments Maurice had tumbled willy-nilly into the case, she was astonished that he had been thoughtful enough to pack her jewellery into the backpack.

Opening it, she frowned and then poked through several sets of tangled costume beads in an increasingly desperate search for what she had expected to find. Her heart stopped dead and her stomach literally heaved. *The Estrada ring was no longer there*...and Rosie lost no time in jumping to the most obvious conclusion. Constantine had been determined to take that ring from her. And, lo and behold, it was now gone! Obviously Constantine had stolen her father's gift from her!

Rosie raced down the long, sweeping staircase barefoot. The light of battle in her furious gaze, she saw

Constantine emerging from a room off the huge hall. 'I want my ring back!' she slung at him full volume.

Startled, Constantine wheeled round to face her. 'What the hell—?'

'The Estrada ring. It was in my jewel case. Now it's gone.'

'*Gone?*' Constantine stressed as he curved a hand round one slight shoulder and pressed her into an elegant reception room. 'Gone where?'

Rosie grimaced. 'I was hoping you wouldn't do this.'

'If you've lost that ring,' Constantine spelt out rawly, 'I'll strangle you!'

'The best line of defence being attack, right?' Rosie looked deeply cynical and her lip curled. 'Look, I know you have the ring and that you are responsible for its disappearance—'

'*Christos*...do you dare to accuse *me* of stealing?' Constantine flared in outrage.

Rosie winced and backtracked a diplomatic inch or two. 'I wouldn't use that term. Let's just say that you have retrieved something which you believe I have no right to retain. But I have every right. Anton *gave* me that ring.'

'I am not a thief. If the emerald is missing we will call the police, but not until I am fully convinced that this is not another ploy.'

'Ploy...what's that supposed to mean?' Rosie splintered.

'It means,' Constantine stated with hauteur, 'that I would not at all be surprised to learn that your boyfriend has the ring. I'm already well aware that you're a liar and a cheat—'

'You swine!' Rosie gasped with a shudder of disbelief.

'And I imagine the ring is heavily insured—'

At that instant, a servant came to the door and spoke

to Constantine while Rosie stood with balled fists of fury.

His arrogant dark head turned. 'You'll have to excuse me. I have a visitor.'

For the space of three minutes, Rosie was frozen to the carpet by that careless dismissal. Either Constantine didn't believe that the ring was genuinely missing or he was being very clever in his pretence of distrust and ignorance. He had to be lying—he *had* to be! Her restive gaze fell on the telephone and stilled. Only then did it occur to her that she didn't know the international code for the UK. A minute search of the room revealed no directory. She didn't even know how to dial the operator in Greece, so how could she contact Maurice?

Frustration currenting through her in a wild surge, she marched out into the hall again and then hesitated, frowning as she heard voices. Constantine and his visitor. His late caller was female and, surprisingly, English. Curiosity took her to the ajar door. She glanced in.

'Louise…' Constantine was saying very, very drily.

A gorgeous brunette with legs as long as rail tracks and even better exposed was reclining on a chaise longue, making very unconvincing play with a frilly handkerchief.

'But to read something like *that* in a newspaper… I was devastated, Constantine! How could you get married without telling me? You said you wouldn't be marrying for years and years and I'm really not at all sure that I can find it within myself to continue as your mistress now that you have a wife,' Louise moaned in a petulant lament, flicking back her glamorous dark mane of hair while her steel-blue gaze carefully judged her effect on the target of her complaints.

Unfortunately that target was out of Rosie's view but that did not inhibit her. Eyes sparkling like emerald gemstones, Rosie pressed the door back and planted herself on the threshold. 'I think I can help you to make up your mind,' she murmured sweetly. 'Come within one hundred yards of Constantine again and I will scratch your eyes out!'

The brunette reared up in comical shock. Constantine spun round, black eyes aflame with sheer incredulity.

'As for *you*,' Rosie breathed, folding her arms with undeniable enjoyment in her role and fixing her full attention on her fake husband, who curiously felt rather more like a husband than he had yet, 'I suggest you remove your ladyfriend from *my* home immediately...because I never make a threat I can't carry through on.'

At the repetition of his own words of earlier in the day, Constantine turned pale beneath his bronzed skin. An incandescent blaze of gold shimmered in his eyes before he veiled them, his sensual mouth compressing into a bloodless line of self-restraint. Constantine silenced. Well, well, well, how the mighty have fallen, Rosie savoured without pity.

The brunette strolled out provocatively slowly past Rosie. She was about a foot taller. Then she paused and glanced back with a curious malicious smile in Constantine's direction. 'It may seem a strange thing to say in the circumstances but your little jailbait bride has just made my day. Why do I get this feeling that life as you know it is over? She'll give you hell and you *deserve* it!'

Rosie watched Louise depart, secretly impressed to death by her cool, dignified exit. As a door slammed in the distance, she sighed, 'I'm so glad you didn't break her heart. Well, how did I do?'

The silence pulsed as if it were about to explode.

'*How...did...you...do?*' Constantine framed between audibly grinding teeth.

'In the newly married woman stakes...was I convincing? I mean, there is just no way a wife would walk past a scene like that in her own home. As you reminded me, I am *not* just a guest here.'

Constantine swung away from her and spread lean brown hands in an unsteady arc of scantily leashed rage. She had the feeling that he couldn't quite believe what had just happened to him. He swore raggedly half under his breath in his own language. Then he murmured, not quite levelly. 'Do you have a single sensitive bone in your body?'

Rosie shook her fiery head. 'Not where you're concerned. I was a bit worried that I might be reading the signals wrong and that your ladyfriend might be sincerely attached to you. But she wasn't, was she? So no harm done.'

'You did it quite deliberately. I am preventing you from contacting that prehistoric ape Maurice and in return you decided to start screwing up *my* private life.'

'Newly married men don't have private lives.'

'You think not?' Constantine purred like a big jungle cat as he prowled round her in an ever-shrinking circle of intimidation. 'Are *you* not a part of my private life? Have you not forced me to acknowledge you as my wife?'

Rosie suffered a sudden alarming loss of confidence, for the first time wishing she hadn't been quite so eager to confess to sins she hadn't committed earlier in the day. 'Constantine—'

'What?'

Rosie took a tiny backward step, her heart thumping somewhere in the region of her throat. 'I think it's time I went to bed.'

'So do I.' Constantine closed his arms deftly around her slim frame and swept her off her feet.

'What do you think you're doing?' Rosie shrieked.

'What I should have done last night!' Constantine started up the stairs with determination.

'Put me down! Have you gone crazy?'

'It's your own bloody fault! *Christos*...you keep on pushing and pushing!' Constantine roared down at her accusingly. 'I put you in a room as far away from me as I could get you and still keep you under the same roof! I was determined not to be tempted by you again. I have tried to keep my distance—'

'Well, you're not trying very hard now, are you?' Rosie snapped back tempestuously. 'And if you don't let go of me right this minute I'm going to hit you so hard you'll be knocked into the middle of next week!'

'Your mouth is bigger than you are,' Constantine growled, his deep voice thickening in a manner that sent Rosie's self-preserving instincts shooting to full power. 'Why not kiss me instead?'

'Because I don't want to kiss you!'

'No?'

'Do I look that dumb?' Rosie spat.

But then Constantine blocked out the light with the hot, hungry heat of his mouth, and the world spun so violently, she gasped and clutched at him. Electrifying heat engulfed her...or maybe it was him. He seemed to be burning up too. Her fingers framed his hard cheekbones and her head went back as he knotted one hand tightly into her hair and kissed her with bruising, demanding thoroughness until she thought she would pass out from lack of oxygen but didn't care because nothing had ever felt so good.

In darkness he brought her down on a bed, and as he released her mouth with a stifled groan of frustration she lay there winded and gasping in air like a drowning swimmer. A light went on and she blinked dazedly. Constantine came down on the bed beside her, wrenching at his silk tie, shrugging out of his jacket. *Run,* a little voice urged her. But she clashed with eyes of searing gold and her whole body turned liquid and unfamiliar, her mind blanking out as an uncontrollable surge of hunger overwhelmed her.

'Don't lie there like a sacrifice, you little witch,' he breathed unevenly. 'Don't let me think…I only want to *feel*—'

His hand wasn't quite steady as he tugged her up to him again. Intense satisfaction filled her, along with a heady sense of power. She snatched in the husky male scent of him so close and every sense thrilled, a desperate wanting that overpowered inhibition driving her hand up to sink wonderingly into the silky black depths of his hair. A tenderness that was new to her made her heart twist and her fingers tremble and his ebony brows drew together in a frown that might have been surprise.

He leant forward and let the tip of his tongue dip between her lips in a heart-stoppingly erotic foray. She shivered violently and then reached for him because she couldn't help herself, finding his carnal mouth again, and instantly he took charge with a husky growl of dominance, kissing her until she was a quivering mass of aching nerve-endings.

A lean hand jerked at the tie on the towelling robe and then closed over one small, pouting breast. The sensation of pleasure was so intense, Rosie almost had a cardiac arrest.

Lifting his dark, tousled head, Constantine smiled sexily down into her shaken face. 'You like that?'

Rosie didn't have words to tell him how much. She was lost in another world, a wholly physical place where only sensation ruled. He sent his tongue skimming over a swollen pink nipple and her back arched, her teeth clenching, her nails clawing into the bedspread beneath her. All she knew was that she wanted more, more of that stunning, heart-racing pleasure, and only he could give it. He lowered his head and tasted her supersensitive flesh and she jerked and whimpered, experiencing a pleasure that blew her mind and reduced her to trembling, gasping submission.

'*Christos*...you're hot,' Constantine groaned, lowering his big, powerful body and shuddering as his hands sank to the swell of her hips, forcing her into contact with the hard, swollen evidence of his arousal and then rolling back from her with a curse of frustration, an impatient hand flying to the belt-buckle of his trousers.

Hot...*hot*? Rosie tensed, her brain flying back into gear. She squinted down at the shameless thrust of her bare breasts, still glistening damply from his lovemaking. For an instant she was frozen there, at a peak of appalled horror that almost equalled her former pitch of excitement, and then she was off that bed so fast, she could have challenged and outrun an Olympic sprinter.

'*Theos*...!' Incredulity exploded from Constantine and took his fluent English with it as he vented a flood of guttural Greek.

Rosie fled into the dark corridor like a lemming charging suicidally at a cliff. *Hot*...cheap, easy, sordid. Dear heaven, how had she let him get that far? One minute she had been shouting at him and the next... Typical Constantine manoeuvre: hit on her one vulnerability and try to use her to level the score. Turn a pitched battle into a sexual orgy and then smirk with macho male superiority. She shuddered in disgust and then registered in horror that the corridor had come to a dismaying dead end.

Constantine stopped ten feet away in a patch of moonlight. Rosie whipped back against the wall, arms spread in sudden instinctive fear, her slender length braced for attack.

'What the hell *is* this?'

'Don't you dare t-touch me...' Her voice was a sick thread of sound.

Constantine stared, incisive black eyes pinned to her frightened face. 'I'm not a rapist,' he said grimly. 'I can take a refusal without becoming violent.'

Trembling, still not quite trusting him, Rosie let her arms slide heavily down the wall and curved them protectively round herself instead, agonisingly aware that she had exposed more than her body to him now in betraying that fear. And a part of her was already acknowledging that she had behaved badly. Lying all but naked on a bed with him and responding with such wild abandon had given him every reason to react incredulously to her sudden change of heart.

'Watching a woman cringe from me as if I am about to attack her has to be the equivalent of ten cold showers at once,' Constantine completed flatly, his nostrils flaring.

'I didn't think you were about to—' she began shakily.

'You *did* think that.'

But only at the height of her appalled turmoil about what had so nearly happened between them. When she had seen him poised there against the darkness, that old subconscious fear had rushed to the surface in response to the sheer physical threat of his masculine power and size.

'I have never had to use force to bed a woman. Nor would I,' Constantine asserted with raw-edged hauteur.

'I led you on...I'm sorry,' Rosie mumbled, frantically wishing he would just go away and leave her to recover in privacy.

'Why?'

That one bald question made Rosie squirm. There was only one answer but it was not an answer she wished to give. Swallowing hard on her reluctance, she muttered,

'I wanted you…' And admitting that to *him* was like drinking a cup of poison.

'Then…?' Constantine prompted without pity.

Her face was now burning so hot, she was convinced she was glowing in the dark like a neon light.

'When you're trying to shrink into a wall, it is a challenge to see you as a natural-born tease, and you *did* almost hit the ceiling in your haste to vacate that hotel bed last night. For a woman with a chequered past, you're strangely nervous when it comes to sex.'

Rosie imagined telling him that she was a virgin and as quickly discarded the mortifying notion with an inner shudder. He wouldn't believe her. He couldn't know how utterly terrifying it was to find herself at the mercy not only of feelings and sexual responses that were new to her, but also at the mercy of a sophisticate like him and realise that she had completely lost control. Constantine made a sensual, seductive feast of lovemaking. Never mind those startlingly eye-catching dark good looks, what about the incredible technique?

Blushing all over again, Rosie forced her dry lips apart and said, 'We don't even like each other.'

'That has a strange, perverse appeal all of its own.'

Rosie swallowed with difficulty at that disturbing assertion.

Constantine watched her with eyes that glittered like diamonds in the moonlight. 'You're running scared, aren't you?' he murmured with sudden amusement.

'I don't understand.'

'You're a control freak and I have found your self-destruct button. I have no doubt that you kept Anton and the throwback spinning in separate orbits with the greatest of ease—'

'The throwback?'

'Maurice…the label fits him like a glove. A great

hulking thicko, whose only talent is inbred cunning for enriching himself,' Constantine extended smoothly.

'Maurice is not thick!' Rosie hissed furiously.

'Of course he is. He's pushed you into my arms. Does he really believe that you'll go back to him after being with me and living in my world?'

'I'm not going to *be* with you in any sense!'

'But the throwback is history. Anton is dead. And you are Mrs Constantine Voulos...for the moment.' Constantine swung on his heel and glanced back at her. 'I won't have to wait long for you to fall into my bed. I would say you are physically incapable of staying out of it!'

He had almost disappeared into the darkness when Rosie raked in an infuriated tone, 'How do I get back to my room?'

Constantine spun round, flung his darkly handsome head back and laughed with raw and unconcealed appreciation of her plight. Rosie thrust shaking hands into her pockets and boiled with loathing. In silence because she didn't trust herself to speak, they reached the relevant corridor.

'I know where I am now.'

'Do you?' His intonation suggested a deeper meaning.

Rosie stiffened, her breath catching in her throat as he curved a staying arm round the base of her slender spine. Raising his hand, he caught a single corkscrew curl and watched with gleaming satisfaction as it coiled obediently round one lean brown forefinger.

Black eyes skimmed direct to hers. 'You're not as tough as you like to make out, are you? In fact, you're on the brink of panic...but think of the potential rewards. Please me and you won't ever have to sell yourself to an older man again!'

Rosie stumbled into her bedroom like a drunk. She was shaking all over. It had been many years since anyone had made her feel weak and powerless. But Constantine had achieved that feat within thirty-six hours. And she wasn't just on the brink, she *was* panicking, with her life suddenly resembling an accident black spot and Constantine continuing to come at her like a particularly deadly juggernaut moving in for the kill.

He had found her Achilles heel and he was already starting to work out what made her tick. She had been a complete fool to keep on challenging a male as sexually experienced as Constantine. And if she ended up in bed with a man who despised her how would she feel about herself then? Wouldn't it be nice to think that she could resist her own most basic urges?

But then it was *him* she couldn't seem to resist. Ignorant, arrogant, macho, *clever* swine that he was. Little rag-doll—oh, yes, she had been behaving just like a little rag-doll. A toy he could push around and play with. And maybe once or twice she had succeeded in outfacing Constantine, but ultimately she had ended up paying very dearly for the privilege.

Why had Anton never warned her that Constantine could be so terrifyingly unpredictable? Or that beneath those smooth, expensive clothes beat the heart and soul of a very primal and passionate male whose every instinct was ruthlessly grounded on a need not only to win but to dominate?

And what about the *other* women in his life? Louise, the mistress, emotionally detached but vindictive enough to delight in the belief that another woman might be giving Constantine his comeuppance at last...and exactly where did the beautiful Italian actress, Cinzia Borzone, who was supposedly his only true love, fit in? Rosie was suddenly even more appalled by her own shameless, reckless behaviour. Evidently Constantine had few morals. And she herself had very nearly fallen victim to his magnetic sexuality as well.

It was time she used the brain she had been born with. Why *should* she have to stay in Greece? It would be madness to risk another uneasy meeting with Thespina. Constantine would simply have to tell her that his bride had already left him. He could even truthfully add that his wife had had a surprise meeting with his mistress…exit wife. Exit where? It didn't take Rosie two minutes to work out the most desirable destination. She would go to Majorca to see Son Fontanal before Constantine sold it again.

An hour later, weighed down only by her backpack, Rosie was lowering herself off the balcony outside her room. She made a slight detour onto a drainpipe to reach the sturdy climber covering the wall and then descended as sure-footed as a cat down onto the paved terrace below. Somewhere too close for comfort, a dog barked. Rosie took off at speed across the landscaped gardens, dodging and weaving like a professional. There was more than one dog barking now and her adrenalin hit an all-time high. As she got near the perimeter wall, some sort of siren screamed and suddenly a man appeared out of the darkness.

Rosie made a rush at the wall. The man got in the way. On the brink of her kicking him, he coughed and she recognised him. 'Taki…?'

He froze in astonishment.

'Taki, *please*,' she pleaded as the dogs got closer.

He gave her a leg-up over the ten-foot wall. By then another alarm was screeching in tune with the siren. Rosie dropped down onto the road and then scudded across it into the cover of some bushes. A police car with a flashing light wheeled to a screeching halt as the electronic gates sprang open. Rosie set off up the road. Eat your heart out, Rambo, she thought smugly. But

Constantine really ought to employ Taki elsewhere. Taki was too impressionable for Constantine's safety.

Why the heck should she care? Well, she might be putting as much distance as she possibly could between herself and Constantine but she didn't want anything *really* bad to happen to him. Her father had been very fond of him. As for her, well, Constantine had taken the ring and severed their agreement. He was on his own now, and so was she, and that was just the way Rosie liked it.

CHAPTER SIX

'WHERE the blazes are you?' Maurice bawled at deafening volume down the line.

Rosie held the telephone at a distance from her ear. 'Majorca—'

'*Majorca?* What the blinkin' heck are you doing there? Constantine's been here…he was frantic! Hell, Rosie, you might have at least left the poor bloke a note! He—'

'Since when did you start feeling sorry for Constantine?' Rosie interrupted in an incredulous hiss.

'Since I saw him demonstrating serious concern for your whereabouts and welfare,' Maurice informed her with nauseating piety. 'You're abroad for the first time in your life, you don't speak the lingo, you don't have any money *and* you disappeared from his home in the middle of the night. I thought you'd grown out of doing moonlit flits.'

'It wasn't like that.' But Rosie flushed furiously.

'Constantine was hopping mad when he arrived because he was so certain you would be here with me. But when he found out that you weren't he started panicking.'

'Constantine is not the panicking type—'

'Where did you get the money to take yourself to Majorca?'

'Never mind that, I want to know *how*—'

'Where are you staying? I'm coming over.'

'Don't be ridiculous—'

'I'm fed up with you and Constantine raving about the globe like a couple of hot-tempered, irrational lu-

natics. Last time I saw him he was mobilising the Greek
police to look for you! If you don't tell me where you're
staying, I'll tell *him* you're in Majorca—'

Five seconds later, Rosie slammed out of the phone
box without even having found out how the news of the
wedding had got into the hands of the Press. It upset her
to be at loggerheads with Maurice but it was time that
he appreciated that she was no longer the terrified thir-
teen-year-old he had once saved from sexual assault. She
clambered back onto the motorbike she had hired, trying
not to think with miserly regret about the secret rainy-
day account she had more than half-emptied in the space
of three days.

Her sparkling eyes hardened as she rode out of the
sleepy little village and back onto the endless mountain
road with its perilous bends and truly terrifying drops.
Knowing that Constantine had flown over to England in
pursuit of her made her feel hunted. It infuriated her too.
Little more than a month ago she had not even met the
swine and now he was acting as if he owned her! So
what if she had fled imprisonment in the middle of the
night? She had done what she had agreed to do in marrying him and he had no right, no right whatsoever, to
try and demand any further sacrifices from her!

By mid-morning, Rosie was studying a battered iron
name-plate hanging by a piece of barbed wire from a set
of seriously rusty gates. Son Fontanal appeared to lie up
a rutted cart track that climbed a steep hill thickly
wooded with pines. Half an hour later, having abandoned the motorbike under the trees, Rosie gazed down
at her father's birthplace in the fertile valley below and
caught her breath in enchantment.

The villa had a faded red roof and ageless peach-
coloured stone walls, the twin wings of the two-storey
building joined by a graceful loggia supported on pillars
lushly entwined by a giant jacaranda. Furthermore there

appeared to be a more passable paved laneway running
to the rear of the building. On the south side, a series of
crumbling arches ran round the perimeter of an overgrown garden studded with palm trees. Not crumbling,
just *old*, Rosie adjusted hurriedly, and maybe there were
a few roof tiles missing here and there and a few cracks
on the walls...but no way was Son Fontanal the ruin
which Constantine had called it!

She hurried down the sloping track, her steps only
slowing as she approached the courtyard entrance. A
plump elderly lady was dozing on a chair in the shade
cast by the loggia. As Rosie drew closer, wondering how
on earth she was to introduce herself, the old woman
woke up and fixed startled eyes on her. Then her creased
face slowly blossomed into a beam of positive pleasure.

Rising with surprising vigour, she opened her arms
almost as if she was expecting Rosie to rush into them.
'Señorita Estrada?' she exclaimed.

Being addressed by her father's name made Rosie still
in astonishment. A torrent of Spanish broke over her as
the old lady surged forward to clasp her hands and kiss
her warmly on both cheeks. Tears shone in her dark
eyes. From the pocket of her pristine white apron, she
withdrew a rather crumpled photograph. '*La hija de Don
Antonio*...the daughter of Don Antonio,' she sighed,
proudly displaying a snapshot of Anton and Rosie together. 'I am Carmina...'

Carmina, once her father's nursemaid. Rosie realised
that she needed no further introduction. This old lady
actually *knew* who she was. When Anton had flown in
to buy Son Fontanal, he had found Carmina still in residence, and in the emotional grip of that reunion and
homecoming he had clearly confessed that he had a
daughter. Rosie's own eyes stung and a tremulous smile
of happiness curved her lips. It meant so much to her

that her father had confided in someone about her existence.

The old woman went back into her pocket and produced a carefully folded piece of newspaper and slowly shook her grey head. 'No señorita…señora,' Carmina stressed with a cheerful smile of self-reproof. 'Señora Voulos…yes?'

Bloody hell, Rosie thought, limp with incredulity and resentment. Halfway up a mountain in a foreign country, she *still* couldn't shake off Constantine and the consequences of that stupid wedding ceremony! Speaking in an excitable mix of Spanish and increasingly confident English now, Carmina went on to enquire anxiously as to the whereabouts of her *esposo*…Spanish for husband, Rosie gathered, her teeth gritting. And almost simultaneously a distant humming noise in the background broke like a thunderclap over the brow of the steep hill she had climbed. Frowning, she looked heavenward.

A scarlet helicopter hung like a giant brash bird against the cloudless blue sky. Rosie left the courtyard to watch the craft circling in search of a landing place. It came down about fifty yards away on the flat ground to the front of the villa. Even before the rotor blades had stopped twirling, a large male figure sprang out. Rosie's heart sank and then gave a paradoxically violent lurch of excitement that interfered with her ability to breathe and filled her with appalled and ashamed discomfiture.

Constantine powered towards her on long, lean, muscular legs. Rosie skidded off one foot onto the other, accidentally clashed with blazing, implacable black eyes and froze, caught like a butterfly pinned live to a specimen board. 'I—' she began in an odd, squeaky, breathless voice she didn't recognise as her own.

As Constantine drew level with her, he stopped dead. Without the smallest warning, he bent and swept her off her feet into his arms. Rosie was silenced by complete shock.

'What I have to say to you does not require an audience,' Constantine splintered in a menacing undertone. 'And isn't it traditional to carry the bride over the threshold?'

Rosie's last view of the helicopter took in Dmitri, whose rock-like visage usually defied interpretation. Not on this occasion, however. Constantine's bodyguard wore a huge appreciative grin.

Scarlet-cheeked, Rosie spat, 'Put me down!'

'*Make me,*' Constantine challenged, stalking through the open doors of Son Fontanal.

Rosie struck his back with two outraged fists.

'You'll have to do better than that, little rag-doll—'

'Don't call me that...I *hate* it!' she launched at him as he started up a wide stone staircase.

'But it is *so* appropriate. If I was the kind of husband you deserve, I would be on the happy brink of beating the stuffing out of you!'

'What's that supposed to mean?' Rosie gasped.

'That I have to come up with another method of punishment—and I have had plenty of time to toy with several interesting possibilities, haven't I?' Constantine murmured in a sizzling purr of threat as he thrust open a carved door. 'In three nightmare days, I have flown from Athens to Manchester, from Manchester to London and from London back to Athens...and then from Athens to Palma. I want someone to pay in spades for that travel itinerary.'

'I don't know why you bothered—'

'Do you want to know what kept me going?' Constantine yanked her off his shoulder, tossed her in the air to clamp two incredibly strong hands beneath her arms and then held her in suspension, face to menacing face. Rosie's immediate surroundings shrank to her own shocked and tiny mirror image in a pair of implacable, glittering black eyes.

'No…' she whispered, dry-mouthed and hypnotised.

'The thought of this moment,' Constantine spelt out not quite evenly as she gazed back at him like a mesmerised rabbit. 'When I show you how a Greek husband treats a runaway wife—'

'Not your wife…' Rosie fumbled with great difficulty to find that disjointed denial. Her brain felt for all the world as though it was set in cement. Not a single rational thought clouded her head. The warm, musky scent of him overlaid with a faint hint of some citrusy aftershave floated into her flaring nostrils, and the more she breathed, the more dizzy and peculiar she felt.

Constantine's intent gaze flashed pure scorching gold. He murmured something rough in Greek and settled her down on the big carved bed that she hadn't even noticed. She sat up again very slowly, her legs and arms oddly unresponsive to her bidding.

Constantine reached down a hand, flipped her gently back against the heaped-up white linen pillows and grated, 'Stay there!'

Rosie stayed put. Wide-eyed, she watched him discard his tie, his jacket and rip at his silk shirt with scant concern for the buttons. Her tongue was welded to the roof of her mouth. A disturbing tremor ran through her tautening length. Her entire attention was nailed to Constantine's bare chest, her spellbound gaze wandering from the gleaming brown skin of his shoulders to the black triangle of curling hair hazing his powerful pectoral muscles.

It was so hard to breathe, even harder to keep her fingers curling into her palms when this insane part of her craved the freedom to shift forward a mere foot to the edge of the bed and *touch*…run exploring fingertips over that smooth golden skin, investigate the undeniable allure of that hard, flat stomach and that truly fascinating little silky furrow of dark hair which started just below his navel and travelled all the way down until it disappeared under the low-slung edge of a pair of black briefs. He was just in the act of hooking a finger into those briefs when Rosie realised in horror that she was gawping at him like a woman at a male strip show.

'Take your clothes off,' Constantine said.

Rosie had twisted her head away so fast, she was all but suffering from whiplash, face as hot as a furnace, gut feelings of shame and shock reverberating through her blitzed brain. So he had a really beautiful body. Was that any excuse to behave like a peeping Tom? But it was even worse to recognise the swollen heaviness of her breasts and the hot liquid sensation of unforgivable excitement burning somewhere she didn't even want to think about. *What* had he said?

Constantine saved her the trouble of plundering her dazed mind for recollection. He said it again. Her bright head whipped back as fast as the head of a swivelling doll, huge green eyes agog at the command.

'OK,' Constantine gritted with savage impatience, and reached for her in one alarmingly fast motion.

'What are you doing?' Rosie screeched as her oversized T-shirt went flying over her startled head and he anchored a businesslike hand into the elasticised waistband of her leggings. Preoccupied by an instinctive need to cover her braless breasts with spread fingers, she was decidedly hampered in the undignified tussle which followed. Her leggings and her briefs were wrenched off together to the accompaniment of her aghast shrieks and breathless and impotent efforts to fight him off.

Clamping a hand like an iron vice to her forearm, Constantine held her fast and flipped the sheet over her frantically struggling body. Sliding into the bed with her, he rolled over and anchored an arm round her waist and yanked her back into electrifying contact with his hot, muscular masculinity. Rosie went rigid. He wasn't wearing a stitch and neither was she and she just could not *believe* that he had forcibly stripped her naked!

'I'll go to the police and report you for this the minute I get out of this room!' Rosie gasped the instant she got oxygen back into her straining lungs.

'Be sure to tell them that I am your husband. I should think they'll laugh themselves sick—'

'You are *not* my husband!' Rosie spat with renewed vigour. 'And if you dare to lay a finger on me—'

'Shut up and go to sleep,' Constantine growled, spreading his big, powerful body across the bed with a deep, luxuriating groan of contentment and forcing her to move with him.

'G-go to sleep?' Rosie queried shakily, every fibre of her trembling body centred in awareness on the bold thrust of his erection against her slender hip.

'I have not slept more than a handful of hours in the past three days. So when I sleep *you* sleep too,' Constantine told her, his deep, dark drawl winding audibly down in speed and volume.

Rosie twisted round in the manacle-like imprisonment of his arm. In a bewildered daze, she surveyed him. His drowsy eyes were darkly shadowed, the crescent lashes as long and luxuriant as a child's already in the act of drifting down towards his cheekbones. Close up, she noticed how pale he was. As she recalled the travel schedule he had outlined, the strangest little pang of guilt nudged at her conscience and provoked a deep flush on her troubled face.

'You don't trust me not to disappear again,' she gathered tautly. 'But I'm prepared to promise that I'll still be in this house when you wake up.'

In unconvinced response, Constantine shifted and snaked his other arm beneath her, forcing her even closer and into, if possible, an even more disturbing intimacy because this time she was facing him and lying half over the outrageously relaxed sprawl of his abrasively masculine frame.

'*Constantine...!*' Rosie shrieked in anguish as he crushed her breasts into the solid wail of his hair-roughened chest and pushed her head down under his chin.

'If you keep me awake I'll get amorous,' he warned her thickly. 'I like to make love before I sleep. Sex is a wonderful antidote to stress and tension, *pethi mou*.'

There was only one tense person in the bed after that assertion and it wasn't Constantine.

Rosie lay as still as a statue with the slow, steady beat of his heart thudding against her breast and the deep rise and fall of his breathing stirring her hair. He had both arms wrapped round her in an entirely asexual embrace. Indeed she might as well have been an inanimate toy. He had dragged her into bed with him only to ensure that she did not get the chance to make a break for freedom again. Now he was sleeping like a big, happy, contented log!

In dismaying contrast, Rosie was in a state of turmoil which was becoming horribly familiar to her in Constantine's radius. Pure panic had provoked her flight from Greece. She winced at the awareness. Even asleep, Constantine reacted to that slight movement of hers, his arms tightening round her as he rolled over, pinning one long, powerful thigh between hers. Her taut nipples throbbed and her stomach clenched with horrendous excitement, her treacherous body responding with a brazen life and hunger all of its own. Rosie simply wanted to *die* of mortification.

He had ripped off her clothes and she had experienced not one decent pang of fear. She had been outraged but not scared and, worst of all, when he had told her to go

to sleep she had been shattered and then…and then…
disappointed? A sexual craving that horrified her still
hungered like a wicked beast inside her. And she felt
even more threatened by the discovery that one glimpse
of Constantine looking exhausted could make her feel
guilty and strangely sympathetic. How could she feel
guilty about a male she loathed? Where had all her anger
gone?

Shaken awake in an only vaguely familiar bedroom,
Rosie slowly lifted her head off the pillow she was hugging, bemused eyes landing on Constantine. Fully
dressed, he was standing by the bed, every vibrant bat-
tery blatantly recharged, energy sizzling from him in intimidating waves. He looked incredibly gorgeous.

'What time is it?' she mumbled, disorientated by the
daylight still flooding through the windows and then
deeply disturbed by the realisation that she had actually
managed to fall asleep in his arms. True, she had not
slept a great deal herself in recent days, but that was no
excuse for relaxing to *that* extent.

'Three in the afternoon. It's time for you to get up.
Lunch is being prepared.'

'By whom…Carmina?' she muttered round a still
sleepy yawn as she stretched.

'Since I was aware that the house had only an elderly
caretaker in residence, I arranged for a number of my
staff to follow me here,' Constantine supplied drily. 'But
since habitable rooms are at a premium they'll be using
the holiday cottages on the edge of the estate.'

Sitting up, Rosie carefully hugged the sheet to her
collarbone. Without shame, Constantine stared. A rosy
red blush started at her breasts and crawled up her throat
before she hurriedly broke back into speech. 'How the
heck did you find out where I was?'

'The passenger manifest of your flight. Is this trip

meant to be some sort of sentimental journey?'
Constantine dealt her a stonily unimpressed appraisal,
openly suspicious as to why she should have chosen to
take refuge in Anton's family home.

'I thought it would be the last place you would look
for me.' Rosie ducked her head, her eyes clouding. A
sentimental journey…if only he knew. But then he
didn't know and he had shot her down in flames when
she had tried to tell him who she was. His contemptuous
dismissal of her claim had bitten deep.

'Where is your wedding ring?' Constantine demanded
so abruptly that she jumped.

'I took it off.'

'Then put it back on again,' Constantine told her
grimly.

'I can't…' Rosie shrugged. 'I dropped it in a bin when
I got off the plane at Palma.'

Constantine slowly breathed in and slowly breathed
out again. Rosie recognised the exercise for what it was.
It was the Voulos equivalent of counting to ten. What
she did not understand was the flare of dark colour over
his hard cheekbones and the momentarily seething look
of a male striving not to react to a personal affront.

'I didn't think I was going to need to wear the
wretched thing again!' she protested in the hissing silence.

'We'll talk downstairs when you're dressed.'
Constantine strode to the door and sent her a slashing
glance. 'You owe me an apology for the manner in
which you chose to leave my home.'

'I wouldn't hold my breath if I were you.' Rosie tilted
her chin. 'I'm not very good at apologising.'

'But you *will* learn,' Constantine spelt out grittily.

Why did he never learn? He was even more stubborn
than she was. Grimacing, she slid out of bed. The
sparsely furnished bedroom rejoiced in a very old-

fashioned adjoining bathroom. The bath was big enough
to accommodate an entire family. Still in possession of
its Victorian shower attachment, it was the sort of bath
which Maurice would have gone into raptures over, but
unhappily there seemed to be no hot water available.

Her teeth were chattering by the time she had finished
washing. Constantine had used both threadbare towels
and discarded them in a sodden heap on the floor.
Presumably he was also responsible for the lack of hot
water. Even Maurice was better trained as a housemate.
She would have to get dressed to fetch her backpack
upstairs and only then would she be able to put on fresh
clothes. However, on her return to the bedroom, Rosie
discovered that she couldn't find a single item of the
clothing which Constantine had unceremoniously ripped
off.

Wrapped in a thin and embarrassingly small wet
towel, Rosie hauled open the bedroom door and shouted
at full volume, '*Constantine!*'

Sixty seconds passed. Her toes began to tap on the
dull, unpolished wooden floor. She yelled again. Steps
sounded on the stairs. Rosie smiled and folded her arms.
But it was not Constantine. Dmitri had been sent to deal
with her. Furious, Rosie ducked back behind the door to
conceal her undressed state.

'Mr Voulos is not accustomed to being hailed by a
shout,' Dmitri said in an apologetic whisper voiced in
fluent English from the landing. 'In fact that form of
address puts him in a very bad mood.'

'He's never in anything else,' Rosie grumbled.

'He still feels the loss of Mr Estrada very deeply.'

That quiet, sobering reminder drained Rosie's face of
colour. No, she hadn't made any allowances for the effects of grief on Constantine's temperament, had she?

'How may I help you, *kiria*?' Dmitri prompted in the
ringing silence.

'It's not important.' Rosie closed the door again and sank down on the edge of the bed.

Since her father's death she had been pretty bad-tempered too, and how many nights had she lain sleepless? Something would happen and she would want to tell Anton about it and then, once more, she would have to come to terms with the fact that he was no longer there to eagerly receive her every confidence and never would be again. After twenty years how much greater that sense of loss must be for Constantine...and surely it was all wrong that they still could not behave like civilised human beings with each other?

A maid knocked on the door and entered, almost staggering under the weight of the garment bags she was carrying. Laying her burden down on a chair, she left the room again. A split second later Constantine strode in with two leather cases.

'Right, obviously you're moving in here...when do I get my clothes back so that I can move out?' Rosie demanded, but after her recent unsettling thoughts her tone was less tart than usual.

'These *are* your clothes,' Constantine responded. 'I bought them between flights on my travels.'

Her fiery head tipped back. 'Why would you buy me clothes?'

'You have nothing appropriate to wear. Consider the new wardrobe a gift.'

Her green eyes glittered. 'That's very generous of you, Constantine...but I would prefer to have my own clothes returned.'

'No. Why do you think I removed them?'

'Removed them...*removed* them? You ripped them off me!'

Constantine dealt her a dark, brooding appraisal, his sensual mouth compressing. 'I find it distasteful that you should wear garments bought by another man.'

'Actually I bought what I was wearing in the cheapest shop I could find in Palma.'

Anger burnished his black eyes. 'You know very well what I am telling you. That dress you wore at the hotel…Anton purchased that, did he not?'

Rosie nodded with a bemused frown.

'So I have made a clean sweep. *Theos*…I can do without the reminder that you were *his* woman first!' Constantine completed in a positive snarl, enraged at being forced to explain his peculiar behaviour.

'Apart from the fact that I am not *any* man's woman—'

'You are mine now.'

'I beg your pardon?' Rosie breathed.

'Anton gave you to me.'

'Say that again,' Rosie invited tremulously, outraged by that particular choice of words.

'And if I am to accept that you are my responsibility I expect you to conform to *my* expectations and respect *my* wishes from now on.'

'I don't conform, Constantine.'

'You will with me.'

'I want my clothes back!' Rosie slammed back at him as she leapt upright, no longer able to stand him towering over her.

He reached for her.

'I hate you…get your lousy hands off me!'

Those same hands framed her wildly flushed cheekbones. Glittering black eyes slashed down into hers in rampant challenge. 'You were clinging to me like a limpet when I woke up, *pethi mou*. I had to give you the pillow to clutch instead.'

'If you weren't so much bigger, I'd knock your teeth down your conceited throat!'

'You see…you're learning already. A week ago you

would have physically attacked me,' Constantine murmured with raw satisfaction.

Rosie shuddered with rage and turbulent confusion. Constantine let both of his hands slowly slide into her bright hair and at the caressing brush of those long brown fingers on her scalp she shivered convulsively, like a woman caught up in a violent storm. He released her with a wolfish smile, dark, measuring eyes scanning her with disturbing intensity. 'You can bite all you like tonight, little rag-doll. I'm very adaptable to new experiences in bed.'

As the door closed, Rosie fell back against the bed for support. Of course he hadn't meant that…he couldn't possibly be telling her that he expected to make love to her tonight. All she had to do was to say no if he made any advances…*all*? Hurriedly, she repressed the suspicion that saying no to Constantine might not be that easy.

What on earth had happened to her barely formed desire to begin trying to civilise relations between them? Within thirty seconds he had had her at screaming pitch again. Why the new wardrobe? And why more clothes than even a rich, spoilt socialite could surely wear in the space of two short months? On their wedding day, Constantine had complained because she wasn't wearing one of the snazzy outfits which he had correctly assumed that Anton had bought her…and *now*?

Now it appeared to be a hanging offence for her to possess a single garment which Anton might have paid for! Her head was aching. It was tension…pounding, throbbing tension and that awful sense of being horribly out of her depth again.

CHAPTER SEVEN

PERSPIRATION dewed Rosie's short upper lip as she walked the length of the big, dark dining room with its massive carved furniture, tracked every step of the way by Constantine's coolly appreciative appraisal. Was it madness to think that there was a gleam of ownership in that look? Was it even greater madness to consider lunging across the table at him to insist that he *stop* looking at her like that?

'I knew that colour would look stunning against that wonderful hair.'

Rosie flushed, murderously self-conscious in her finery. Expensive or not, it was a plain little green summer dress and she had chosen it in preference to half a dozen more revealing outfits, only to discover that once the fabric was filled with living female flesh it outlined every slim curve with disturbing clarity.

'Why did you bring staff here...surely you're not planning to stay long in a house you described as a ruin?' Rosie prompted tautly as she took a seat opposite him.

'The other wing of the house is uninhabitable but I believe we can manage to exist with the privations in this wing for a few weeks—'

'A few *weeks*?'

'Why not? What could be more conventional than a newly married couple seeking the seclusion of a mountain villa?' Constantine watched her bridle with the indolent cool of a sunbathing big cat.

'Why do you have to keep on reminding me about that stupid wedding ceremony?' Rosie snapped.

Disturbing amusement flared in his brilliant dark gaze. 'I think it's time we called a truce.'

'A...truce?' Rosie echoed uncertainly.

Constantine released his breath in a hiss of impatience. 'I had every excuse to be outraged by the terms of Anton's will. Possibly I overreacted but Anton was more dear to me than my own father. It was a great shock to learn that he had another woman in his life.'

'He didn't. How many times do I have to say it? I was *not* his mistress! You were in that house,' Rosie pressed in a tone of frantic appeal. 'You must have noticed that we had separate bedrooms!'

Constantine shifted a broad shoulder in a fluid shrug but his strong face hardened. 'Your sleeping arrangements were of no interest to me.'

'*But—*'

Constantine slung her a chilling look. 'I have never slept a night through in a woman's bed. Does that mean that I am a celibate?' he traded with sardonic emphasis.

It did not but the information somehow stabbed Rosie like a knife. She veiled her eyes from his but nothing could wipe out a fleeting, distressing image of Constantine sliding out of the lovely Louise's arms in the early hours to head home. 'You're such a cold fish,' she condemned helplessly. 'The minute you've had what you wanted, you take off. You should be ashamed to admit that.'

An arc of faint colour scored Constantine's cheekbones. His mouth clenched hard. 'Sex is an exchange of mutual physical pleasure—'

'Wham-bam, thank you ma'am. No romance, no affection, no feelings. No wonder Anton was mortified by your attitude to women!'

Constantine went white beneath his bronzed skin. '*Christos...*' he ground out raggedly, hanging on to his temper by a hair's breadth.

In similar shock at the attack she had made on him, Rosie dropped her fiery head. But imagine falling in love with a guy like that! she thought. Her mind ran on unstoppably… A cold, unfeeling swine who talked smoothly about exchanging physical satisfaction and who desired no deeper connection in a relationship. Listening to him made her blood curdle in her veins.

'I see nothing wrong in my views.'

'What about love?'

'I have never been in love…' Constantine dealt her a slashing look of driven impatience. 'I don't believe in it. Now, if you were to talk to me of infatuation or lust—'

'No, thanks. I think you've let yourself down enough for one day.' Rosie picked up her knife and fork to embark on the first course of her meal. Somehow she just didn't want to look at Constantine any more. He had *never* been in love? Even with Cinzia Borzone? But then he probably wouldn't recognise the emotion unless it came with a fat price tag attached and was offered via his mobile phone!

Her preoccupied gaze strayed from the elaborately presented dish to the ring lying on the white linen tablecloth. She dropped her cutlery with a noisy clatter, snatched up the Estrada emerald and whispered uncertainly, '*Why* are you giving it back to me?'

'Don't flatter me. I was merely the courier. You left it behind in England.'

'The last time I saw this ring, it was in my jewel case.'

'I think not. Maurice found it on the windowsill in the kitchen.'

Rosie reddened with guilty discomfiture as she threaded the ornate gem back onto her finger. 'I don't remember leaving it there. I honestly did think that I had put it away. I'm sorry I accused you of taking it,' she muttered in a very small voice.

'He also accepted full and complete responsibility for that newspaper article.'

Rosie's chin came up, her wide eyes pained. *'No!'*

Constantine studied her shocked face with cool, dark, incisive eyes. 'You're incredibly naïve in some ways,' he mused. 'You put Maurice in possession of a story worth a great deal of money. He went for the money—'

'I can't believe that...I just can't!'

'He admitted it to me.' Constantine held her distraught gaze steadily. 'I owe you an apology for calling you a cheat.'

Rosie dropped her head again. 'It doesn't matter.'

'It matters to me,' Constantine murmured levelly. 'I misjudged you. But why did you pretend that you *were* responsible?'

Rosie struggled to swallow the thick lump forming in her throat. 'I...I—'

'Every move you make seems to be based on a pathetic need to protect a man who betrayed you without a second's hesitation,' Constantine drawled with derision.

Rosie rose almost clumsily upright. 'I'm not feeling very hungry,' she muttered unsteadily, and walked out of the room as fast as her feet would carry her.

It hurt so very, very much to believe that Maurice could have sold out their friendship for profit. Yes, she had always known that money was important to Maurice and that he was very ambitious, but his business was booming and he was anything but short of ready cash! Peering with tear-filled eyes into a room that seemed to be bustling with people fussing with office equipment, Rosie cannoned blindly into a uniformed maid and then fled out of the open front doors into the sunlight. Even the courtyard wasn't empty, and she raced past the van being industriously unloaded and out into the garden, seeking cover and privacy in the same way that an in-jured animal seeks darkness.

A convulsive sob was torn from her then. She covered her working face with her spread hands and from behind her came two supporting arms which inexorably turned her round. Gasping, she went rigid, a long shudder of repressed emotion quivering through her.

'Don't be scared, *pethi mou*...it is only me,' Constantine murmured roughly, as if it were the most natural thing in the world that he should attempt to hold her close in a comforting embrace. 'It hurts when people let you down...'

'He's the only man I've ever trusted...apart from Anton,' Rosie framed, fighting a losing battle against the tears pouring down her cheeks.

Constantine drew her hands down from her face but with a sudden jerk Rosie pulled away, turning her narrow back defensively on him.

'How long have you known Maurice?'

'Since I was thirteen... And it was weird,' she whispered thickly in recollection. 'Before I got to know him, I was more scared of him than I was of any of the other boys in the home.'

'What home?'

Rosie loosed a choky laugh. 'When my mother died, my stepfather put me into care.'

'Why?' Constantine shot at her with fierce incompre-hension.

'Because I wasn't his. He only found out that Mum was expecting me *after* he married her.'

'Yet he stayed married to her...why didn't he divorce her?' Constantine demanded.

Rosie compressed her lips. Nothing was ever that sim-ple. Tony Waring had been her mother's first serious boyfriend. He had pleaded with her to marry him before she'd gone down to London to find a secretarial job.

When she had returned home and said yes, he had been too overjoyed to question her sudden change of heart. Her mother had told her that bit of the story more than once in an effort to make Rosie understand that her stepfather was entitled to be bitter, that he had been wronged and that it wouldn't be fair to expect him to treat Rosie the same way as he did his own two sons.

'He loved her but he just could never get over her doing that to him,' Rosie muttered tightly. 'They had two kids of their own and he still couldn't forget, so once she was gone there was no way he was going to keep me.'

'What age were you?'

'Nine. I went into a council home and then a lot of short-term foster homes. I kept on running away, so I got a name for being difficult. The place I finally ended up in had some very rough inmates.'

'Including Maurice?'

'He was only there because the authorities had to keep him close to the hospital his mother was in. His sister was fostered but not too many families want to foster teenage boys. I don't want to talk about this...' Rosie started walking away, too upset to be able to understand why she had told Constantine embarrassing, private things that were absolutely none of his business.

'You really love that profiteering ape,' Constantine breathed with savage incredulity. 'And he's a low-life bastard who would rent you out by the hour if he could get away with it!'

Rosie spun round, her tear-wet face appalled. 'How dare you say that?'

'He thrust you at me. He set the two of us up. Did he care what kind of man I was? Or how I might treat you when that story broke?'

'He couldn't have thought—he just couldn't have...' Rosie argued brokenly.

'You say one more word in his defence and I'll fly over to England and rip him apart with my bare hands!' Constantine roared at her in a thunderous, seething fury that shook her so much that she stared wide-eyed. 'And before you ask me why I didn't do that the day before yesterday remind yourself that he knows the *whole* story and not just the tiny part that was published! I have no desire to wake up some day soon to the tale of your sordid affair with Anton!'

Constantine stalked off and then as swiftly turned back again and strode with daunting purpose back across the rough grass. He closed a lean hand over hers. 'You are coming back inside to finish your meal—'

'No.'

'My wife is not going to skulk in the garden and snivel for the entertainment of my staff!'

Rosie gulped. 'Why are you so angry?'

'That is a very stupid question. In fact that may go down in history as the most stupid question I have *ever* been asked!'

Constantine produced an immaculate white handkerchief and dabbed with ruthless but surprising gentleness at her damp cheeks. Rosie studied him with reddened, bemused eyes. 'Oh, *right*,' she muttered, believing she had found the answer to behaviour that was plunging her into ever deeper confusion. 'You don't want the pretend marriage to fall apart this obviously so soon—'

In response, Constantine bent his arrogant dark head and ravished apart her startled lips in a plundering, passionate kiss. Fire leapt into her limp body and blazed through every skin cell with explosive efficiency. Reeling dizzily with the force of her response, Rosie met blazing golden eyes as he lifted his head again.

Screening his gaze, Constantine surveyed her with disturbing calm. 'We'll dine out at the Formentor tonight. That should give the staff time to get the house into some sort of order.'

Garbed in a divinely sophisticated evening gown in glistening pearl-grey, Rosie was surprised to appreciate just how much she was enjoying herself. The hotel was fabulous and she had even recognised one or two famous faces amongst the other diners. But Constantine was undeniably the most gorgeous-looking male present. That spectacular bone structure, that golden skin and those incredibly compelling dark, long-lashed eyes…

There wasn't a woman in the place who hadn't looked at him at least twice and yet amazingly he was feeding *her* champagne and flattering *her* with his undivided attention. He hadn't even spared a glance at the arrival of an only minimally dressed blonde bombshell who had turned every other male head in the room.

'You're very quiet, *pethi mou*,' Constantine murmured.

It took a terrifying amount of will-power to drag her disobedient gaze from him. Angry with herself, her colour heightened, Rosie watched candlelight twinkle across the slender platinum wedding band on her finger. A frown pleated her brow. Earlier that evening, a jeweller had arrived at Son Fontanal with an extensive selection of rings and a replacement had been picked. Constantine had actually laughed about the fact that she had binned the first ring. Why was he being nice all of a sudden?

'Rosie…what are you thinking about?' He said the abbreviated version of her name for the very first time and somehow it sounded so different the way he said it. That honey-dark drawl made her stupid heart skip a beat.

Studying her champagne glass, Rosie drew in a deep, steadying breath. 'I was thinking about Maurice,' she

lied, shaken that she had so easily forgotten what had
hurt so much only hours earlier.

'*Theos*…' Constantine breathed with flaring impatience. 'The throwback haunts us!'

Her head tilted back, eyes bright with anger. 'He may
not have your education or your status but when I
needed him Maurice was always there for me.'

'Only not when your needs conflicted with his ava-
rice.' Lounging fluidly back in his chair, Constantine
slung the reminder at her with contempt.

'You can't expect anyone to put you first all the
time…even Anton didn't,' Rosie conceded with difficulty. 'But when I most needed Maurice he didn't let
me down…' Her voice trailed away and in a nervous
movement she drained the champagne in her glass.

'I'm still listening,' Constantine prompted drily.

Her face stiff with strain, Rosie swallowed hard.
'When I was thirteen, two boys forced their way into
my room and tried to assault me… Maurice stopped
them and because there were two of them he took a hell
of a beating doing it.'

Constantine had paled but his gleaming gaze was
veiled in the thunderous silence, his sensual mouth twisting. 'Do I start calling him St George instead of the
throwback? Maybe you should answer one question before I decide… How long was it before he took with
your agreement what the others tried to take by force?'

Rosie flinched as though he had struck her. 'Why…is
that how *you* would have behaved?'

Registering her distress, Constantine frowned and
abruptly stretched a hand across the table to reach for
her tightly coiled fingers. 'Rosie, I—'

In stark rejection of that gesture, Rosie trailed her fingers free and said starkly, 'I reminded him of his kid
sister. When he was a child, he had to look after Lorna
because their mother was an alcoholic. But after they

went into care Lorna was adopted by her foster family and Maurice was left out in the cold. They let them stay in contact but it wasn't the same. So if you want an explanation for why he stuck his neck out for me that night think *clean*—or would that be too much of a challenge for you?'

Tears brightening her eyes, Rosie didn't even look at him as she thrust her chair back and walked out of the dining room. He caught up with her in the foyer, a lean hand curving round her rigid spine and settling on her waist to still her. 'Rosie—'

'*Constantine!*' a female voice shrilled ecstatically.

Constantine froze and winced as Rosie's head spun round. The blonde bombshell in the unbelievably tiny black dress was bearing down on them, full breasts heaving, voracious blue eyes glittering with satisfaction. 'When did you arrive?' she demanded, literally wrenching him free of Rosie to plant an intimate and lingering kiss full on his mouth. 'Doesn't *this* bring back memories of Monte Carlo, darling?' she moaned throatily, running caressing hands over any bit of him she could reach and trying for a place or two that no lady should aim at in public.

Constantine detached himself with distinct hauteur, the faintest colour accentuating the hard slant of his cheekbones as his black eyes skimmed with curious expectancy to Rosie.

'Justine...this is my wife, Rosalie,' he drawled with supreme self-command.

'Oh, don't mind me,' Rosie said sweetly. 'I'm not the tiniest bit possessive about you.'

'You've got married? *You*?' Justine looked thunderstruck and finally took Rosie under her notice. 'To *her*?' she gasped in stricken incomprehension as she gawped at Rosie. 'But why?'

'If you get me in the right mood, I even loan him

out,' Rosie imparted with a slanting smile beneath which
she boiled with rage. Then she turned on her heel and
stalked out into the night air. Momentarily her head
reeled and she knew that she had drunk a little too much
champagne.

But no wonder Constantine hadn't looked at the
blonde bombshell falling out of her dress! Been there,
done that…and the creep had had the neck to call *her* a
tart! Rosie did not flaunt herself half-naked and she
would cut off her hands sooner than make such a blatant
pass at any man in front of an audience of interested
spectators.

Several steps beyond the doors, Constantine reached
her and closed a hand over her forearm. '*Christos*…how
dare you refer to our marriage and to *me* in such terms?'
he gritted rawly.

'Let's get this straight, Constantine…' Rosie stopped
dead, her oval face flushed with equal fury. '*We are not
married.* Got it? If ever I do get married, I will get married in church and the groom will be someone I at least
like and respect. He will not be a hypocritical, insensitive, conceited swine who can't think beyond the level
of a one-night stand! So go take a hike!'

'Don't speak to me like that!' Constantine seethed.

'And your taste in women is *pitiful*!' Rosie seethed
back, unable to restrain her overwhelming need to pass
on that opinion. 'So why waste your time being nice to
me all evening? You must have had a far better time in
Monte Carlo, *darling* Constantine! You're a womaniser
and I wouldn't touch you with a barge-pole!'

'*Theos*…is that a fact?' Constantine roared.

'Yes, that is a fact, *darling*!' Rosie mimicked with
vicious pleasure.

A flash of bright light temporarily blinded her and she
blinked in bewilderment, straining to focus on a man in
a white shirt darting away with a camera. Constantine

took advantage of her stasis to grab her with two furiously angry hands and bring his mouth down hotly on hers. *Whoosh*! It felt as if the top of her head was flying off, closely followed by the rest of her startled body taking off into orbit with it. I *lied*, was the last thought she had as her angry fingers knotted fiercely into his thick black hair and held him to her, wanting him, hating him, needing him with a savage passion that was utterly outside her control.

Afterwards, she didn't remember getting into the car. Dmitri had looked suitably grave head-on but from the back seat and through the thick glass separating them Rosie watched his big shoulders give a betraying little quiver and looked hurriedly away again, mortification eating her alive.

'I was offensive and you were justifiably angry but when I followed you out of the dining room I intended to apologise,' Constantine admitted with raw-edged clarity.

'Wow,' Rosie said, but she was still trembling and deep down inside she was a stricken bag of nerves. She had been *jealous*, jealous for the first time in her life! Justine's familiar advances to Constantine had filled her with rage and she had lost her head. Now the paparazzi had a photo of them having a stand-up fight outside the hotel.

'Your behaviour was…' Constantine seemed to be struggling to find the right word in English.

'Appalling,' Rosie slotted in heavily. 'But maybe we should try to look on the bright side of this—'

'*Christos*…you sound like Anton…the roof has fallen in, let us be joyful that the walls still stand!' Constantine grated incredulously. 'What bright side?'

Rosie coiled her trembling hands together. 'If that picture is published, it'll accelerate the break-up, won't it?'

Constantine frowned without comprehension. 'The break-up?'

'When our fake marriage ends. I mean, obviously if we're so badly matched we're at each other's throats within days of the wedding and we've got the publicity to prove it, we shouldn't need to wait a whole two months to split up and go for a divorce,' Rosie pointed out tightly.

'There is a cloud in every silver lining.'

'You've got that the wrong way round.' Suddenly Rosie was feeling horribly depressed and wondering if it was that awful loss of temper which was responsible or the decided awareness that she definitely did not hate Constantine the way she had believed she did. What she hated and feared was the extraordinary power he had over her emotions.

'Have I?'

A strained silence stretched.

'When I asked how long it was before you became intimately involved with Maurice, I spoke without thought. I was not being as insensitive as I may have sounded,' Constantine framed in a roughened undertone. 'I was very disturbed to learn that you had endured a vicious assault at that age but I do not see Maurice as your saviour beyond that one gallant act...in fact I now see him as a yob who took advantage of your hero-worship and gratitude.'

From throwback to yob. Had Maurice risen from rock-bottom in Constantine's estimation? It was hard to tell. But she herself had definitely sunk and shrunk in stature. Constantine no longer talked as if he thought she was the more dominant partner in the relationship. Now she sounded like a poor little victim.

'I am not intimately involved with Maurice,' Rosie muttered, biting hard at her lower lip.

'Not now, not any longer,' Constantine stated with

grim emphasis, his strong jawline clenching as he shot her a sardonic glance. 'And when we go our separate ways, if I have anything to do with it, you will not be crawling back to him! He's a bad influence on you.'

'I'm twenty, not ten, Constantine.'

'But you still tell as many lies as a child.' As the car drew to a halt in the courtyard at Son Fontanal, Constantine murmured drily, 'Do you really think I could believe that you haven't slept with *either* of the men you were living with? Or that Anton forced me to marry you over anything less than his honest belief that you were expecting his child?'

'Don't you dare call me a liar!' Springing out of the limo, Rosie stalked indoors.

'I console myself with one reflection,' Constantine drawled as he drew level with her in the stone-flagged hall. 'Had you been pregnant by Anton or indeed *had* there been a blood-tie between you—' a derisive laugh expressed his opinion of that possibility '—I would have been trapped in this marriage for the rest of my days.'

Disbelief halted Rosie in her tracks. 'That's…that's a crazy thing to say.'

'Crazy?' His winged brows drew together in genuine astonishment at the charge, his black eyes frowning. 'In either of those circumstances it would have been a matter of honour that I should fully accept the obligation he laid upon me.'

'But that's outrageous…' Rosie condemned unevenly.

'To you, perhaps,' Constantine conceded wryly. 'But Anton brought me up and I had enormous respect for him. I owe him a great deal. He had a very strong sense of duty towards his family. That kind of loyalty *should* take precedence over personal feelings.'

A jerky little laugh fell from Rosie's dry lips as she found herself blindly studying her feet. Suddenly she was very grateful that she had not repeated her claim that she was Anton's daughter. She had a vision of Constantine hog-roped and tied to her out of respect for her father's last wishes. 'A matter of honour', he called it. She winced at the demeaning concept but a tinge of curiosity remained.

'Are you actually saying that you would have married a stranger and stayed married to her just because that was what Anton asked you to do?' she prompted.

'I have married a stranger…only you become more familiar and yet more strange with every minute I spend in your company,' Constantine confessed with a sudden fierceness that made her shiver. 'I do not understand you…and I will not be satisfied until I do!'

Rosie moved away a step. She wasn't even looking at him. Already she had learnt that defence but it wasn't working now. The darkly passionate rasp of his voice made her feel all hot and sort of quivery and even a foot from him she knew she was still too close for safety.

'Look at me…' Constantine invited softly.

Rosie was in retreat. 'I think I—'

'I am not a womaniser.'

'If you say so.'

'I had a brief and foolish affair with Justine when I was only twenty-one.'

'Gosh…you must have made some impression!' Accidentally meeting his intent golden eyes, Rosie became alarmingly short of breath. Without fully appreciating what she was doing, she started up the staircase backwards.

'My wealth made the deepest impression.' Constantine spread eloquent and dismissive hands as he strolled towards her with the fluid prowl of a lion tracking a nervous prey. 'Yet it appears to mean little to you. That is a new experience for me and a most surprising response from you.'

'Really?' Rosie's strained query wobbled as she

flipped up two whole steps at once, tightly gripping the worn balustrade for support. 'Why surprising?'

'Had you been as avaricious as I believed, you would have played on the attraction between us. You would have been eager to share my bed in the expectation of profiting from that intimacy,' Constantine responded with a slow, devastating smile. 'But while the flesh was weak the will was stronger still and you were not tempted by the thought of what surrender might bring you.'

'Constantine,' Rosie said slightly shrilly, still heading up and back but utterly powerless to disengage her mesmerised gaze from the dark lure of his. 'Hasn't it occurred to you that I might be the kind of devious woman who thinks that you could thrive on a challenge?'

'But you know that truth as if you were *born* knowing it, *pethi mou*,' Constantine savoured with disconcerting amusement, raking her with burnished eyes of appreciative gold. 'Why else would you fight with me?'

'Because...because...' Rosie fumbled wildly for a reason as she reached the landing and tried to step up. She might have lost her balance had Constantine not reached out and swiftly steadied her with strong hands. 'Because you irritate the hell out of me...that's why I fight with you!' she managed in a surge of frantic rebellion.

'You fight with me,' Constantine traded in a husky growl of disagreement, 'to hold me at bay. But you've used that ploy once too often, and I may have been a slow learner but, believe me, when I catch on I'm faster than the speed of light and from now on every time you shout at me I will cover your mouth with mine.'

'It won't work...I'm naturally argumentative!' Rosie asserted even more tautly.

Golden fire in his molten appraisal, Constantine swept her up into his arms to carry her into the bedroom.

'*Christos*…of course it will work. And once we have made love, once you have lain in my arms and tasted the pleasure we can share, you will never mention the throwback again. I may not be perfect but I'm way beyond him in the reliability stakes.'

Rosie looked up at him, her heart racing so fast, it thundered in her ears. 'We c-can't do this,' she stammered.

'We can…let me show you *how*,' Constantine groaned achingly against the corner of her mouth, his breath fanning her cheek. A hunger she couldn't fight shot through her with the shattering shock effect of a lightning bolt and, reacting on pure instinct to the almost pleading quality of that deep, dark drawl, she turned her mouth under his…and burned.

CHAPTER EIGHT

ROSIE surfaced from that kiss to find herself on the bed. Her dress started falling off as she pulled herself up on one elbow and she snatched at the wildly dipping neckline which was threatening to expose her breasts. A vaguely exploring hand discovered the reason for that lack of suspension. Her zip was down. In a daze she focused on Constantine.

Already he was half-undressed and he was watching her intently, a curious smile playing about his wide, wickedly sensual mouth. 'Why do you act so shy? Do you only make love in the dark?'

A flush of pink ran up beneath her skin. Meeting those brilliant black eyes, she found it was so incredibly hard to breathe or to think but oh, so easy to *feel* the pulse of throbbing excitement that beat in tune with her racing heart. Do I want to do this? Rosie asked herself in sudden turmoil. Oh, yes. Should I? *Definitely not.* Hitching her dress with an unsteady hand, she snaked a foot slowly towards the edge of the bed.

Constantine strolled forward with immense calm and tugged her shoes off. His mobile phone buzzed. He tensed. Rosie watched him expectantly as he reached for it. The buzz stopped. 'What are you doing?' she whispered.

'Switching it off—'

'But it might be an important call!'

Beneath Rosie's deeply shaken gaze, Constantine shrugged. 'It can wait until morning, *pethi mou.*'

A whole night in Constantine's arms, Rosie found herself savouring, and then she stopped herself dead. There was no such thing as a whole night with Constantine. As soon as he had satisfied his lust, he would be off to sleep elsewhere. *His lust.* Dear heaven, how could she even be thinking of making love with him? That anguished question had little hope of a rational answer when she discovered that she could think of nothing else.

'You're very nervous,' Constantine murmured with a frown as he slid out of his well-cut trousers.

'I am not nervous,' Rosie stated with a shrill and desperate stab at dignity as she finally worked up sufficient will-power to scramble off the bed, hotly flushed and contorting herself to struggle with her zip. 'But I'm afraid you can't buy me with dinner and a new wardrobe...or even a reasonable pretence of being human for five minutes—'

Constantine intercepted her, confident hands closing over her rigid shoulders. 'You don't have to be scared of me. I'm not rough in bed,' he told her huskily. 'Not unless you want me to be...'

Finding herself backed up against the bed, Rosie stammered. 'C-Constantine...'

'Your heart is going crazy, *pethi mou.*'

In the act of clamping a guilty hand to the offending organ, Rosie discovered that Constantine had got there first. A warm palm curved against the pouting swell of her breast and she trembled at that light yet possessive touch, her eyes involuntarily closing on a tide of sexual awareness so powerful that her legs threatened to buckle beneath her. *'Don't!'* she gasped strickenly.

But he slowly slid the straps of her dress all the way down her arms and simultaneously pressed his mouth to the precise spot where a pulse was flickering wildly at the base of her throat. A faint moan escaped Rosie as he simply lifted her out of her dress and settled her back on the bed again.

'I'll be very gentle,' Constantine promised thickly, with emphasis.

Her lashes flew up to encounter molten gold enquiry. One look and her bones felt as if they were melting beneath her skin. He came down beside her, lithe and dark and naked, and her heart gave a reactive lurch as she ran wondering, curious eyes over his impressive, powerful length. Her startled eyes widened at the bold, hard thrust of his manhood and she ran out of breath all at once, hot colour and alarm seizing her in a twin attack as, curiosity more than satisfied, she made an entirely instinctive move to escape again.

Constantine rolled over so fast to prevent that that she found herself trapped under him instead, a position that made her even more overpoweringly aware of what she had decided she ought to avoid. '*Theos…*' he grated as he stared down into her anxious, evasive eyes. 'I wish I had smashed Maurice's face in…what the hell did he *do* to you in bed?'

'Nothing!'

'I am not going to hurt you…' Constantine ran a caressing finger along the tense compression of her soft, full mouth, brilliant golden eyes shimmering over her, mesmerically sentencing her to stillness. 'I bet he's never heard of foreplay… Even if it takes me all night to prove it, I swear you will enjoy every moment with me, *pethi mou.*' With the tip of his finger he pressed apart her lips and gently probed the moist cavern within while she stared up at him, lost in those compelling eyes of his, and her lips curved round that finger, laving it with her tongue.

Constantine smiled. Rosie's heart flipped. He withdrew his finger, dropped his dark head and traced the fullness of her lower lip with the teasing tip of his tongue. She wanted him to kiss her. It was an instantaneous need and she shifted beneath him, all of a quiver with helpless impatience, her body taut with sudden screaming tension. Her hands flew up of their own volition and her fingers sank into his black hair to try and drag him down to her by force.

With a husky laugh, Constantine resisted her urging and instead let his tongue dip between her readily parted lips. 'Foreplay,' he whispered provocatively.

But, in the grip of hunger, Rosie wasn't that easily quelled. She reached up until she found his sensual mouth for herself, forcing the pace by wrenching him down to her, not satisfied until he kissed her long and hard and then learning that she still wasn't satisfied. But he was ahead of her then, shifting down her trembling length and letting knowing fingers glance over her swelling breasts and linger like the kiss of fire on the straining thrust of her taut nipples.

All the breath left her lungs in a strangled moan of tortured pleasure. Gazing down at her, Constantine made a husky soothing sound deep in his throat. It was incredibly sexy. He bent his head, long fingers pressing the pouting mounds together, and licked the rosy peaks gently and then more rapidly until her back arched on a long, sighing gasp. As he toyed with those achingly sensitive buds, Rosie whimpered and jerked, flames of tormented excitement building in an uncontrollable surge. Her hands skimmed with wild indecision over every part of him she could reach, tangling in his hair, smoothing over his blunt cheekbones, clutching at the smooth, muscular expanse of his shoulders.

Constantine rolled over, carrying her with him so that she was lying on top of him, and plundered her soft mouth with a force of passion that splintered through her squirming body at storm force. Meshing a hand into her mane of hair, he tugged her head up to look at her with burning golden eyes. 'Would you like five minutes to cool down?' he asked thickly.

'Cool down?' Rosie echoed breathlessly as if he were talking in a foreign language, the throbbing tips of her breasts grazed by the rough black curls on his chest, making her eyes slide shut again on a silent shiver of utterly boneless pleasure. She moved so that she could rub herself against him again and moaned.

A thick flood of Greek was wrenched from Constantine, his long, hard frame shuddering beneath hers in enforced response. Hard hands closed round her hips and dragged her up his extended length, parting her thighs so that she straddled him. 'I need to cool down...no, I *need*—' And he closed his mouth hungrily over a rosy nipple, jolting her with such a shock of intense sensation that she cried out, her head falling back.

He splayed long fingers over the ripe curve of her behind to settle her exactly where he wanted her and rock her back and forth over the velvet-smooth thrust of his arousal with an earthy groan of satisfaction. Rosie moaned in shivering, startled reaction to that new source of excitement, out of control and irretrievably lost in the violent surge of pleasure he was giving her. She burned and ached and craved more with a hunger that threatened to tear her apart.

'*Please...*' she gasped.

Constantine flipped her back onto the mattress and kissed her again, his tongue delving in electrifying imitation of an infinitely more invasive possession. At the same time he ran a knowing hand down the straining slender expanse of her inner thigh, making every tiny muscle in her entire body jerk, and fleetingly skimmed the moist, throbbing centre of her.

'You feel like hot satin,' he groaned against her swollen mouth.

Touched where she had never been touched before, Rosie was incapable of a vocal response. Her whole being was centred on the tormenting exploration of those skilful fingers. She wanted to thrash about and he wouldn't let her. Her heart slammed like a hammer against her breastbone as she sobbed for breath, driving to such a wild pitch of excitement that she was convinced she was being deliberately tortured.

And then, at the height of that teeth-clenching, agonising pleasure, Constantine pulled her under him and plunged into her with the ravishing force of an invading army. Rosie let out a yelp of pain that would have woken the dead and then sank her teeth vengefully into a hard, muscular shoulder. He cursed and flinched into sudden stillness. As the level of agony subsided to a dulled but still perceptible throb, Rosie unclenched her teeth and looked up at him accusingly.

'*Theos*...' Constantine rasped, black eyes expressively awash with guilty, angry bewilderment as he snatched in a ragged breath. 'I'm sorry...you excited me so much, I lost control.'

Incredibly touched by the look of bemusement in those magnetic dark eyes, Rosie's tension gave. 'I—'

His dark, tousled head swooped down, the tender, seductive caress of his mouth feathering against hers in silken persuasion of the cruellest kind. 'But you feel like heaven on earth,' he confided with a sinuous, slow and infinitesimal shift of his hips that sent a rise of reawakened pleasure travelling through her startled body. 'Trust me, *pethi mou*...'

Rosie melted like frost in sunlight, heat surging back in a stabbing little surge of excitement. The next time he moved she was waiting for that feeling and a second after that she was shocked to realise that she was desperately craving more of that astonishingly sensual sensation which sent every pulse racing.

'OK?' Constantine husked.

OK? It was more than OK, it was...it was glorious and so deeply intimate that she felt possessed. Squeezing her eyes shut, Rosie felt the excitement rocket almost terrifyingly fast until all she could do was gasp and cling in abandoned surrender to the hungry, diving stroke of him inside her. And then, before she could even grasp what was happening to her, the heat mushroomed and stars exploded in a multicoloured frenzy behind her eyelids. As he shuddered above her in the grip of his own climax, the tidal wave of extraordinary pleasure still rocking her was mindless in its intensity.

She didn't want Constantine to move and disturb the incredible sense of peace and happiness filling her. And he was inextricably bound up with those feelings, she registered in confusion, instinctively loving the heat and weight of him and the achingly familiar scent of his damp skin.

He lifted his dark head and stared down at her with stunning intensity. Rosie was held fast by that scrutiny and the raw tension now tautening his muscles but his black eyes were utterly unreadable. His mouth twisted. 'You felt like a virgin.' He vented a harsh, almost bitter laugh. 'Or how I *imagine* a virgin would feel! *Christo*, what would I know about that?'

Releasing her from his weight with startling abruptness, Constantine sprang off the bed. 'I need a shower.'

'Constantine...?' Rosie whispered shakily.

'I am sorry I hurt you,' Constantine breathed roughly on the threshold of the bathroom without turning round to look at her again. 'But right now I don't feel good about this development.'

In a shock made raw by a crawling sense of humiliation, Rosie lay listening to the shower running. Constantine regretted the 'development'. Sexual hunger satisfied, Constantine couldn't escape the scene of the crime quickly enough. A great lump closed over Rosie's throat and her eyes stung and burned. She could have stopped him; she could have said no. But she had stu-

pidly indulged herself, indulged him and refused to face
up to what she was doing. Yet in her worst imaginings
she could not have expected so devastating and immediate a rejection of their intimacy...or the feeling that
she was being ripped slowly in two by the strength of
her own turbulent emotions.

Constantine emerged from the bathroom again. He
banged through every piece of furniture in the room.
Curiosity finally drove Rosie's head up. Light glim-
mered over the long, golden sweep of his back. He was
pulling on a pair of jeans, electric tension sizzling like
wildfire from every jerky, impatient movement.
Fascinated against her will, Rosie stared.

'I'm going out,' Constantine gritted over one brown
shoulder.

'Be my guest,' Rosie managed, turning away again
and feeling more alone than she had ever felt in her life
before. She had felt she knew Constantine but now she
knew that she didn't know him at all. She didn't know
why he was behaving as he was. She didn't know what
was on his mind. Self-loathing boiled through her slender frame. Well, that was what you got when you went
to bed with a stranger.

After lying awake for hours, Rosie finally slid into an
exhausted sleep around dawn. Shortly after nine, voices
below her window woke her up. Workmen were assem-
bling to repair the roof. She had a shower, made unimpressed use of the extravagant number of luxurious new
towels available, and while she wondered where
Constantine had slept she despised herself for caring.

Downstairs she passed by a closed door beyond which
she heard Constantine and a ringing phone. Her strained
mouth compressed as a maid directed her into the dining
room. Breakfast was served but Rosie had little appetite.

She was finishing her coffee when Carmina appeared, beaming behind a huge bouquet of flowers.

'Forgive me,' it said on the card.

Two high spots of colour flared over Rosie's taut cheekbones. Forgive him? Not if he crawled and begged for a hundred years! Her teeth gritted. 'Get her some flowers,' he had probably said to Dmitri. Oh, what a big effort Constantine had made! Why? He was stuck up a mountain, supposedly on his honeymoon, and sexually available women were thinner than hens' teeth on the ground. The threat of celibacy undoubtedly struck horror into his oversexed bones. Had Constantine now decided that he had been too hasty in regretting their intimacy?

Rosie thrust wide the door of the room being used as an office. As an entrance it failed. Everyone was too busy to notice her. A svelte brunette in her thirties was taking notes while standing up. Constantine was dictating in bursts of low-pitched Greek, while simultaneously conducting a conversation on the phone. A young man was seated, muttering over a computer terminal, while another was ripping several feet of paper out of a fax machine.

Rosie crossed the room to the electric shredder, hit the button and started stuffing flowers into the metal jaws. The shredder chewed up the first few inches of the floral sacrifice, wedged shut on the stalks and cut out with a complaining beep of warning. Silence slowly spread and Rosie spun round.

Constantine had lowered his phone. She saw only him, raging green eyes connecting with glittering black as he sprang upright. Sheathed in a lightweight suit in pale grey, he looked devastatingly handsome. As their companions melted out of the room without being asked, Rosie sucked in a deep breath, found it insufficient to cool her temper and battered the remaining blooms in seething frustration against the inanimate shredder be-

fore flinging them to the floor in a violent gesture of
contempt.

'You unbelievable creep! How *dare* you give me
flowers?'

'Last night shouldn't have happened,' Constantine
gritted between clenched teeth, brilliant black eyes un-
flinching. 'But what is done is done.'

Disconcerted by that initial statement, Rosie paled,
and even though she knew she ought to agree with the
sentiment expressed she was attacked by an amount of
pain that tensed every muscle in her slender body. Her
lashes dipped to conceal her confusion. 'You were determined to get me into bed,' she condemned.

'*Theos*…given the overwhelming attraction between
us, that conclusion was inevitable! But I'm not very
proud that last night I wasn't able to keep my hands off
my guardian's mistress,' Constantine stated with fierce
candour.

Belated comprehension sank in on Rosie, making her
marvel at her lack of perception. Once again,
Constantine's firm belief that she had had an affair with
Anton had made its prejudice felt…and *how*, she reflected painfully, recalling the bitter force of his rejection
only hours earlier. But with understanding came an odd
sense of relief and then a rise of stark frustration. Her
chin came up, green eyes flashing a direct challenge.
'How many times do I have to tell you that Anton and
I were not lovers?'

Shimmering dark golden eyes collided ferociously fast
with hers. Constantine expelled his breath in a driven
hiss. 'There's a fool born every minute but I'm not one
of them.'

She could go and drag in Carmina and ask her to show
that photograph and repeat what Anton had told her, but
how embarrassing that would be for all of them…and
then what? Even if she actually managed to convince

Constantine that she was Anton's daughter, where did they go from there? She might want to clear her name but she couldn't forget what Constantine had admitted with such impressive conviction the night before.

If he knew who she *really* was, would he start thinking of her as some sort of ghastly obligation and out of respect for Anton feel forced to change his behaviour accordingly? She cringed from that idea. At least on these terms they met on level ground. The time would certainly come when she would try to prove her identity but that time was not now, when she couldn't bear to think that owning up to being Anton's illegitimate child might make Constantine pity her.

Staring into those scorching dark eyes, Rosie felt her heart lurch and her mouth run dry. Constantine gazed back at her in the pounding, pulsing silence. Without warning it was incredibly difficult to breathe. Shock reeled over her because this time she couldn't even pretend that she didn't know what was happening to her.

'You told Anton that you were pregnant,' Constantine contended in a ragged, dark growl as he drew inexorably closer. 'It was a cheap trick but that is why he demanded that I marry you.'

'I don't play cheap tricks,' Rosie told him breathlessly, struggling to hang on to her wits as her skin heated and her breasts swelled into throbbing sensitivity. She pressed a betraying hand to the pulse flickering a crazy beat at her collarbone.

'*Christos*...you play me like a witch casting a spell!' Constantine countered with sudden glancing rawness. 'I want you even more now than I wanted you last night—'

'Tough,' Rosie said with tremulous bite, a quiver of deep overpowering longing sheeting over her with the efficacy of a mind-blowing drug, leaving her more dizzy and disorientated than ever. Her dazed green eyes clung to his hard, dark face in a tormented craving that cut like glass through her pride and slashed it to ribbons.

In response, Constantine reached out, curved his fingers firmly over her stiff shoulders and pulled her across the floor into his arms. And since that was where every inch of her wanted to be she couldn't fight. He crushed her to him in a shatteringly sexual embrace, a powerful hand pressing her into intimate contact with the bold, hard thrust of his arousal. Rosie shivered violently, her legs turning hollow. He took her mouth with hot, hard hunger and the heat of desire blanked out every thought. She clutched at his broad shoulders, knit frantic fingers into his thick black hair and feverishly kissed him back.

He sank down into his swivel chair with her on top of him, lean hands roving beneath her loose T-shirt, skimming over the smooth, taut skin of her ribcage in search of the pouting mounds above. Encountering her bra, he groaned with frustration against her reddened mouth, released the fastening with dexterity and spread both hands possessively over her bared breasts. Fierce sensation engulfed her in a wild tide of shuddering response. If she had been standing up, she would have fallen down.

Meshing a hand into the tumble of her hair, Constantine held her back from him, his breath coming in tortured bursts. The phone was ringing off the hook, the fax still noisily spewing paper. A flicker of disconcertion drew his winged ebony brows together. Momentarily he closed his eyes as if he was fighting for control, a muscle pulling taut at the corner of his sensual mouth. His thumb rubbed over an achingly erect pink nipple and Rosie trembled and gasped as if she were in a force-ten-gale, bowing her head over his, resting her forehead in his luxuriant hair, torn apart and weak as water with need.

'You are driving me off the edge, *pethi mou*,'

Constantine confided with ragged bite. 'Possibly a working honeymoon was not one of my brighter ideas.' Suddenly he stood up, both arms anchored around her, and
set her down on the edge of the desk, sending papers
flying with a decisive sweep of one arrogant brown hand.
'But then if I want to make love to my wife in the middle
of the day that is *my* business.'

Rosie's lashes fluttered. 'I'm not your...' she began,
yet her voice trailed away again, wiped out by the
change she'd discovered within herself, the sea change
that had crept up on her without her noticing. *His wife,*
she savoured in a sudden stark surge of possessiveness
that shook her.

Tugging the wide-necked T-shirt down her arms to
entrap her and then slowly extracting her hands,
Constantine delved his tongue between her parted lips
with a growl of immense satisfaction. The hunger he
could heighten with just one more kiss blazed a fiery
trail that plunged her into quivering sensual oblivion. He
skimmed caressing fingers over the straining pink buds
of her nipples, making her burn and shift and moan with
pleasure beneath his mouth, and then he was pressing
her back, his hands skimming up her thighs to drag her
cotton skirt down out of his path as he pulled her to him.

Clenched by an excitement that made breathing a torment to her struggling lungs, Rosie focused on him with
wondering eyes, her racing heart threatening to arrest as
she drowned in the passionate intensity of his gaze.
Utterly entrapped, she arched her spine like a willing
sacrifice.

'You make me *ache*...' His deep, dark drawl was ragged with arousal as he lowered his mouth to her pouting
breasts. 'I want to be inside you so badly, I'm shaking,
pethi mou.'

The hot pleasure took her by violent storm, strangled
moans torn from deep in her throat as he worked his

way slowly down her quivering length, and by the time
he reached the tensing, jerking concavity of her stomach
Rosie was just a mass of melting, gasping nerve-endings,
only managing to stay on the desk because he had her
pinned there. He was torturing her and she couldn't bear
it. He hooked his fingers into the waistband of her high-
cut cotton panties and she was on the very brink of ex-
ploding with the sheer force of her anticipation when,
without the smallest warning, Constantine froze, grabbed
up her T-shirt and flung it across her. Her startled eyes
flew wide.

Constantine strode towards the opening door at the
same time as a thunderous crash of smashing china and
rattling metal sounded in the hall outside.

In shock, Rosie jumped a foot in the air. Other noises
which she had tuned out swam back into her awareness.
The phone was still ringing, the fax still buzzing. She
blinked in frantic bemusement. Only one item of clothing stood between her and complete nudity, she registered strickenly. In broad daylight, she was spread across
Constantine's desk like a brazen trollop. Oh, dear
heaven…

Constantine snapped the door softly shut again. 'One
of the maids was bringing in coffee. Dmitri intercepted
her. He gave her such a fright she dropped the tray. I
haven't done anything like this since I was a teenager,'
he murmured with sudden rueful amusement.

Rosie refused to look at him. 'Go away!' she said
shakily.

'Why?'

She was burning alive in an agony of mortification.
'Get out of here while I get my clothes on!'

'Don't you think that would be just a little absurd in
the circumstances?'

'Bloody hell…can you never do *anything* I ask you

to do?' Her strained voice cracked on the demand. 'Do you always have to argue about it?'

The door closed with a definitive thud.

Pale as milk, Rosie shot off the desk like a shoplifter caught red-handed in the glare of spotlights. In a mad rush she fumbled clumsily for her bra and her skirt and then crawled about the floor until she finally located a missing canvas pump lying under a chair. As she dressed, tears drenching her distraught eyes, she studied the open window, and then, in sudden decision, pressed it wider to facilitate her exit. It was the work of a moment to hoist herself over the sill and out into the fresh air, thereby cravenly avoiding any immediate further contact with Constantine. Before she dealt with Constantine, she conceded painfully, she needed to deal with what was happening inside her own head.

As she clambered over the stack of roof tiles in her path and worked her way round a ladder, she heard a car coming up the drive. It was a bright yellow four-wheel drive. Drawing the brash vehicle to a halt, the driver vaulted out, blond mane gleaming in the sunshine as he looked curiously around himself. Rosie froze.

'Maurice?' she whispered shakily, and then she shrieked, *'Maurice!'* and closed the distance between them in ten seconds flat to fling herself at him with a strangled sob of welcome.

CHAPTER NINE

ENVELOPING Rosie in a bear hug, Maurice scanned her damp-eyed pallor beneath her wildly tousled hair, an anxious frown in his bright blue eyes. 'You look bloody awful...what's been going on?' he demanded.

'Let's go for a drive!' Pulling free of him, Rosie dived into the passenger seat of the four-wheel drive and looked at him expectantly. 'What are you waiting for?'

'Constantine.' Maurice mimicked the soundtrack from *Jaws*.

'Oh, stop being funny!' Rosie cried as she cast hunted glances in all directions, her nerves shot to hell by an absolute terror of Constantine appearing and dragging her back out of the car. 'I think I'm in love with him!'

There it was, *said*, out in the open, Rosie's worst nightmare come true, and Maurice didn't even have the decency to look surprised.

'What on earth are you doing over here?' she asked belatedly.

Maurice swung the brightly coloured vehicle into an unhurried U-turn. 'I've been promising myself a holiday for a long time. The minute you said you were in Majorca, I saw sun and sand and I realised where you had to be heading. From there it was only a matter of studying the map.'

While he drove down the steep mountain road at the crawling speed of someone terrified of heights, easing round every zigzag bend with an agonised death-grip on the steering wheel, Rosie thought feverishly about Constantine until her head spun and pounded with tension.

Bang! He had stolen her tranquillity and her security. And what had he given her in return? A hideous sense of inadequacy and self-loathing and a temper as unreliable as an active volcano. If threatened by Constantine, *shout*. Only last night he had been telling her that she argued with him to hold him at bay! He had seen inside her and understood something she hadn't understood herself and that was terrifying.

The minute she had found herself holding fire on protesting her identity, the minute that she had found herself wishing that their marriage were a real marriage, she should have known that she was in love with him. But all Constantine had ever wanted from her was sex. She found him irresistible, he found her...available. If that tabloid hadn't exposed their secret wedding, Constantine would've walked away from her that morning without a backward glance.

'Aren't you even curious about that newspaper article?' Maurice prompted between grinding teeth of strain. 'Or didn't Constantine tell you that I took the blame for that? It's true, it *was* my fault. I shot my mouth off to my sister—'

'Lorna?' Dredged from her introspection, Rosie's head spun round.

'She used to see this bloke, Mitch, in the pub. He was a reporter on the local paper. Apparently, she'd been trying to get off with him for ages,' Maurice explained grimly. 'So she spouted the story to try and impress him with the idea that she had interesting connections, invited him back to her flat for coffee and let him borrow that photo she took of you.'

Only then did Rosie recall that the day she and Maurice had moved into the cottage it had been his sister wielding the camera. Lorna had given *her* a souvenir copy of that photograph.

'And that was the last she saw of him. Mitch swopped

the scoop for a job on a London tabloid. It's a lucky thing that I only told Lorna you were marrying Constantine and nothing else. She thinks you met him down in London,' Maurice proffered heavily. 'If she'd known about Anton or the will, that slimy reporter would've got the whole damned lot out of her!'

Rosie sighed. 'You lied to protect her.'

'Constantine is a very confrontational bloke. In fact, he comes out of nowhere like a rocket attack,' Maurice groaned, staring fixedly into the driving mirror.

Rosie stiffened, dismayed to discover words in defence of Constantine brimming to her lips and hurriedly swallowing them back. 'I'm probably just infatuated with him. I'll get over it,' she swore, striving to save face on the subject of a relationship that had no future whatsoever.

'I hope so. Only a maniac with no respect for human life would sit on my bumper on a road as dangerous as this!' Sweat was breaking out on Maurice's brow.

'You mean...?' Rosie's head whipped round at the exact same moment as a low-slung scarlet sports car flashed past them at speed on the brow of the bend and screeched to a tyre-squealing halt.

Panicked by the manoeuvre, Maurice hit the brakes of the four-wheel drive in an emergency stop. Constantine sprang fluidly out of the sports car and strode back towards them.

'He raced cars for a while when he was a teenager,' Rosie explained shakily. 'Thespina persuaded him to give it up.' He took up women instead, she completed inwardly.

'He's walking inches from the edge of a thousand-foot drop without looking where he's going!' Maurice gritted, his appalled gaze glued to the sight.

'Can't you drive on past or something?'

'Are you as crazy as he is?' Maurice demanded in a

defensive burst of incredulity. 'I'd need a death wish to try and outrun a Ferrari on this road!'

Constantine stilled three feet from the car and removed his sunglasses, sliding them into the pocket of his exquisitely tailored jacket. Ice-cold black eyes dug into Rosie and she shivered, intimidated more by that chilling, silent menace than she would have been by rage.

Maurice skimmed a rueful glance between the two of them and slowly shook his head. 'Get out of the car, Rosie,' he murmured flatly. 'I'm only a hero on level ground…and, aside of that, Constantine *is* your husband.'

Shock made Rosie's generous mouth fall inelegantly wide.

'Unless, of course, you were about to tell me that he knocks you about…' Maurice dealt her a doubtful but enquiring glance.

A terrible desire to lie assailed Rosie and then she clashed with the raw outrage in Constantine's fulminating stare and shrank with shame. 'But you can't just—'

'I'm sorry, but I'm not taking sides.' With an air of decided finality, Maurice hit the release button on her seat belt.

'How wise,' Constantine purred like the predator he was as he strolled round the bonnet.

'I'll be in touch,' Maurice sighed.

Disdaining the use of the door, Constantine lifted Rosie out of the passenger seat with two powerful hands. 'I can walk,' she snapped, her burning face a picture of temper and mortification. 'Put me down, for heaven's sake!'

In intimidating silence and paying no heed whatsoever to her fevered protests, Constantine strode back down the road and settled her into the Ferrari.

'How dare you treat me like that?' Rosie gasped as he swung in beside her.

'What did you expect…applause for making a fool of yourself?'

'And what's that supposed to mean?'

'Conscience might have brought Maurice over here to check up on you but he wasn't prepared to force the issue with me. Clearly you were telling the truth when you said that you weren't lovers…but the absence of the sexual element wasn't for want of trying on your part, was it?' Constantine slashed her a look of biting derision. 'It is obvious to me that you settled for friendship only because *he* wasn't interested in anything else.'

'That's nonsense…' Rosie began heatedly.

'And then you threw yourself at Anton because you needed to prove to yourself that you were capable of attracting other men! Or was the affair with Anton and the move to London planned as a desperate last-ditch attempt to make Maurice jealous and sit up and take notice of you?'

'Don't be ridiculous…I'm not in love with Maurice.'

'You certainly weren't in love with Anton. But then no doubt he was a father figure,' Constantine responded with sardonic bite.

Rosie froze, her anger decimated by pain. 'That's exactly what he was,' she mumbled.

'And within minutes of that memorial service you weren't lusting after any ghost!'

Rosie reddened fiercely at that earthy reminder of the way Constantine had affected her that day. 'Don't you have any decency?'

The powerful car shot to a halt in the courtyard. Constantine killed the engine and turned his head to look at her, black eyes as hard as jet in his vibrantly handsome face. 'It took a hike when you took off in a tantrum with Maurice. He's your security blanket and I think you're old enough to do without him. Times have changed and don't try to tell me differently, *pethi mou*. It's me that you want now...'

Always and for ever, she thought fearfully, clenched by a bone-deep sense of her own vulnerability. She wanted much more than she had any hope of achieving.

Constantine lifted a lean hand and caught a colourful handful of corkscrew curls gently between his fingers. He tipped her troubled face up to the onslaught of his starkly assessing gaze. 'And I want you,' he completed with lethal brevity. 'So what's the problem? As I see it, it's a simple and perfectly straightforward relationship.'

Rosie snatched in a sustaining breath, almost drowning in the evocative scent of him so close, a whole chain of little reactions making her head swim and her body quiver. 'But then you only think with your hormones—'

'*Theos*, I can't think with anything else around you,' Constantine admitted thickly, unconcerned by her censure.

Rosie struggled to suppress a shiver of excitement. Shame engulfed her and she swept up an unsteady hand to detach his fingers from her hair and pull back. 'I know there are no guarantees in life but that's not enough for me,' she said tautly.

'This is beginning to sound like a negotiation and negotiations invariably end with a price.'

'Feelings don't come with prices attached.'

He threw back his arrogant dark head, ebony brows raised in challenge above cool, watchful black eyes. 'Are you sure of that? I've already given up my freedom and, strange as it might seem to you, that feels like a pretty hefty concession when I've never done it before.'

Refusing to be driven into retreat by the warning chill in the air, Rosie tilted her chin. 'You haven't given up anything for my benefit. You only married me because

of the will and we're only here together now because
the Press found out. Do you have any idea how that
makes me feel? Well, I'll tell you how it makes me
feel…like the flavour of the month for a casual sexual
interlude,' she asserted with steadily rising volume in the
face of his dauntingly impassive appraisal. 'And it might
surprise you but I value myself a lot more highly than
that!'

A silence punctuated by the audible hiss of her quick-
ened breathing fell.

'Then we would appear to have nothing more to discuss,' Constantine concluded softly.

Rosie frowned in bemusement. 'But…'

Constantine elevated a winged brow. 'You don't want
a casual sexual interlude…and I don't want anything
else.'

The flush on Rosie's cheeks slowly drained away,
leaving her as white as his shirt-front. That cold-blooded
assurance cut right into her like a knife. Nothing had
ever hurt her so much. She clambered out of the Ferrari
like a drunk trying to act sober, choosing each movement with infinitesimal care. Her stomach churned with
nausea.

She could not believe that she had clumsily exposed
herself to that level of rejection. Like a frantic teenager
in love, she had slung her fear and insecurity at him in
the hope of drawing a reassuring response. But
Constantine did not appreciate being put on the spot and
he had had no inhibitions about brutally matching her
foolish candour.

'Of course,' Constantine added softly, smoothly as he
studied the rigidity of her slender back, 'you could always try to change my mind, *pethi mou.*'

Rosie shuddered as the knife slid deeper still into her
unprotected heart. In that selfsame moment, she also

learnt that when provoked she could still hate almost as much as she loved.

'And permit me to offer some advice,' he murmured. 'You are not going to do it by chasing off down a mountain with the throwback.'

Rosie lifted her fiery head high and turned round to face him again. 'As far as I'm concerned, you don't exist any more. You are beneath my notice,' she stated with tremulous, driven dignity. 'And I don't want anything more to do with you.'

Anguished pain and flagellated pride weighted her as she walked indoors, shoulders square, chin high. Maybe it was just as well that she had been so painfully and naïvely frank, she told herself heavily. At last she now knew where she stood. And she knew how he saw her now too. She might not have enjoyed having her worst suspicions confirmed but knowledge was protection...*wasn't it*?

'Oh, you shouldn't have!' Rosie scolded when she glanced up and found Carmina hovering over her with a glass of freshly squeezed lemonade. 'I could have come inside to get something.'

'When you are inside?' the old lady grumbled. 'You come inside only when it is getting dark.'

Standing up, Rosie straightened, and her aching back protested. She rubbed her damp hands down over her grubby shorts and grasped the glass with a determined smile. 'This garden...it's beginning to look good again, don't you think?'

Carmina settled down on the flight of stone steps rediscovered only the day before as a result of Rosie's industrious labour and folded her plump arms. Her wrinkled face was troubled as she surveyed the pruned shrubs and the border of old climbing roses which now stood revealed where there had once been only a tangled thicket of undergrowth. She sighed. 'The marriage...it is not looking so good.'

Wincing, Rosie tilted her tense face up to the sun and then drank deep of the lemonade. It quenched her thirst but the effort of forcing liquid past her tightening throat muscles hurt. 'Carmina—'

'This is not what your father wanted,' Carmina told her stubbornly. 'You and Constantine...this marriage was his dream for the future.'

'Dreams don't always work out...' In fact, Anton's dream had plunged her into a real nightmare, Rosie reflected wretchedly.

Over the past three days, living under the same roof as Constantine had become an agonising ordeal and no matter how hard she tried she had found it impossible to rise above that rejection and behave as if nothing had happened. She just couldn't bear to be in the same room as him. She just couldn't bear to look at him or speak to him. She could only suppress her turbulent emotions in hard physical work, and at night she was so darned tired, she ought to have been sleeping like the dead...but she *wasn't*.

She tossed, she turned and then she slid into an uneasy doze, only to wake up in hot-faced shock from dream after erotic dream about Constantine. What she did to him, what he did to her and the incredible number of unlikely places in which they carried out these shameless fantasies of hers ensured that her nights were far more exhausting than her days. And her inventive imagination made it even more impossible for her to meet Constantine's eyes.

'He does not know that you are Don Antonio's daughter,' Carmina complained in a tone of reproof. 'That is a very big secret to keep from your husband.'

'I know what I'm doing, Carmina.'

'How can you say that? There is no peace in Son

Fontanal. We all creep about the house…no smiles, no laughter. That fancy cook…he says if one more meal comes back to him uneaten he will leave!'

'Constantine has a filthy temper.'

'With a wife labouring in the garden all day, he has reason. You are neglecting your husband.'

Not in her dreams, she wasn't. 'He thrives on neglect.'

With a disapproving clicking of her teeth, Carmina shook her head and got up to go. 'You are as stubborn as he is.'

Rosie settled back down to her weeding with renewed vigour. If her father was looking down on her and Constantine now, she knew he would be blaming her too. But from the moment that Constantine had asserted that had she been related to Anton he would have felt obligated to stay married to her Rosie had been determined not to try to attract and hold him on that basis.

Having smoothly seduced her into bed, Constantine had then freely admitted that his sole interest in her was sexual. Had he known she was Anton's daughter, he would have tried to pretend that there was more to their relationship but all the time he would've been feeling trapped and resenting her like mad. And to try to tell him now when they were at daggers drawn and when she had no real proof to offer…what would be the point?

'Why did you send away the gardeners I engaged?'

Startled, Rosie twisted round on her knees. A big black shadow had blocked out the sun. She focused on Constantine's hand-stitched Italian loafers and looked no higher. 'I prefer to do the work myself.'

'There are several acres of ground here.'

'Well, I've got plenty of time on my hands, haven't I?' Her treacherous gaze started wandering up from the hem of his beautifully tailored grey trousers to the extensive length of his lean, hard thighs. Her stomach clenched and turned over.

Constantine released his breath in an explosive hiss. 'You won't go out to lunch, you won't go out to dinner...you won't even go out for a drive...'

They did nothing so safe in Rosie's night-time fantasies. Her guilt-stricken appraisal strayed to the hard, muscular flare of his hip and the taut flatness of his stomach then lower again and she closed her eyes in absolute anguish as she realised that she was eating him up with her eyes. 'I'd be wasting my time and yours.'

'You nourish a grievance like a child revelling in a monumental sulk!'

'I'm not sulking. I just don't think we have anything left to say to each other. You said it *all*.'

'*Christos*...at least stand up and look at me when you're speaking to me!' Constantine grated rawly, bending down without warning to close one strong hand over hers and tug her upright.

Rosie pulled herself free and backed away several steps. Involuntarily her evasive gaze clashed with diamond-hard dark eyes. It was even worse than she had feared. That collision cost her dear. It was like being run over by a truck, thrown into the air with heart fearfully hammering and the breath wrenched from her body, all control wrested from her.

She shivered, every muscle taut as the hunger hit her in a stormy, greedy wave, a desperate, obsessive wanting that paid no heed to pride or intelligence. She wanted to touch him so badly, her fingernails bit sharp crescents into her hands. The simmering tension in the atmosphere heightened, until she could hear the accelerated thump of her heart in her ears.

'What I said to you...' Brilliant dark golden eyes challenged her levelly, his sensual mouth twisting. 'Has it occurred to you that perhaps I wasn't ready to answer questions about us?'

She wanted to believe him—she wanted to believe

him so badly, she could almost taste her own desperation. But it had taken him too long to come up with that justification and suddenly Rosie despised herself for even listening. She started walking away. 'I need a bath—'

A lean hand whipped out and closed round her forearm to stay her. 'Is that all you have to say to me?' he gritted.

Angry green eyes flashed into his. 'You miscalculated, Constantine. You're so used to saying and doing whatever you like with women that you thought you could do the same with me.'

'What the hell are you talking about?' he growled.

A bitter little laugh was dredged from her tight throat. 'You assumed that you could be honest and get away with it. In fact, not only did you think that, you actually thought that putting me down would make me try harder to please...' Her strained voice shook and she compressed her lips to silence herself.

For a split second, Constantine stared down at her, inky black lashes low on his stabbing gaze. 'That is not true—'

'I don't believe you. You're arrogant and selfish and inconsiderate of other people's feelings,' Rosie asserted unsteadily. 'And I don't care how rich or how powerful you are...I wouldn't give daylight to any man who talked to me like that!'

'Is that a fact?' Reaching out for her with two determined hands, Constantine urged her up against him and sent every skin cell in her taut body leaping. 'You will give me a lot more than daylight before I am finished, *pethi mou!*'

His vengeful mouth was hot, hungry and hard and her knees gave way. His tongue delved between her lips with an erotic thrust that tore a whimper of delight from her. Raw excitement electrified her, releasing the uncontrollable flood of her own hunger. She shuddered convulsively and her heart raced so hard and fast that she clung and clutched at him to stay upright.

And then just as suddenly she was freed, left to find her own support on wildly wobbling legs, dilated green eyes pinned to him in shock. That separation was as painful and as unwelcome as an amputation when every shameless, sensitised inch of her quivering body craved more—so much more that she was in torment.

She focused in appalled fascination on the grimy set of fingerprints which now marred his silk shirt, sweeping up from his waist, glancing across his broad chest in an obviously lingering caress and then indenting clearly across his wide shoulders where she had clung. Those marks were now exhibited for all to see, like a public badge of her shame and surrender.

'You need to change your shirt,' she mumbled shakily.

'I shall wear it with pride,' Constantine confided with disconcerting amusement. 'There don't seem to be many parts of me that you overlooked—'

'Change it,' Rosie muttered in a heartfelt plea, hurriedly sidestepping him to head back towards the house. 'I'm going for a bath.'

'I'll see you upstairs,' Constantine murmured smoothly.

She stiffened and then grasped his meaning. He had to change and half his clothes were in the wardrobe in her room, even though he slept in a bedroom across the landing. Her head was still spinning. One kiss and she had been so far gone, Constantine could have done anything with her! Not a bit of wonder he was laughing! She was his for the taking and he knew it.

A taxi was waiting in the courtyard and as Rosie entered the hall a maid was showing a grey-haired man with a briefcase into the drawing room. Momentarily, the man stilled, shooting Rosie an almost startled glance. Then, just as abruptly, his keen dark eyes veiled and he inclined his head in a polite nod of acknowledgement before disappearing from her view.

Rosie looked curiously at Dmitri where he stood below the stairs. 'Who was that?'

'Theodopoulos Stephanos. Mr Voulos's lawyer.'

No doubt the man had stared because she looked such a fright in her gardening clothes...hardly the image he might have expected from Constantine's wife, temporary or otherwise.

In the bathroom, she stripped off. An agony of self-loathing engulfed her and for long, anguished minutes she simply stood there, tasting the painful reality of her supreme unimportance in Constantine's life...

Not a wife, not a girlfriend, not even a mistress. You're a puddle of self-pity, a little inner voice scolded drily as she washed herself. Maybe he *had been* telling the truth when he'd said he just hadn't been ready to answer questions about their relationship. Maybe, in her defensive insecurity, she was her own worst enemy. Angry confusion shrilled through her then. Now she was making excuses for Constantine and blaming herself!

Anchoring a fleecy towel round her in a careless swathe, she walked back into the bedroom...and stopped dead. Her bed was occupied. Constantine was in it, every muscular line of his lithe body fluidly indolent, his bronzed skin startlingly dark against the pale bedlinen. Eyes huge, Rosie gaped at him. A smile of intense amusement curled his wickedly sensual mouth.

'I don't know what you think you're doing here—'

'*Theos...*' Constantine ran deceptively sleepy eyes of gold over her and her heart took a frantic, convulsive leap against her breastbone. 'You need me to state my intentions?'

'I've got a very fair idea of your intentions,

Constantine,' Rosie spluttered, stalking over to the door, intending to throw it wide in an invitation for him to leave.

'It's locked.'

Rosie spun round. Constantine displayed a large, ornate key for her inspection. 'We wouldn't want to startle the staff again.'

'Give me that key!' Rosie launched at him furiously.

'Come and get it…'

Rosie hesitated.

Constantine dealt her a wolfish grin, white teeth gleaming against golden skin. 'Didn't I tell you that you'd learn caution around me?'

That one taunt was sufficient to overcome it. Rosie landed on the bed in a flying leap of temper and made a wild snatch at the key. Constantine flung it across the room and snaked two powerful arms round her slender waist to entrap her. 'I knew you would rise to the bait.'

Clamped to his hard, lean length in impotent stillness, Rosie flung her fiery head back and glowered down at him. 'Let go of me!'

'Self-denial doesn't come naturally to me. And I wouldn't say that you were a rousing success in that department either.' Constantine surveyed her with thickly lashed eyes screened to a mocking sliver of knowing gold. 'Ten hours a day with a hoe you use like a machete! I have to confess that no woman has ever gone to that amount of effort to resist me, *pethi mou*.'

'I just don't want to be anywhere near you!' Rosie snarled, feeling the naked heat of his intimidatingly relaxed length striking her through the thin sheet and the rumpled towel that separated them. Terrifying little shivers of seething sexual awareness were already pulling her skin tight over her bones and strangling her breathing processes.

'Because you don't trust yourself,' Constantine savoured with raw satisfaction. 'And, watching you bend and stretch in those shorts, I was equally challenged. You have the most provocative heart-shaped derrière, little rag-doll...and when you shake your T-shirt because you're getting too warm those beautiful little breasts bounce and push against the damp cotton until your nipples—'

'Stop it!' Appalled to realise that he had been watching her and noticing such things, Rosie was mortified.

Brilliant dark golden eyes intent, Constantine appraised the hot pink flush on her cheeks. 'You still blush like an innocent. That turns me on even harder,' he confided huskily as he fluidly shifted to kick the sheet away and yanked at her towel to detach it.

Taken by surprise, Rosie made a mad grab at her only covering just a second too late and found herself swung over lightning-fast onto her back with Constantine looking down at her instead. *'No!'*

'Christos...you smell of soap—all clean and scrubbed and sweet. But even when you're dirty and sweaty and too warm you excite me. The scent of you, the feel of you, the *taste* of you,' he growled sexily, a lean, hair-roughened thigh deftly parting hers as he brought his weight down on her and shamelessly acquainted her with the smooth, hard thrust of his erection.

A burst of burning heat ignited low in the pit of Rosie's stomach. 'Your lawyer's waiting to see you downstairs!' she gasped in sudden recall, fighting her own weakness with all her might.

'Theo's already gone.' A slight frown drew Constantine's winged brows together. 'Crazy of him to come all this way only to deliver some papers and then refuse to even stay for lunch.' Golden eyes smouldered down at her hectically flushed face. 'But remarkably tactful.'

Transfixed, Rosie stared back up at him, great rolling

breakers of excitement making her heart thunder and her limbs quiver. Her breasts felt swollen and tender, the taut peaks aching for his mouth and his hands, and never had she been more agonisingly aware of the moist, throbbing centre of need between her thighs.

'We don't need other people around us, *pethi mou.* They get in the way and I am far too distracted to work. Say something,' Constantine invited encouragingly.

Rosie parted dry lips and managed only one word, so intense was her arousal. *'Please…'*

Primitive triumph flashed in his glittering gaze. He ran slow, seeking fingers over the pouting mounds he had bared for his pleasure. As his thumbs glanced over the stiff pink buds straining up to him, she gasped and rose against him, every nerve-ending in her body screaming in response. He thrust her flat with a devouringly passionate kiss. She kissed him back with desperate urgency, everything she had held back for long, endless days suddenly betraying her in a stormy flood of possessive need. Her hands ran over him, smoothing over warm golden skin sheathing whipcord muscles, and a hungry moan of impatience escaped her.

'You are always in a rush…'

Rosie twisted and squirmed, on fire with wanting him, not a shred of self-restraint left or even recalled. Clenching her fingers into his thick, silky black hair, she shifted her legs in an aching invitation more blatant than speech.

With an urgent groan, Constantine sank his hands to her hips and hauled her under him. Then he hesitated. 'I don't want to hurt you again.'

'You don't argue with me in my fantasies…you don't stop…you don't make me wait!' Rosie sobbed in explosive frustration.

The silence thundered. She closed her eyes in horror. Oh, no, I didn't say that…*did I*? she asked herself.

'What do I do?' he murmured.

'What I want,' Rosie mumbled.

Constantine vented a ragged laugh of appreciation. The velvet-hard thrust of him surged teasingly against her, gently probing the slick, damp welcome awaiting him.

Rosie was on a high of such shivering excitement, she couldn't have vocalised to save her life. What she wanted was even more thrilling in reality. He entered her so slowly that she raked her fingernails down his back. The pleasure was so intoxicatingly intense, she lost herself in the bold feel of him stretching her with delicious force.

'Open your eyes,' Constantine ordered.

Rosie lifted lush lashes to see the blazing gold command in his eyes and drowned. She was drugged into silence by sensation, feverish, all-absorbing sensation, as he withdrew and then thrust into her all over again. He was slow and then fast, smooth and then rough. She couldn't do anything but cling with impassioned hands and moan and sob her incredible pleasure. He went on and on and on, driving her to mindless heights until the pulsing, tormenting heat inside her exploded and unleashed a shattering tidal wave of satisfaction.

As he shuddered in the protective circle of her arms, an aching flood of tenderness consumed Rosie and she pressed her lips lovingly to a smooth brown shoulder. Drinking in the hot, musky scent of his damp skin, she felt utterly at peace.

Constantine released her from his weight and bent over her. 'Where are you under all that hair?' he groaned, lean fingers brushing the tangle of bright curls gently off her brow.

Compelling dark eyes probed her dreamy face. His fingertips lightly traced the delicate curve of her jawbone and she turned her cheek slowly into his palm, a wondering light in her gaze as she recalled his eagerness to leave her the first time they had made love. In the heart-stopping silence, he rearranged a straying curl to his own satisfaction and let his thumb lightly caress the reddened pout of her lower lip.

He collided with her fascinated scrutiny and a faint, rueful smile curved his wide mouth. 'I can't stop touching you…'

That charismatic smile turned her heart over and inside out.

'And I want you all over again,' he confided.

As he pulled her back into his arms, she quivered in helpless response. Her fingers delved into his luxuriant hair. Held fast by his dark golden eyes, she was conscious of an extraordinary surge of happiness.

'It was a really good idea to give the staff the rest of the day off,' Rosie mused, seated on the edge of the scrubbed table, watching Constantine struggle to find a tidy way of finishing off the doorstep-sized sandwich she had made. 'But I didn't realise you would be so helpless without a chef.'

Constantine looked wary. 'I thought you could cook.'

'I know, and look where it got you. I live on salad, fruit and convenience food. Your chef does not use convenience food and he deserves a medal for serving up such wonderful menus on that prehistoric cooker. Still, at least I can make coffee,' she murmured with dancing eyes, flicking a meaningful glance at the undrinkable tarry brew he had prepared when challenged.

'You also look very good on a kitchen table,' Constantine told her.

Rosie swung up her jean-clad legs and lay on her side, posing like a fifties film starlet, her bright head propped on the heel of her hand. A slow smile curved his mouth and he laughed. 'You like sending me up, don't you?'

'You've only just realised?'

'Slow learner,' he murmured, studying her with appreciative eyes as she slid in one fluid, impulsive movement off the table again. 'But I hope you're not heading for a window, *pethi mou*.'

'A window?' And then she reddened and ran her fingers restively through her hair, recalling the manner in which she had left his home in Greece and the quick escape she had made the day she'd gone down the mountain with Maurice.

'In certain moods you're like a cat burglar.'

'I've had a lot of practice over the years.' She laughed uneasily, not liking the turn the conversation had taken.

'Running away? It's a waste of time with me,' Constantine informed her with deep conviction. 'The more you run, the harder I chase. It's an elemental response. I can't seem to beat it.'

'You just want to catch up with me so that you can tell me what you think of me for doing it in the first place.'

'You only do it when I have upset you,' he returned with a perception that shook her. 'Or got too close. Now I can stop doing the first but I'm definitely not going to stop doing the second.'

'Is that a threat?'

He tugged her into his arms with insistent hands. 'I don't make threats any more,' he said softly. 'I make promises. I want to know everything there is to know about you, *agape mou*.'

The tenderness in his steady dark appraisal made her heart sing. He was being so open, so honest. A little twinge of shame filled her as she lowered her own gaze. She was the one with the secrets, not him. Soon she would need to tell him all over again that she was Anton's daughter...but not just at this moment when she was revelling in the awareness that he couldn't take his eyes off her.

The thunderous slam of a door jolted Rosie awake. Blinking bemusedly in the lamplight, she pulled herself up against the pillows and focused hazily on Constantine where he stood at the foot of the bed, bare-chested, only a pair of faded tight jeans riding low on his lean hips. A tender smile curved her lips. He looked so spectacular, he *always* looked so spectacular, that she could even forgive him for carelessly wakening her up from the first sound sleep she had enjoyed in days.

Ferocious dark eyes slashed into hers. Rosie stiffened in dismay, her smile dying, her tummy muscles clenching. Seething tension emanated from Constantine in waves.

'What's wrong?' she whispered.

'I was hungry. I got up to get something to eat and on the way downstairs I began wondering what was so important about those papers that Theo thought it necessary to fly over and personally place them in my hands...and if they *were* worthy of that importance why didn't he say so and why was he so keen to make an exit again?'

Rosie's attention slowly dropped to the bulky brown envelope clasped in one lean brown hand. Her heart jumped into her mouth.

'But now I understand. Theo was embarrassed,' Constantine continued in the same murderously quiet drawl. 'Because when I gave him the licence to empty a certain safety-deposit box held in Anton's name neither one of us was expecting anything of a confidential nature to emerge...'

He lifted his other hand and something fluttered down onto the bed. Rosie snatched the item up. Her hand trembled. She was looking at a small colour snap of herself as a toddler.

Black eyes blazed condemnation at her, his lean, dark features clenched hard. 'You wanted revenge, didn't you? You were going to wait right to the bitter end to throw your paternity in my face!'

CHAPTER TEN

REVENGE? Stunned by the accusation, Rosie reacted on instinct. Sliding out of bed at speed, she made an unwittingly pleading movement towards Constantine.

'Forget it. The last thing on my mind right now is that deceptively tempting little body of yours!' Constantine asserted with biting derision.

Swept by abrasive dark eyes, Rosie suddenly felt appallingly naked. She grabbed up the towel lying on the rug by the bed and hurriedly wrapped it around her. 'Where did you get that photo from?'

In answer, Constantine withdrew a whole handful of photos from the envelope and cast them down on the mattress like a thrown gauntlet. 'Rosie from birth to the age of nine. And not a happy child according to this pictorial account. You've got tears in your eyes in half of them and what look like slap marks all down your leg on another.' His deep, dark drawl wavered slightly and his eloquent mouth compressed hard. 'I imagine Anton was suitably tortured in receipt of such heartbreaking reminders of your existence. *Theos*...your mother must've been bitter!'

'Maybe.' Her tortured breath caught in her throat. 'I did try to tell you who I was—'

'And your mother taught you that same bitterness,' Constantine stabbed as if she hadn't spoken, murderously bright golden eyes lancing into her.

'What are you talking about?'

'You were planning to unveil yourself as Anton's child only when Thespina was present to enjoy the full effect of your revelation.'

166

Rosie's eyes flew wide, shock freezing her facial muscles. 'I would never have done that! *Never!*'

'Well, you certainly weren't about to waste any time trying to convince me of your true identity, not once you'd had the opportunity to think the idea over,' Constantine condemned between gritted teeth. 'Keeping quiet was much more fun, wasn't it?'

Hopelessly confused by his attacks, Rosie gasped, 'I still don't understand—'

In one powerful stride, Constantine reached her and closed two strong hands round her slender forearms to force her closer. '*Christos*…you were waiting for your moment and hoping to cause the maximum damage. You weren't prepared that day in London when Thespina arrived without warning. But you told me—you just blurted it out like a bad joke and then you never referred to the subject again. OK, I didn't listen, but you made no real attempt to convince me that you were serious! What was I supposed to think?'

'I had no way of making you believe me. I have no proof of who I am!' Rosie protested fiercely.

'Anton had the proof and you must have known that. You didn't even care that this file might have fallen into Thespina's hands!' In unconcealed disgust, Constantine thrust her back from him again.

'I didn't even think about it, for heaven's sake. Do you think I was *expecting* my father to die?' Rosie prompted jerkily. 'And Anton never mentioned any file to me… What's in it?'

'Your history from birth. Evidently he knew every damn thing about you before he even approached you!'

The news shattered Rosie. There had been so many painful events in her life which she had deliberately not shared with her father. She had wanted to protect him. And yet all the time he had known exactly what her life had been like.

'How did Anton get involved with your mother?' Constantine demanded.

Rosie's legs wouldn't hold her up any longer. She sank down dizzily on the side of the bed. 'His secretary was sick. Mum was an agency temp. Their affair only lasted a few weeks before he finished it—'

'Because my parents died and Anton and Thespina became my legal guardians. I imagine you've often thought how *very* different your life might have been had that not happened.'

It was strange, Rosie registered in deep shock, but she had never made that final connection until Constantine made it for her. Almost twenty-one years ago, she had been accidentally conceived when Anton's marriage was on the rocks. And then ironically, within weeks of her conception, a tragic car crash had quite miraculously given her father and his wife the child they had both been longing for. A nine-year-old boy had become their shared responsibility and had effectively healed the breach between them. And that little boy had been Constantine.

'I never appreciated that timing before...not properly,' she admitted tautly. 'But Anton had no idea that my mother was pregnant when they parted. He didn't find out until it was far too late for him to try and help her.'

'No, he got a photo and a cold little note through the post telling him that he was the father of a daughter he could never know because your mother had married another man. When the photos stopped coming, I assume that he couldn't live with his curiosity any longer and he started looking for you.'

'He didn't even know my stepfather's name...he had so little to go on and a couple of times he gave up.'

'*Christos*...you must hate *me* as much as you hate Thespina for the life you have led!' Constantine ground out half under his breath. He swung violently away from her as if he could no longer bear to look at her. Every powerful line of his lean, muscular body sizzled with whip-taut tension.

'I don't hate anyone.' But Rosie still felt ashamed because she could remember occasions before her father's death when her resentment of his legitimate family had risen to explosive proportions...only that had been before she had met Constantine and Thespina and before she had made herself face reality.

'Anton didn't love my mother,' she pointed out tightly. 'He never stopped loving Thespina. Even if he had known about me, he wouldn't have divorced her for my mother. I think she knew that and that's why she never gave him a choice.'

'You didn't give *me* a choice either,' Constantine condemned with ringing bitterness. 'You allowed me to go on thinking that you had slept with Anton. Even when you knew that that belief was tearing me apart, you let me go on believing it!'

'I kept on telling you that we weren't lovers—'

'While being aware that that made no kind of sense! The only other possible explanation for Anton's will was the one I came up with. And you only have yourself to thank for the way I treated you.' His hawk-like profile rigid with repressed emotion, Constantine dealt her a raw-edged glance. 'But I have to live with the awareness that I cruelly and cynically misjudged Anton and did everything I could to evade the responsibility that he trusted me to accept. And that responsibility was for his daughter. I betrayed his trust in every way possible.'

'You didn't betray anything...it was outrageous of him to demand that you marry me!' Her anxious eyes clung to the fierce cast of his features. 'I know he had good intentions but it was still crazy!'

'I was one bloody mixed-up kid when the Estradas

got landed with me… They put up with me and straightened me out. Without their love and guidance, I'd have
gone off the rails. You can never repay a debt like that.'
Pale beneath his dark skin, Constantine compressed his
lips and turned away from her again to stride over to the
window and yank open the curtains on the clear moonlit
night beyond. The savage tension in his wide brown
shoulders made her drop her aching eyes.

It was something of a shock for Rosie to appreciate
that Constantine's early years with his own parents
might have been less than perfect. Yet she remembered
him admitting that Anton had meant more to him than
his own father. She stifled her curiosity because she was
already squirming with all kinds of incredibly guilty
feelings. Constantine had interpreted her silence as evidence of malice and a vengeful desire to put him in the
wrong. He had even cherished the suspicion that she had
been lying in wait for some kind of spiteful showdown
with Thespina.

'I'm sorry…maybe I should've spoken up again
sooner, but you really cut me off that day when I tried
to tell you, and then later, when you started talking about
debts and stuff,' Rosie framed tremulously, 'I just
couldn't face—'

Abruptly, Constantine wheeled round and strode back
across the room. Alarmingly strong hands closed over
her shoulders and dragged her upright. Blazing golden
eyes swept her shaken face in smouldering fury. 'You
were a virgin…but you would have died sooner than
give me the pleasure of knowing that you had not been
Anton's woman first! Every way you could, you turned
the screw on me! What a cold, vindictive bitch you are,'
he grated thickly. 'And what a bloody fool I was to think
differently!'

As the door thudded shut on his exit, Rosie stood there
with slow, painful tears tracking down her quivering

cheeks. Only hours earlier she had gone to sleep in his arms. She had felt so close to him, so…cherished. *Cherished?* A hiccuping sob escaped her, and then another. Why did she kid herself like that? Why was she so wretchedly naïve? So Constantine was fantastic in bed and he was experienced enough to make a woman feel incredibly special, but that was *all*. It didn't mean he had been falling in love with her or wanting to make their marriage a real one.

And now, he despised her. It had never occurred to her that the information she was withholding might have such a devastating emotional effect on him. What had she expected? Well, at the very least she had expected the chance to tell him herself and she had expected him to be incredulous and then probably apologising all over the place for not believing her claim the first time she had made it.

Constantine…filled with remorse and humility, shamefacedly apologising? Rosie squirmed. At the back of her mind, hadn't she been looking forward to that highly imaginative moment and feeling slightly smug that he was in for a major shock? Hadn't she been determined that he should want her for herself and not because she was Anton's daughter? And hadn't she even secretly hoped that by the time she got around to breaking the news at a carefully chosen optimum moment it might finally strike Constantine as *terrific* news? She winced in remembrance.

All along she had blithely ignored the nature of the male animal she was dealing with. In her hurt pride and insecurity, she had been selfish and insensitive. Constantine made a real virtue of candour and plain speaking. Her continued silence *had* been a form of deception and he could scarcely be blamed for assuming the worst about her motives.

After pacing the floor for what felt like hours, Rosie

tried to get some sleep, but she found it impossible to still her uneasy conscience or to suppress the suspicion that she had made a poor showing in her own defence. Switching on the bedside light, she discovered that it was almost three in the morning. Would Constantine be asleep? Or would he be lying awake like she was?

Clad in a faded cotton nightshirt, Rosie tiptoed across the landing and slowly opened the door. Moonlight shone through the windows onto the untouched bed. From the stairs, she saw a dim light showing beneath the drawing-room door. In the hall she hesitated, wondering what on earth she was going to say when she couldn't bring herself to admit that she was head over heels in love with him...

Right now he hated her, and even if he got over that aversion the announcement that she was in love with him might scare him all the way back to Greece. A male who had never been in love and who was extremely wary of commitment was unlikely to feel comfortable with being loved, even by a temporary wife, who would be lying in her teeth if she said she didn't have a hidden agenda.

Rosie tilted her chin and opened the door. Only one lamp was lit, leaving most of the vast room in gloomy dark shadow. Constantine was lying on a sofa. She crept over to him just as he muttered something slurred in Greek. His dense black lashes lifted and it appeared to be a struggle for him to focus on her.

'Constantine?'

He blinked twice, a slow frown drawing his ebony brows together, and he responded to his name in his own language.

His black hair was tousled and a heavy blue-black shadow of stubble obscured his hard jawline. But it was the look of desolation in his eyes which punched a hole in Rosie's heart. She dropped down on her knees by the sofa and reached for one lean brown hand. 'I'm so sor—'

A flicker of movement stirred in the shadows · and Rosie gasped, almost jumping out of her skin. Having risen from his seat behind the door, Dmitri strolled forward. 'I'll look after him, Mrs Voulos.'

'Is he ill? I mean...' She fell silent as she belatedly picked up the strong smell of alcohol. Her attention skimmed to the whisky bottle and glass lying abandoned on the rug and she froze in dismayed comprehension. 'He's...*he's*—?'

'A little under the weather. Go back to bed,' Dmitri urged flatly. 'I'll stay with him.'

'Does he make a habit of this?' Rosie managed shakily, her small fingers curving possessively round one lean, unresponsive thigh.

'I have never seen him like this before.' Even in shock that Constantine could do something as uncharacteristic as get paralytically drunk, Rosie would have had to be blind to miss the coolness in the older man's eyes and the protective way he hovered at the head of the sofa, as if she were some sort of a threat to his employer's safety.

'What's he talking about?' she pressed as Constantine shifted and muttered some more.

'Rabbits,' Dmitri informed her with extreme reluctance.

'Rabbits?' Rosie queried weakly.

'I'll take him up to bed...' Dmitri stepped forward, forcing Rosie to relinquish her hold and scramble upright.

'I'll help you.'

'Thank you but that won't be necessary.'

Rosie backed away, dismayed by the bodyguard's barely concealed hostility. He hesitated, clearly determined not to subject Constantine to the indignity of his assistance while she lingered. From the door, she glanced back. 'It's not the way you think it is,' she said helplessly.

'It's not my place to think anything, Mrs Voulos.'

But condemnation was written all over him, his usual quiet friendliness chilled out by what she recognised as fierce defensive loyalty to Constantine. Only the conviction that Constantine was too damned macho and proud to want her around him when he was in that condition spurred Rosie back to her room.

She lay in bed, watching dawn break the skies. He was really upset…he had to be to have drunk like that. And Rosie tried so hard to understand. Wasn't she herself equally guilty of betraying Anton's trust? She had only agreed to marry Constantine under duress, and would have run a thousand miles had she known what fate had in store for them in the morning after the ceremony.

And it wasn't as if Constantine had tried to disinherit her or anything like that. Anton had got himself into serious financial hot water raising the loan for the Son Fontanal estate. Constantine must have used his own money to bail out his guardian's business ventures and even the house needed a fortune spent on it. Indeed being Anton's heir had undoubtedly proved to be a most unprofitable undertaking, but Constantine, famed in the business world for his ruthless pursuit of profit, would never admit that because to do so would be disloyal.

So why had her Greek tycoon drunk himself into a stupor? Guilt at not rolling out a red carpet for Anton's daughter? Or suicidal depression at the knowledge that if he carried out his guardian's last wishes he would be stuck with Rosie for ever?

Her sensitive stomach lurching, she got out of bed again. Pulling on jeans and a fresh cotton top, she paused only to drag a brush through her mane of fiery hair. She

needed some fresh air and space. The motorbike she had
hired was parked below the steps in the courtyard. She
hadn't been out on it since her arrival and maybe a ride
down that mountain would blow the cobwebs away…

It was still very early when Rosie stopped in the shade
of some sweet-smelling pine trees and ate the snack she
had brought with her. The canned drink and the long
bread roll filled with ham and luscious wedges of tomato
satisfied her appetite but the hollow feeling inside her
wouldn't go away. She was struggling desperately hard
to convince herself that there would be life after
Constantine. What did they have in common, after all?

He was a domineering, arrogant, workaholic tycoon.
He was everything she wasn't. Rich, educated, pedi-
greed. He was far better-looking than she was. He also
had loads of women running after him and Rosie was
not the type to compete in a race. She had her pride, not
to mention the painful experience of being brought down
to earth with a severe bump only hours earlier.

If Constantine had had any feelings for her, she had
killed them. So there was no point in concentrating on
the more positive aspects of his personality. Like the fact
that he could be incredibly charming and entertaining
and give the most astonishing impression of being caring
and supportive. That sort of stuff wasn't relevant. That
was her foolish heart talking, not her head. They didn't
have a real marriage. And their temporary arrangement
was currently at breaking point.

A big black shiny limousine was parked outside Son
Fontanal. Rosie rode past it into the courtyard and
slowly, stiffly dismounted. She was removing her helmet
when Constantine strode down the steps. Her treacherous
heart performed a somersault. Attired as he was in an
Italian-cut double-breasted cream suit that highlighted

his black hair and golden skin, one look made her melt like chocolate left out in the sun.

Brilliant dark eyes swept over her and lingered, a curious stillness etched into his strong, dark face. 'Did it even occur to you that I might be worried sick about you?'

Rosie reddened with discomfiture. 'I was away before I thought about that.'

'Where the hell did you get the bike?'

'I hired it for a fortnight the day I arrived.'

'I assumed it belonged to one of the workmen. Dmitri will see that it is returned. I don't like the idea of you out on a motorbike on these roads,' Constantine delivered, the faint pallor beneath his sun-bronzed complexion emphasising the tense line of his mouth.

As he stared at her, holding her there by sheer force of will, the silence mounted, thick and heavy. And suddenly she understood. He hadn't thought she would be coming back but for some reason he wasn't saying one half of what he wanted to say on that subject.

'Thespina arrived ten minutes ago,' he breathed in taut explanation.

Rosie stiffened and lost every scrap of colour. 'Oh, no…'

'I have decided that we have no option other than to tell her the truth,' he admitted with grim emphasis. 'Too many people know your identity now. A slip of the tongue and any lies or half-truths would be exposed. I cannot take that risk.'

Shock glued Rosie's feet to the worn paving stones. Constantine closed a big hand round hers and drew her up the steps into the hall. Rosie tried to pull free then. '*You* do it!'

'This particular confession needs to come from both of us, *pethi mou*.' His lean fingers retaining their determined grip, Constantine led her into the drawing room before she could utter another word of argument.

Thespina rose to greet her with a pleasant smile. Rosie's stomach lurched and sank to her toes. Oh, dear heaven, she just could not face what was to come!

'Come and sit down beside me,' Thespina invited, settling back onto the sofa and patting it cosily.

A maid entered with a tray and began to pour coffee. Positioning himself by the big stone fireplace, Constantine embarked on a somewhat strained conversation. Everyone having been served, the door closed on the maid.

Thespina turned to look at Rosie and, with a slow shake of her dark head, she said gently, 'I really feel this charade has gone on long enough. I have to confess that there was something rather endearing about Constantine's efforts to explain the inexplicable and protect me but I should've spoke up sooner. Even as a boy, he could never lie and look me in the eye.'

In the act of sugaring his coffee, Constantine straightened so fast that half the contents of his cup slopped onto the saucer. He set it down with a stifled oath. 'Are you saying that—?'

'I've known about Rosie's existence for almost twenty years,' Thespina confirmed, tactfully removing her gaze from Constantine's stunned visage and affecting not to hear Rosie's strangled gasp. 'You'll have to forgive me for not immediately recognising you, Rosalie. But I knew that you were Anton's child the instant Constantine said your name. The combination of your hair and that unusual name was too much for me to overlook and the two of you behaved very oddly. I'm afraid that I couldn't help but know that you weren't telling me the truth.'

'Twenty years...?' Constantine repeated in flat astonishment, still staring at the calm little Greek woman.

'Anton was never very good at hiding his feelings. He was dreadfully upset after he received that first photograph of Rosie,' Thespina proffered with a grimace. 'I found it in his desk with her mother's letter and then I understood. I was very distressed by what I learnt but in the end I was most concerned with keeping our marriage intact. I could've confronted him but what would I have achieved? His guilt and his fear of discovery were very obvious to me. I didn't want to lose him. Perhaps I was wrong not to bring it all out into the open—'

'No...he could not have handled that and stayed,' Constantine conceded half under his breath.

'He had already had so much to bear.' The older woman looked at Rosie and sighed heavily. 'All my life I'd received everything I wanted without effort. When my son was stillborn, when I finally had to accept that I was unlikely ever to give birth to a living child, I took my bitterness and my anger out on my husband and I rejected him. I told him I needed to be alone and I drove him away. I had less right than most to complain when he turned to another woman...'

Constantine frowned darkly. 'I had no idea your marriage had ever been in trouble.'

'It was before you came to us. And I allowed Rosie to remain a secret to conserve my own pride too. I also knew that her mother was married and I felt safe. As the years passed, I always made a point of seeking out those photos. Anton only placed them in a safety-deposit box shortly before he died.'

'All this time...you knew about me,' Rosie whispered in a daze.

'But it never occurred to me that Anton had found you. I was aware that he had attempted to trace you when you were younger and reached a dead end. When he became so buoyantly cheerful six months ago, I even suspected that he was having another affair.' Thespina surveyed the younger woman with wry but warm eyes. 'But I'm not sorry that he found you, Rosie. I'm glad that he was able to spend time with you before he died. I do know what that must have meant to him.'

Rosie licked her dry lips. 'You're being very understanding.'

'Secrets make everyone so uncomfortable,' Thespina pointed out ruefully. 'I am also now aware of the terms of my husband's new will. I would be *very* grateful if one of you would now tell me whether you are genuinely married or only pretending to be married for the sake of that will.'

Rosie swallowed the giant lump impeding her voice. 'We're faking it—'

'Like hell we are!' Constantine shot at Rosie in raw, angry disagreement.

'Perhaps I was a little premature with that question.' Setting down her empty coffee-cup with a faintly amused smile, Thespina stood up. 'But if you feel you could stay together long enough to supply me with a grandchild I would be very much obliged. I've been waiting a long time for that pleasure.'

Rosie studied her feet, burning colour in her cheeks. She couldn't bring herself to look at Constantine but she also realised what her father's widow was trying to tell her. Thespina was letting her know that she was ready to accept her as part of the family.

'Where are you going?' Constantine demanded of his stepmother.

'This was only intended as a flying visit to clear the air. I shall come back and see Son Fontanal some other time. By the way, Rosie…'

Rosie glanced up nervously. Thespina smiled again. 'Your father managed to persuade his mother not to sell the family portraits with the house. I would be happy to see them hung here where they belong.'

'Thespina could run rings around Machiavelli,' Rosie mumbled as the limousine disappeared from view. 'She wiped the floor with us both.'

Still in shock, she started back indoors. And then it hit her: Thespina knew everything. There was no further need for pretence, no necessity to wait before seeking a divorce. All of a sudden, Rosie's lower limbs felt like toothpicks struggling weakly to wade through a swamp. Thespina had dissolved the artificial boundaries within which their relationship had been formed. They had run out of time.

'How could you tell her that our marriage was a fake?' Constantine condemned wrathfully. 'Did you really think that was necessary?'

With difficulty, Rosie straightened her slumped shoulders and dug deep into her reserves of pride as she forced herself round to face him. 'I told the truth. After she had been so frank, anything less would have been an insult.'

Glittering black eyes centred on her with near-physical force. 'How was it the truth? Are we not married? Are we not lovers?'

Rosie's nerves were jangling like piano wires. 'You made it very clear how you felt about me last night.'

'*Christos*...I thought I did but now I'm not so sure. You put me through hell for no good reason. I may have wounded your pride by dismissing your claim to be Anton's daughter but you must have realised that the concept struck me as so incredible, I didn't even pause to consider it!' Shimmering dark eyes intercepted her evasive gaze. 'OK...I was in the wrong, but what I don't understand is your failure to repeat that claim once we knew each other better.'

'I didn't see that it would make any difference—'

'It would've made one hell of a difference if I'd known! And stop acting dumb!' Constantine bit out in frustration. 'I was shattered by the contents of that file. You seemed so open yet you had hidden the very essence of yourself from me...'

Her fingers clenched in on themselves as she faced the prospect of never seeing him again. Just walking away as if they had never been together, as if the past weeks had never happened. Acid burned her aching throat. The fear that she could not control her turbulent emotions drove her to say, 'It doesn't matter now, does it? We don't need to pretend for anyone's benefit now. We can get a divorce.'

Constantine perceptibly froze, his strong face clenching. 'I don't want a divorce.'

A great flood of pain and bitterness welled up inside Rosie, threatening her fast splintering control. And then the dam broke as she shot him a look of fierce condemnation. 'I'm not staying married to you just because you've got this stupid macho *thing* about keeping faith with what my father wanted!'

Constantine glowered at her in apparent incredulity. 'This is not a macho thing, Rosie,' he said drily.

A sob rollicked about like a death rattle in her chest. 'Call it what you like. I'm going upstairs to get packed!'

She raced out of the room and upstairs as if all the hounds of hell were on her trail. In fact they were inside her head. A weak, seductive little voice which she loathed was already pointing out that Constantine was offering himself on a plate. If he was stupid enough to do that and she wanted him, why shouldn't she hang onto him any way she could? Pride would be a cold, lonely bedfellow and there was nothing cold about Constantine. She dashed an angry hand over her tear-filled eyes.

'Rosie...?'

'I'm not staying with you because you're great in bed

either!' she blistered accusingly before she could bite the words back.

Thrusting the door shut and leaning back against it, his lean, powerful body rigid with tension, Constantine stared darkly back at her. 'But that attraction could be a beginning, a foundation—'

'Last night you called me a cold, vindictive bitch!' Rosie reminded him painfully.

Inky black lashes dropped low on fiercely intent golden eyes. '*Christos*, I didn't mean a word of it. I...I was...' He hesitated, teeth gritting. 'I was so...'

'You were what?' Rosie demanded.

'*Hurt*... You ripped my guts out!' Constantine shot back in a raw explosion of emotion that silenced her. 'How would you have felt? I thought we were getting close, and then all of a sudden I find out you're not even the person I thought you were...and then...*Theos*...I wake up with the most incredible hangover and I know that you still are...'

'You *still* think I'm a bitch?'

Constantine threw his arms wide in furious frustration. 'Of course not! That's not what I meant!'

'It's what it sounded like,' Rosie mumbled chokily as she stalked over and began pulling out drawers.

'Last night I thought you had to hate me and I haven't had much practice at talking about feelings. I attack first. I couldn't think straight until this morning and then when I got up you'd vanished...'

Hearing the ragged, raw strain in his deep, dark drawl, Rosie ached but refused to look at him, her hands shaking as she mounded clothes willy-nilly into a huge pile. He didn't love her but he certainly had loved and respected her father.

In the dragging silence his mobile phone buzzed.

'Go on...answer it!' Rosie hissed nastily over one shoulder.

With a strangled, driven imprecation, he did so. Rosie listened but she didn't even recognise the language. It wasn't Greek or French... And then she heard him say 'Cinzia' as clear as a bell and sheer murderous rage just exploded like a blazing fire-ball inside her. Scrambling up, she launched herself at him, ripped the mobile phone from his hand and plunged it into the carafe of cold water beside the bed.

'You can talk to Cinzia when I'm gone, not before!' she condemned strickenly. 'I hope the two of you rot in hell... I hope her husband catches you with her and kills you!'

As she spun away again, shaking and trembling like a leaf in a high wind, a pin-dropping silence thundered all around her.

'Cinzia and I split up years ago. We're still friends,' Constantine said almost conversationally. 'If I allowed Anton and Thespina to assume it was an ongoing affair, it was only because it became very embarrassing to be presented with marriageable young women every time I went to dine with them.'

Rosie blinked and sucked in a slow, steadying breath.

'Both of them were painfully keen for me to marry and settle down. I wasn't interested. Cinzia made a good cover story and they stopped lining up blind dates for me.'

In horror, Rosie surveyed the mobile phone sunk at the foot of the glass water container.

'There's no need for you to be jealous of Cinzia. That was over a long time ago.'

Intense mortification engulfed her. 'I'm not jealous!'

'If you say so...' Disturbingly, a thread of tender amusement softened Constantine's response. 'But I do feel that I ought to point out that every time I have had anything to do with another woman you have seen her off with the efficiency of a hit man!'

'I was pretending to be a wife... *just* pretending.'

'I don't want you to pretend any more. If you walk out that door, I'll feel like my life's going to end...'

Stiffening in disbelief, Rosie brushed a wavering hand across her damp cheeks and twisted round. She saw him through a haze of tears. His compelling dark golden eyes were fixed on her with such intense hunger and hope, she trembled.

'I know you still think you're in love with Maurice,' Constantine framed hoarsely. 'But I think you'll grow out of that if I'm patient. I can't face losing you. I tried to last night and all I ended up with was this sense... this knowing that really nothing else mattered as long as I still had you...'

Rosie licked her dry lips and waited, fingers rolled into feverish fists because she was so desperate to fling her arms round him but she wanted to hear the words first.

Constantine breathed in slowly like a non-swimmer about to plunge into a deep pool without a lifebelt. 'I love you like crazy—'

Rosie hurled herself at him. 'I'm not in love with Maurice, I'm in love with you... and I'm sorry I hurt you but I couldn't stand for you to want to stay married to me just because Anton was my father,' she gasped out in a confiding rush, fingers flexing joyously over wide, strong shoulders she had never thought to explore again and lingering in a deeply possessive hold.

He closed his arms round her so tightly, she could barely breathe. 'Didn't you realise that I loved you last night? Why do you think I got so damn drunk?'

'I never even dreamt that I could affect you like that.'

'And now that you know you're not going to allow me to forget it.' Constantine tipped her head up and searched her eyes for confirmation of what he so badly wanted to believe. A brilliant smile drove the last of the tension from his dark features and his gaze gleamed possessively over her.

'The first time I saw you it was like hitting a wall at two hundred miles an hour. I lost my head when I found you at Anton's house because you were the very last woman I wanted to find there. I wanted you to be mine and I wouldn't admit that to myself.'

'I really got on your nerves at the start.' Rosie's fingers were happily engaged in unknotting his silk tie and yanking it off.

'You wouldn't let me ignore you and then I began making excuses for you...didn't you notice that?' Helpfully he detached himself long enough to shrug free of his jacket. It fell unnoticed to the floor for they only had eyes for each other.

'Excuses?' Rosie queried, unbuttoning his shirt with a frown of concentration.

'On your behalf, I began to come up with all sorts of understandable reasons for you to have ended up as an older man's mistress.'

'Like that Maurice was a bad influence who had taken advantage of me, that I was in love with him and flung myself at Anton in despair,' Rosie recounted for herself, a faintly dazed light in her eyes as she marvelled at her own lack of perception and dragged his shirt down his arms and off. 'You were making terrific excuses for me even before we ended up in bed.'

'You didn't notice...I did,' Constantine confided, watching with slightly bemused eyes as Rosie embarked on his belt. '*Theos*...it really shook me that you could have that much effect on my brain. And I was eaten up with jealousy of Maurice. You never shut up about him. Every time I thought I might be getting somewhere with you, *he* came into it again.'

'He's my best friend and there's never been the tiniest spark between us. You misjudged him,' Rosie scolded,

gaining in confidence by meteoric degrees as she spread
a smile of unconcealed admiration over Constantine's
bare chest.

'Misjudged him?' Constantine shuddered as Rosie
moved on to more physical ways of demonstrating her
love and appreciation. She muttered a distracted explanation about Maurice's sister, Lorna, and her unfortunate
experience with the journalist she had fancied. It became
very involved and eventually petered out entirely.

She ran blissful hands across his hair-roughened chest
and down over his long, powerful thighs before sliding
them up to the hard bulge straining at his zip. He
groaned out loud as she let her fingers shape him. And
then he grabbed her up to him and plundered her mouth
with hungry need. They fell backwards on the bed. He
ripped her clothes off. This time Rosie helped and returned the favour...

A long while later, they were wrapped together in a
gloriously happy haze of mutual satisfaction and the
sheer wonder of loving each other, an abstracted frown
clouded Rosie's brow. 'There's just one thing I don't
understand...*rabbits*? Why did Dmitri tell me you were
talking about rabbits?'

Constantine shifted a little tautly and faint colour
darkened his blunt cheekbones. 'There are two whole
crates of them downstairs.'

'Excuse me?' Rosie stared down at him.

'Those Sylvac rabbits you collect...you remember
that one I broke? Last week I got on the phone and spoke
to a dealer and he put the word out, and you are now
the owner of probably the most expensive collection of
ceramic rabbits in the world today.'

A delighted grin illuminated Rosie's face. 'That's so
sweet, Constantine. You must have been really desperate
to impress me.'

'You're such a diplomat, Rosie.' His dark golden eyes

glittered over her and a slanting, wicked smile curved his mouth. 'I'll be equally tactless. When are you planning to tell me exactly what I do in these fantasies of yours?'

Rosie went pink. 'I don't want to shock you.'

'Did I say a word when my mobile phone went swimming?' Reaching up to tug her insistently down to him again, Constantine kissed her breathless. An almost soundless little sigh of contentment escaped her. She wondered how much he would enjoy playing a gangster...

Helen Bianchin was born in New Zealand and travelled to Australia before marrying her Italian-born husband. After three years they moved, returned to New Zealand with their daughter, had two sons then re-settled in Australia. Encouraged by friends to recount anecdotes of her years as a tobacco sharefarmer's wife living in an Italian community, Helen began setting words on paper and her first novel was published in 1975. An animal lover, she says her terrier and Persian cat regard her study as much theirs as hers.

NO GENTLE SEDUCTION

by

HELEN BIANCHIN

CHAPTER ONE

HOT, humid southern hemispheric temperatures prevailed, shrouding Sydney's tall city buildings in a stultifying summer heat-haze capable of frazzling the most even temperament.

Traffic in all city-bound lanes had slowed to a standstill, and Lexi spared a quick glance at her watch as she waited for the queue of cars to begin moving again.

A faint frown furrowed her smooth brow, and her lacquered nails played out an abstracted tattoo against the steering-wheel as she pondered her brother's telephone call of the previous evening. The serious tone of David's voice had proved vaguely perturbing, and no amount of cajoling had persuaded him to reveal any information.

Lexi shifted gears as the lights changed and she sent the sports car forward with a muted growl from its superb engine.

The movement of air teased tendrils of dark auburn hair loose from its careless knot atop her head, and she lifted a hand to brush them back from her cheek. Designer sunglasses shaded golden hazel eyes, and her attractive fine-boned features drew several admiring glances as she made her way into the city.

A wry smile twisted the edges of her generous mouth in the knowledge that as much of the envious speculation was for the aerodynamic lines of her

5

brother's near-new red Ferrari 348 as it was for the girl driving it. Wealth wasn't everything, she silently derided, and natural good looks could prove a handicap—something she'd discovered to her cost.

Such thoughts were detrimental, and she determinedly shut out the past by deliberately concentrating on negotiating the heavy inner-city traffic.

Ten minutes later a soft sigh of relief escaped her lips as she turned into the car park beneath a towering modern block housing her brother's suite of offices. Using extreme care, she eased the red sports car down two levels and brought it to a smooth halt in its reserved parking bay.

Gathering up her bag, she slid to her feet just as another car pulled into a nearby space, and her eyes widened fractionally at the sight of an almost identical Ferrari. The coincidence of two expensive Italian sports cars parking within such close proximity was highly improbable, and she watched with detached interest as the driver emerged from behind the wheel.

He was tall, she noticed idly, with an enviable breadth of shoulder evident beneath the flawless cut of his jacket, and he moved with the lithe ease of inherent strength. His hair was dark and well-groomed, and the broad-chiselled bone-structure moulded his features into rugged attractiveness.

Features that were vaguely familiar, and yet even as she searched her memory there was no spark of recognition, no name she could retrieve that would identify him.

As if sensing her scrutiny he lifted his head, and she was unprepared for the dark probing gaze that raked her slim curves in analytical appraisal before returning to settle overlong on the soft fullness of her mouth. Then his eyes travelled slowly up to focus on her startled expression.

She felt a surge of rage begin deep inside, and its threatened eruption brought a fiery sparkle to her beautiful eyes. How *dared* he subject her to such blatantly sexual assessment?

Impossibly angry, she turned towards the car, locked the door and activated the alarm, then she crossed to the lifts to jab the call-button with unnecessary force, silently willing any one of three lifts to descend and transport her to the fifteenth floor.

It irked her unbearably that she should still be waiting when he joined her, and she stood silently aloof until a faint hydraulic hiss heralded the arrival of a lift. As soon as as the doors slid open she stepped forward with easy grace into the electronic cubicle, pressed the appropriate digit on the illuminated panel, then stood back in silence, mentally distancing herself from the man's physical presence.

A faint prickle of apprehension feathered the surface of her skin, which was crazy, for he posed no threat. Yet she was frighteningly aware of his studied evaluation, and she hated the elusive alchemy that pulled at her senses. She was damned if she'd give him the satisfaction of returning his gaze. Who did he think he was, for heaven's sake?

A sobering inner voice silently derided that he knew precisely who he was, and without doubt his action was a deliberate attempt to ruffle her composure.

Somehow she expected him to voice any one of several differing phrases men inevitably used as an opening gambit with an attractive woman, and when he didn't the rage within only intensified, for it gave her no opportunity to deliver a scathing response.

It took only seconds to reach the fifteenth floor, but it felt like minutes, and so intense was her need to escape that she stepped from the lift the instant the doors slid open, unable to prevent the feeling that she was fleeing from a predatory animal.

A sensation that was as totally insane as it was out of perspective, she mentally chided as she entered the foyer of her brother's suite of legal offices.

'Good morning, Miss Harrison,' the receptionist greeted warmly. 'Mr Harrison said to go straight through.'

'Thanks,' Lexi proffered with a faint smile as she continued past the central desk and turned down a corridor leading to a large corner office which offered panoramic views of the city and inner harbour.

'David,' she greeted as the door closed behind her, accepting the affectionate brush of her brother's lips against her cheek before she subsided into a nearby chair. 'Thanks for organising my car into the repair shop. I've parked the red monster in its usual space.'

David's eyebrows rose in a gesture of feigned offence. '*Monster*, Lexi?'

A faint grin curved her generous mouth. 'Sorry,' she corrected, aware that the Ferrari represented an unaccustomed flamboyance in his otherwise staid existence as one of Sydney's leading barristers. 'Your magnificent motoring machine.'

As the son and daughter of one of Australia's most respected financial entrepreneurs, they had each achieved success in their own right, choosing to decline any assistance afforded them by virtue of their father's considerable wealth and position.

'Have you any plans for tonight?'

Her eyes widened slightly. 'I can't imagine you need to resort to your sister's company through lack of a suitable female partner.'

His glance was level and strangely watchful as he offered a light bantering response. 'Now that your decree absolute has been granted I thought we might celebrate by having dinner together.'

An entire gamut of emotions flitted in and out of her expressive eyes, and for a moment he glimpsed her pain before a wry, faintly cynical smile tugged the edges of her mouth.

Despite her reluctance, memories sharpened into startling focus. The dissolution of her marriage meant that she no longer bore any affiliation, legal or otherwise, to a man who had deliberately pursued her for the fame of her family name and the considerable fortune he imagined would be his to access at will as the husband of Jonathan Harrison's daughter.

Paul Ellis had epitomised every vulnerable young girl's dream and every caring parent's nightmare, Lexi reflected with grim hindsight. Within weeks of returning to Australia from a two-year working stint in Europe she met Paul at a party, and became instantly attracted to him. Blindly infatuated, she had discounted her father's caution, disregarded David's advice, and married Paul three months later in a whirl of speculative publicity.

To Jonathan's credit he had concealed his concern and provided a wedding that had proved to be the social event of the year.

Mere days into a Caribbean honeymoon Lexi's dream of marital bliss had begun to fragment as Paul voiced a series of protests. The home her father had presented them with as a wedding gift was considered by Paul as too small for the sort of entertaining he had had in mind, and his disappointment in Jonathan's failure to appoint his son-in-law to the board of directors had been compounded when Lexi had refused to exert any influence in Paul's favour. His sudden enthusiasm for a child had raised doubts in Lexi's mind, and when she had elected to defer pregnancy for a year he'd lost his temper and the rift between them had become irreparable.

Paul, when faced with the *fait accompli* of legal separation, had filed claim for a huge financial settlement and threatened court proceedings if his demands were not met.

One of David's colleagues had conducted such superb legal representation that Paul's case was thrown out of court.

Concentrating on her modelling career, Lexi had declined her father's offer to occupy his prestigious Vaucluse mansion, opting instead to live alone in a beautifully furnished apartment at Darling Point overlooking the inner harbour.

At twenty-five she was considered to be one of Sydney's top models, and work provided a panacea that helped relegate Paul to the past.

The experience had left her with a cynical attitude towards men to such an extent that she chose not to date at all, preferring the company of Jonathan and David on the few occasions it became necessary for her to provide an escort.

Now Lexi met David's steady gaze with equanimity. 'That's the momentous news you wanted to discuss with me in person?'

He was silent for a few long seconds as he chose his words with care. 'Part of it.'

Her eyes widened fractionally at his hesitation.

'Paul has somehow discovered Jonathan is at present undertaking extremely delicate negotiations with a Japanese consortium to finance a proposed tourist resort on Queensland's Gold Coast,' he revealed slowly, and Lexi cast him a puzzled glance.

'In what context can Paul pose any threat?'

'He has made a demand for money.'

'Why?' she demanded at once.

David seemed to take an inordinate amount of time in answering. 'He is threatening to sell his story of the marriage break-up to the Press, detailing how he was discarded by the Harrison family without a cent.' His lips twisted. 'The fact that Paul deliberately set Jonathan's fortune in his sights and preyed upon your emotions is immaterial,' he informed cynically. 'The Press, at Paul's direction, will have a field-day. Especially when it can run a concurrent story of the extent of Jonathan's financial involvement in the Japanese deal.'

Lexi didn't need to be told just how Paul's supposed plight would be highlighted. Without doubt he would portray the injured party to the hilt, invoking reader sympathy against the plutocratic Harrison family. As long as there was some basis of fact the truth was unimportant with some tabloids, and the major criterion was saleable copy.

'But surely the Japanese consortium is astute

enough not to allow personalities to enter into any business dealings?'

'Indeed,' he agreed drily. 'However, they will acquire their tourist resort regardless of whether Jonathan's company is the majority shareholder or not. There are other viable companies which would clutch at any straw in their struggle for power.'

Lexi didn't need to be enlightened as to her ex-husband's duplicity. 'The price for his silence is a financial settlement,' Lexi concluded, her eyes hardening until they resembled dark topaz. 'A settlement he was legally unable to obtain when we separated.'

'Unfortunately it isn't that simple,' David declared slowly. 'Jonathan is as yet unaware of Paul's intention. With your help I intend to keep it that way.'

Her eyes flashed with brilliant gold. 'Paul has no scruples whatsoever, and I'm damned if I'll allow you or Jonathan to pay Paul what amounts to blackmail on my account. It would only be the beginning, and you know it!'

David moved to stand beside the wide expanse of plate-glass, his expression pensive and incredibly solemn as he appeared to admire the view. After what seemed an age he turned towards her and thrust hands into his trouser pockets.

'The Japanese deal is important to Jonathan.' He effected a negligible shrug. 'But its failure or success is immaterial in the long term. There are other deals, other opportunities. However, in this particular issue the element of timing is crucial, and with Jonathan's health at stake I'll do anything in my power to prevent him from suffering any unnecessary stress.'

A painful hand clutched at her heart, and her voice

became husky with concern. 'What's wrong with Jonathan?' Her eyes clung to his. 'Why haven't you told me?'

'Because there was no point until all the tests were conclusive,' David said gently. 'His only option is a triple bypass, and surgery is scheduled for the beginning of January. Timed,' he added wryly, 'at Jonathan's insistence, to coincide with the anticipated conclusion of the Japanese negotiations. In the meantime it's essential he leads a quiet life with minimum stress.' He drew a deep breath as he surveyed her pale, stricken features. 'I hardly need to tell you what effect Paul's threatened publicity will have on Jonathan if we're unable to prevent it from erupting prior to surgery.'

The fact that her indomitable human dynamo of a father was victim of a heart disease was more than she could bear. 'It's that serious?'

David reached out and caught hold of her hand. 'You must know he'll have the best surgeon,' he reassured gently. 'And such operations are now considered routine.'

Lexi could only look at him blankly, her mind filling with conflicting images and an unassailable anger that anything Paul attempted might damage her father's health. 'What possible solution have you come up with?' she managed at last.

David seemed to take his time, then offered quietly, 'Paul's adverse publicity attempt will look extremely foolish if you were already heavily involved, even engaged, to a man who is sufficiently wealthy to finance the necessary fifty-one-per-cent stake. A man who could present the role of adoring fiancé with conviction.' Seeing her silent scepticism, he lifted his hand in a dismissive gesture as he sought to assure. 'With careful orchestration and the right publicity we could ensure that any demands Paul sought were seen to be merely a case of sour grapes.'

'Since I'm not romantically involved with anyone, just *who* do you propose to link me with?' she queried with deceptive calm, then said with categoric certainty, 'It won't work.'

'It has to work,' David insisted. 'I can provide sufficient delaying tactics for a week or two on the premise of considering Paul's demands.'

'And the man, David? Just who is this paragon who will give his time to act out a charade?' A faint bitterness crept into her voice. 'And what's *his* price?'

'Georg Nicolaos,' he revealed slowly. 'And there is no price.'

'I find that difficult to believe,' she replied with scepticism. 'Everything has a price.'

'Jonathan's association with the Nicolaos family is well known. He has entered into several joint financial ventures with Alex and Georg Nicolaos in the past. It will come as no surprise if, now that your divorce from Paul is final, Georg Nicolaos is seen escorting you to a variety of functions during the rundown to the festive season.' A faint smile tugged the corners of his mouth. 'It will be alleged in the gossip columns that you and Georg have enjoyed a clandestine relationship for some time, and now that you're legally free Georg is losing no time in staking his claim.'

'Are Alex and Georg Nicolaos involved in this particular venture?'

'Yes.'

'And what if Paul suspects it's merely a smoke-screen?'

'I will utilise all my legal ability to persuade him we're more likely to take a magnanimous view of his demands now you're considering marriage with Georg. I can gain time with negotiations by insisting that Paul sign a document indicating he has no further financial claim on acceptance of an agreed amount.'

She gave him a look of scandalised disbelief. 'So you *do* intend to pay him?'

'A token sum, commensurate with the length of time he was married to you.' His good-looking features hardened into a mask of distaste. 'Added to the car and furniture he spirited out of the house within hours of your leaving him, the total value will be more than generous under the circumstances.' His expression gentled. 'Four weeks, Lexi—five at the most. Surely it's not too much to ask?'

She hesitated, unwilling to voice her own reluctance for fear it would sound ungrateful in light of the caring support her father and brother had each given her during the past two years. 'I can hardly refuse, can I?' she said at last, and glimpsed the relieved satisfaction in his eyes.

'In that case, I'll contact Georg and arrange for him to meet us this evening.'

So soon? Yet logic demanded there was no reason for delay.

Almost as if he sensed her reserve, he gave her hand a reassuring squeeze. 'I'll call for you at six-thirty.'

She possessed a wardrobe filled with designer

clothes, and she mentally reviewed them in an attempt to make an appropriate selection. 'I imagine you require me to present a dazzling image?'

'You look fantastic in anything.'

'Now that's what I call brotherly love,' Lexi accepted with a contrived smile. Sparing her watch a quick glance, she rose to her feet and delved into her bag to extract a set of keys which she pressed into his hand. 'Thanks for the loan of the Ferrari.'

David tossed them down on to his desk and reached into a nearby drawer. 'Here's yours. It's parked on level three, close to the lifts.'

'Give me the bill,' she insisted, 'and I'll write you a cheque.'

He made no demur and merely extracted the itemised account, watching as she wrote in the amount and attached her signature with unaffected flair.

Collecting her keys, she made her way towards the door. 'I have a modelling assignment at eleven. Jacques will have a fit if I'm late.'

The Mercedes sports car purred to life at the first turn of the key, and Lexi exited the car park, then headed towards the eastern suburbs.

The address she'd been given was for a restaurant venue in Double Bay whose patron had generously donated to charity the cost of providing food for the seventy ticket-paying guests.

It was, Jacques assured, a long-standing annual event for which the particular charity involved was dependently grateful.

Parking was achieved with ease, and Lexi locked up, activating the car alarm before walking towards the main street.

She located the discreet restaurant display-board without difficulty, and traversed a wide curving staircase to the main entrance, where an elegantly gowned hostess greeted and directed her to a makeshift changing-room.

'Lexi, you're late,' a harassed voice announced the instant she entered the small room, and she checked her watch with a faintly raised eyebrow.

'By less than a minute,' she protested as she deftly began discarding her outer clothes. 'The fashion parade isn't due to begin for another half-hour.'

'Time which must be spent perfecting the hair and make-up, *oui*?'

The models were due to take to the catwalk at precisely eleven-thirty, displaying a variety of exclusive labels for an hour, after which lunch would be served, followed by customary speeches and the giving of a few token awards.

Thank heaven today's modelling assignment was being held indoors in air-conditioned comfort, Lexi consoled herself more than an hour later as she hurriedly discarded an elegantly tailored suit and reached for a superb evening gown, the final selection in a superb fashion range.

Yesterday had involved a beach, searing sun, hot sand, and a gathering of ogling, wolf-whistling young men intent on upsetting her composure.

Modelling was hard work, and often the antithesis of its projected glamorous image, Lexi mused as she took her cue and moved out on to the small makeshift stage. Her hazel-gold eyes were wide and clear, and she portrayed graceful dignity as she took to the catwalk, pausing momentarily as she executed a series of choreographed movements; then she returned to the stage to effect one final turn before slipping through the curtain to backstage.

'The restaurateur has set a table aside for those of you who wish to eat,' Jacques informed them as he carefully slid the last garment into its protective cover. 'Of course, there is no obligation to stay.'

The three other models opted to remain, while Lexi shook her head in silent negation. 'I can't. I have a dental appointment in half an hour.'

He gave a typical Gallic shrug. 'Tomorrow at three, Lexi,' he reminded her, and she nodded in acquiescence as she cast her reflection a quick glance before collecting her bag.

'I must fly, or I'll be late.'

Slipping out of the changing-room, Lexi quickly manoeuvred her way between tables, inadvertently bumping into a solid masculine frame which seemed to appear out of nowhere.

Her hand clutched his arm in an instinctive attempt to steady herself, and a faint smile parted her lips accompanied by a few words in murmured apology.

Words that froze in the back of her throat as she recognised the man with whom she'd shared a lift only a few hours earlier.

This close she could see the fine lines fanning out from the corners of his eyes, the deep groove slashing each cheek.

He possessed an animalistic sense of power, as well as an indefinable sensual quality that was infinitely dangerous to any sensible woman's peace of mind.

There was a degree of mocking amusement evident

in the depths of his gaze, and Lexi became aware that she was still clutching his arm.

She snatched her hand away as if burned by fire, and her eyes flared to a brilliant gold as she regained the power of speech. 'I'm sorry. Excuse me,' she added in a huskily spoken afterthought as she made to move past him.

'You are not staying?'

His drawled query held the faintest accent, and the sound of it sent a tiny shiver of alarm scudding down the length of her spine.

'No.'

His gaze was steady, his brown eyes dark, inscrutable depths in which it would be all too easy to become lost, and there could be no doubt that he possessed sufficient sensual expertise to melt the hardest heart.

But not hers, she assured herself silently. Definitely not hers. She'd travelled that particular road before, and there was no way she intended being hurt again. By *any* man.

He made no comment, and merely inclined his head in silent mocking acceptance of her decision.

The desperate need to get away from him surprised her, and she lifted a hand to push back the length of her hair in a gesture that was born from nervous tension.

A fact that was unsettling, given her exclusive schooling, she acknowledged as she made her way towards the foyer. And after her disastrously short marriage to Paul she had managed to acquire a protective façade she considered virtually impregnable.

It was after five when Lexi entered her luxurious

Darling Point apartment, and her arms were laden with an assortment of brightly coloured carrier-bags that held Christmas gifts for Jonathan and David, as well as an exquisite new perfume she'd bought for herself.

With a sigh of relief she closed the door behind her, eased off her shoes, then carried her purchases through to the spare bedroom. From there she made her way into the kitchen and poured herself a long cool drink of orange juice, then she drifted into the lounge and sank into one of several soft leather chairs.

It had been an unsettling day, fraught with surprises, and she needed ten minutes in which to relax and *think*.

Blind dating—if dining with Georg Nicolaos could be termed that—was something in which she'd never indulged, and she was reluctant to begin, even given such an essentially worthy cause.

Any choice she might have in the matter was a mere fallacy, for there *was* no choice, she decided wryly. Somehow she had to endure being in the constant company of a man she'd never met for the next five weeks; to smile and laugh, and generally give the impression that she was relieved and delighted that their romance, which had supposedly been kept under wraps for months, was now out in the open.

Without doubt it would tax her acting ability to the limit.

With a sigh of resignation she stretched her arms above her head and flexed her shoulders, then rose to her feet and made her way into the bedroom, where she stripped, and took a shower in the adjoining *en suite* bathroom.

Lexi was ready a few minutes before six-thirty, her long hair confined into a knot atop her head from which she deliberately teased free a few soft-curling tendrils. Make-up was deliberately understated, with the accent on subtle shadings of eyeshadow, a touch of blusher, and soft clear rose colouring her lips. The gown she'd chosen was black with a cleverly designed ruched bodice and figure-hugging skirt. It came with a stole which she casually draped across her shoulders, and her feet were encased in black Jourdan slender-heeled shoes.

'Beautiful,' David complimented warmly when she opened the door at his summons.

'Thanks,' she accepted without guile as she preceded him into the lounge. 'Would you like a drink?'

'I told Georg we'd meet him at seven.'

Lexi cast him a quick glance before collecting her evening-bag from a nearby mahogany table. 'In that case, I guess we'd better not keep him waiting.'

Double Bay was a popular 'in' place to eat, hosting a variety of exclusive restaurants, and it wasn't until David led her to a familiar flight of stairs that she realised their destination.

'I was here this morning on a modelling assignment.'

'Really? Georg is known to favour a few worthy charity organisations.'

A brief flicker of surprise lit her features. 'Georg Nicolaos owns the restaurant?'

'It belongs to the Nicolaos family,' David corrected. 'Georg assumed a personal interest in it after the death of his father. If you remember, Alex and I attended university together.'

A darkly handsome figure sprang to mind, formidable and intensely Greek. 'I seem to recollect hearing Alex had married.' A faint gleam sparkled in the depths of her eyes. 'His wife has my sympathy.'

'Dear lord, *why*?'

Lexi gave a husky laugh. 'Oh, for heaven's sake, David! Alex is one of the most frighteningly sexy men I've met. The woman who managed to snare him must be quite something.'

'Samantha is charming,' David allowed, before giving his name to the hostess at the desk.

'Ah, yes, Mr Harrison.' Her smile was practised, bright, and deferential. 'Mr Nicolaos has instructed me to let him know the moment you arrive. If you'd care to follow me, I'll direct you to your table. Mr Nicolaos will join you shortly.'

'You seem to be very much in favour,' Lexi teased minutes after they had taken their seats, and David effected a self-deprecatory shrug.

'I've known the family a long time. Alex waited tables between college and university semesters in the days when his father headed the restaurant. As did Georg and Anna.'

'I find it strange that, although I've met Alex on a number of occasions over the years, I have yet to meet his brother.'

David leaned well back in his chair, a habit he unconsciously adopted whenever he was about to choose his words with care. Lexi wondered if he was aware of it, and why he should do so now.

'Perhaps because Alex chooses to adopt a stand on certain political issues, and enjoys a prominent social existence.'

'And Georg doesn't?' she queried idly.

'Not to the same degree.'

Her eyelids flicked wide. 'Why? Is he a recluse? Or does he not enjoy the company of women?'

David's gleaming humour was somehow directed to a point somewhere beyond her left shoulder.

'On the contrary,' a deep slightly accented, vaguely familiar voice interjected in a silky drawl. 'I very much enjoy the opposite sex.'

Lexi turned slowly to find her worst fears were confirmed, and a silent scream of rejection rose against the irony of fate that Georg Nicolaos and the driver of the red Ferrari were one and same.

CHAPTER TWO

LEXI'S eyes flared briefly in silent resentment as David effected an introduction.

'Mr Nicolaos,' Lexi acknowledged, hating the way her stomach began to knot in sheer reaction to his presence.

'*Georg*, please,' he insisted, holding her gaze a few seconds longer than was necessary before switching his attention to the man seated opposite. 'David.'

A waiter appeared the instant Georg folded his lengthy frame into a chair, and he hovered with intent solicitude as his employer enquired about his guests' choice of wine while Lexi sat stiffly upright as every last nerve-ending tingled alive in silent antipathy.

Not even in her wildest imagination had she envisaged being placed in the invidious position of having to act out a charade with someone of Georg Nicolaos's calibre.

Part of her demanded an escape *now*, while she still had the courage to do so. Except that she was impossibly bound to remain, and she viewed him surreptitiously under the guise of perusing the menu.

In his late thirties, he managed without effort to portray a dramatic mesh of blatant masculinity and elemental ruthlessness—a facet that was obviously a family trait, she decided uncharitably, recalling Alex's formidable features.

The menu was extensive, and she opted for a

24

chicken consommé, followed it with a salad, and waived dessert in favour of the cheeseboard.

'I can't persuade you to sample even one dish from our selection of Greek cuisine?'

Lexi met Georg's dark gaze, and was unable to read anything from his expression. His faint smile held a degree of warmth and was doubtless aimed to put her at ease. Yet beneath the façade she detected a lurking cynicism, and it rankled.

Her eyes held his with deliberately cool regard. 'Thank you, but no,' she refused quietly.

'Another occasion, perhaps?'

She wanted to tell him that there would be no other occasion, but the reality of the next few weeks emerged with vivid clarity.

Lifting her glass to her lips, she savoured its excellent contents, then set it down on to the table, unconsciously tracing the patterned cloth with the tip of her elegantly shaped nail.

Mockery appeared to be her only defence, and she utilised it mercilessly. 'Do we each bring out our figurative engagement books, and consult?'

A gleam of humour sharpened his dark eyes. 'You have your engagement book with you?'

It was crazy to feel so vulnerable, yet she was supremely conscious of every single breath, and it wasn't a sensation she enjoyed.

'Like the advertisement for a well-known credit card,' she responded, 'I never leave home without it.'

'For tomorrow night,' Georg drawled, 'I have tickets for the opera.'

Lexi shook her head. 'I have a photographic modelling session tomorrow afternoon.'

'Which is due to finish—when?'

She effected a faint shrug. 'Five, six,' she hazarded. 'Maybe later. Peter is a perfectionist. He'll take as many shots as he needs to capture precisely the right image.'

'Dinner is obviously out. I'll collect you at seven-thirty.'

She regarded him coolly. 'I could have made other plans.' She heard David's audible intake of breath and registered his protest before he had the opportunity to voice the words.

'Lexi—'

'Perhaps you could check?' Georg interceded in a deep, faintly accented drawl, and an icy chill feathered across the surface of her skin.

Lexi knew she was behaving badly, yet she was unable to prevent herself from searching for her pocket diary and riffling through its pages until she reached the appropriate one. 'Drinks with Elaine, seven o'clock,' she read out, then spared him an apparently regretful glance. 'Sorry. Not the opera.' A shaft of remorse prompted her to offer a slight smile. 'Unless I miss the first act and join you during the second?'

'Alternatively, we could both miss the first act,' Georg declared silkily.

It was a clash of wills, and she was determined to win. 'I wouldn't dream of allowing you to make such a concession. If you let me have the ticket I'll meet you there.'

'Surely you could cancel Elaine?' David intervened, shooting her a cautionary look that ordinarily she would have heeded.

'Arrangements were made weeks ago for a number of friends to meet for a few pre-Christmas drinks,' she explained. 'If I opt out she'll be hurt. Besides,' she qualified, unable to prevent a faint tinge of bitterness entering her voice, 'once my supposed romance with Georg hits the gossip columns there will be no peace at all. At least permit me another day of relative freedom.'

'I should remind you that Georg is under no obligation whatsoever,' David declared heavily.

'Perhaps not,' she tempered sweetly. 'Although, business-wise, I doubt if either Alex or Georg wants this particular deal to fall through. Therefore, Georg *does* have an interest. Am I not right?' She spared her brother a winsome smile before switching her attention to his companion. 'Unless, of course, he's bored with life and not averse to a little subterfuge by way of adventure. Is that the reason you've agreed to act as a mythical knight in shining armour, Georg?' She deliberately gave his name its correct phonetic pronunciation, so that it fell from her lips as 'Jorj'.

His eyes swept her features in raking assessment, then locked with hers for a brief instant before assuming an expression of bland inscrutability. 'My life is far from boring,' he acknowledged with velvet-smoothness, although only a fool would have failed to perceive the steel evident.

'Yet you are willing to reorganise your social life to the extent of putting it entirely on hold for a month.' She let her eyes travel at will over each and every one of his visible features in an appraisal that was meant to diffuse the sheer overwhelming presence of the man. 'Your current—er—companion,' she accorded with delicate emphasis, 'must be extremely understanding.'

Georg regarded her steadily until she almost felt impelled to wrench her gaze away from those fathomless dark eyes, then his eyelids lowered slightly, successfully masking his expression as he proffered a faintly mocking smile.

'You're a very attractive young woman,' he drawled. 'Being your escort for a few weeks in an attempt to perpetrate an illusion will provide no hardship at all.'

It was as well the waiter arrived at that precise moment with their starter, and Lexi spooned the excellent chicken consommé with little appetite, and merely picked at her salad.

The wine helped soothe her nerves, although she refused to allow her glass to be refilled and opted for chilled water throughout the remainder of the meal.

It was almost ten when David indicated that they should leave, and Lexi experienced considerable relief that the evening was almost over.

'Your ticket for the opera,' Georg indicated as he withdrew a slim envelope from his jacket pocket and handed it to her.

She took care that their fingers didn't touch, aware from the faint gleam of amusement evident that he *knew*. 'I'm not sure what time I'll get there,' she ventured, determined not to rush away from Elaine's party before she was ready.

'Try to make it before the final act,' he advised in a cynical drawl. 'And take a taxi,' he added. 'We'll go on to a night-club afterwards.'

Her lashes swept up as she cast him a cool glance. 'Is that necessary?'

'It is if we're to be seen together, photographed and captioned in the gossip columns.' His smile was totally without humour. 'Our supposed "romance" won't have much credence if we depart in separate vehicles.'

She felt her stomach give a sickening lurch at the reality of what she was about to undertake. Yet any visible sign of apprehension was unthinkable, and she tilted her chin fractionally as she proffered a brilliant smile. 'I'll endeavour to dazzle.'

'You appear to do that without effort,' Georg accorded drily as he rose to his feet, and Lexi followed suit, collecting her evening-bag as he escorted them both to the lobby.

'Really, Lexi,' David chastised her the instant they were out of earshot. 'You were incredibly rude—'

'I know everything you're going to say,' she intercepted a trifle wearily, glad that they had reached the street. 'Treat it as a temporary aberration.' Her voice assumed an unaccustomed asperity. 'I just hate the degree of my own involvement in this ill-fated scheme.' Especially with someone like Georg Nicolaos, a tiny voice taunted.

David shot her a perceptive look. 'Georg is unlikely to proposition you, if that's your concern.'

Oh, *David*, she longed to deride him. If only you knew how emotionally insecure I feel—how afraid I am to get close to *any* man, even if it's only to participate in an inglorious charade!

Yet she said nothing, and merely walked at his side

to the car, opting to remain pensively silent as he drove her the short distance to her apartment block.

'Ring me at the office on Wednesday. Jonathan mentioned something about our both joining him at home for dinner.' His kindly eyes pierced hers in the dim interior of the car. 'Georg will make a welcome guest. Invite him along.'

She was caught in a trap, and already she could feel the first tinge of pain. 'I'll mention it,' she compromised, slipping easily from the low-slung vehicle the instant it pulled to a halt. 'Goodnight.'

'Darling, *must* you?'

The words appeared to be sincere, but in reality masked boredom and lack of interest, and Lexi wondered why she'd stayed at Elaine's party for so long.

Sheer perversity, born from a desire to tread the edge of Georg Nicolaos's self-control; something that was akin to total madness, she decided as she declared that she really *must* leave.

'I'll just say goodnight to Elaine,' she murmured, then drifted towards a group of three women deep in animated conversation near the door.

Kisses, a few shared hugs, the exchanged avowals to enjoy a really great 'Chrissie', then Lexi managed to slip away.

The taxi she'd ordered was parked outside, waiting, and the driver merely shrugged in complacent resignation as she directed him to the Opera House.

Lexi checked the ticket—something she hadn't bothered to do until now—and saw that the reservation was for *Madame Butterfly*.

The torturous and incredibly sad aspects of love,

no matter how beautifully enacted, could hardly be her favoured selection. Yet a quirk of sardonic irony permitted her to see humour in the unwanted parable. The question that sprang immediately to mind was whether Georg Nicolaos's choice was deliberate or merely happenstance.

Some thirty minutes later Lexi was led unobtrusively to a section which comprised some of the best seats in the house, and with a murmured apology she moved along the aisle and sank down into the reserved space.

Her hand was captured almost at once, and she instinctively pulled against the strength of Georg's fingers as he threaded them through her own.

'Seated behind us, to your left, is Anaïs Pembleton,' he cautioned softly as he leaned closer, and she closed her eyes in frustration that one of the city's leading matrons should have chosen tonight of all nights to visit the opera. Worse, that the society doyenne should be seated in the immediate vicinity. Sharp-eyed and acid-tongued, Anaïs Pembleton had a nose for gossip to the extent that she was accorded the status of the uncrowned queen of the gossip-mongers. Lexi hardly needed Georg to remind her to behave.

'How…opportune,' she murmured, hating his close proximity, the faint helplessness at having her hand enclosed within his own, and the sheer animal magnetism he managed to exude without any seeming effort.

'Try to smile,' he drawled, and she could sense his cynical amusement. 'The curtain is about to fall.'

A minute was all she had to prepare herself, and

for one brief second her eyes felt incredibly large, their poignant depths strangely dry as she fought to quell the faint trembling of her lips.

'Would you prefer to remain seated?'

He was quite devastating when he deliberately set out to charm and she endeavoured to match the warmth reflected in his smile. 'Could we mingle in the foyer?' At least then she could move around, and there was always the chance she might meet an acquaintance, thus providing an opportunity to focus her attention on someone other than *him*.

Georg rose to his feet without a word, leading her through a throng of fashionably attired men and women.

Lexi had chosen to wear a formal gown of rich red velvet, its body-hugging lines emphasising her soft feminine curves. A wrap in matching velvet added undeniable elegance, and she'd utilised two side-combs to sweep the hair back from her face. Her only jewellery was a diamond pendant on a slim gold chain, and matching ear-studs.

'A drink?' he queried as they reached the foyer.

'Lime and soda, with a dash of bitters.'

'Ice?'

'Please,' she acceded, watching as a waiter appeared at their side as if by magic.

Georg Nicolaos emanated an infinite degree of power of a kind that commanded instant attention. Yet there was no arrogance apparent, just a compelling omnipotence that scorned all forms of weakness.

It was little wonder that women were held enthralled by him, she perceived wryly. Even if he wasn't extraordinarily wealthy, he would still manage to snare most feminine hearts.

He smiled, and deep grooves slashed his cheeks. 'How was the party?'

She looked at him carefully, analysing the broad-sculptured bone-structure, the steady wide-spaced dark eyes. 'Fine.' A faint moue appeared momentarily, then it was gone, and she effected a slight shrug. 'Am I now supposed to enquire about your day?'

'Are you in the least interested?' he queried, watching as she lifted her glass and took a small sip.

'I know very little about you,' Lexi ventured, and her eyes flared as he reached out and threaded his fingers through her own. Her initial instinct to pull free was thwarted, and she retaliated with a surreptitious dig from her long hard nails.

'Why, Georg,' a breathy feminine voice intruded, 'how wonderful to see you! Are you going on to the club afterwards?'

Lexi turned slowly and met a vision of brunette perfection attired in black silk that shrieked an exclusive designer label only the favoured few could afford.

'Louise,' he acknowledged, then performed an introduction.

'Your face is familiar, yet I'm sure we've never met,' the brunette declared with a faint frown.

'Lexi is a model,' Georg revealed smoothly, clasping Lexi's hand even more firmly within his own.

The gesture didn't go unnoticed, and Lexi caught the sharpness apparent in Louise's beautiful blue eyes before the expression was carefully masked.

'Harrison. Are you any relation to Jonathan Harrison?'

There was no point in denying the truth. 'His daughter.'

There was instant, inevitable knowledge evident in the other girl's exquisite features. 'Of course. Now I remember. Your marriage and divorce achieved notoriety in the Press.'

During the past two years Lexi had encountered several occasions such as this one, and had become accustomed to dealing with them. Pride lifted her chin, and her lashes swept down to form a partial protective veil. 'At the time it was a seven-day wonder,' she allowed with quiet dignity.

'A sensation,' Louise corrected with sweet emphasis. 'No sooner was the honeymoon over than so was the marriage.' There was a delicate pause as she waited for Lexi's comment, and when none was forthcoming a glitter of malice appeared briefly before it was quickly masked. 'I imagine it was a difficult time for you.'

Lexi felt she owed no one an explanation, and any comment was superfluous.

'Finish your drink, darling,' Georg drawled, 'and we'll return to our seats.'

Lexi heard the cool bland words, yet they barely registered. *'Darling'?*

'You'll excuse us, Louise?'

Lexi's glass was taken from her hand, and beneath her startled gaze she watched as he calmly placed it, only half-empty, down on to a nearby tray.

Within seconds she found herself being drawn towards the auditorium.

'Do you mind unshackling me?' she demanded in a vicious undertone.

'Behave,' Georg adjured quietly. 'If you continue to struggle you'll only hurt yourself.'

'Damn you, let me go! I'm not a child in need of a restraining hand!'

It was a relief to reach their seats, and she was glad of the subdued lighting. It hid the faint angry flush that lay along her cheekbones and the glittering sparkle in the depths of her eyes.

A furtive but strong tug of her hand did no good at all, and the breath stilled in her throat as she felt the slight pressure of his thumb caressing the fast-pulsing veins at her wrist.

She turned towards him, only to find he had leaned sideways and his face was mere inches from her own.

'Have you no shame?' Lexi hissed, incensed almost beyond words as she saw his attention deliberately centre on the fullness of her mouth.

Slowly his eyes travelled up to meet her own, and she had to restrain herself from hitting him at the glimpse of mocking amusement apparent in their depths.

'None whatsoever.'

It was as well that the house lights dimmed then as the curtain rose for the third and final act, she decided vengefully. Otherwise she would have been tempted to slap his hateful face!

The dramatic conclusion to Cio-cio-san's tragic romance with an American naval officer was splendidly performed, and the depth and agonising pathos portrayed brought a lump to Lexi's throat as she was held enraptured by the sheer magical spell of the Japanese girl's emotional trauma.

Lexi was unable to prevent thoughts of her own disenchantment with Paul, the loss of trust, the deliberate deception, and her eyes began to ache as she sought to suppress the tell-tale shimmer of tears.

Dear heaven, what was the matter with her? Why tonight, of all night, did she have to fall prey to such maudlin emotions?

Because, an inner voice taunted, you've been thrust into a damnable situation where you're forced to conform to a set of circumstances with a man whose sense of purpose is nothing less than daunting.

Members of the Press were waiting in the foyer to photograph the more famous of the opera devotees, and any hope Lexi held for being able to slip away undetected died even before it was born as camera lenses were thrust in her face and a hard-voiced journalist asked a host of probing questions.

Georg handled it all with urbane charm, and Lexi had merely to smile. At last they were free, and she moved quickly at Georg's side as he led her through a side-door and down into the car park.

It wasn't until they were in the car that she began to relax, although her relief was short-lived as she realised that the Ferrari was heading towards the city.

'I'd prefer to go home, if you don't mind.'

He turned his head slightly and spared her a brief, inflexible glance, then concentrated on negotiating the traffic. 'Half an hour at the club will provide the opportunity for more publicity.' His voice assumed a silky drawl. 'I think you'll agree that's the main objective?'

'I would have thought the news hounds would be satisfied with our appearance at the opera,' she offered with a touch of cynicism, becoming impossibly angry when he offered no comment.

She maintained an icy silence until Georg brought the car to a halt in a city car park, and she slid out from the passenger seat, then closed the door with a firm clunk before flicking him a cool aloof glance.

'Thirty minutes,' she vouchsafed. 'Any longer and I'll call a taxi.'

He could annihilate her in a second. It was there in his eyes, the firm set of his mouth, and Lexi wondered at her own temerity in acting like a spoilt bitch.

'We either do this properly, or we won't do it at all,' Georg stated with chilling cynicism.

The desire to rage against his implacability was paramount, and her eyes warred openly with his, longing to consign him to hell. Never could she remember feeling so intensely angry; not even with Paul.

Without a word she moved away from the car and began walking towards the flight of stairs leading up to the carpeted lobby.

It wasn't surrender—more a case of restrained capitulation, she assured herself, supremely conscious of several patrons waiting for a lift to transport them to the trendy night-club situated on the top floor of the building.

The venue was crowded, attesting to its popularity, and intent on playing host to a plethora of 'beautiful' people who were more interested in being 'seen' as they flitted from table to table in the pursuit of compliments regarding their designer-label clothes and the success of their latest business dealings.

'What would you like to drink?'

Lexi's eyes flashed with a mixture of resentment and silent antipathy for one brief second before long thick lashes swept down to form a protective veil. 'Do I look as if I need one?'

'You look,' Georg drawled in a silky undertone, 'as if you've been thrown into a den of lions.'

He was too perceptive by far! The music was loud, the band excellent, and she let her gaze rove round the room, recognising at least half a dozen familiar faces.

'Georg, you decided to come. Louise said you would, but I hardly dared believed her.'

Lexi turned slightly to encounter an exquisite blonde whose appearance was as sexually blatant as her voice.

'Brigitte,' he acknowledged in an amused drawl. With casual ease he curved a possessive arm around Lexi's waist as he effected an introduction, and it took considerable effort on her part to proffer a brilliant smile.

'Are there any women you *don't* know?' she queried the instant Brigitte moved out of earshot.

'Shall we attempt the dance-floor?'

Oh, he was the very limit! 'Do I have any choice?'

Without a word he drew her towards the centre of the room, and she instinctively stiffened as he caught her close.

His hold was hardly conventional, and she wanted to tear herself away. *Pretend,* an inner voice chided. In all probability he no more wants to dance with you than you do with him! So just close your eyes, and follow his lead.

Except that it wasn't that simple. The cool crisp smell of his cologne mingled with the slight muskiness emanating from his skin, stirring alive an elusive chemistry that made her want to move even closer within his grasp.

It was almost as if she were in the grip of some magnetic force, and she gave an imperceptible start as she felt the brush of his lips against her temple.

Her eyes flew wide open, and for one brief second those brilliant depths mirrored a mixture of pain and outrage before assuming an opaqueness that shuttered the windows to her soul.

It was totally insane, but she felt as if somehow with subtle manipulation Georg Nicolaos had assumed control of her life, and it rankled unbearably.

Sheer will-power helped her survive the next half-hour as they alternately drifted round the dance-floor and paused to converse with fellow guests.

Lexi even managed to smile as they bade good-night to a few of Georg's acquaintances, and she suffered his arm at her waist as they traversed the lobby, rode the lift and ultimately reached the car.

Safely seated inside, she simply maintained an icy silence as he fired the engine and sent the car purring towards street level.

Traffic was moderately light, and she stared sightlessly out of the windscreen as he headed for Darling Point.

Lexi reached for the door-handle the instant the Ferrari slid to a halt outside the entrance to her apartment block, and she cast Georg a look of disbelief as he switched off the ignition and calmly stepped out of the car.

'Where do you think you're going?'

'Escorting you safely indoors, where you'll make me some coffee, which will take at least half an hour to consume.'

'The hell I will!' She was so furious she could have hit him, and she wrenched her arm in a fruitless attempt to be free of him. 'I'm tired, and I want to go to bed. I have an early-morning photographic shoot, and I need to look good!'

He was leading her inexorably towards the entrance. What was more, he'd calmly retrieved her security-coded card and a set of keys from her hand. Before she could voice any further protest they were indoors and heading towards the lift-shaft.

'A car tailed us all the way here,' Georg informed her silkily. 'Without doubt an enthusiastic journalist from one of the less salubrious tabloids.' He jabbed the call-button and the doors immediately slid open. 'We've brought a supposedly clandestine affair out into the open, and it will seem contradictory if I merely drop you off and drive away, don't you think?'

Safely inside the cubicle, she let loose some of her rage. 'I could have a headache!'

His hard, rough-chiselled features assumed mocking cynicism. 'Have you?'

'You, David—this whole wretched farce gives me a headache!' Lexi retorted waspishly.

The lift came to a halt, and she stepped quickly out and headed towards the furthest of two doors situated to the left.

Georg was there before her, the key in the lock, and she turned to face him as soon as the door closed shut.

All the pent-up fury erupted with potent force, and, unbidden, her hand snaked towards his face, the small explosion of sound seeming to rebound in the silence of the room.

His eyes gleamed with glittery anger, and for one horrifying second she thought he meant to strike her back.

He stood curiously still, in perfect control, yet Lexi only barely managed to suppress an involuntary shiver. Never in her life had she felt so threatened, and she unconsciously held her breath, her eyes wide and unblinking as she stood transfixed in mesmeric horror.

'Does that make you feel better?' Georg drawled with dangerous softness. He conducted a slow, deliberate appraisal of each and every one of her physical attributes, and she almost died at the expression in those dark eyes as they returned to meet her own, reflecting a savage ruthlessness that made her want to turn and run.

'Be warned,' he cautioned with icy remoteness. 'I will not be your whipping boy.' His eyes speared hers, activating an angry defiance deep within, turning her golden-hazel eyes a brilliant topaz with the sheer force of it.

'And I won't tolerate any tyrannical behaviour,' she retaliated, uncaring of the tiny flaring from the centre of those hard brown eyes.

'I am here in the guise of an ally, not your enemy,' he reminded her implacably.

'And it would be much easier if I were amenable?' She felt as if she were on a roller-coaster, experiencing the tumult of emotional fear and exhilaration that went with the thrill of courting danger.

'While I can understand your aversion to men in general,' he drawled, 'you would be advised to remember that I am not cast from the same mould as your ex-husband.'

'That doesn't mean I have to like you.' Her attempt at cool anger failed dismally in the face of his mocking cynicism.

'My dear Lexi, you don't know me well enough to judge.'

She wanted to lash out, physically *hit* him, and be damned to the consequences. One transgression had been ignored, and she knew without doubt that another would bring retaliation of a kind she'd be wise to avoid.

'Will you please leave?'

'I'll make the coffee.'

He appeared so indomitable, so in control, that it was almost more than she could bear, and she was consumed with boiling rage as she followed on his heels into the kitchen.

'This is *my* home, dammit,' Lexi vented furiously, 'and I want you out of it!'

Georg assessed the well-designed kitchen with one sweeping glance, then reached for the percolator, extracted a drip filter, and set about grinding the coffee beans.

Lexi viewed his back with angry vexation. '*Damn* you, don't you listen?' She reached for his arm in an attempt to drag him round to face her, and felt the sheer strength of well-honed muscle beneath her fingers.

'I heard you.' He transferred the percolator on to the element and switched it on.

'Don't you dare ignore me!'

Georg turned slowly to face her, and suddenly she was supremely conscious of his close proximity, the powerful breadth of shoulder beneath its civilised sheath of expensive tailoring.

'If you continue to behave like a belligerent child I'll treat you like one.' The words were silky-soft, and dangerous with the threat of intent.

'Oh? What particular form of punishment do you have in mind?' She was so angry that she really didn't care any more. 'Be warned that if you so much as touch me I'll have you up for assault.'

His eyes became almost black, and his mouth tightened into a thin line. Without warning he caught hold of her shoulders and drew her inextricably close. So close that she was made aware of every tautened muscle and sinew.

'Don't—'

It was far too late to bargain with him, and she cried out as his head lowered to hers, his mouth fastening with unerring accuracy over her own as he forced her tightly closed lips apart.

A silent moan failed to find voice as he initiated a brutal assault on her senses, and she struggled against him, beating her fists against his back, his ribs—anywhere she could reach.

Her jaw ached from the sheer force of his possession, and she could have screamed with frus-

trated rage as every attempt she made to struggle free
was halted with effortless ease.

Timeless minutes later he relinquished her mouth,
and she stood in shocked silence as she made a
conscious effort to regain her breath, hardly aware
that her face was waxen-pale and her eyes were large
luminous pools mirroring a mixture of pain and disbelief.

His features appeared blurred behind the slow well
of tears, and she blinked rapidly to dispel their threatened spill.

If he'd wanted to deliver a lesson in male superiority he had succeeded, although her spirit wouldn't
permit him the satisfaction of knowing the depth of
her shaken emotions.

Sheer unadulterated pride was responsible for the
slight tilt of her chin, while a degree of dignity and
self-respect lent her eyes a fiery blaze.

'If you don't leave I'll walk out of the door and
book myself into a hotel for the night,' Lexi declared
in a deadly calm voice.

His appraisal was swift and clinically analytical as
he surveyed her beautiful features, and she hated the
knowledge she glimpsed in his gaze, the sure, un-
abating regard that was a perplexing mixture of ruthlessness and shameless sensuality.

His eyes held hers for what seemed an age, then
they slid slowly down to settle on the soft fullness of
her mouth before lifting to meet her startled defiant
gaze.

Then he turned and walked towards the door,
opened it, and closed it quietly behind him.

Somehow she had expected him to overrule her,

and, although she desperately wanted him gone, his departure was something of an anticlimax.

Damn him! She was so impossibly angry she almost wished he were still in the apartment so that she could vent some of her rage.

Except there was the pain of her ravaged mouth as a vivid reminder, and she felt a sudden chill shiver down the length of her spine in the knowledge that Georg Nicolaos would never allow himself to be subservient to any woman, much less *her*.

The frantic bubbling of the percolator penetrated her mind, and she reached forward to switch off the element, opting instead for hot milk with a generous dash of brandy.

When it was ready she carried it through to the lounge and sank into one of the large leather sofas, slipping off her shoes and nestling her feet up beneath her as she slowly sipped from the mug.

A heavy silence permeated the room, almost as if the man who had not long vacated it had left something of his presence behind, Lexi brooded as she gazed sightlessly into space.

He was everything she hated in a man, she decided with damning frustration: self-assured, arrogant, and impossibly iron-willed.

If it weren't for Jonathan she'd condemn Georg Nicolaos to the nether regions of hell without so much as a second thought.

A long heartfelt sigh escaped her lips. Five weeks, David had intimated. It would be a miracle if she survived the distance.

The brandy began to soothe her fractured nerves, and when the laced milk was finished she drifted into her bedroom, stripped off her clothes, removed her make-up, and slipped into bed to sleep deeply until seven when the alarm shrilled its loud insistent summons to the start of a new day.

CHAPTER THREE

THE photographic session went way over time, with endless extra shots being required—to such an extent that it was all Lexi could do to contain her impatience as she obediently performed for the camera.

As much as she admired Peter's professional expertise, this morning for some reason his seemingly endless search for perfection proved tiresome, and she longed for the moment he would call a halt.

'That's good, darling. Chin a fraction higher. Now turn slowly towards me. *Great*. Smile. Sultry, sexy— that's the look I want. Pout a little. Sweep down with those eyelashes. Good. Now open. Look at me.' The shutter clicked with increasing rapidity. 'That's it, darling. I've got all I need.'

With a sigh of relief Lexi stepped away from the backdrop with its concentration of lights angling in from various points on the set. The heat they generated added at least ten degrees to the temperature inside the studio, and she longed for a cool shower.

She quickly effected a change of clothes in a dressing-room at the rear of the set, and, aware of the time, Lexi simply caught up her bag and emerged to cast Peter and his two assistants a hasty grin.

'Got to dash. I'm due to model at a fashion auction at one. *Ciao*.'

It took ten minutes to reach her apartment, a further fifteen minutes to shower and dress, then she slipped back into the car and drove towards the exclusive suburb of Woollahra.

Traffic seemed unusually congested, and she managed to miss almost every set of traffic-lights at each consecutive intersection. Consequently, by the time she had parked the Mercedes she had five minutes to spare before the auction was due to begin.

Held in an exclusive boutique and organised by its owner to aid of one of Lexi's favoured charities, with guest attendance strictly by invitation, it was a twice-yearly event for which she waived her normal fee. Designer labels were displayed by three professional models and individually auctioned at a cost price reserve. Considered a 'must' by the social élite, it was definitely an occasion, with champagne and hors-d'oeuvres offered by hired staff, followed at the auction's conclusion by a sumptuous array of savouries and continental cakes served with coffee and tea.

Organised chaos reigned in the small changing-room, and Lexi murmured a quick apology as she began pulling on a pair of sheer tights.

'*Lexi*. For heaven's sake, we thought you weren't going to make it in time!'

Anxiety coloured the older woman's voice, and Lexi proffered a soothing smile. 'Relax, Renée. Jacqueline is just now beginning her welcoming introductory speech. It will be at least five minutes before she's ready to announce the first of the collection.' She stepped into a silk half-slip, then dressed in the stunning ensemble that represented an exotic and expensive line in resort wear. With skilled fingers she swept her hair up into a casually contrived knot atop her head, added adept strokes with shadow and liner to highlight her eyes, blusher to her cheeks, then outlined her mouth and brushed colour over the contour of her lips. 'There. All done.' A quick check in the mirror, a practised smile at her own reflection, then she slid her feet into slender-heeled pumps and stood waiting with poised assurance for Jacqueline's call.

Possessed of an ebullient personality and an enviable degree of showmanship, Jacqueline was very much in charge of the auction, which soon assumed the theatrics of a stage production. Without doubt she held her 'audience' in the palm of her hand, and, suitably relaxed by a generous flow of fine champagne, her guests entered into the spirit of it all with a display of friendly rivalry as they attempted to outbid each other in their race for a bargain purchase.

Elegant day-wear soon gave way to a sophisticated line of tailored business-wear, and was followed by the after-five range.

Lexi completed her walk, gave a final turn, then moved quickly into the changing-room, effecting a smooth exchange of garments with swift professional ease.

The background music was muted, a tasteful selection that didn't compete with Jacqueline's spirited auctioneering, and Lexi emerged on cue in an absolutely stunning creation that could easily have been created for her alone.

Adopting a practised smile, she moved with easy fluidity to pause, turn, then repeat the process at three-metre intervals until she'd completed the pre-arranged circuit.

As she turned to face the guests her eyes were

caught by a tall figure standing on the periphery of her vision.

Georg Nicolaos. What the *hell* was he doing here?

Looking incredibly arresting in a dark business suit, his pale blue shirt worn with a sombre silk tie, he represented an alien force in what was surely a feminine sphere.

Lexi forced herself to meet his gaze and hold it for a few seconds before transferring her attention elsewhere as the bidding became fiercely competitive.

'Two hundred and fifty.'

'Four hundred.'

Heads turned as if in synchronisation at the sound of a deep masculine drawl, and Jacqueline, with immediate recognition and an impish sense of humour, broke into tinkling laughter.

'Darlings, we *are* honoured this afternoon. For those of you who haven't read this morning's papers, Georg and our darling Lexi are an item.' She paused slightly and made a delicate fluttering movement with her elegantly manicured hands. 'Don't you think it's just marvellous?' Her smile held genuine warmth as she turned towards Lexi. 'I'm so pleased for you both.' Turning back towards her guests, she lifted her hands in an expressive gesture. 'Now, ladies, is anyone going to compete with Georg?'

'Four hundred and fifty.'

'Six hundred.'

Lexi's eyes widened fractionally as she forced herself to maintain a slight smile. Inside, she could feel the onset of helpless frustration and anger at his deliberate actions.

'Seven,' followed in feminine determination.

'One thousand,' Georg drawled, lifting one eye-brow in a gesture of musing indulgence at the sound of a few gasps.

He was deliberately attempting to set a precedent in their purported relationship. His appearance here would be regarded as juicy gossip, Lexi seethed, and as such it would be discussed, embellished, and cir-culated with wildfire speed.

Damn him!

'Eleven hundred.'

'Twelve,' another feminine bidder added, while yet another topped it by a further two hundred dollars.

Dear lord in heaven. They were caught up with the need to outbid each other, turning a civilised event into a circus.

'Two thousand,' Georg called calmly, and there was a hushed silence.

Would anyone else dare bid? Somehow Lexi doubted it. Even the most frivolous of the women present would balk at paying three times the gown's wholesale price.

'Sold,' Jacqueline declared with a delighted clap of her hands. 'Thank you, Georg.' She turned towards Lexi and directed an ecstatic smile. 'You, too, dar-ling.' With professional ease she commandeered her guests' attention. 'Now, ladies, please prepare your-selves for the evening-wear selection. Then I have a little surprise in store.'

Lexi escaped into the changing-room, and her fin-gers shook as she slid out of the gown and handed it to the assistant before donning a strapless and prac-tically backless figure-hugging creation in patterned silk.

Any hopes she held that Georg might have made an unobtrusive exit were dashed as she re-emerged, and in silent defiance she directed him a deliberately sultry smile before veiling her eyes.

It was almost half an hour before the last evening gown was sold, and with each passing minute Lexi felt as if her nerves were being stretched to breaking point.

Georg had declined to make another bid, and his presence merely whipped speculation to fever pitch. Lexi's sensory perception was so acute that she could almost *hear* what they were thinking.

'Now, darlings, I've added an extra line as a little titillation.' Jacqueline paused, allowing her words to have maximum effect. 'What you've seen so far will certainly gain your favourite man's attention. Now, for the grand finale we'll play an ace with a range of sleep-wear guaranteed to raise his—' she hesitated with theatrical precision, then a husky voluptuous laugh escaped her lips '—blood-pressure.' From the degree of laughter filtering through to the changing-room, the guests were in fine form, their normal reserve loosened somewhat by several glasses of champagne.

Lexi cast the final rack an experienced eye, and inwardly cringed. Exclusive, ruinously expensive, the items displayed represented the finest in silk, satin and lace, and were guaranteed by the designer to be original and unduplicated.

Even attired in the exquisitely fashioned teddy, she would be just as adequately covered as if she were modelling a swim-suit. Yet there was a wealth of difference in the degree of projected provocativeness.

For a moment she considered refusing, but there were three models and consequently three of every line. If she opted out Georg, as well as every guest present, would be aware of it, and she was damned if she'd give him that satisfaction.

With professional panache she took each call, modelling first the satin lounge pyjamas, following them with a silk nightgown and négligé set in soft peach-coloured silk. The nightgown was so exquisitely designed it could easily have been worn as an evening gown, and she gave the patrons full benefit of its delightful lines by removing the négligé and completing another round.

The teddy, with an ankle-length wrap in matching satin, was left until last and presented as the *pièce de résistance*.

Lexi was the last of the three models to emerge, and she unconsciously lifted her chin a fraction higher as she moved slowly around the room, deliberately not casting so much as a glance in Georg's direction.

'Remove the wrap, darling,' Jacqueline instructed, and Lexi shook her head as she conjured forth a witching smile.

'I prefer a little mystique, Jacqueline.' The wrap had no ties, and she was careful to ensure that the lapels covered each peak of her satin-and-lace-clad breasts. Her long slim legs were beautifully smooth and lightly tanned, and with considerable grace she lifted a hand to her head, released the weight of her hair so that it cascaded in a rippling flow of thick curls down her back, then she held out the edges of her wrap and executed a slow turn before moving towards the changing-room, not caring that she was breaking with one of Jacqueline's preferred rules.

'One thousand dollars.'

No one glimpsed the flash of fury in her lovely golden eyes at the sound of that deep, faintly accented masculine voice, nor the faint tightening of her lips as she heard Jacqueline's subtle teasing and Georg's evocative drawl in response.

Instead she concentrated on changing into her own clothes, and deliberately ignored the other two models' curiosity as she re-fastened her hair into a casually elegant knot at her nape.

She would have given anything to have slipped out of the side-door and make good her escape, but Jacqueline, Lexi knew, preferred her models to mix and mingle for at least ten minutes, during which she presented each with a fashion accessory for donating their time without fee to such a worthy cause.

The social conclusion to the afternoon gave her assistants time to discreetly collect payment and distribute purchases.

Perhaps Georg had already left, Lexi decided darkly, for only the strongest man would opt to stay in a room full of animated chattering women.

She was wrong, of course. Worse, he didn't appear to be even vaguely ill at ease, and she took her time in joining him as she paused to talk with first one guest and then another as she slowly moved towards the door.

Eventually there was nowhere else for her to go, and she tilted her head slightly, centring her attention on the bridge of his aristocratic Grecian nose.

'Georg.' Her voice was a deliberately husky drawl,

and she slanted one eyebrow in a gesture of teasing mockery. 'What *are* you doing here?'

His features creased into a seemingly warm, intimate smile, and his eyes were so dark it was impossible to read their expression. 'I patronise the charity organisation which benefits from this auction,' he informed her, and, lifting a hand, he casually pushed a stray tendril of hair back behind her ear. 'Knowing you were one of the models was sufficient incentive for me to put in a personal appearance.'

Dear heaven, he was good! Too damned good, she decided darkly, aware they were the focus of attention.

How had he known she'd be here this afternoon? David? As close as she was to her brother, she didn't communicate to him her every move. Therefore Georg must have deliberately sought to discover her whereabouts. The thought rankled unbearably.

'Another brilliantly calculated ploy?' Lexi arched with deliberate softness, and saw his eyes narrow fractionally.

'Five minutes,' he cautioned quietly. 'Then we'll leave.'

A slow sweet smile widened her provocatively curved mouth. 'Any longer and I won't be able to sheathe my claws.' She was so angry it was almost impossible to still the faint shakiness of her hand as she accepted a glass of chilled water from a dutiful waitress, and she kept her eyes veiled beneath long fringed lashes in an attempt to hide her true feelings.

If he so much as *dared* to present her with his purchases in front of all these women she'd be hard pressed not to throw them back at him!

A hollow laugh rose and died in her throat. It would be ironic if they weren't for her at all. No matter how much *she* hated him, there could be no doubt he was held in considerable awe by members of the opposite sex.

'You haven't forgotten we're dining with Jonathan this evening?'

Lexi spared him a level glance. 'No.' Thank heaven David would be there to act as a buffer, for sitting through an intimate family dinner would tax her acting ability to its very limit.

'News of our...relationship has reached my mother.' His eyes probed hers, seeing the faint flaring of defiance, the latent anger simmering beneath the surface of her control. 'I have been severely chastised for not having brought you to meet her.'

Her fingers tightened round the stem of her glass, and she took a steadying breath. 'I'm not sure I can stand such devotion to familial duty.'

'Lexi! *Georg!*'

It was too much to hope that they might be left alone, and Lexi had to stop herself from physically flinching as the man at her side altered his stance so that his arm pressed against her shoulder.

'Jacqueline,' he acknowledged. 'How are you?'

'Absolutely fine, darling.' Her smile was genuine, and she case Lexi a warm glance. 'You were outstanding, as always. That touch of originality at the end was quite stunning.' Her eyes lit with a hint of mischievous humour. 'Georg was suitably appreciative.'

'Overwhelmed,' he drawled in musing acknowledgment as he extracted and handed Jacqueline his cheque. 'And understandably anxious for a private encore.'

Lexi was dimly aware of Jacqueline's tinkling laughter as she proffered two gold signature-emblazoned carrier-bags.

'A lovely addition to your wardrobe, darling,' Jacqueline accorded, and, leaning forward, she brushed her lips lightly against Lexi's cheek. 'I couldn't be more delighted.'

Lexi had never felt more like screaming with vexation in her life. Yet she had to smile and pretend that Georg's gift was warmly received. The moment they were alone, she promised herself, she would verbally *slay* him.

'If you'll excuse us, Jacqueline?' Georg said smoothly.

Lexi murmured a farewell and followed it with a captivating smile, then she turned and preceded Georg from the boutique, waiting until they were on the pavement and at least ten paces from its doors before expelling a deep breath.

'You were utterly *impossible*!'

'Where are you parked?'

'Don't you *dare* ignore me!' Frustrated anger filled her voice, and, even though she pitched it low, there could be no doubt as to the extent of her fury.

'I have no intention of ignoring you,' Georg replied with deceptive calm. 'But the footpath of an exclusive shopping centre is hardly the place for a slanging match.' He directed her a look that held infinite mockery. 'Unless, of course, you have no objection to an audience of interested bystanders.'

'Where would you suggest?' she threw vengefully.

'Your apartment,' he drawled. 'After which we'll visit my mother and then join Jonathan for dinner.'

In a moment she'd erupt! 'I'm sure your mother is delightful, but I'd rather delay meeting her for a few days if you don't mind.'

'Ah, but I do mind.' He was so darned imperturbable that she felt like slapping him! 'She is expecting us at five.'

'You can call her and cancel.' Lexi walked quickly along the street in an attempt to out-pace him, and it irked her unbearably that his stride appeared leisurely by comparison.

'She is elderly and very fragile. She is also irascible, speaks her mind, and likes to have command over her children.' His voice held musing affection. 'We tend to indulge her.'

She reached the car park, and crossed to her silver Mercedes. 'Your mother may have issued a royal edict, but right now I've had about as much of you as I can stand.' She extracted her keys and unlocked the door. 'Believe that if I could opt out of dinner tonight with Jonathan, I would!' In one graceful movement she slid in behind the wheel and fired the engine.

Easing the vehicle forward, she sent it moving swiftly towards the exit without sparing so much as a glance in her rear-view mirror, and she headed towards Darling Point, uncaring as to whether he followed or not.

He really was the most insufferable, antagonistic, *frightening* man she'd ever met, Lexi fumed as she reached her apartment block and swept below street level to her allotted parking space.

Within minutes of her entering her apartment the doorbell pealed, and she flung the door open to see Georg's tall frame filling the aperture.

'How did you get past security?' she demanded instantly.

'I produced credentials, and exerted sufficient influence.' He extended two carrier-bags. 'Yours,' he declared with dangerous softness, and her eyes flared brilliantly alive with frustrated rage.

'I can't possibly accept them.'

There was a leashed quality about his stance as he entered the lounge, a silent warning evident that only a fool would choose to disregard. 'Consider them a gift.'

'For which you paid an exorbitant amount,' Lexi vented furiously, 'under the guise of a charitable donation.'

'The purchases were immaterial.'

'The main reason for your appearance at the boutique was abundantly clear,' she accorded bitterly. 'By tomorrow the society grapevine will have relayed every little detail plus embellishment and supposition.'

'Without doubt.'

Her eyes flashed. 'You don't give a damn, do you?'

He looked at her in silence, his gaze unwaveringly direct, and there was an element of ruthlessness apparent when he spoke. 'Go and get changed.'

She drew a deep, angry breath. 'I am not visiting your mother. At least, not today.'

'She's expecting us.'

He made her feel like a recalcitrant child, and she

was neither. 'I don't like domineering, autocratic men who relegate women to second-class citizenship merely because of their sex.' She glimpsed a tiny flare of anger in the depths of his eyes, and chose to ignore it. 'Will you please leave? I'd like to shower and change.'

'What do you imagine I'll do if I stay?' Georg mocked cynically. 'Invade your bedroom and subject you to a display of unbridled passion?'

She managed to hold his gaze, although there was nothing she could do to prevent the soft tinge of pink that coloured her cheeks. Remembering the force of his kiss was sufficient to enable her to imagine precisely how uninhibited his lovemaking would be.

Effecting a careless shrug, she turned and walked towards the hallway, reaching her bedroom with seemingly unhurried steps where she carefully closed the door.

Damn him! Why did he ruffle her composure? Worse, why did she allow him to succeed?

Twenty minutes later she added the last touch to her make-up, then stood back from the mirror to view her image with critical assessment.

The slim-fitting dress of peacock-blue silk accentuated her slight curves, and provided a perfect foil for her dark auburn hair worn in a smooth knot at her nape with a small bow in matching blue.

Perfume, her favourite Givenchy, was sprayed to several pulse-points, then she gathered up her evening-bag and made her way to the lounge.

Georg was standing by the window, and he turned as she entered the room, his eyes conducting a sweeping appraisal that brought forth an unconscious lift of her chin as she issued coolly, 'Shall we go?'

Lexi didn't offer so much as a word as they took the lift down to street level, and she maintained an icy silence as Georg sent the Ferrari east towards Vaucluse.

As much as she wanted to rail against him, there seemed little point in continuing an argument she couldn't win.

Several butterflies inside her stomach began a series of somersaults as Georg eased the Ferrari into a wide circular driveway and brought it to a halt behind a large Mercedes.

'Relax,' he advised quietly as he slipped out from behind the wheel and moved round to open her door, and Lexi directed a brilliant smile at him as she stepped out, and walked at his side towards the imposing entrance.

'I'm perfectly relaxed,' she assured. Her eyes challenged his—wide, gold and apparently guileless.

The front door opened and they were welcomed inside by a formally suited man whose demeanour was politely deferential. 'The family are assembled in the lounge, if you would care to go through.'

Georg smiled at the butler. 'Thanks, Nathaniel.'

Lexi drew a calming breath, and drew courage from the strength of her convictions.

'Georgiou! You are late! Everyone else is here!'

A tiny figure attired entirely in black was the visual attestation of an elderly matriarch, and despite her advanced years her eyes were surprisingly alert behind gold-rimmed glasses as she sat rigidly upright in a straight-backed chair.

Lexi proffered a conciliatory smile. 'The fault is mine.'

The dark brown eyes sharpened and conducted a swift analytical assessment. 'Indeed?'

'Georg informed me less than an hour ago that you were expecting us.' Her eyebrows rose fractionally and she effected a deprecatory gesture with her hands. 'I had just finished a modelling assignment and I needed to go home and change.'

'Georgiou, are you not going to introduce this young woman to us all?'

'Of course, Mama,' Georg conceded with lazy humour. 'Lexi Harrison.'

'Lexi? What name is that?'

'My mother's favoured derivation of Alexis,' she informed her calmly, refusing to be fazed in the slightest.

'You are divorced.'

'Yes, I am.' What was this—an inquisition, for heaven's sake?

'Mama,' Georg admonished with musing indolence. 'You presume too much.'

'I agree,' a deep voice drawled, and an older version of Georg moved forward, his smile warm and welcoming. 'Lexi, how are you?'

'Alex,' Lexi acknowledged, allowing her answering smile to encompass the slim attractive-looking woman at his side.

'My wife Samantha,' he introduced. 'And this,' he paused to indicate the little girl cradled in the curve of his arm, 'is our daughter Leanne.'

'She's beautiful,' Lexi complimented, for it was

true. The wide-eyed sable-haired imp was utterly adorable.

'Yes,' Alex agreed, and his eyes settled on his wife with such infinite warmth that Lexi almost caught her breath. 'I am a very fortunate man.'

'Anna and Nick are not able to be here,' Mrs Nicolaos informed them. 'Tomorrow night we will have a celebratory dinner.' Her eyes did not leave Lexi for a second. 'Precisely what do you model, young woman, and when and where did you meet Georgiou?'

The elderly woman was persistent, and 'irascible' wasn't the right word! 'Clothes,' Lexi answered with every semblance of outward calm. 'The winter, spring, summer and autumn collections of well-known designers; photographic stills for fashion magazines, and the occasional television commercial.' It wasn't in her nature to be outrageous, but the temptation to shock was irresistible. 'I don't pose in the nude, nor do I resort to the type of photography that portrays women in a state of provocative dishabille.'

Mrs Nicolaos didn't bat so much as an eyelid. 'Of course not. Your father would have disowned you.'

Lexi effected a slight moue in silent agreement. 'I met your son—'

'At a party,' Georg intervened smoothly. 'Lexi was accompanied by her brother.'

'Hmm. I do not approve of divorce.'

'Neither do I,' Lexi responded evenly. 'If I'd had any sense I would have lived in sin instead of opting for marriage. Then I could have walked away relatively unscathed.'

'And Georgiou? Do you intend walking away from him?'

This was getting worse by the minute! 'I would walk away from any man who mistreated me,' she said quietly. 'Whether he was your son or not.'

There was a palpable silence during which Lexi held the older woman's direct gaze, and for a brief moment she glimpsed a softening in those dark eyes before they moved to settle on her youngest son.

'Georgiou, open the champagne. Alexandros, relinquish my granddaughter so that she may sit with me a while.'

Leanne, who surely should have been terrified of her grandmother, ran to her side the instant Alex set her down on her feet, and the transformation on Mrs Nicolaos's face was unbelievable as Leanne caught hold of her hand. The elderly woman spoke softly in Greek, and the child gazed at her in open adoration.

'She's a darling,' Samantha said gently, interpreting Lexi's glance. 'She also guards her family like a lioness. If it's any consolation, she attempted to tear me apart the first time Alex brought me here.'

'Champagne,' Georg announced, handing Samantha and Lexi each a slim crystal flute, while Alex crossed to his mother's side.

'Sit down. Why is everyone standing?' Mrs Nicolaos demanded, directing both Alex and Georg a fierce look.

'Out of deference to you, Mama,' Alex declared gently. 'If it pleases you for us to be seated, then we shall do so for a short while. Then we will leave, and you must rest.'

'Bah! I am not an invalid!'

'You are infinitely precious to us all. That is why our visits are designed not to overtax your strength.' Alex leaned forward and brushed his lips against the lined cheek. 'Now, shall we have our champagne?'

It was almost six when they made their farewells, and, seated in the Ferrari, Lexi leaned back against the head-rest as Georg fired the engine and eased the car down the driveway behind Alex's Mercedes.

'You didn't tell me it was going to be the Nicolaos family *en masse*,' she berated him the instant the car entered the street.

He gave her a dark, penetrating glance before returning his attention to the road. 'Does it matter that Alex and Samantha were there?'

'This whole thing is beginning to getting out of hand,' she retaliated, hating the degree of deception involved. In the beginning it had seemed relatively uncomplicated, and now she wasn't so sure.

'Yet you were aware when you agreed that it was all or nothing,' Georg reminded her silkily.

'At the time I had little conception of what "all" would involve,' Lexi opined drily.

Only a few blocks separated his mother's home from Jonathan's exclusive residence, and they reached the elegant tudor-styled mansion in less than five minutes.

David's Ferrari was nowhere in sight, and Lexi wasn't sure whether to be relieved or disappointed at being the first to arrive.

'Before we go inside I suggest you slip this on.'

'This' was a brilliant square diamond set on a slender gold band, and she looked at him in consternation. 'You can't be serious?'

'Very.'

'Don't you think it's taking things a bit too far?'

'If we've been keeping our affair under wraps until your divorce was finalised, now that we've gone public surely the next logical step is a formal announcement of our forthcoming marriage?'

'*No.*'

'You don't think Jonathan will rest easy until he has proof that my intentions are honourable?'

Her eyes glittered with unspoken rage as he calmly slid the ring on to her finger. 'Damn you,' she accorded bitterly.

'Shall we go in?' There was an edge of mockery apparent. 'I imagine Sophie has heard us arrive, and your father will be curious as to why we're taking so long.'

CHAPTER FOUR

JONATHAN greeted them at the door, and Lexi returned his affectionate embrace with enthusiasm, smiling as he put her at arm's length.

'Come inside. I thought we'd relax out on the terrace. David will be delayed by about ten minutes, and Sophie has organised dinner for six-thirty.'

Home. The house where she had grown up, she mused as she followed Jonathan indoors. It was amazing how secure she felt within these walls, how protected.

It took only a few minutes for him to notice the significance of the ring on her finger. His pleasure brought her close to tears, and she could hardly protest when he brought out a bottle of Dom Perignon to celebrate the occasion.

'I'm delighted to have you both as my guests.'

The genuineness of her father's enthusiasm couldn't be doubted, and Lexi managed a suitable smile in response.

Georg, damn him, stayed close to her side, and even David's arrival did little to diminish his attention.

The warmth of his smile appeared so honest it was all she could do not to reel from its impact, and she was forced to suffer the touch of his hand on her elbow as he led her into dinner.

Sophie served the first course, a delicious beef consommé, and followed it with deep-fried prawns in a nest of finely shredded lettuce. The main course was a superb duck *à l'orange* with tiny roast potatoes, honeyed carrots, courgettes and beans.

David took care to ensure that the appropriate wine accompanied each course, although Lexi sipped at the contents of her glass and declined to have it refilled, opting for chilled water instead.

Conversation flowed, touching on a variety of subjects that pertained primarily to business and mutual acquaintances, and to all intents and purposes it appeared to be a convivial family gathering.

It proved, Lexi perceived a trifle wryly, what excellent actors they were.

'When do you go into hospital, Daddy?' It was a question she had to ask, and there was nothing she could do to mask her anxiety.

'Sunday week, darling,' Jonathan revealed gently. 'Surgery is scheduled for the following day.'

'You've always been so careful, eating the right foods, not smoking, exercising each day. I can't believe something like this could happen to you.'

'Let's admit it, Father is a human dynamo,' David declared with a slow smile. 'Always accepting a new challenge, fighting to make it succeed. Continually pitting his wits against unforeseen obstacles.'

Lexi captured her father's eyes and held them with her own. 'I think you'd better re-evaluate your life and slow down.' Without thought, she added with a light laugh, 'I want you around to appreciate your grandchildren.'

'Indeed,' Georg acceded with musing enthusiasm, and there was nothing Lexi could do in protest as he lifted her hand to his lips to kiss each finger in turn—a deliberately blatant gesture that taxed all her strength not to snatch her hand from his grasp.

'Grandchildren,' Jonathan repeated bemusedly. 'I like that idea.'

'You'll forgive me if I agree,' Georg declared with a husky chuckle, leaving no one in any doubt just where his thoughts lay.

Lexi reached out and deliberately traced the tip of her highly polished fingernail across the back of his left hand as she directed him a brilliantly warm smile. 'Steady, darling. I've only just accepted your engagement ring.'

As if sensing her protest Georg lifted a hand and his gaze was infinitely disturbed as he touched a finger to her lips. 'Something which has made me a very happy man.'

She wanted to *kill* him. Yet all she could do was smile.

'Have you made any plans for the wedding?'

'We thought a quiet affair, confined to family and close friends. Five weeks from now,' Georg indicated, and, on hearing Lexi's slightly audible gasp, he leant forward and bestowed a fleeting kiss on her as she opened her mouth to protest. 'If I had my way we'd obtain a special licence and marry within a matter of days.'

How could he sit there and announce such a thing? Lexi was so utterly furious that it was a wonder she didn't erupt with rage.

He turned towards Jonathan, totally ignoring her. 'That will give you time to recuperate sufficiently from surgery. Are you happy to leave all the arrangements to me?'

Her father couldn't have looked more delighted. 'Of course. I can't begin to tell you both how happy this makes me. Now I can enter hospital with a clear mind, knowing that if anything happens Lexi will be taken care of by someone who has my utmost respect.'

Oh, dear lord! After such fulsome enthusiasm how could she possibly refute it? Lexi groaned with frustration. But how far did it have to go? Surely specific arrangements for a wedding were hardly necessary?

'A church wedding, darling?'

'I don't think so, Daddy,' she negated quietly. 'I had all that before.' She lifted a hand and smoothed back a stray tendril of hair in a purely defensive gesture.

'The gardens are lovely—so colourful at this time of year,' Jonathan enthused. 'Would you consider marrying at home?'

'A marvellous idea,' Georg conceded, slanting Lexi such a warm glance that she almost reeled from its implied intimacy. 'Early afternoon? Followed by champagne and hors-d'oeuvres. Unless there is any objection, I would prefer the reception to be held in the restaurant. It is regarded as something of a family tradition, and would give my mother immense pleasure.'

The tension robbed her of her appetite, and she declined dessert and the cheeseboard, and opted instead for coffee laced with liqueur and cream.

Consequently her nerves had tightened almost to breaking point by the time they took their leave.

'Take good care of Lexi for me,' Jonathan bade Georg as he escorted them to the door.

'I fully intend to,' Georg declared with quiet emphasis, and Lexi was forced to suffer his arm about her waist as he led her down to the car.

Almost as soon as they were clear of the driveway she burst into angry, voluble speech.

'Did you *have* to be so—' she paused as words momentarily failed her '—proprietorial?' Her fingers clenched until the knuckles showed white as she gripped the clasp of her evening-bag. 'You sat there so damned *calmly*, looking at me as if...' She trailed to a frustrated halt, loath to say what Georg had no compunction in voicing.

'I couldn't wait to get you home and into bed?' he completed in a drawling tone, adding with cynical mockery, 'Is it so surprising that I might want to?'

'Discussing a wedding and prospective grand-children!' Outrage brought her anger to boiling point. 'It was totally ridiculous!'

'If I remember correctly, it was you who brought up the subject of grandchildren,' he alluded in droll tones, and she clenched her hands in an effort not to physically *hit* him!

'What on earth do you think you're *doing*, for heaven's sake?'

'Driving you home.'

An impossible fury rose within. 'Don't be face-tious!'

'We'll discuss it rationally over coffee.'

'You're being deliberately evasive, skilfully utilising boardroom tactics to avoid the issue!' she accused heatedly.

'I am merely attempting to defuse your temper sufficiently until I'm in a position to satisfactorily deal with it.'

'Don't you dare patronise me. I won't stand for it!'

He didn't respond, and she sat in angry silence for several seconds before turning towards him. 'Stop the car. I'll hail a taxi.' She was so incensed that she reached for the door-handle without even caring that the car was travelling along the main arterial road towards Rose Bay.

'Don't be a fool!'

His words were harsh, demanding obedience, and she instinctively braced her body as he brought the Ferrari to a smooth halt alongside the kerb.

The handle refused to function, and she pulled at it fruitlessly for a number of seconds before becoming aware that he'd activated the locking mechanism.

'Release it, damn you!'

'I will, when you've calmed down,' Georg voiced implacably, switching off the engine and turning sideways to face her.

Incensed almost beyond endurance, she turned and lashed out at him, an action that was swiftly stilled as he caught hold of her hands and held them in a bone-crushing grip.

'You unspeakable fiend!' Topaz eyes glittered with fury as she made a futile attempt to break free.

His hands tightened, and she cried out in pain. 'You'll only succeed in hurting yourself.'

Part of her was appalled by the enormity of her actions while the other deplored the extent of her behaviour. 'Then let me go.'

His hard, intent stare played havoc with her nerve-ends, and she stifled a silent scream at the strength of purpose in those chilling depths. 'Your hands, yes,' he agreed, relinquishing them, and she rubbed them to ease the bruised bones.

She felt like a steel rope that had been rendered taut almost to breaking point. At any second she was in danger of snapping. Her mouth quivered as she drew a deep calming breath, and her hands shook uncontrollably.

'Perhaps you would care to tell me why you react so violently at the thought that a man might want to make love to you?'

Her thoughts scattered into a deep dark void where she couldn't retrieve them, and she stared blankly out of the windscreen, unable to summon her voice through the physical lump that had risen in her throat.

No one, not even Jonathan—dear lord, especially not Jonathan—knew just how deep were the scars from her association with Paul. The night she'd left him would be indelibly imprinted in her brain for as long as she lived. The explosive argument, one of many they'd had over money, had resulted in her expressing an intention to leave him and had ended in physical abuse of the worst kind. Paul had forced her to submit to sex, and afterwards she'd simply pulled on some clothes and ordered a taxi to take her to a motel. The next day she'd rung Jonathan and David and told them the marriage was over.

Lexi had little idea of the passage of time. It could have been five minutes or fifteen; she retained no recollection. At last she moved her head slightly, and her pale profile stood out in sharp contrast against the night's darkness.

'There's a beach not far from here. I'd like to walk for a while.'

Her voice sounded strangely quiet, almost disembodied, and she wasn't conscious of him reaching for the ignition until she heard the refined purr of the engine.

She sat in silence as he traversed the distance then pulled to a halt alongside a short flight of steps leading down on to the sandy foreshore.

Georg slid out from behind the wheel and walked round to open her door, watching with narrowed eyes as she slipped off her shoes.

He followed her actions, pushing the elegant hand-crafted imported shoes on to the floor before bending low to turn up the cuffs of his trousers. Then he straightened and locked the car, taking care to activate the alarm before moving to the head of the steps where he stood, impossibly tall and vaguely forbidding, silhouetted against the skyline.

The stretch of beach appeared deserted, and she longed for solitude. 'I can walk on my own.'

'I go with you, or you don't go at all,' Georg declared inflexibly.

Without a further word she moved past him, and, once down on the sand, she wandered out towards the gentle out-going tide, then began following its edge as the bay curved towards an outcrop of rocks.

There was a faint breeze, and she felt it tease loose a few strands of hair so that they brushed against her face.

The sand was wet beneath her bare feet, and there was just the soft sound of water lapping gently against the distant rocks. Every now and then a car sped past on the road, but the noise was far enough away not to intrude.

Somehow she expected Georg to attempt conversation, but he walked at her side in silence, and she was grateful for his perception.

On reaching the rocks, they turned as if by tacit agreement and began retracing their steps. Lexi felt the cool air on her face, and in an unbidden gesture she lifted her hand to her hair and freed the knot so that its length fell down her shoulders.

A sense of peace invaded her being, rather like the calm after a storm, and she tried to tell herself that it had nothing to do with the man at her side.

Instinct warned her that he was someone she would infinitely prefer to have as a friend than an enemy, for in opposition he'd prove a formidable force.

A slight shiver shook her slim frame, although it had nothing to do with feeling cold, and she gave a start of surprise when he shrugged off his jacket and placed it around her shoulders.

His fingers brushed her nape as he lifted her hair free, and Lexi spared him a quick glance, unable to read anything from his expression, and her murmured thanks sounded indistinct on the night air.

For some strange reason she felt as if she'd been enveloped in a security blanket, and she wasn't sure whether to feel alarmed or relieved.

The smooth jacket-lining was silky against her skin, and still held the warmth from his body. It was far too big for her, and its weight brought an awareness of his height and breadth. Evident, too, was the clean smell of the fine woollen material and the elusive woody tones of his cologne.

They reached the short flight of steps leading up
on to the road far too quickly, and after dusting sand
from their feet they each retrieved their shoes prior to
sliding into the car.

Within a matter of minutes the Ferrari drew to a
halt in the courtyard adjoining her apartment block,
and she was powerless to prevent him from following
her indoors.

Any argument seemed futile, and she simply
extracted her key while they took the lift to her
designated floor.

'Coffee?'

Lexi closed her eyes, then slowly opened them
again in utter frustration. 'If you want coffee, *you*
make it!'

He took the key from her fingers and unlocked the
door, then he pushed her gently inside. 'I fully intend
to,' he drawled. 'I merely asked if you would like
some.'

'Oh—go to hell!'

His eyes speared hers, dark and fathoms deep with
the silent threat of an emotion she didn't even begin
to comprehend. 'Believe that I could take you there,
and you would hate every second of it.'

Her whole body froze in seemingly slow motion,
and her eyes became wide as they assumed a haunted,
hunted quality. A glaze seemed to dull their expression as she stared sightlessly ahead, oblivious to her
surroundings, the man a few feet distant—*everything*
except a vivid event that would never be erased from
her memory.

When he lifted a hand towards her she visibly
flinched and averted her head to one side, instinc-

tively shielding her face with her hands, and therefore missing the brief hardness that flared in his eyes.

'*Cristos!*' The harsh, softly husked oath sounded savage in the silence of the room, but it barely registered. He made a compulsive movement, then checked it as he demanded in a dangerously soft voice, 'Did Paul *hit* you?'

She blinked slowly, and the glaze gradually dissipated. A shiver shook her slender frame, and she hugged her arms together across her breasts in an attempt to contain it.

'Answer me, Lexi.'

The quietness of his voice didn't deceive her, and she stood, hesitant, loath to resurrect that fateful night.

'Yes.'

'Nothing more?'

She looked at him fearlessly as the silence between them became a palpable entity. Her breath hurt in her throat, constricting it almost beyond the ability to speak. 'Does it matter?'

She sensed his inner rage as he murmured something viciously explicit in his own language, and her chin lifted in an unbidden gesture as she sought a measure of strength.

'I think I'd like that coffee,' she indicated, meeting his compelling gaze with courage and dignity.

Georg's stance didn't alter for several heart-stopping seconds, then he turned and made his way towards the kitchen.

When he returned he placed a tall handled glass into her hands. 'Drink all of it.'

Lexi tasted the contents, and effected a faint grimace in recognition of the measure of brandy he'd added to the cream-topped brew. She almost never touched spirits, and it was more than a year since she'd had to resort to taking the occasional sleeping-pill. Obediently she sipped until the glass was empty, then set it down on a nearby table.

'Would you mind leaving now? It's late, and I'd like to go to bed.'

He slowly drained his glass, then held it between his hands. 'Have lunch with me tomorrow.'

'Today,' Lexi corrected absently. 'And no, I think I'd rather be alone.' The beginnings of a faint smile tugged one edge of her mouth. 'We're dining with your mother. I'll need to harness all my resources.'

'My family is not in the least formidable.'

She moved towards the lobby, and paused by the front door. 'That's a matter of opinion.'

Gentle fingers lifted her chin, and her lashes swiftly lowered as she felt his fingertips trace the outline of her mouth. Beneath his feather-light touch she was unable to control the slight trembling, and she stood very still as he brushed his lips against her temple.

'Be ready at six.'

As soon as he had gone she locked up and moved back into the lounge, activating the television set in a bid to discover a programme that would catch her interest until exhaustion set in and provided an escape into oblivion.

CHAPTER FIVE

LEXI chose to wear a stunning gown in emerald-green silk, its smooth lines hugging the delicate curves of her breasts, her waist, then flaring out from the hips to fall in generous folds to calf-length. Matching shoes and evening-bag completed the outfit, and her make-up was deliberately understated. In a last-minute decision she opted to leave her hair loose, using side-clips to hold its thick length away from her face.

The doorbell chimed just as she emerged into the lounge, and she moved quickly towards the lobby to answer its summons.

Georg stood framed in the aperture, attired in an immaculate dark suit and white linen shirt, and exuding a combination of dynamic masculinity and raw virility. 'Punctuality is one of your virtues,' he greeted her with a slow disturbing smile, and Lexi effected a faint shrug.

'Not always. Shall we leave?'

George headed the Ferrari towards Double Bay and slid to a halt adjacent to the shopping centre.

'Why are you stopping here?'

'Quite simply because this is where we're dining.'

'The restaurant? I thought we were dining with your mother,' Lexi said, faintly perplexed at the change in plan.

'Mama suggested that we celebrate according to

Greek tradition,' Georg informed her smoothly. 'So tonight the restaurant is closed to all but family and close friends.'

'A party?'

'Specifically to celebrate our forthcoming marriage.'

She felt the nerves in her stomach clench in painful rejection. 'This entire débâcle gets worse with every passing day,' she opined wretchedly.

His appraisal was swiftly analytical as he raked her slim form. 'Relax.'

'How can I relax?' she retorted. 'Your family and friends will examine and dissect my every word as they attempt to determine whether I'm worthy of acceptance into the Nicolaos clan.'

'There can be no doubt that they will approve my choice,' he mocked, and she gave a short laugh.

'No one would dare oppose you.'

'You do,' he drawled.

'Only because you have the ability to make me impossibly angry!'

'We're almost there,' Georg declared imperturbably.

'And it's smile-time,' she said with a trace of bitterness.'

'You do it so well.'

'Oh, stop being so damned cynical!' She was almost at the end of her tether, and being faced with the prospect of a celebratory party where they would be the focus of attention was almost more than she could bear.

Yet somehow she managed to portray a combination of gracious sincerity and suitable bewitchment with the youngest Nicolaos son.

There was a variety of food to tempt the most critical palate, and sufficient of it to feed an army. Beneath Georg's persuasive touch, Lexi sampled several delicacies and followed it with a light white wine.

At times she thought she was a little over the top, and Georg merely compounded the situation by playing the part of adoring lover to the hilt.

Her ring was admired and commented upon, and inevitably the question arose as to a possible wedding date.

'The end of January,' Georg revealed, and laughed softly at Lexi's obvious surprise. 'Do you blame me? I have no intention of allowing her to slip through my fingers.'

'And the honeymoon?'

'Greece. Where else?'

Where else, indeed?

'Are you *mad*?' Lexi demanded in a subdued voice the instant they had a moment alone. To any onlookers they must appear a loving couple, drifting close together on the dance-floor. Bouzoukis played softly in the background a haunting melody that seemed filled with pathos, as were many of the Greek songs.

'All of these people are very dear friends,' Georg murmured close to her ear.

'There can be no mistake that they imagine this to be an engagement party.' She was so angry that her whole body shook with it. 'They've brought gifts, which will have to be returned. And why did you have to give out a wedding date?'

'In a few minutes the music will change. The

women will sit at the tables and watch as the men take to the floor and dance.'

Lexi looked at him with helpless frustration. 'Including you?'

'Especially me,' he informed cynically, 'in an attempt to convince everyone I am a strong virile man who will promise his prospective wife many fine sons to carry the Nicolaos name.'

'The dance is a feat of strength?'

'Symbolic endurance,' George drawled, and his dark eyes gleamed with amusement as twin flags of colour stained her cheeks. 'Come, you will sit with my mother, Anna and Samantha.'

'I'll probably walk straight out the door.'

'Be sure that I will follow and drag you back.'

The threat of his intent was without doubt, and, unbidden, her eyes moved to rest on the sensual curve of his mouth, widening slightly and assuming momentary vulnerability in memory of the havoc he'd wrought the previous evening.

His gaze narrowed, then he lowered his head down to hers.

No one could possibly have heard what they were saying, and there wasn't one guest present who doubted the reason behind the brief seemingly passionate kiss the prospective bridegroom bestowed on his bride-to-be in the middle of the dance-floor before leading her to sit in the bosom of his family as the music assumed a traditional slow lilting beat.

Lexi sat perfectly still, a smile fixed permanently in place, as each of the men removed their jackets and rolled back their shirt-sleeves before taking up their positions on the dance-floor.

Together, with arms outstretched and in perfect unison, they began to move in time to the music, their steps quickening as the beat slowly increased, until only the very fit were able to sustain the rapid tempo.

Alex and Anna's husband Nick remained with Georg, as well as a few of the younger men, and Lexi found herself unconsciously holding her breath as the impossible beat continued.

There was a crash of broken crockery as a plate hit the wooden floor, quickly followed by another, until it was difficult to distinguish the sound of each plate.

'Lexi. Here is one for you.'

Turning, she saw the proffered plate extended in Samantha's hand.

'Throw it as a gesture of appreciation.'

'You're joking.'

'It will be noticed if you don't,' Samantha cautioned softly. 'By everyone.'

'Greek tradition?'

A mischievous smile lit Samantha's beautiful features. 'Feminine enthusiasm.'

Taking the plate, Lexi looked at Georg and calmly threw it on to the floor. For her it was a gesture of suppressed anger, and, without thinking, she picked up another for good measure and sent it following in the path of the first.

It was only when she had another plate pressed into her hand that she realised the significance of the numbers thrown.

Georg, damn him, merely laughed, his dark eyes alive with devilish humour, and Lexi wanted to curl up and die as Mrs Nicolaos took up a plate and extended it.

To refuse would have been incredibly rude, and, forcing a smile, she took it and sent it crashing to the floor.

'Well done,' Samantha accorded softly. 'You've now been officially accepted into the family.'

The music reached a crescendo, then abruptly stopped, and Lexi soon saw why as several waiters with brooms appeared and began clearing up the debris, while the men had glasses of wine pressed into their hands to quench their thirst.

It wasn't long before the bouzoukis were taken up again, and this time the men fetched their womenfolk on to the dance-floor.

Georg's skin felt warm beneath her fingers, his arms hard with corded muscle, and there was nothing Lexi could do to prevent being held close in against his body. She could feel the powerful beat of his heart, and sense the musky aroma of his cologne.

'Soon Alex and Samantha will take Mama home, then gradually everyone will leave,' Georg informed her as he led her among the dancing couples.

'Your mother is amazing,' she told him.

'Be sure that she has rested all day, and tomorrow will not be permitted to rise from her bed.'

'You're extremely protective of her.'

'Mama is a very special woman,' he accorded quietly. 'Her husband, his dreams; the children, and now the grandchildren. Together they have been her reason for living.' She sensed his faint smile. 'You have her approval.'

'Should I feel flattered?'

'Without question.'

'I wonder why,' Lexi mused. 'Could it be because

I stand up for myself, and don't pretend you're God and any number of sacred saints all rolled into one?'

He slanted her a wry look that was tempered with humour. 'Perhaps she sees, as I do, a girl whose inner beauty surpasses her physical attributes.'

The breath caught in her throat. 'I don't think either of you knows me well enough to reach an adequate conclusion.'

'No?'

She felt defeated, and stiffened slightly as his lips brushed her temple. 'Please don't.'

'What a contrary combination of words,' Georg mocked. 'The first encourages, while the second is a refusal.'

'Perhaps I unconsciously chose them because I am a contrary creature!'

Gently he withdrew his arms, and her eyes reflected the sudden loss of security before she successfully masked their expression. 'Alex is about to leave with Mama,' he informed. 'Come, we will bid them good-night, then stand together and thank our guests as they leave.'

It was an hour before they were able to get away, and in the car Lexi simply leaned well back and let her head sink against the head-rest. As Georg fired the engine, she closed her eyes, and didn't open them until he brought the car to a standstill outside the entrance to her apartment block.

'There's no need for you to come in.'

'Nevertheless, I will see you safely indoors.'

It was far too late to protest, and she was overcome with helpless frustration as she passed through the entrance lobby *en route* to the lifts.

'Don't you ever *listen*?' she burst out scant minutes later as he withdrew her set of keys, selected one and inserted it into the lock of her apartment.

'Always.'

'Then why are you *here*?'

He took time to close the door carefully before turning back to face her. 'Would you believe— because I want to be?'

Lexi closed her eyes, then slowly opened them again. 'Doesn't it matter that *I* don't want you here?'

He reached forward and brushed his fingers lightly along the edge of her jaw, then slipped to cup her chin. 'Precisely what are you afraid of?' Georg queried with cynical mockery, and her eyes assumed the hue of brilliant gold.

'Will you please leave? I'm tired and I want to go to bed.'

'Are you working tomorrow?'

'No. I intend sleeping in, then taking a picnic lunch to the beach, where I can enjoy a few hours of un- interrupted solitude.'

'In preparation for the party we're to attend tomorrow evening,' he drawled, and, leaning forward, he kissed her on the mouth, a hard, passionate possession that left her wide-eyed and faintly hurt. 'Sweet dreams, Lexi.'

Then he turned and left, closing the door quietly behind him.

Lexi chose a beach more than an hour's drive north of the city, and, with Christmas only a matter of days away, there were very few people electing to spend valuable shopping time lazing on a sandy foreshore.

For a number of hours she simply stretched out beneath the shade of a beach umbrella and read a thick paperback, then she applied a liberal dose of sunscreen and cautiously exposed herself to the sun's rays for a short space of time.

At four she packed everything into the boot of the Mercedes and drove back to Darling Point, where she showered and shampooed her hair in preparation for the evening ahead.

The party was a perfectly splendid affair, Lexi mused as she stood with apparent ease at Georg's side in a sumptuously appointed lounge of a harbourside mansion noted for being one of the city's finest. The guests numbered among the social élite, and each of the women appeared to have spent several hours, if not the entire day, on their appearance, so exquisitely perfect were their hairstyles and make-up. Collectively their designer clothes would have cost a small fortune, and a king's ransom was represented in jewellery.

She took a small sip of an innocuously mild spritzer, then gave a faint start of surprise as she saw Anaïs Pembleton moving determinedly towards them.

'Lexi, *darling*, how are you?' Without pausing for breath, the society matron greeted Georg. 'I'm so pleased you've managed to persuade this beautiful, beautiful girl back on to the social scene.'

'Anaïs,' Georg acknowledged, his expression politely bland.

'Congratulations are in order, I hear. May one ask when the wedding is to take place?'

'Oh, there's no hurry,' Lexi hastened to reply

swiftly, only to be caught by Georg's look of musing indulgence.

'I am not a patient man,' he offered with a warm smile. 'If I had my way it would be tomorrow.'

Lexi seethed in silence, angry beyond belief at Georg's deliberate ploy. The sound of the society matron's laughter was the living end, and she gave into temptation and uttered sweetly, 'You know what they say about "once bitten, twice shy".'

'Oh, yes, darling. But this time, surely it's different?' The emphasis was there, and it succeeded in rousing her temper almost to boiling point. 'I mean, Georg is impossibly rich, whereas Paul…'

There was a faint pause, and Lexi finished with seeming sweetness, 'Was a Lothario and a leech?' Her eyes contained a dangerous sparkle. 'Why not say it to my face, Anaïs? It's no secret that it's been said behind my back.'

There was a faint gasp, then the older woman drew herself up to her full height as she mentally bore down on the slim young girl facing up to her with far more courage than she'd ever imagined possible. 'My dear Lexi,' she purred softly, 'you're surely not accusing me of anything?'

Lexi's smile was the epitome of innocence. 'Now why should you imagine that?'

'I am no rumour-monger,' Anaïs Pembleton assured with chilling hauteur.

'Merely a purveyor of purported fact.' Lexi attempted to defuse the strength of her stinging words with a solemn and faintly sad smile. 'If you'll excuse me, I really must powder my nose.' There was no need for any part of her exquisitely made-up features to be retouched, but if she didn't escape now she'd end up saying something totally regrettable.

The powder-room was empty, and Lexi withdrew several tissues, dampened them, then pressed the refreshingly cool pads against both temples before standing back to examine her features.

Her eyes looked incredibly large and luminous, and there were twin flags of colour high on each cheekbone. Her mouth looked far too full. Luscious, she decided, twisting the curved edges into an expression of self-derision.

She possessed the kind of looks most girls would have killed for, and a figure that was the envy of any self-respecting female. Nature, she accorded, had certainly been extremely gracious in her endowment. Add a successful career, bankability, considerable assets, and it all added up to something that was almost too good to be true.

On an impulse she lifted her hands and tore out the restraining pins from her hair, letting its length cascade down her back in a glorious thick mass of curls.

Gone was the slender-necked society belle with her air of fragility, for now Lexi resembled a contender in the promiscuity stakes.

A quirk of amusement lifted the edge of her lips. It was amazing what a different hairstyle and a change in expression could do! It remained to be seen whether Georg would appreciate the difference.

There was a gleam of defiance in her eyes as she entered the lounge, and she saw him at once, standing tall in a group of elegantly suited men.

It was marvellous how men gravitated towards

each other on the pretext of discussing business. Jonathan was a prime example, as was David.

Perhaps it was time to give Georg a taste of his own medicine. A social occasion was meant to be exactly that—social, she determined, as she threaded her way through the guests to where he stood. And *she* could play charades equally as well as he could!

Deep in conversation, he turned slightly, then his gaze narrowed fractionally as he caught sight of her.

'Darling,' Lexi greeted, a deceptively soft smile parting her mouth as she placed fingers on the sleeve of his jacket. 'I'm dying of thirst.' Her eyes were wide and deep as she gazed up at him. 'Would you mind getting me another drink?'

'Of course,' Georg acceded as he excused himself from the group. 'Wine, or something stronger?'

'Stronger, definitely.'

'That bad?' he quizzed lightly. 'You sound as if you're planning an escape.'

Her lashes swept high and wide, and she attempted a singularly sweet smile. 'Only cowards cut and run, and I won't allow Anaïs Pembleton the pleasure.'

His gleaming gaze did strange things to her equilibrium. 'Then why not forgo the drink, and we'll drift out on to the terrace and dance?'

Lexi swallowed the sudden lump that had risen in her throat. 'No, I don't think so.'

'Afraid, *darling*?'

Her chin lifted fractionally. 'Of you, Georg?' She tilted her head slightly in the pretence of examining his features. 'You're so shockingly powerful, one derives the impression you have only to blink and the markets tremble. Yet I don't fear you.'

'Perhaps you should.'

Her eyes didn't waver. 'If you don't want to fetch me a drink I'll get one myself.'

Without a word he moved towards the bar, and returned with a vodka and orange juice.

'Did Jonathan never spank you as a child?' he queried mildly as she took the glass from his hand.

'He never had to,' Lexi retorted swiftly.

His mouth curved into a musing smile. 'The perfect juvenile, hmm? Picture-book pretty, with a complexion like porcelain, and impossibly long auburn hair bound in plaits.'

'Talk to David. He'll tell you I walked in his shadow, always wanting to play.'

'Did he allow you to?'

'Most of the time,' she answered, quietly reflective, yet her voice held a tinge of wryness. 'All his friends thought I was cute, and I survived puberty without braces or acne.'

'Is it such a handicap being beautiful?' he queried with soft cynicism, and she shot him a dark pensive glance.

'Sometimes I could scream for people to see beyond the façade, to be liked for *me*, everything that is Alexis Honore Harrison. Not simply Jonathan Harrison's daughter, or David Harrison's sister. Or even Lexi Harrison, model.' She effected a helpless shrug. 'There was a time when I thought of hiring a four-wheel drive and travelling north to Kakadu Reserve,' she continued broodingly as she sipped from her glass.

'Tracking kangaroos and crocodiles, dressed in khaki and wearing an akubra hat?' He lifted a hand

and touched the tip of his forefinger to the edge of her nose. 'Living life in the rough and exposing this beautiful skin to the heat and dust and other unmentionable elements.' His finger slid down to the curve of her upper lip, then gently traced its outline. 'The trouble with running away is that eventually you have to return. And the problems you wanted to escape from still remain. It's better to stay and deal with them.' His smile was warm and completely disarming. 'Believe me.'

It was impossible to still the faint trembling of her mouth. 'You sound like Jonathan and David.'

He reached out and caught her arm in a light clasp. 'Come out on to the terrace. It's cooler, and we can talk without half the room watching our every move.'

He was weaving a subtle magical spell, and the crazy thing was that she drew great comfort from the touch of his hand. It was almost as if he represented a large stable rock to which she could cling, and be safe from the storm-tossed sea threatening to engulf her. Yet that in itself was a parody, for Georg Nicolaos represented a far bigger threat than she'd ever encountered, and she wasn't sure precisely how she was going to deal with it.

He was right, she accorded a few minutes later. The terrace was cooler, and it was nothing less than sheer bliss to be free of the surreptitious glances and the mild exasperation of knowing she was the subject of conjecture.

'Shall we dance?'

'Must we?'

He took the glass from her hand and placed it down on the wide ledge of the balustrading. 'I think so. I shan't bite,' he drawled with hateful mockery, and she stiffened as he drew her close.

'If you even dared,' Lexi warned with soft vehemence, 'I'd—'

'What? Bite me back?'

Damn him, he was amused! *Yes!*

'I'm almost tempted. The result could prove—' he paused deliberately '—interesting, shall we say?'

He held her impossibly close, and she felt consumed with futile anger. 'Damn you!' she burst out in a furious undertone. 'This isn't dancing!'

'Why not relax?' Georg queried imperturbably, restraining her efforts to wrest herself free with galling ease.

'The only way I can relax is when I'm ten feet away from you!' she declared vehemently.

'That's quite an admission. Have you stopped to consider why?'

His silky drawl was the very limit, and her head reared back as she sought to deliver a bitter invective. Except that the words never found voice as his mouth closed over hers in a kiss that took all her fine anger and tamed it into subdued submission.

'Don't ever do that again,' Lexi said shakily several long seconds after he'd relinquished her mouth. That long, infinitely slow possession had been one of the most evocative, erotic experiences of her life. Eyes closed, she had wanted it to go on and on, and never stop. And she'd wanted so much more than just the mere coupling of their mouths.

For the first time since those initial heady days with Paul she wanted, *needed* a complete satiation of the senses that went way beyond mere seduction. Not just with any man. *This* man, a tiny voice taunted.

And he knew. It was there in his eyes, the soft curve of his mouth, the possessiveness of his hands as they moved lightly down her back to curve her close against the hard length of his body.

She unconsciously pleaded with him, her eyes large luminous pools that shimmered with the threat of crystalline tears. 'Let me go.'

His gaze darkened fractionally, and his mouth moved to form a sensual curve. 'What if I refuse?'

She felt as if she were caught up in a swirling vortex of emotion so treacherous that she was in danger of drowning. 'Please.' The effort it cost her to summon a faint smile was beyond measure. 'I—' she hesitated, and her lips trembled slightly as her eyes silently beseeched him '—I don't want to play this particular game.'

His head lowered, and his lips brushed the length of her jaw to settle at the corner of her mouth. 'Who said it was a game?'

A single tear overflowed and slowly trickled down her cheek. 'You're not playing fair.'

'That depends on your definition of the word.'

If she didn't attempt to instil some levity into the situation she'd fragment into a thousand pieces. 'Shall we go back indoors?'

He lifted his head. 'Do you particularly want to?'

'I think so,' she said steadily. 'We've stayed out here sufficiently long to make our absence convincing.'

His eyes gleamed darkly in the shadowy light. 'One look at you will be enough to convince anyone,' he mocked gently as he lifted a hand and smoothed back a few wayward tresses.

For a moment she appeared stricken by his implication; then her features assembled an expressionless mask as she withdrew a tube of coloured gloss from her evening-bag and skilfully smoothed it over her lips.

Without a word she stepped away from him and walked slowly along the terrace to a double set of doors.

For what remained of the evening Georg was never far from her side, and she circulated among the guests, chatting, smiling with such conviction that it was doubtful anyone guessed that inside she was a mess of shattered nerves.

Everyone appeared to be enjoying themselves, but Lexi wondered darkly if it was just a façade. The smiles, the expressed interest all seemed so incredibly false, so artificial. Were any of them true friends, or merely trading as superficial acquaintances? A hollow laugh rose unbidden, then died in her throat. Should anyone present tonight suffer a change in financial status, their social standing would diminish to zero.

'Shall we leave?'

Lexi turned towards Georg and proffered a solemn smile. 'Is it awfully late?'

'Almost two.'

She managed an expression of mock surprise. 'Good heavens. I had no idea.'

A warm, sloping smile tugged at the corners of his mouth. 'Behave, Lexi,' he bade her, and, taking hold of her hand, he led her towards their hosts.

In the car he drove competently, slipping a cassette

into the stereo system so that conversation wasn't a necessity, and when he drew to a halt outside her apartment block she made no demur as his hands closed over her shoulders.

She knew she should flee *now*, before she became lost, but it was far too late as his lips brushed hers, settling with unerring ease over their delicate curves, savouring the sensual softness; then she gasped as he caught hold of her lower lip and pulled it gently into his mouth. Her tongue darted forward in a gesture of protective defence, then sprang back in shocked disbelief as he caught its tip between his teeth and gently drew it forward.

She swallowed convulsively, and made a strangled demur in resistance, only to have his mouth open over her own as he took possession in a manner that left her in no doubt as to his ultimate intention.

She reached for his shoulders and used all her strength to push against him, gaining a slight degree of freedom only, she suspected, because he permitted it.

'Please.' The word came out as a tortured whisper.

'You could ask me in.'

'If I did,' she managed shakily, 'you'd read more into the invitation than I intended.'

'And you'd hate yourself in the morning?'

'Something like that.'

She could sense his faint smile a few seconds before his lips brushed hers, then she was free.

'We'll dine out tomorrow night.'

Lexi looked momentarily startled, and was about to refuse when she caught his faintly brooding smile. 'What if I've already made plans?'

'Cancel them,' he instructed cynically.

'I may not want to,' she felt empowered to state, and glimpsed the mockery evident in the depths of his eyes.

'Do it, Lexi. I'll collect you at seven.'

'Do you usually *tell* your female companions what your plans are, and expect them to pander to your every whim?'

His eyes became tinged with musing warmth, and a sloping smile tugged the corners of his mouth. 'For some reason they seem intent on pleasing me.'

She didn't doubt it for a minute. There was an inherent quality about him that was wholly sensual, and something else that made her want to run and hide. Except that she couldn't, and maybe that bothered her more than she was willing to admit.

It was almost as if he was playing a game, she decided with an intuitive flash of speculative knowledge. His manipulative force in the business sector was legendary, and the Press dutifully recorded his every move.

'Why wouldn't they?' Lexi returned sweetly, uncaring of his deep probing glance. 'You're an exceptionally wealthy man, you drive an exotic car, and you're reasonably attractive—if you happen to like a surfeit of brooding Greek magnificence.' She tilted her head to one side as she subjected him to a pensive appraisal. 'I hope I won't damage your ego when I say that it wouldn't really matter if you were fifty, paunchy and bald. The women would still flock to your side.'

One eyebrow slanted in musing cynicism, and she caught a gleam of laughter in the depths of his eyes.

'Perhaps I should return the compliment. There are any number of men waiting to beat a path to your door—if only you would let them.'

Her eyes widened fractionally, then became veiled by the swift downward sweep of her lashes. 'Now you're being facetious.'

'Perhaps we should be grateful that neither of us possess any illusions,' he drawled.

Lexi reached for the doorknob. 'Goodnight.'

She was totally unprepared as he leant forward and covered her mouth with his own.

This time there was no hard possession, more a mixture of evocative control and blatant intention.

She had no defence against the explorative probe of his tongue as it traversed the inner contours of her mouth, and an electrifying awareness tingled through her veins as his touch became so intensely erotic that she had to physically restrain herself from allowing her body its instinctive inclination to lean close in against him and deepen the kiss.

It was madness, and just as she thought she could stand it no longer he lifted his head and slowly pushed her to arm's length.

'Sleep well, Lexi,' he taunted lazily, and in her anxiety she didn't hesitate to escape.

He waited until she was safely through the security doors before restarting the engine, and Lexi walked towards the lift without so much as a backward glance.

How could she *sleep*? He aroused a complexity of emotions, and not one of them was enviable.

Her mouth felt slightly swollen, and she ran the tip

of her tongue over the lower curve as she entered her apartment.

Damn Georg Nicolaos, she cursed irreverently. Damn him to hell.

CHAPTER SIX

'YOU'RE late,' Lexi greeted Georg the instant she opened the door the following evening.

He pulled back the cuff of his jacket and examined a distinctive gold Rolex. 'Seven minutes. Is it an unforgivable sin?'

It was immaterial that she hadn't been ready until two minutes ago, and she had no intention of informing him of that fact. 'I'm starving,' she declared truthfully, sweeping past him.

'Had a bad day?'

She wanted to hit him, and, enclosed within the confines of the lift, she wondered if there was some dark reason behind the temptation to resort to physical violence whenever she was in his company.

'Shall I start from the beginning?' Even to her own ears she sounded faintly harassed and on edge.

He unlocked the Ferrari and saw her seated inside before going round to slip in behind the wheel and fire the engine. 'Please do.'

'You're amused,' she accused him.

'Intrigued,' he amended as he concentrated on negotiating traffic.

Events of the totally chaotic day rose up to taunt her, and she grimaced in memory. 'The Mercedes had a flat tyre, and I changed it myself. So I was late. That disrupted Jacques's schedule. He swore so... graphically that I thought he was going to cancel

100

the entire session. And nothing went right. They sent the wrong-sized clothes, and the accessories didn't match. He ordered a few stills in black and white, then stormed out in a temper, leaving us to make the best of it. Monique blasted him with a blistered riposte that would have made a navvy blush.' Her mouth assumed a rueful moue. 'I missed lunch, discovered that the spare tyre I'd substituted this morning had developed a slow leak, and I had to catch a taxi into the city. The modelling academy kept me way beyond the projected time, and do you know how *impossible* it is to get a taxi between five and six?' She suddenly became aware of their whereabouts. 'Where are you taking me?'

'To my apartment.'

'For dinner?'

'Are you unaware that I am an accomplished chef?'

There was nothing she could do to guard against a sharp intake of breath. If she said she'd prefer to go to a restaurant he would imagine she was afraid to be alone with him. And she wasn't. At least, fear didn't motivate the state of her emotions.

'You've been slaving in the kitchen all afternoon?' she countered as he turned beneath an impressive apartment block and sent the Ferrari growling into a reserved bay. 'Don't you have to spend your weekend in an office directing a large slice of the city's finances?'

His smile was faintly cynical. 'I have access to hi-tech equipment in a number of offices, one of which is based in my apartment. Communication in the nineties is becoming increasingly portable. All it takes is the flick of an electronic button.' He switched off the ignition and slid out of the car, waiting until she joined him before walking towards the lifts. 'The restaurant is managed by a team of extremely competent chefs, who kindly permit me to work with them whenever I feel the inclination.' He jabbed the callbutton and when the doors slid open he inserted a key to allow private access to the penthouse apartment. 'And slaving is scarcely applicable in preparing a dinner *à deux*,' he concluded as the lift came to a smooth halt.

The penthouse was magnificent, and she said so, complimenting him with genuine sincerity on the tasteful blend of cream, beige and muted shades of brown and Wedgwood blue skilfully used in the décor. Deep-buttoned leather furniture in chocolate brown lent a masculine touch, and contrasting colours were implemented in expensive works of art gracing the walls.

'Sit down,' Georg bade her, crossing to the cocktail bar. 'What can I get you to drink?'

Without doubt there would be wine to accompany their meal, and she had the feeling she needed to be in total control of her senses. 'Something long, cool and non-alcoholic.'

'Playing it safe, Lexi?'

Her eyes caught his, and her chin lifted a fraction in defiance of his drawling tones. 'It's the only way.'

'You sound defensive,' he accorded, slanting her a musing glance. 'Will it help if I assure you that you have nothing to fear?'

Maybe, just maybe she might have believed him if it wasn't for some elusive sixth sense that warned he was skilfully indulging in a contest where he was the mastermind and she merely a pawn. It was crazy, and totally without foundation, but the thought had infiltrated her mind and refused to be dislodged.

'You mean, I'm safe from any so-called "fringe benefits" you might consider your due as a participant in this diabolical scheme?'

His gaze didn't waver, although his eyes darkened measurably, and his voice when he spoke was deliberately mild, yet she detected an edge of steel beneath the velvet-smooth surface. 'As safe as you choose to be.'

If that was assurance it was unsuccessful, and she watched as he put ice in a tall glass, then added lime-juice, a dash of bitters and topped it with soda before handing it to her.

'Good luck.'

Educated in the best private schools, and fashionably 'finished', she was adept at dealing with almost any given situation, commanding an enviable repertoire of stock-in-trade social small talk. Yet with Georg Nicolaos she alternated between raging at him in temper and behaving like a tongue-tied teenager. It was ridiculous, she chided silently.

'Tell me about yourself.'

Lexi looked momentarily startled, and took an appreciative sip from her glass. 'A personal profile from birth until now?' Her lips widened to form a bitter-sweet smile. 'Including a run-down on my disastrous marriage?'

'I consider Paul to be immaterial,' Georg dismissed drily, and she felt a slight shiver feather its way down the length of her spine.

She looked at him carefully, noting the dark busi-

ness suit, immaculate white linen shirt and sober navy
blue silk tie. Character analysis just had to be his
forte, for he appeared every inch the wealthy executive, exuding an animalistic sense of power with chilling ease.

'What made you decide to take up modelling?'

Lexi gave a careless shrug. 'It happened by
accident. I attended a fashion parade with a friend
three years ago. Just after I returned from two years
abroad. The mother of another friend owned one of
the boutiques supplying the parade with clothes. One
of the models failed to show, and I was there—the
right height and size. Before I knew it I was out on
the catwalk trying to look as if I'd modelled clothes
for years.'

'With obvious success,' Georg conceded.

'I enjoyed it,' she admitted. 'Sufficiently so to
agree to participating in another fashion parade held
a few days later. Jacques was there. He seemed to
think I possessed a natural flair. So I began to look
at it seriously, enrolling at a modelling academy to
learn all the tricks of the trade, and, as they say—the
rest is history.'

'It hasn't occurred to you to venture into the field
of design?'

'No. It's a cut-throat trade, and you need to be a
true artist. I prefer accessories. Matching up shoes,
belts, whether to add a scarf and, if so, how it should
be worn.' Her eyes had darkened with enthusiasm,
and her voice held genuine warmth. 'Jewellery—even
the right hairstyle, make-up. The entire composition.
I often suggest changes, and Jacques usually goes
along with them.'

'All in aid of making women appear beautiful.'

Lexi looked at him, deliberately searching for mockery, yet, if he had intended any, it was carefully hidden.

'A woman's true beauty comes from within,' she revealed slowly. 'It radiates through her skin, shows in her smile, and is reflected in her eyes. If she's not happy with herself, or lacks self-esteem, then it is generally apparent in mannerisms. Body language.' Her gaze became startlingly direct. 'With care and skill a woman can learn to make the best of her natural attributes, no matter what her size or age.'

'Gilding an outer shell, which, with expert marketing, grosses enormous profits for the various merchandisers.'

'Perhaps. But it isn't confined to women. Men like to present the outer trappings of their success in fine clothes.' She ran an experienced eye over his suit. 'Unless I'm mistaken, that's tailored by Ermenegildo Zegna. And your shoes are hand-stitched—either French or Italian imports.'

His smile proved to be a disruptive force, curving his mouth and lightening the harsh lines of his chiselled features. 'Are you implying that I project a required image?'

She responded with a winsome smile. 'Definitely.'

'Which is?'

'An astute entrepreneur,' she ventured quietly. 'Someone who wouldn't suffer fools gladly.'

'What about Georg Nicolaos, the man?'

For some reason she felt as if she'd skated on to dangerously thin ice. 'A contradiction between cruelty and kindness.'

'Ah—*honesty*.' Georg laughed softly, and one glance at those gleaming dark eyes revealed that he wasn't fooled in the slightest.

'Shall we have dinner?'

Lexi needed no second bidding, and she allowed him to lead her to the elegantly appointed dining-room, where within minutes he transferred serving dishes from the kitchen on to the table.

There was soup as a starter, a delicately flavoured leek and potato which tasted like liquid ambrosia, followed by luscious prawns in a delicate sauce served on a bed of rice.

The portions were temptingly small, so that she consumed every morsel, and the main course was an exquisite *coq au vin*.

There was wine—a clear sharp white—and chilled water, and dessert was a superb crème caramel.

'That was—perfect,' Lexi complimented, leaning back in her chair, fully replete.

'A compliment?'

'You can't possibly cook like that every night,' she declared in wistful disbelief, and caught his slow musing smile. 'Do you ever eat alone?' she asked, genuinely curious.

'Not often,' Georg responded indolently. 'I make a practice of dining with Mama once a week, and Samantha and Alex insist I join them on frequent occasions. Anna and Nick, also. Then, of course, the restaurant, and the inevitable social interludes...' He let his voice trail off as he effected an elegant shrug. 'However, there are times when I enjoy a quiet evening at home.'

'Samantha is charming,' Lexi voiced with sincerity.

'She is a very beautiful woman. Genuine, caring. Exceptional.'

Her eyes widened, and she glimpsed the darkness reflected in his own, then he smiled. 'Shall we have coffee?'

'Let's dispense with the dishes first,' she said, getting to her feet and beginning to stack plates together.

'Leave them. My housemaid, Carla, is due tomorrow. She'll attend to them.'

'It won't take long.' She spared him a quick glance. 'Unless you're particularly protective about a woman invading your kitchen?'

Shrugging off his jacket, he tossed it carelessly over a nearby chair, and she watched as he removed cufflinks and folded back the sleeves of his shirt.

'In that case, we'll do them together.'

The kitchen was a delight, spacious and boasting every modern convenience imaginable. Apart from a collection of saucepans drying in a dish-rack atop the draining-board, there wasn't a thing out of place.

'I'm impressed.'

'With the kitchen?'

His faint mockery did strange things to her equilibrium, and she concentrated on rinsing the crockery and cutlery while he stacked the dishwasher.

'What made you decide to be a chef?'

'My parents emigrated from Greece when Alex, Anna and I were very young. Papa owned three restaurants in Athens, and it was a natural progression for him to pursue the business here.' He filled the percolator with water, extracted a filter and spooned in freshly ground coffee beans. 'We all helped, waiting tables, the dishes, cleaning. Before school, after

school, during semester breaks. Like all parents, they
wanted great things for each of their children, and I
followed Alex into university and studied for a business degree. Papa was taken ill not long after I graduated, and for a few years I worked in an office by
day and managed the restaurant at night. Now we
keep it for Mama's sake. It represents so many memories for us all.'

'She must be very proud of you.'

'We are a very close family.'

The strength of her own familial ties was such that
she'd consented to an impossible charade with a man
who was the antithesis of harmless.

'All done.' Lexi dried her hands, then watched as
Georg set cups on to their saucers, then extracted
sugar, liqueur and cream. His hands were large, and
his forearms firmly muscled and liberally sprinkled
with dark hair. Their actions displayed an economy
of movement, and there was strength apparent as well
as a degree of sensitivity.

'Come into the lounge.'

Said the spider to the fly, she echoed silently, wondering what quirk of cynical humour had promoted
that thought to mind. 'I must leave soon,' she murmured out loud, and incurred his dark slanting glance.

'Must?'

'I need my beauty sleep,' she quipped lightly as
she followed him and settled comfortably into a single
armchair.

'We also need to plan the next week,' Georg
indicated as he took an opposite chair. 'It was the
reason I brought you here, so that we could discuss

it rationally rather than risk argument in a public restaurant.'

'I don't argue,' Lexi retaliated, only to give a rueful smile as she caught his raised eyebrow. 'Well, not usually.'

'I'm the exception?'

She looked at him carefully. 'Just because I recognise the necessity for this...deception—' she paused deliberately '—doesn't mean I have to like it.'

The dark eyes sharpened, and for some inexplicable reason she had difficulty holding their concentrated gaze.

'You find me—dislikeable?'

She suddenly felt as if she'd stepped from the safe shallows into water way over her head. 'No,' she said honestly.

'Yet you're afraid.'

It was a statement she didn't deny. She had genuinely enjoyed his company tonight, even if she had been slightly on edge. And, if she was fair, she could only accord that fault as entirely her own.

'I don't feel entirely comfortable with you,' she admitted, and saw his eyelids droop slightly, successfully veiling his expression.

'Could that not be because we have yet to forge a friendship?'

Could a woman ever be mere *friend* to someone like Georg Nicolaos? Somehow she doubted it.

'You mentioned collaborating on our social calendar.' Lexi broached the subject in an attempt to steer the conversation into safer channels.

'There are the inevitable invitations issued at this time of year,' he drawled, 'few of which I usually accept. However, there is a party to be held at the home of a friend which I think we should attend. Samantha and Alex have requested that we join them at a society ball, the proceeds from which are donated to make Christmas a more joyful occasion for a number of terminally ill children. It is considered to be *the* social event of the season.'

'Good heavens,' Lexi said faintly. 'I'm due to fly to the Gold Coast on Thursday morning for a photographic shoot organised by the Mirage Resort. It will be followed early in the New Year by another at the sister resort in Port Douglas.'

Georg's eyes narrowed faintly. 'How long will you be away?'

She gave a slight shrug. 'Overnight, on each occasion.'

'Apart from that do you have any social obligations?'

She looked at him, noting the apparent indolence, and wasn't fooled in the slightest. 'Jonathan, David and I usually attend a few pre-Christmas functions together.' A faint sigh whispered from her lips. 'I think I prefer an evening of solitude with a good book, or tuned in to a VCR.'

'I can think of an infinitely more pleasurable way in which to spend the night hours,' Georg drawled, and saw the faint blush of pink that crept into her cheeks.

'I'm sure you can,' Lexi managed equably. With unhurried movements she stood to her feet. 'Would you mind if I phoned for a taxi?'

His eyes trapped her own for far too long, and she

had to glance away from that disturbing gaze. 'You haven't finished your coffee.'

He was imperturbable, so maddeningly calm, and totally impervious to the agitation welling deep inside her. Lexi suddenly felt as if she were treading on eggshells.

'Please.' She attempted to keep her voice light and devoid of a degree of mounting tension. 'I'd really like to leave.'

'As soon as I finish my coffee I'll take you home.'

Reaching forward, she picked up the cup and saucer, spacing her movements so they appeared calm and unhurried as she sipped the remaining brew, then she carried the cup out to the kitchen and carefully rinsed it.

When she turned he was there, and her pulse began an erratic beat as he moved close to place his cup and saucer in the sink. It simply wasn't fair that she was overly sensitive to his potent brand of sexuality.

'Ready?'

She gave an indicative nod, and without a further word he turned and preceded her from the apartment.

In the car she sat in silence, consumed by an acute sense of vulnerability. A number of conversational gambits rose to mind, but she ventured none of them, and she sat trapped in silence for a few interminable seconds as he brought the Ferrari to a halt outside her apartment block.

'Thanks for dinner.' Good manners insisted that she acknowledge his hospitality.

'So—thank me.'

She looked at him carefully, and wondered why she

should suddenly feel threatened. All she had to do was reach forward and place her lips to his cheek.

Except that he turned his head and her lips touched his mouth, and before she could retreat he lifted his hands to capture her head, and it was he who took command, *he* who turned what began as a casual salutation into an evocative embrace that made her aware of a magical, elusive alchemy.

A treacherous weakness invaded her limbs as he wrought havoc with a ravaging exploration that brought a thousand tiny nerve-endings leaping into pulsating life, arousing feelings too complex to distinguish any one as she clung to him unashamedly.

It was almost as if every pore of her skin became suffused with sweet aching pleasure beneath his mercilessly erotic plunder of her senses, and when at last he slowly released her she could only look at him in complete bewilderment.

Without a word she reached for the door-handle and slid out from the passenger seat.

The door snapped shut with a refined click, and she crossed to the main entrance without a backward glance, using her security card to gain access; it was only when she was safely indoors that she heard the muted roar of the Ferrari's engine as it purred down one half of the semi-circular driveway.

It was a relief to enter her apartment, and she secured the lock before crossing to the windows to close the curtains against the night sky.

She felt incredibly restless, and far too emotionally uptight to sleep. Perhaps a long, leisurely soak in the spa-bath might ease some of her tension, and without further thought she wandered into the bathroom and filled the capacious tub.

Half an hour later she emerged to towel herself dry, then, attired in a short cotton nightshirt, she slipped into bed to lie staring into the darkness for what seemed an age, before exhaustion finally claimed her in a deep, troubled sleep from which she woke late, dark-eyed and drained.

During the following few days Lexi deliberately maintained a low profile. She consulted with Jacques over the forthcoming shoot at the Gold Coast's tourist resort, met Jonathan for lunch, completed some Christmas shopping, and spent an hour stretched out on a lounger beside the pool each afternoon, perfecting a tan. For two consecutive evenings she conjured up a suitable excuse to avoid seeing Georg, and on the third night she answered the doorbell to find him standing in the hallway.

'Have you eaten yet?' he drawled, and Lexi looked at him with exasperation as he moved into the lounge.

'I planned on spending a quiet evening at home.'

One eyebrow slanted in quizzical disbelief. 'You've already done that two evenings in a row.'

She heaved a faint sigh. 'Is that an indication we should go out and play?'

'What if I say…you get to choose the venue?'

'You're taking an awful risk,' Lexi declared. 'I may decide on a rock concert.'

'Out of sheer perversity?'

'Yes, I think so.' Humour lent her hazel-gold eyes an impish sparkle and she tilted her head to one side. 'You'll have to change. Where we're going, anything else but jeans, T-shirt and joggers will be a fashion mis-statement.'

'You have tickets?'

A wide smile curved her mouth. 'Indeed. Jacques did an outrageously successful shoot a few years ago for one of the leading agencies in town. Ever since, they've presented him with half a dozen tickets to each top promotion.'

'I hardly dare ask which bands are featured,' he drawled, almost wincing as she named two; then she added insult to injury by following them with three artists known for their explosive style on stage. 'This is revenge, I gather?'

'I sat through *Madame Butterfly*,' she reminded him, and saw his eyes darken with cynical humour.

'I doubt there is any comparison.'

'It starts at eight.'

'You're determined?'

The thought of having him suffer through hours of impossibly loud rock music was too great a temptation to miss! 'Yes.'

'Then get changed, and we'll go back to my apartment.'

'After which, when you've changed into casual gear, we'll go straight on and grab a hamburger or eat something there.' She saw his look of disbelief and managed to appear completely guileless. 'Be a devil for once. I'm sure your digestive system will survive.'

'More pertinent: will my eardrums?'

'Oh, I think so,' Lexi declared solemnly. 'I've been to a number of rock concerts, and my hearing is still intact.' She gestured towards the drinks cabinet. 'Fix yourself something while I go change.'

Ten minutes later she emerged clad in faded denims, a white T-shirt, white jogging shoes, and a denim jacket slung casually across her shoulders. Make-up was minimal and she'd twisted her hair into an elaborate pleat at her nape.

'I suspect I'm in for a culture shock,' Georg drawled as he followed her out of the apartment, and she spared him a laughing glance.

The Ferrari traversed the short distance between Darling Point and Double Bay in record time, and Lexi watched the news on television while Georg effected a swift change of clothes.

'Hmm,' she accorded musingly as he re-entered the lounge a short while later. 'You look almost—human.'

He certainly looked different, having discarded the image of impeccably attired businessman for something infinitely more casual. Hip- and thigh-hugging jeans worn with a pale cotton shirt beneath a contrasting designer jacket was perfectly suitable attire in which to attend a rock concert. Yet somehow it failed to disguise the essence of the man and his innate ability to project an aura of power.

'It would take only minutes to grill steak and prepare a salad.'

'Hamburgers,' Lexi negated firmly, moving towards the lobby.

'Junk food.'

'Surveys report there's not as much junk in *junk* food as we're led to believe. It can actually be quite high in nutritional value.' She wrinkled her nose at him. 'Relax, Georg. You may just enjoy yourself.'

That Lexi did was without doubt. The music was loud, but the sound-effects were without distortion, emitted at their sophisticated best and an audible attestation to superb technology. She clapped and sang with the rest of the audience, oblivious for the most part to the man who sat at her side.

'Isn't he great?' Lexi enthused as one of Australia's better-known vocalists took the stage for a popular encore—a song that had won him an Entertainer of the Year award the previous year. He was married, a devoted husband and father, and affectionately held his doting public in the palm of his hand. 'He doesn't just *sing*—he puts everything into it and becomes a part of the music itself.' She turned towards Georg and was disconcerted to see that his attention was centred on her, not the band or the vocalist on stage. For a moment her breath locked in her throat as she became trapped by the expression in those dark eyes, then she swallowed and said fiercely, 'The proceeds of this concert go to charity.'

'You don't need to justify anything,' Georg drawled. 'And you're right. I am enjoying myself— watching you.'

She felt incredibly vulnerable, and everything else faded as she glimpsed something she dared not define before she managed to tear her gaze away.

The musicians caught her attention, but for the remainder of the evening she was supremely conscious of his presence.

It was late when the concert wound down, and the exits became jammed with a river of people attempting to vacate the venue. It was even worse trying to leave the car park.

Consequently it was after midnight before the Ferrari was able to move freely in traffic, and Lexi leaned well back in her seat and closed her eyes as she mentally reviewed the concert and its artists.

'Do you want to go somewhere for supper?'

She opened her eyes and turned to look at him. 'Are you hungry?'

'Peckish.'

'We're not exactly dressed for any of your usual haunts,' she ventured.

'I know of a place. Trust me.'

When the car slid to a halt she checked their whereabouts and shot him a cheeky grin. 'I don't believe this.'

'Come on. Out.' He slid from behind the wheel and went round to open her door. 'A fitting end to the evening, wouldn't you say?'

The café was intimately small and spotlessly clean, and the smell of food was tantalising. They sat opposite each other in a booth, and ordered steakburgers, fries and salad. Afterwards they washed it down with surprisingly good coffee, then Georg paid the bill and drove towards Darling Point.

It had been a wonderful evening, and she told him as much as he drew to a halt outside her apartment block.

'I agree.'

Something in the tone of his voice arrested her attention, and she turned towards him in seemingly slow motion as his hands caught hold of her shoulders.

'Georg—don't. Please,' she whispered as he impelled her forward, and the butterflies in her stomach began an erratic tattoo, making her frighteningly aware of the electric tension between them.

Lexi felt herself begin to tremble as he lowered his head and touched his lips briefly against her temple.

Any further protest became lost as his mouth slid down to cover hers in a kiss that was tantalising, tender, yet with a hint of controlled passion, and to her utter chagrin it left her feeling vaguely bereft and wanting more.

'I really must go,' she said a trifle shakily.

'Don't forget we're attending the charity ball tomorrow night,' Georg reminded her as she made to step out from the car. 'We're meeting Samantha and Alex there at eight. I'll pick you up at seven-thirty.'

She murmured agreement, then activated her security card to pass through the main doors, and when she turned back all she could see was the twin red tail-lights as the Ferrari swept down the street.

CHAPTER SEVEN

LEXI dressed with care, and her mirrored reflection gave visual satisfaction that her choice of gown was a success.

In midnight-blue silk, it accentuated her slim curves by hugging them shamelessly from breast to knee before flaring out in a generous fold that fell to ankle-length. Matching shoes and evening-bag completed the outfit, and for jewellery she'd opted to wear a glorious sapphire pendant encircled in diamonds and matching ear-studs.

Her hair was worn swept back from her face and caught together at one side so that a thick mass of curls cascaded down on to her left breast. Make-up had been skilfully applied to highlight her eyes, and a deep dusky rose coloured the generous curve of her mouth.

Perfume—Jean-Louis Scherrer—completed the required image, and at the sound of the doorbell she moved through the lounge to answer its summons.

'Beautiful,' Georg accorded softly, after conducting a slow appreciative appraisal that brought a defiant sparkle to her eyes.

'Wearing clothes is an acquired flair,' Lexi qualified with a faint defensive lift of her chin as she met his warm gaze.

'You do it extremely well.'

Perhaps she'd overdone it, she decided wryly. Except that tonight of all nights, given such an auspicious occasion, she felt the need to excel. The charity ball would be patronised by the cream of Sydney's society, and Lexi Harrison's affair with Georg Nicolaos was hot gossip. She would be examined in detail from the tip of her shoes to the top of her head, discussed and dissected, her behaviour observed and criticised. From the moment she stepped out of Georg's car she would need to *shine*.

'Would you like a drink?' she queried. 'Or shall we leave?'

'Oh, leave, I think,' Georg intimated with husky humour. 'Otherwise I shall probably be tempted to dissuade you from moving one step out of this apartment.'

The only way she could cope with him in this frame of mood was outright flippancy. 'And waste all the time and effort I've expended in adopting this glamorous image? Not on your life.'

'Shame,' he drawled. 'Now I shall have to exercise the utmost control during the entire evening.'

She proffered a wide sweet smile. 'I have no doubt you'll manage.'

He stood to one side, allowing her to precede him into the lobby.

The venue was a plush hotel in the inner city, and, although she had attended many such functions in the past, tonight it was impossible to dispel a feeling of nervousness.

Georg Nicolaos had a lot to answer for, she decided

darkly as they moved into the foyer, where their tickets were scrutinised and marked off an impressive list before they were ushered into the elaborately decorated function-room.

Drinks and canapés were served by a bevy of hovering waiters, and Lexi drifted at Georg's side as they slowly mixed and mingled with a variety of acquaintances.

'Lexi; Georg.' Alex, with Samantha at his side looking incredibly lovely in black velvet. Lexi greeted them both warmly, accepted Samantha's compliment and promptly returned it. 'Shall we take our seats at the table?' Alex enquired. 'It looks as if most of the guests are intent on becoming seated.'

The food was superb, and Lexi forked a few mouthfuls from each course, declined wine in favour of mineral water, and opted for fresh fruit salad instead of the cheeseboard. There were the usual salutary speeches lauding the charity chairperson, the secretary, and a brief résumé of the charity's successful endeavours and anticipatory projections. Then it was clearly party-time as a band took up its position and began to play.

'Would you excuse me while I freshen up?' said Lexi.

'I'll come with you,' Samantha indicated, rising to her feet, and together they began threading their way across the room.

The powder-room was crowded, and it took considerable time before Samantha was able to occupy a spare cubicle. Lexi gave her place to an expectant mother who obviously needed to use the facilities more urgently than she did.

'Don't wait,' Lexi bade Samantha with a helpless smile. 'I'll rejoin you as soon as I can.'

It was at least five minutes before she emerged, and she paused as someone called her name, then stood politely as a woman she barely knew insisted on offering her congratulations.

An acquaintance of Jonathan's restricted her passage, enquiring after his health, and she turned to retrace her steps to the table.

Afterwards she couldn't recall quite what made her conduct a sweeping appraisal of the function-room and its guests. She certainly wasn't conscious of doing it deliberately. There had to be at least thirty people present whom she knew reasonably well, and more than fifty who were social acquaintances.

Even as her eyes skimmed the crowd, it never occurred to her that she might number her ex-husband among the invited guests.

Lexi felt the blood drain from her face at the sight of Paul standing on the far side of the room. Even from this distance she could see the wicked, faintly malevolent gleam in his eyes, the cynical twist of his mouth.

She saw him murmur to his companion, then he began threading his way through the gathered groups of guests.

'Well, hello,' Paul greeted softly, and she cringed beneath his deliberate raking appraisal. 'It's been ages, my sweet. I see you're inhabiting the social scene again,' he intoned hatefully. 'The gossip around town is that you and Georg Nicolaos are an item. Are you?'

Careful, she cautioned silently. The last thing she wanted was a scene. Perhaps if she was polite he'd be satisfied and leave her alone.

Lexi took her time in answering, letting her lashes sweep up as she met his stare with unblinking solemnity. 'Yes.'

His lips curved to form a vicious sickle. 'Why, Lexi, darling, whatever are you thinking of? Georg eats little girls for breakfast.'

'I'm no longer a little girl, Paul,' she said steadily. 'You personally saw to it that I grew up.'

'Do you imagine for one minute it will be any different with Georg Nicolaos? He's a hard corporate executive, too attuned to business interests to be much concerned with *you*, except when it suits him, of course.'

'As you were, Paul?'

'My, my,' he accorded with slow deliberation. 'Tell me, sweetie,' he began, pausing as he set his weapons ready for the figurative kill, 'are you still an inhibited, frigid little bitch in bed? Or hasn't Georg been able to persuade you into his yet?' He reached out a hand to push back a tendril of hair behind her ear, and laughed softly as she reared back from his touch as if from flame.

'You would be advised not to cause trouble, Ellis,' a too-familiar voice intimated with icy disdain, and Lexi felt faint.

'I have an invitation to this soirée,' Paul said mockingly, his eyes moving slowly from Georg to Lexi.

'Obviously,' Georg conceded with studied ruthlessness. 'Otherwise you would not have been admitted.' He paused, before adding with killing softness, 'However, if I hear of your bothering Lexi again I can promise that you will live to regret it.'

Lexi shivered at the degree of ice evident in Georg's tone, and she glimpsed the malevolent gleam in Paul's eye as he ventured cynically, 'Physical violence, my dear chap?'

'Nothing so uncivilised.'

Paul's gaze swept down to the ring on Lexi's finger, then he lifted his head to slant her a mocking glance. 'Congratulations, darling. Daddy will be pleased.'

It was evident that Paul had deliberately sought this very scene, and Lexi was supremely conscious of the curious looks cast in their direction, the avid, all-too-seeing eyes alight with speculative conjecture. Inside she was shattering into a thousand pieces, but she was darned if she'd give Paul the pleasure of glimpsing any visible signs of her distress.

'Yes,' she agreed quietly, 'he is.'

'Better luck this time, sweetie.'

'We'll excuse you,' Georg said silkily. 'There can be no doubt this conversation has reached its conclusion.'

'I wouldn't dream of continuing it,' Paul declared with ill-concealed mockery, then he turned and strolled with apparent nonchalance to rejoin his friends.

Pride was a damnable thing, and she lifted her head, tilting her chin in an unconscious gesture of defence. Georg's eyes seemed to tear down the barriers she had erected, and after a few interminably long minutes she lowered her gaze to a point somewhere above his left shoulder.

Without a word he reached out and caught hold of her hand, and she shifted her attention, meeting his unfathomable expression with a clear, direct gaze, hiding the pain buried deep inside. She even managed a slight smile, although she was unaware that it appeared to be tinged with sadness. 'The only regret I have where Paul is concerned is that I was foolish enough to be taken in by him in the first place.'

'You were young and susceptible, were you not?'

Lexi gave an imperceptible shrug. 'Nothing alters the fact that I made a terrible misjudgement of character, which was only compounded by my unwillingness to heed my father or David.'

'You paid for your mistake.'

It wasn't a query, merely a statement of fact, and her lashes swept down to shutter the sudden flaring of pain.

'Not all men are callous, insensitive brutes,' Georg offered quietly.

'Possibly not.' She paused, her eyes wide and startlingly direct. 'But I've never been sufficiently inclined to set out on a wild bedroom romp in an attempt to disprove Paul's accusations of my frigidity!'

'Ludicrous,' Georg drawled, and her eyes flashed with sudden animosity. 'That you could possibly be frigid,' he elaborated.

'And you're an expert on the sexual exploits of men and women?'

His faint smile held amused cynicism. 'I can guarantee that my experience is infinitely more vast than yours.'

'I wouldn't dream of doubting it!'

He lifted her hand to his lips and idly brushed her fingertips in a gesture that was blatantly evocative, and she felt so impossibly angry it was all she could do not to snatch her hand from his grasp.

'Stop opposing me,' he berated quietly.

'How can I *not* oppose you? At first it appeared I was agreeing to a simple collusion,' she said wretchedly. 'Now I'm wearing an engagement ring, and you've told Jonathan and the gossip columnists that we're getting married within weeks!'

'Would it be so disastrous if we did?'

Her eyes widened with incredulous disbelief. 'You can't be serious?'

'Very serious.'

'But—*why*?'

'Why not?' Georg countered smoothly. 'I look at Alex and Samantha and I know that I want what they have. A caring relationship; children.'

'That's no basis for marriage,' she responded, utterly shocked by his reasoning.

'Isn't it better to have a marriage based on friendship and mutual trust than chase an illusion?' His eyes were dark and fathomless. 'I have amassed considerable assets. Do you think for one moment that women solicit my attention for reasons other than with an eye to a generous expense account, travel, and the gift of limitless jewellery?' His query was wholly cynical, and she looked at him carefully.

'You would be content with such a relationship?'

'Yes.'

Her expression registered an entire gamut of emotions, and she struggled to contain them. Could she marry him? *Dared* she? Once she had chased a fairy-tale and fallen flat on her face. Maybe this time she should use her head instead of her heart.

He smiled, and everything else seemed to fade as he leant forward and brushed his lips against her forehead. 'I'll get you a drink,' he said solemnly. 'And then we'll mingle.'

Lexi accepted a glass of champagne, then walked at his side as they mixed with the guests, pausing to converse with one group and another before eventually rejoining Samantha and Alex.

'Shall we leave them to it?' Samantha queried with a cheeky grin as the two brothers became engaged in deep conversation, and Lexi agreed, watching as Samantha briefly touched Alex's shoulder.

Georg caught the unobtrusive gesture, and his eyes pierced Lexi's for a second before he returned his attention to the man at his side.

Together Samantha and Lexi threaded their way towards a table where two waitresses were dispensing coffee.

'Oh, this is heaven,' Samantha breathed as she sipped the aromatic brew. 'It has been a successful night. All the tickets were sold out last week.'

'Another notable charity,' Lexi accorded. 'Georg seems to be an active patron of several.'

'Georg is a very special man,' Samantha offered with deep sincerity.

'He complimented you in much the same manner.'

A dimpled smile turned Samantha's features into something quite beautiful. 'We are—*simpatico*. There was a time when Alex was impossibly jealous. Completely without foundation, I might add.'

'Of course.'

Samantha laughed. 'You sound so sure.'

'One has only to look at you and Alex together to know no one else in the world exists for either of you.'

'Yet it wasn't always like that.'

Lexi didn't know what to say, and sagely maintained her silence.

'I found myself married to Alex without any choice,' Samantha revealed quietly. 'I was very young, and at first I rebelled. Rather badly, I'm afraid. The first few months were—' she paused, effecting a faint grimace in memory '—difficult.'

'You weren't in love with him?'

'Not at first, no.'

'I find that very hard to believe.'

'Now I cannot imagine my life without him.'

Lexi looked at her carefully. 'What are you trying to tell me?'

'That Georg is the one man, aside from Alex, whom I would trust with my life,' Samantha said simply.

'You think I'm not sure of Georg?'

'I think,' Samantha corrected, 'you're unsure of yourself.'

'Oh, my,' Lexi declared with a defenceless little shrug. 'Next you'll say that love can come after the marriage, and I should leap in where any self-respecting angel would fear to tread!' Her eyes kindled with rueful cynicism, and Samantha laughed.

'Are we permitted to share the joke?' a deep voice drawled from behind, and Lexi turned to see Alex and Georg had rejoined them.

'Most definitely not.'

'Ah—woman-talk, I presume,' Alex declared, shooting his wife a dark probing glance that held latent warmth.

'We were talking about men,' Samantha reported gravely.

Her husband seemed interested, rivetingly so. 'Indeed?'

Georg began to laugh softly, and caught hold of Lexi's hand. 'I think we'll leave you two alone.' He tugged gently, and drew her towards the dance-floor.

'I'm not sure that I want to dance,' Lexi protested, yet somehow she was in his arms, and the music was slow, the lights low, and it was all too easy to forget everything except the moment.

His hold was less than conventional, and after a few minutes she gave in to temptation and let her head rest against the curve of his shoulder. If she closed her eyes she could almost imagine this was real, and somewhere deep inside was born the longing for it to be more than just a pretence.

There were as many reasons why she should marry him as there were reasons for her to refuse. She thought of Samantha and Alex, and their daughter Leanne; of a home, with Georg in the role of husband, lover, father.

'You're very quiet.'

Lexi lifted her head and gave him a rueful smile. 'I was just about to suggest we leave. It must be after midnight, and I have to catch an early-morning flight to the Gold Coast.'

'We'll find Samantha and Alex, and bid them goodnight,' Georg declared, relinquishing his hold.

Ten minutes later they were in the car, and Lexi sat in silence, listening to the slight swish of tyres traversing a road wet with a sudden summer shower of rain. The air smelt fresh and clean, and the sky was a clear indigo blue, almost black, and even as she looked there was a sprinkling of stars to herald the promise of a clear new day.

Georg brought the Ferrari to a halt outside the entrance to her apartment block and switched off the engine.

'I'll ring you as soon as I get back,' Lexi indicated as she released the seatbelt.

'Ring me when you arrive,' he drawled, releasing his own and shifting slightly to face her.

He seemed to loom large, a vaguely threatening force, and she mentally chided herself for possessing too vivid an imagination.

'I have to pack,' she said quickly.

'And you merely want to escape.'

She looked at him carefully, seeing his rough-chiselled features, the stark strength apparent. 'It's quite late.'

'Then kiss me goodnight, and run upstairs to bed.'

She felt her eyes widen, and wondered at the degree of indolent sensuality apparent in his voice.

'Why so hesitant, Lexi?' he drawled. 'Have I suddenly grown horns?'

She shook her head. 'Of course not,' she negated slowly.

'Yet you find it difficult, hmm?'

You can't begin to know *how* difficult, she longed to respond, then she gave herself a mental shake. This was crazy. Tentatively she reached up to brush her lips against his cheek, and found he'd moved his head so that instead she encountered his mouth.

For a moment she froze, then she pressed her mouth lightly against his in a fleeting kiss.

'That isn't exactly what I had in mind.'

His faint mockery brought a flood of colour to her cheeks, and she opened her mouth to fling a stinging retort at him only to have it possessed by his in a kiss that rocked the very foundation of her being. 'Possessed' was the only word adequate to define it, and some devious alchemy had to be responsible for the traitorous way she began to respond. Her breathing became rapid and uneven, and she was aware of the pulse thudding at the base of her throat. Every inch of skin tingled alive, heightening her senses and making her feel achingly aware of him until she wanted more than a mere melding of mouths.

The restriction of clothes—his, *hers*—seemed an impossible barrier, and her fingers shook as they hovered close to his shirt buttons, then fell away in distracted dismay as she realised how close she was to wanting him totally.

With a murmur of distress Lexi tore her mouth away. Her eyes were impossibly wide and hauntingly luminous and her cheeks tinged with pink as she encountered his dark glittering gaze.

'If you don't want me to come upstairs and invade your bed I suggest you get out of the car before I discard my noble instincts,' Georg taunted with husky amusement.

Lexi needed no second bidding, and she heard his soft chuckle an instant before she closed the door behind her and ran lightly towards the entrance.

CHAPTER EIGHT

IT HAD been quite a day, one way and another, Lexi mused thoughtfully as she entered the luxurious apartment. The sun at its zenith had been hot—at least three degrees higher than Sydney temperatures, and she needed a cool shower and an icy drink.

The Gold Coast was one of her favourite places, its relaxed lifestyle and long hours of sunshine providing a magnet for the many tourists who flocked to the famed coastal strip in search of golden sands and sapphire-blue sea with spume-crested waves rolling in from the Pacific Ocean. Many of the shopping complexes favoured seven-day trading, and it was all too easy to lose track of time exploring exotic boutiques in any one of several malls.

With a faintly weary gesture Lexi reached a hand to the long thick length of her hair and lifted it away from her nape. The apartment's air-conditioning cooled the heat from her skin, which, despite liberal use of sunblock during the long hours spent in the sun, showed visible signs of exposure.

The photographic shoot had been successful, and a brief session in the morning should wrap it up, then she would be able to catch the next available flight home.

A strange anticipatory thrill coursed through her veins at the mere thought, and she was forced to admit reluctantly that Georg was the main cause.

His image was never far from her mind, and she had only to close her eyes to instantly recall his strong features, the depth of his eyes and the degree of lazy warmth in his smile.

Was it all merely a pretence in their scheme of make-believe? she wondered as she stripped off her clothes and stepped into the shower cubicle. Selecting shampoo, she began working it into the thick length of her hair.

There were times when she rather wistfully longed for their supposed romance to be real, yet that was akin to chasing an impossible dream. The reality was more...comfortable, she decided. If 'comfortable' was a description one could apply to Georg Nicolaos! He possessed the ability to set her emotions into pure turmoil with the least amount of effort.

Lexi sluiced shampoo from her hair, then repeated the process and worked in conditioning lotion.

It was impossible to dispel the fact that he probably regarded her as an attractive addition to his life; if they married she would assume the role of hostess and companion who conveniently fulfilled his sexual needs.

Could such an arrangement work? Would she be able to live with him, accept his physical lovemaking without becoming too emotionally involved?

Damn. The soft curse was lost beneath the sound of the shower as she deliberately cast such evocative thoughts aside and concentrated on completing her ablutions.

Several minutes later she donned a silk robe before plugging in the hairdrier to style her hair.

A time-consuming task, which she had almost completed when the doorbell rang, and a puzzled frown momentarily creased her forehead as she moved through the lounge. She hadn't ordered room-service, and she certainly wasn't expecting anyone.

The tall dark frame filling the aperture was incredibly familiar.

Her surprise was evident, and several differing emotions chased fleetingly across her expressive features. 'Georg! What are you doing here?'

'Aren't you going to ask me in?'

His slight smile did strange things to her equilibrium, and she stood aside at once. 'Of course.' She pushed a hand through her hair, and gave a faint grimace. Tumbled tresses, no make-up, and attired in only a robe. He couldn't have caught her at more of a disadvantage if he'd tried. 'I haven't long emerged from the shower.'

His eyes were strangely watchful as he reached forward and trailed his fingers down the smoothness of her cheek. 'You look about sixteen,' he said quietly, and she wrinkled her nose at him in silent admonition, feeling suddenly gauche at the degree of drawled amusement in his voice, and a little nervous.

'This is a surprise,' she declared lightly. 'Can I get you a drink?'

'I'll fix myself something while you get changed.'

Something in his tone ensured that he was the total focus of her attention, and her eyes flew to his with a mixture of concern and outright fear.

Unbidden, her hand rose towards him, then fluttered down to her side. 'It's Jonathan, isn't it?'

'He collapsed this afternoon,' Georg revealed gently. 'At this very moment he's in surgery. I chartered a private jet from Sydney, and a limousine is waiting outside. All you have to do is slip into some clothes.'

'David—'

'Is waiting for us at the hospital.' He leaned forward and brushed his lips against her temple. 'Jonathan will be fine,' he reassured. 'He has the best team of vascular surgeons in the country, and they're confident of success.'

There wasn't a thing she was capable of saying, and she turned away from him blindly, her movements completely automatic as she walked swiftly into the bedroom.

Retrieving a bag from the wardrobe, she hurriedly tore clothes from their hangers, then she slipped into clean underwear and donned eau de Nil cotton trousers and matching top, slid a brush through her hair and slipped her feet into casual shoes. She could attend to her make-up in the limousine, she decided, gathering up toiletries and her make-up bag.

'I've arranged your check-out,' Georg informed as she emerged into the lounge. 'Is there anyone here you should contact before we leave?'

'The cameraman. He's staying in a unit at the resort.'

'Give me his name, and we'll arrange for a message to reach him.'

Two hours later they arrived at Sydney airport, and it was after eight when they reached the hospital to find a weary, but mildly exuberant David waiting to greet them.

Lexi flew into his embrace at once, and was

soundly hugged before being gently pushed to arm's length.

'Jonathan's OK,' David reassured her before she could voice the query. 'Surgery was successful, and he's in intensive care.'

Intensive care sounded vaguely frightening, and she stood still, hugging herself in a defensive gesture as she looked askance from one to the other in silence.

'Standard procedure,' Georg assured her quietly. 'They'll keep him there for a few days until he stabilises, I imagine.'

A shiver shook her slim frame. Life was so tenuous, so incredibly fragile. The thought of losing Jonathan was more than she could bear. 'Can I see him?'

'I'm sure the medical staff would advise against it,' Georg said gently. 'He'll be heavily sedated, and hooked up to various machines.'

She turned towards her brother. 'David?'

'Georg is right, sweetheart. There's nothing we can do.' He reached out and gave her shoulder a gentle squeeze. 'Let Georg take you home. The hospital has my number, and if there's even the slightest change I'll call you at once.'

In the car she sat in silence, and it was only when the Ferrari drew to a halt that she withdrew from reflective thought sufficiently to recognise her surroundings.

Indoors, she made for the lift, conscious that Georg walked at her side, and she made no demur when he took her keys and unlocked the apartment.

'Thank you,' she said with genuine gratitude. 'For

ensuring that I reached Sydney as quickly as possible.'

'I'll fix a snack,' Georg indicated. 'You ate nothing on the plane.'

'I don't feel hungry.'

'Something light,' he insisted as he shrugged off his jacket, and, placing it over a nearby chair, he rolled up each sleeve-cuff and walked into the kitchen. 'An omelette?'

Lexi slowly followed him, watching as he deftly set the pan to heat, whisked eggs in a bowl, then sliced up bacon, cheese and tomato.

Within minutes she found herself seated at the table, forking delectable pieces of food into her mouth. It was delicious, and she said so, shooting him a slight smile as he made the coffee.

'You're more than just a handsome face,' she accorded lightly.

'Ah—a compliment,' he drawled as he poured the aromatic brew into two cups. 'Usually you are swift to upbraid me for some imagined misdemeanour.'

She spared him a direct look, and was disconcerted by his unwavering gaze. 'We—strike sparks off each other,' she ventured in explanation, and heard his husky laugh.

'Have you ever paused to consider *why*?'

'I resent you,' Lexi responded swiftly. 'For attempting to rule my life—*me*.' Replacing her cutlery on her plate, she pushed it towards the centre of the table. 'In a minute we'll be arguing again.'

'Something at which you seem to excel.'

She looked at him carefully, seeing the strength apparent and an indomitable measure of self-will. 'I don't feel inclined to be at cross purposes with you tonight.'

'In that case, let's take our coffee into the lounge and watch television together.'

She shrugged slightly. 'Why not?'

For the next hour they sat in separate chairs, watching the second half of a film, and when it finished Georg got to his feet.

A strange sense of desolation assailed her at the thought that he was about to leave, and she rose from the chair, then stood hesitantly as he took the few steps necessary to bring him within touching distance.

He had only to reach out, and she waited, almost afraid to breathe, alternately craving solace and unwilling to accept its price.

For a long time she just looked at him, watching with detached fascination as he lifted a hand and brushed his fingers across the delicate planes of her cheek, then lowered his head.

His kiss held an infinite degree of *tendresse*, and she felt the ache of tears. Never had she felt quite so alone or so incredibly forlorn, and she badly needed to hold on to his sheer physical presence.

He held her gaze, and she stood mesmerised, unable to look away from those deep dark depths as if her life depended on it. He tilted her face, framing it between his hands, and his gaze was steady. 'Do you want me to stay?'

'I—don't think I could bear to be alone,' she whispered, feeling shaky and ill-equipped to deal with him.

Her lips parted, trembling a little as he idly traced their lower curve. Unbidden, her eyes filled with tears, and he swore softly as they spilled over and ran slowly down each cheek. Lexi shook her head slightly, and rubbed the back of her hands across each cheek. 'It's just reaction.'

He pressed a forefinger against her mouth, and his eyes darkened as he felt her lips tremble beneath his touch.

'I'll heat some milk and brandy,' he said gently.

She was powerless to prevent the lump that rose in her throat, and she merely nodded in silent acquiescence, watching as he left the room.

Dear heaven, she was weary. If she could just close her eyes for a few minutes…

When Georg re-entered the lounge she was asleep, curled up on the sofa, looking as guileless as a young child.

A slow smile tugged at the edges of his mouth, and he carefully eased her slight body into his arms and carried her through to the bedroom.

She stirred faintly, but didn't wake as he slipped off her outer clothes and placed her between soft percale sheets.

He stood looking down at her for a very long time, then he moved quietly into the main bathroom and showered before switching off the lights with the exception of one in the hallway.

Lexi slept deeply, caught up in the spell of differing dreams, some more vivid and vaguely disturbing than others, and she was barely aware of a source of enveloping strength as she hovered increasingly closer to wakefulness.

There was something different apparent, but she was unable to pinpoint exactly what, until the powerful heartbeat beneath her cheek gradually penetrated her subconscious, and she froze, becoming aware with shocking clarity that she was not only in bed, but held lightly imprisoned against a male body. What was more, one of her arms curved across the hard musculature of his ribcage, while one of *his* closed possessively over her hip.

'You're awake.'

If she lay perfectly still maybe her immobility would persuade him he was mistaken.

'Don't pretend,' Georg drawled. 'Your heartbeat has just gone into overdrive.'

As if to prove his point he trailed a hand to the rapidly beating pulse at the base of her throat.

With infinite slowness her lashes swept slowly upwards. Her lips felt impossibly dry, and she drew in the lower curve in an attempt to moisten it. Inside she was as nervous as a kitten, and her eyes clung to his as he tilted her chin.

'What are you doing here?' Her voice quivered slightly, and her eyes widened as she viewed him with unblinking solemnity.

The reflection from the lighted hallway provided subdued illumination, and she glimpsed his faint smile.

'Your apartment, specifically, or your bed?'

Her throat ached, and the words came out in a husky undertone. 'Don't—tease.'

His fingers trailed a gentle exploratory path across the delicate hollows at the base of her throat.

His touch was familiar, and so very sure, that the blood drained from her face. He hadn't—surely they hadn't—? No, it wasn't possible. She would have woken, would have known—

'You think I would attempt to steal from you in sleep what you would not willingly give when you were in total possession of your senses?'

Dear lord, was she so transparent? Heat flooded her cheeks, and her lashes swept down to form a protective veil.

His warm breath fanned her temples. 'Lexi?'

She heard the softly voiced command, and was held immobile by the wealth of seduction apparent. She looked at him, and she wanted to cry, but no tears would come.

Capturing her head between his hands, he leant forward and covered her lips with his own, softly and with such tenderness that it made her catch her breath. There seemed no urgency to deepen the kiss as he gently traced the outline of her lips, savouring their sweet fullness until her mouth parted of its own volition.

Without conscious thought her hands slid to his shoulders, then crept up to encircle his neck, and his mouth hardened in possession as he sought a devastation that left her weak-willed and malleable.

It seemed an age before he relinquished her mouth, and he trailed his lips down the sensitive cord at her neck to explore the hollows at the base of her throat, then edged lower to the curve of her breast.

The top she wore was easily dispensed with, as was the silk and lace that comprised her bra, and she gasped as he captured one tender burgeoning peak between his teeth and rendered such exquisite pleasure that it was all she could do not to cry out. Her fingers raked through his hair, silently begging him to desist as her whole body began to pulsate with molten fire, and she became mindless, lost in a wealth of sensuality so intense that there was no room for anything else but the need to subside into the swirling vortex of emotion.

There could be no turning back, and she told herself that nothing else mattered, only *now*, as he gently removed every last vestige of her clothing.

His hands and his mouth became evocative instruments as he sought to awaken a tumultuous response, his lips grazing down over her ribcage on a destructive path towards the central core of her femininity.

Her shocked protest went unheeded, as with deliberate eroticism he taught her to enjoy an experience so fraught with sensual ecstasy that she cried out, alternately pleading for more and begging him to desist, until, just as she thought she could stand it no longer, his mouth began a slow upward trail, tantalising, teasing, tasting.

Slowly, with care, he gained entry with one sure thrust, then he deliberately sought a response she was afraid to give.

Her pleasure began as a spiralling sensation that swelled into an intense throbbing ache as she became completely and utterly absorbed in his deep rhythmic possession.

Mindlessly exultant, she scaled the heights of ecstasy and knew she never wanted to descend from this elusive sensory plateau where sheer sensation ruled.

Her faint whimper of distress was very real as he

began to withdraw, and she held him close, unwilling to have it end.

His lips moved to her shoulder, caressing the delicate curves and hollows, before wandering with tactile sensuality to tease the edge of her mouth; then he lifted a hand to her chin and forced her to meet his gaze.

There wasn't a single word she was capable of uttering, and her eyes felt like huge liquid pools mirroring the degree of deep slumberous passion she'd experienced beneath his touch.

Gently he lifted her hand to his lips, and there was nothing she could do to prevent the slight quivering of her mouth as she glimpsed the warmth reflected in the depths of his eyes.

It was impossible for him to be unaware of her unbridled response to his lovemaking, and a faint tide of pink coloured her cheeks as she glimpsed his slight smile.

This, *this* was so different from Paul's selfish insensitivity, Lexi decided wondrously, feeling bewitched and bemused by the awakening of her own sensuality. She had read once that good lovemaking was nature's ultimate aphrodisiac, and it was true, for she felt tremendously and utterly *complete*.

Her eyes widened slightly as Georg slid out of the bed, and anything she might have said was lost beneath the brief pressure of his mouth; then he straightened and walked towards the *en suite* bathroom. She let her lashes drift, down, unwilling to move so much as an inch.

Minutes later her eyes flew wide open and she

made a slight sound in protest as she was lifted out of the bed and carried into the bathroom.

Without any effort he stepped into the round spa-bath and lowered her to sit in front of him. Deliciously warm water lapped her shoulders, and it was pure reflex action that sent her hands to her hair, lifting, twisting its length into a knot atop her head.

She wasn't capable of uttering a single word as he collected soap and began slowly sponging her skin. The action was gently erotic, and she felt a traitorous warmth unfurl deep within and steal treacherously through her veins.

His lips grazed across her exposed nape and settled in the soft curve of her neck, then travelled to the tip of her shoulder and trailed back again. One hand cupped the slight fullness of her breast, while the other traced an evocative pattern across her ribcage, then ventured lower to settle with unerring ease on the nub of her femininity.

Nothing seemed to matter except the resurging desire spiralling through her body, emcompassing and all-consuming, and she gave a startled gasp as he lifted her round to face him.

He kissed her, gently at first, then with tantalising evocativeness, choosing not to allow her to deepen the kiss until she murmured a protest and captured his head with her hands.

His eyes gleamed with lazy passion as she moved forward, and he allowed her licence to initiate a foray that somehow became his to control, then he gently broke the kiss, smiling faintly at her disappointment.

For a moment she was unsure of his intention, and her eyes widened in disbelief as he carefully positioned her to accept his male length, and he watched several fleeting emotions chase expressively over her features as his manhood swelled inside her.

Then his hands slid to her breasts, shaping the soft curves before rendering exquisite torture to their engorged peaks.

Just as she thought she could stand it no longer, he slid one hand to her nape while the other tangled in the mass of her hair as he pulled her head down to his, and this time his kiss was an erotic possession that gave no quarter until she became a mindless supplicant in his arms.

It was a long time before they emerged to towel each other dry, then they walked arm in arm to the bedroom and slid into bed to continue the long slow exploration until sleep claimed them at the edge of a new day's dawn.

CHAPTER NINE

LEXI felt a featherlight touch tracing a delicate pattern along her collarbone, and she opened her eyes slowly, unwilling to come fully awake in case what she'd experienced last night had been little more than a figment of her vivid imagination.

'Wake up, sleepyhead.'

Dreams didn't have voices that sounded like a deep, teasing faintly accented drawl belonging to a certain Greek—at least, none of the dreams she'd ever experienced.

Slowly she let her eyelashes sweep upwards, and her eyes widened slightly as they met the lazy warmth reflecting in his.

'Good morning,' Georg greeted her gently.

She couldn't think of one coherent word to offer, and his mouth assumed a sensual curve that tripped her pulse-beat and sent it racing at a rapid rate.

Thanks, she wanted to say, for the most beautiful night of my life. Except that her throat was dry, and she doubted that any sound would emerge.

'Orange juice? Coffee?' he slanted musingly, shifting slightly to prop his head with one hand.

She wanted both, except she was loath to move, and he laughed softly as he reached out to push several tumbled tresses back behind her ear.

'Time to rise and shine,' he mocked huskily. 'I

have a meeting to attend at nine-thirty, and I imagine you want to ring the hospital.'

Jonathan. Dear lord, how could she possibly have forgotten? Her eyes mirrored her anguish, and he leant forward to brush his lips across her mouth.

'David hasn't rung, so Jonathan's condition will be stable.' He pushed the sheet back and bent to bestow a lingering kiss on her breast. 'Let's take a shower, then we'll share breakfast.'

There was nothing she could do to prevent the faint tinge of pink that flew to her cheeks at the promise of shared intimacy, and the colour deepened as Georg slid out from the bed, unconcerned by his nakedness, and walked round to scoop her into his arms.

'Put me down,' Lexi protested half-heartedly, and he merely laughed as he carried her through to the bathroom.

Reaching into the shower-cubicle, he turned on the taps then let her slide to her feet in front of him.

'You're shy.'

As a statement of fact it was without equal, and she gave a slight ineffectual gesture of assent.

'Don't begin erecting barriers, Lexi.'

She felt utterly defenceless, and she swallowed convulsively as her mouth began to tremble. 'I'm not—used to this,' she said shakily.

His eyes flared, and she saw the pupils darken and change as he caught her close. Then his mouth opened over hers in a kiss that possessed every nuance of erotic mastery, skilfully absorbing her until nothing else mattered except *now*.

She had no idea how long they remained locked together, and when he slowly broke the kiss she could only stand in total bemusement as he reached for a shower-cap, pushed the mass of her curling hair beneath it and gently pulled her into the cubicle.

Half an hour later they were both dressed and seated opposite each other at the breakfast table.

Jonathan, the hospital reported, was stable and had spent a comfortable night. Visitors were limited to five minutes and restricted to immediate family.

Almost as soon as she had replaced the receiver David rang through with the same news and suggested she meet him for lunch.

'I'll see you tonight about seven,' Georg bade her as he drained the last of his coffee.

'Where?' Lexi queried idly as she walked with him towards the door, and he smiled down at her.

'My apartment...yours—does it matter?'

Her eyes lifted to meet his, and she looked unsure, not really wanting him to leave, yet knowing that he must.

'We'll discuss it tonight. Take care,' he said quietly as he opened the door.

Then he was gone, and Lexi closed the door behind him before wandering back into the kitchen.

The day held a dream-like quality as she attended to routine chores, made a few calls, rang David and confirmed arrangements for lunch, then drove to the hospital.

Jonathan was still heavily sedated, and, although he opened his eyes during her brief visit, she doubted her presence registered.

David was already seated when she entered the small restaurant, and he rose to his feet with a warm smile creasing his attractive features.

'I had trouble parking,' she explained with an expressive shrug as she brushed her lips to his cheek. He shook his head as he told her, 'I've only been waiting a few minutes. Will you have something to drink?'

'Mineral water.'

They each ordered from the menu, and Lexi opted for a garden salad followed with fresh fruit.

'How are you getting on with Georg?'

'Reasonably well,' Lexi acknowledged cautiously.

'Jonathan is absolutely delighted you've both opted for marriage,' David ventured, shooting her a deep probing look that didn't fool her in the slightest. 'You must know you have my blessing.'

She took a leisurely sip from her glass, then replaced it carefully down on the table. 'I'm sure you and Jonathan are immensely relieved.'

David appeared to choose his words carefully. 'We've both known the Nicolaos family for many years.'

'How is the business deal progressing with the Japanese consortium?'

'Extremely well. Alex and Georg have managed to elicit a signed preliminary agreement, which I have perused and sanctioned. As soon as Jonathan is well enough the documents will be presented for his signature.' He lifted his shoulders in an expressive gesture. 'Aside from time-consuming technicalities, it is virtually a *fait accompli*.'

She picked at her salad and forked a few morsels into her mouth before venturing, 'And Paul? Presumably you've managed to come to an amicable arrangement with him?'

'We're in a state of negotiation.'

'He's pressing for a larger settlement, and you're stalling,' Lexi deduced with a wry grimace.

'For a few more days, until the deal is due for a Press release,' David agreed.

'After which he will have no room for further negotiation.'

'Precisely.'

It was impossible to refrain from cynicism. 'And all loose ends will be successfully tied.'

'A propitious start to a productive new year.'

'It's Christmas the day after tomorrow,' Lexi murmured, and her expressive eyes dulled slightly as she became lost in reflective thought, remembering previous years at home with numerous gifts piled beneath an enormous decorated tree and Sophie dishing up a veritable feast of festive fare. 'It won't be the same with Jonathan in hospital.'

'I've already spoken with Sophie, and we'll have lunch together at the house, then spend time with Jonathan. Georg, I'm sure, will insist you share the evening with his family.'

She was gripped with a sudden need to confide her own doubts and insecurities. 'David...' she paused, unsure whether her choice of words would sound inane '...I'd rather this marriage was planned for months down the track, instead of the mere weeks Georg is insistent upon.'

Her brother assumed a look of professionally bland inscrutability. 'It's perfectly understandable you should experience doubts, given the circumstances. Why not discuss them with Georg?'

'Because he's equally clever as you, if not more

so,' she acknowledged quietly, and he offered her a slightly whimsical smile.

'Shall we order coffee? I'm due in court at two.'

'David—'

'Marry him, Lexi,' he advised gently. 'I'm confident you'll never have cause to regret it.'

How could something appear so simple and logical, yet be fraught with innumerable complexities? Lexi pondered as she drove to the hospital and called in on Jonathan.

This time he was awake, but extremely drowsy, and she was cheered by his faint smile and the reassurance by nursing staff as to his progress.

What remained of the afternoon she spent shopping, and she returned to her apartment laden with various coloured carrier-bags and packages which she spilled on to the bed in the spare bedroom.

It was hot—so hot, in fact, that Lexi decided to change into a bikini and swim several leisurely lengths of the swimming-pool in an effort to cool off and relax, before returning to her apartment to shower and wash her hair.

Would Georg want to dine in, or go out? Out seemed infinitely safer, for she needed time to think about their shared intimacy and all that it implied before accepting a state of domesticity and shared domicile.

She was ready a few minutes before seven, dressed in an elegant cream strapless silk gown with matching accessories. A silk wrap completed the outfit, and she added a slim gold choker, bracelet and ear-studs. A last-minute check in the mirror lent reassurance that she'd made the right decision in adopting an intricate upswept hairstyle, and her make-up was understated, with skilled application of shadow and liner to emphasis her eyes.

For some reason she felt consumed by nervous tension, and when the doorbell pealed she took a deep breath before crossing the lounge.

Georg looked the epitome of the sophisticated executive, and she let her eyes sweep over the impeccable tailoring of his suit before lifting her gaze to meet his.

Then she immediately wished she hadn't, for she wasn't quite prepared for the lazy warmth evident in those dark eyes or the sensual curve of his mouth. It brought a vivid reminder of all that they'd shared through the night, and her senses leapt at the thought of what lay ahead at the evening's end.

'I wasn't sure what you had in mind,' Lexi offered helplessly, and a husky chuckle left his throat.

'Oh, just an enjoyable meal in your company,' he drawled, adding softly, 'for now.'

Her eyes widened at his unspoken implication, and she was powerless to prevent the feeling of acute vulnerability. 'Would you like a drink?'

His smile deepened, and her stomach seemed to execute a series of somersaults as he caught hold of her hand. 'If you're ready we'll leave.'

The restaurant Georg had chosen was one of the city's élite establishments, and he ordered expensive champagne, then asked her choice of food before selecting what proved to be an epicurean delight.

They conversed, discussing the highlights of each other's day among other things, and afterwards Lexi had no clear recollection of a single topic.

All she was aware of was Georg. His expressive features, the wide-spaced dark eyes, the broad well-defined bone-structure, and his mouth, which seemed to compel an almost hypnotic fascination.

It was after ten when they left, and Lexi was grateful when he slotted a tape into the cassette-player, for it meant she didn't have to search for something adequate by way of conversation.

On reaching her apartment block, he simply parked the car and together they took the lift to her designated floor. She was incapable of making any demur when he retrieved her keys, unlocked the door, then ushered her inside.

All evening she had been conscious of his indolent regard, the degree of latent passion evident, and now she felt like a finely tuned violin waiting for the maestro's touch. It was crazy to be so acutely aware of another human body and the effect it could have on her senses.

'You look so incredibly fragile I am almost afraid to touch you,' Georg mused as he lifted a hand and trailed his fingers down her cheek. He traced the curve of her mouth with a gentle forefinger, then lowered his head to bestow a fleeting kiss on her mouth.

Her lips parted involuntarily, trembling as she caught his indrawn breath, and she felt a sense of loss as he drew back and stood regarding her with disruptive sensuality.

'Will you object if I unpin your hair?'

She shook her head in silent acquiescence, and when the curls lay in a thick mass below her shoulders he slid his fingers through their length.

'I've wanted to do this all evening.'

And I've waited all day, she assured silently, and felt vaguely shocked at the truth of her thoughts.

Then he kissed her, gently at first, and afterwards she had little recollection of who was in command as passion flared and demanded assuagement.

With a husky exultant laugh Georg swept her into his arms and carried her through to the bedroom, where he took infinite care to remove every last vestige of her clothing before beginning on his own.

Lexi behaved like a shameless wanton beneath his touch as he sought to strike an unhitherto heard chord, and she cried out as the deep rhythm of his possession took her to the heights of ecstasy and beyond.

Long after he had fallen asleep at her side she lay awake, too caught up with introspection to cull an easy somnolence.

Even now it seemed a fantasy, some wild imaginative dream that had no part of reality. Potent, dangerous, and—in its aftermath—destructive.

Just as she'd thought the pain and degradation Paul had inflicted was unacceptable, this—passionate *possession* Georg evoked was everything she'd been led to believe, and more.

Had *he* felt like that? Was he able to command such a mindless response from every woman he took to bed? Or was it merely sexual chemistry at its zenith? She'd been so caught up with her own reactions that she hadn't given a thought to his.

A shudder shook her slender frame in the realisation that she'd taken everything he'd chosen to give, and given nothing in return. It had been *her* pleasure, her climactic orgasm that had been all-important, the desperate need to have him continue arousing those spiralling sensations until she felt almost *driven* by a wholly consuming desire.

In the night he stirred and reached for her, settling her into the curve of his body, and she woke late to find an empty space beside her and a scrawled note on the adjoining pillow, which read, 'Dinner tonight my apartment—I'll cook. Georg.'

Lexi showered, then, dressed in casual clothes, she drove to the supermarket, battling against weary mothers with young children and middle-aged matrons in an effort to traverse the numerous aisles and fill her trolley with necessary groceries. She visited Jonathan in hospital, then she returned home to tidy up before driving back to the hospital mid-afteroon.

It was almost six-thirty when she buzzed Georg's apartment from the lobby, and within minutes the lift descended to transport her to the uppermost floor.

She had elected to dress casually, choosing a straight black skirt and white knit top, and her hair was caught up at her nape with a fashionable black bow.

'Mmm, smells heavenly,' Lexi greeted him as soon as Georg opened the door, and she almost melted at the warmth reflected in his eyes.

'Tonight you will sample a selection of traditional Greek cuisine.'

'And afterwards can we watch the carol-singing on television?' she ventured, wriggling her nose at him as he slanted her a quizzical glance. 'It's Christmas Eve.'

He, too, was in casual attire: dressed in designer

jeans and a cotton-knit shirt, he projected a raw virility that was arresting.

For a starter he served vine-wrapped parcels of minced lamb accompanied by a delicate sauce, which he followed with moussaka. Dessert was baklava, and afterwards they dispensed with the dishes before taking their coffee through to the lounge, where they watched a number of artists, accompanied by a choir, sing a variety of carols, recorded live from a large city park.

'I must go,' Lexi intimated when the programme came to a close.

'Why must you?' Georg drawled.

'Tomorrow is Christmas Day,' she said helplessly as he reached forward and undid the bow fastening her hair. 'I'm visiting Jonathan in the morning, and meeting David at the house at midday. After lunch we'll both go to the hospital, and—'

'Stay with me,' he interceded. 'And in the morning we will visit Jonathan together.'

She looked at him carefully, then opened her mouth to speak, only to have him press her lips closed.

'Indulge me. I cannot think of a nicer Christmas present than to wake and find you in my bed.'

A long time afterwards she wondered why she hadn't protested, but by then it was far too late to rationalise her decision.

Christmas Day was filled with love and laughter, the joy of gifts and giving, *family*. Hers, his. And Jonathan was progressing with such speed that it seemed there was little cause to doubt his ability to recover fully from surgery.

The days leading up to New Year passed all too

quickly. Lexi spent each morning and afternoon visiting Jonathan, and the nights were spent with Georg,
at his apartment or her own. Sometimes they ate out,
dining with Samantha and Alex, or with Mrs
Nicolaos, and when they stayed home they took it in
turns to prepare the evening meal.

'I'll cook tonight,' Lexi declared as she followed
him to the door of his apartment a few days before
she was due to fly north for the photographic shoot
at the Port Douglas Mirage Resort. She had something special in mind, and teased lightly as he moved
towards the lift, 'Will you mind if I use your kitchen?'

'Carla is due to arrive about nine,' he warned as
he pressed the call-button.

His housekeeper was Spanish, matronly, and came
in two days a week to clean, stock up the pantry and
refrigerator from Georg's list, and take care of the
laundry. She was a delight, voluble, and possessed of
a wicked sense of humour.

Lexi retreated into the kitchen and poured herself
a second cup of coffee, then planned a menu and
checked ingredients before making out a list of what
she needed.

At ten she visited Jonathan, then went on to complete her shopping, and most of the afternoon was
spent preparing food.

Carla left at five, and Lexi hurriedly changed into
white evening culottes and a patterned top before returning to the kitchen to anxiously oversee the various
dishes alternately simmering atop the elements and
the oven. Then she was able to centre her attention
on setting an elegant table in the dining-room.

When Georg arrived shortly after six everything

was ready, and she felt inordinately pleased with the result.

'Hmm, is this is a sample of what I can look forward to in the future?' he drawled as he caught her close, and she returned his kiss with such fervour it left her slightly breathless.

'I felt like surprising you,' she said simply, and her bones seemed to melt at the warmth reflected in his eyes.

'Mental telepathy, perhaps?' Georg slanted as he moved across to the cabinet to pour them both a drink. 'I have decided to surprise you by having an agent line up a few properties for us to inspect tomorrow.'

Her expressive features portrayed a gamut of emotions. 'You intend buying a house?'

'Yes, Lexi. *Ours.*'

She took the slim crystal flute from his hand and sipped the contents. 'I assumed if we married that we'd live here.'

His gaze probed hers. '*When*, not if. And we shall live here until such time as the redecorating and refurbishing of the house is completed.'

The breath caught in her throat, and for a moment she was lost for words. 'I barely become accustomed to one concept when you confront me with another,' she managed shakily.

He reached out and tilted her chin. 'I thought I had managed to dispense with all your doubts.'

She gave a light shrugging gesture. 'Most of them.'

Gently he bent his head down to hers and trailed his lips over her cheek. 'Could it be that you need reassurance?'

'The kind of reassurance you have in mind will mean we get to miss dinner,' she reproved him with a helpless smile, and he laughed softly.

'Tonight you have gone to too much trouble for that, hmm?' His kiss was hard and brief, then he stepped back and caught hold of her hand. 'Let us eat.'

If not exactly of cordon bleu standard, the meal was a complete success, and Lexi basked in the glow of Georg's praise as he sampled one course after another before sitting back, replete, with a glass of superb port.

Together they dispensed with the dishes, and after a leisurely coffee Georg simply swung her into his arms and carried her through to the bedroom.

CHAPTER TEN

THERE was no doubt which house held the most appeal. Lexi fell in love with its Federation-style architecture and multi-coloured leaded windows, the many rooms with wide glass doors opening on to a magnificent terrace, and the panoramic view of the harbour. Possessed of an air of tranquillity, it seemed far removed from the city's hustle and bustle, and with its gardens pruned and replanted it would soon be restored to its former glory.

'This is it?' Georg queried, smiling at her enthusiasm.

'It has so much potential,' she breathed. 'What do *you* think?'

'I'll contact the agent this afternoon.'

'I have a few things to do,' Lexi declared as Georg headed the Ferrari towards Double Bay. 'Shopping.' She really could not leave selecting a suitable gown for the wedding any longer, and she knew of just the boutique where she might find exactly what she had in mind. 'And I'll call into the hospital to see Jonathan, then head back to my apartment.'

'Don't forget we're dining out tonight,' he reminded her. 'I'll collect you at six.'

It was after four when Lexi entered her apartment, and she moved through to the kitchen to retrieve a cool drink from the refrigerator. As much as she adored shopping, to do so in the heat of sub-tropical summer proved an enervating experience.

The insistent burr of the telephone sounded loud in the stillness of the apartment, and she quickly crossed the room and picked up the receiver.

'Lexi?'

The sound of Paul's voice was totally unexpected, and her fingers tightened until the knuckles showed white.

'You must know I have nothing whatsoever to say to you,' she reiterated hardily.

'You don't need to, darling. Just listen is all I ask.'

'Hurry up and get it over with, Paul. I haven't much spare time.'

'Jonathan's precious deal has gone through. Although I guess you know that. And I've been paid off,' he drawled. 'Not as handsomely as I'd like, but adequately enough.'

'Is that it?'

'Don't hang up, Lexi. This conversation is entirely for your benefit.'

She gave a heavy sigh. 'I find that almost impossible to believe.'

'Ah, but you see, darling,' Paul informed her hatefully, 'what you fail to comprehend is that the ultimate joke in this entire débâcle is on you. *Yes*, my sweet—' he paused to give his words sufficient emphasis '—a masterly scheme, conveniently compounded by *my* coincidental involvement, for, after your initial disastrous foray into matrimony with me, it became essential such an error was not repeated. Your dear father and brother, in cohorts with Georg, conspired to utilise Jonathan's forthcoming surgery as a reason to arrange an eminently suitable marriage for you—with none other than Georg Nicolaos.' His laugh was totally without humour. 'And you, in your innocence, played right into their hands.'

She felt sickened, almost to the point of being physically ill. It took considerable effort to keep her voice calm, but she managed it—just.

'I don't have to listen to any of this.' She had surpassed anger, and was fast approaching a numbed state of limbo.

'Check it out with David,' Paul exhorted cynically. 'I doubt he'll deny it.' Lexi didn't bother to comment, and he continued in a hateful voice, 'Will you think me facetious if I wish you happiness in your second marriage? Such a pity its basis is no more to do with *love* than your first,' he accorded, and there was a slight click as he hung up.

Lexi stood where she was for several long seconds, then she depressed the call-button and punched out a succession of digits.

'David Harrison,' she requested as soon as the receptionist answered. 'Lexi Harrison speaking.'

'Mr Harrison is engaged with a client. Can I get him to call you?'

'It's urgent,' Lexi insisted, and seconds later David came on the line. 'Paul rang to tell me he'd been paid off,' she began without preamble. 'He insists Jonathan deliberately conspired with you and Georg to trap me into marriage. Is it true?'

There was an imperceptible silence, and her stomach gave a sickening lurch.

'Your happiness has always been Jonathan's prime concern,' David responded cautiously.

'Don't play the courtroom tactician with me, David,' she said tightly. 'At least have the decency to confirm or deny it.'

'It's clearly evident you and Georg are happy together.'

'Damn you!' she cursed. 'That doesn't excuse anything!'

'I'll call Georg—'

'Don't interfere,' she warned fiercely. 'If you do I'll never speak to you again!'

She replaced the receiver and almost immediately the telephone burred an insistent summons. For all of ten seconds she determined not to answer, and only the thought that it might be Jonathan motivated her to pick up the receiver.

'Lexi?' Georg's deep faintly accented voice sounded so close he could have been in the same room. 'I'll be delayed by about half an hour.'

Oh, heavens, they were supposed to be dining out! She closed her eyes, then slowly reopened them. 'I was just about to ring you,' she declared, inventing with no scruple whatsoever. 'I can't make it tonight. Jacques needs me. One of the models reported in sick.'

She closed her eyes momentarily against the slight throbbing that began in the region of her right temple.

'Where is the assignment? I'll meet you there.'

An inner voice screamed out in silent rejection. She couldn't face seeing him tonight. If she did she'd never contain the anger that was seething deep inside. 'No, Georg.' Time enough tomorrow to face a confrontation. By then she might have gathered sufficient courage to be able to adopt a cool rationale. 'I have to go. I'm running late.' She replaced the receiver before he had a chance to comment. Crossing into the bedroom, she stripped off her outer clothes, then selected designer jeans and a loose cotton top at random from her wardrobe. Dressed, she caught her hair into a loose knot, picked up her bag, and made her way out of the apartment.

Quite where she was heading she wasn't sure. Anywhere would do, as long as she had some time alone in which to think. Somewhere where no one could contact her.

In the car she slotted a compact disc into the music system, then sent the Mercedes up to street level. Taking a left turn, she simply drove, uncaring of her direction or destination.

Sheer driving skill and instinct kept her within the speed limit and observant of the road rules. Either that or divine guidance, she decided wryly as she finally brought the car to a halt on the side of the road.

She had no idea where she was, for how long or how far she'd travelled, and she rested her forehead on the steering-wheel in a gesture of infinite weariness.

Perhaps there was a motel somewhere nearby where she could book in for the night. It was either that or face a long drive back to her apartment.

A strange light-headedness assailed her, and she wound down the window to let in some fresh air. Now that she thought about it, the last time she'd eaten was at midday, and then it had only been a light salad.

A glance at her watch revealed that it was nine o'clock. She'd been driving for more than three hours.

It was hardly likely that anything would be open at this time of night, although she vaguely remembered passing a petrol station a short while ago. Maybe they ran a fast-food outlet where she could pick up hot coffee and a filled roll.

Without further thought she switched on the ignition and fired the engine, swinging the car in a semi-circle on to the northbound highway.

Half an hour later, suitably revived by two cups of strong coffee and a surprisingly wholesome meal, she made the decision to drive home.

It was almost one o'clock when she took the lift up to her apartment. As the doors slid open she stifled a yawn, weary almost beyond belief.

At first she didn't see the tall figure leaning against the wall outside her apartment door. It wasn't until a slight movement caught her attention that his presence registered, and she faltered mid-step, then froze as Georg's muscular frame unfolded.

Shock, resentment, *anger*—all those emotions seemed to register at once, and her tiredness vanished.

'What are you doing here?'

One eyebrow slanted in silent query. 'Whatever happened to "hello"?' His gaze was dark and infinitely formidable beneath its steady appraisal. 'I contacted Jacques, only to be told that, if there was a fashion parade on in the city tonight, he certainly wasn't running it.' His eyes seemed to mesmerise hers. 'If you didn't want to dine out you had only to say so.'

Lexi didn't blink. 'You would have asked questions and demanded answers.'

His silence accelerated her nervous tension to a point where she was sure he must see the pulse thudding at the base of her throat. 'Do you consider it so strange that I feel I have a right to know if something bothers you?'

His drawled query seemed like the last straw! Her anger snapped, and she could feel it erupt inside her like a volcano. *'Right?'* she exploded. 'You have no rights where I'm concerned!'

His gaze narrowed, and a muscle tensed along the edge of his jaw. 'The hallway is hardly the place for a slanging match. Where are your keys?'

Ignoring her protest, he took her bag and searched inside it until he discovered her keyring, then he calmly put an arm around her waist and hoisted her over his shoulder.

'Put me down, you fiend!' She tried to kick him and one of her shoes fell to the carpeted floor. 'Let me go, *damn you!*'

There was nothing she could do to stop him unlocking the front door, and, once inside, he closed it with an almost silent click before allowing her to slide down to her feet.

His eyes held hers, dark and incredibly watchful. 'Now, suppose you explain?' he demanded in a voice that was dangerously soft.

'Explain?' she vented, furious almost beyond belief. 'You thought you were very clever, didn't you? Together with Jonathan and David, you played both ends against the middle and manufactured a conspiracy in which you were not only a perpetrator, but a

willing participant.' Her eyes gleamed with a fine rage. 'You conniving, uncaring, diabolical *bastard*! Who do you think you are, attempting to play God?' She took a step forward and began railing him with her fists, hitting him anywhere she could connect—his chest, his arms, his shoulders…beating him with an anger that brought tears streaming down her cheeks until hard hands caught hold of her own, stilling their actions with galling ease.

'That's enough.'

'I hate you!' she stormed vehemently. '*Hate* you, do you understand?'

His hands tightened their grasp on her wrists, and she struggled powerlessly against him as he drew her close. Effortlessly he caught both her hands together, then slid his hand through the length of her hair, exerting sufficient pressure until there was no other option but for her to meet his gaze.

Lexi was aware of every muscle in the taut length of his body, and she wanted to scream and rage against him.

Broken dreams, a cynical inner voice taunted; the destruction of the hope that Georg could possibly feel about her the way she felt about him, that such a tenuous, precious emotion as *love* might be shared.

Yet pride forbade acceptance of any logic, and she pulled away from him, straining against hands that held her firmly at arm's length.

'Let me go,' she demanded, attempting to wrest free from his grasp and failing miserably.

'So that you can run away again?'

'I didn't run,' she disclaimed heatedly, and glimpsed the wry twist of his mouth.

'No?'

'Will you please leave?' she countered with un-accustomed hauteur. 'I'm tired, I have a headache, and I want to go to bed.' Her eyes resembled fiery shards of sheer topaz, a brilliance that refused to be daunted beneath his probing gaze. She felt mentally drained, and completely enervated. The headache was no fabrication, and she raised a shaky hand to her left temple in an attempt to ease the pain.

'I would have thought you impervious to any element of gossip,' Georg drawled with soft inflexibility.

Her eyes didn't waver from his for a second. 'Paul was terribly convincing.' She saw the dark flaring in the depths of his eyes, the faint bunching of muscle at the edge of his jaw. 'Yes, *Paul*. But then, you know, don't you? I have no doubt David called you, in spite of anything I said to the contrary.' She lifted a hand in an involuntary gesture as he would have spoken. 'Don't. Please don't compound the situation with any meaningless qualification.' She even managed a faint smile. 'It's amazing, really. Beneath the anger, the sheer *rage* that my life, my future, should be treated with such clinical detachment and utter high-handedness, I can still see the logic of it all from Jonathan's point of view. The youngest child, his adored little girl, couldn't be allowed to drift through life alone. A man had to be found: the *right* man. Someone above reproach, of considerable financial standing, and preferably of a similar calibre to Jonathan himself.' Her features assumed a deliber-ately winsome expression. 'Even fate took a hand in providing the perfect opportunity to have me collab-orate. Bypass surgery is sufficiently serious to warrant

respect and a willingness to ease the patient's mind.
I can even understand Jonathan's need to tie it all up
beforehand, so that *he* could undergo surgery safe in
the knowledge there would be someone to care for
me should things go wrong. What I fail to comprehend,' she continued slowly, 'is *your* involvement.
You don't need my share of my father's money.
You're so self-sufficient, you certainly don't need *me*.
And I refuse to believe you'd consent to marry merely
to honour the close friendship of a business partner.'
She drew in a slight breath, not caring just how brutal
her analytical dissection became. 'There is, of course,
the possibility you had reached an age where you
were inclined to make the clinical decision to take a
wife and sire a son to follow in your footsteps. In that
respect I guess I qualify. I'm from the right side of
the track, educated, personable. We're even physically—'

'Compatible?'

Remembering exactly to what precise degree they
were sexually in tune almost proved to be her undoing, and a faint tinge of pink rose to define her
cheekbones. 'Yes.'

'Is that how you see me?'

Her chin lifted fractionally as she accorded without
guile, 'I have to give you full marks for sensual expertise.'

His eyes seared hers, almost as if he could see
through to her soul. 'You think that's all it was?' he
demanded in a voice that sounded like steel razing
silk asunder.

'Good sex,' she conceded matter-of-factly. Inside
she was slowly dying. 'I doubt it comes any better.'

'The mechanical coupling of two consenting adults who indulge in an act of physical lust? Not making love, where each partner takes infinite care to caress and arouse until they ache with an awareness so acute it transcends mere pleasure? And even then the pleasure is extended until the fire becomes unbearable, like a mindless passion demanding the release that only they can give—to each other?'

Lexi wanted to close her eyes and shut out the images his voice evoked, to still the shivers that slithered across the surface of her skin as memory provided a graphic reminder of the nights they'd spent in each other's arms.

'Tomorrow I fly north to Cairns for the photographic shoot at Port Douglas. I plan to stay on at the resort for a few days.' She managed to hold his gaze without wavering. 'I need some peace and tranquillity in my life.'

'You imagine I'll let you walk away?'

Pride, together with an innate sense of self-preservation, was responsible for the steadiness of her voice. 'There is nothing you can do to stop me.'

He stood looking at her for what seemed an age, and the breath caught in her throat, seeming to formulate into a lump which made it impossible for her to swallow.

Dark eyes hardened with frightening anger, and for one heart-stopping moment she thought he was going to *shake* her.

'Have your time alone, if that's what you think you need.' His voice was controlled, yet as hard as tensile steel. 'However, if you intend opting out of our impending marriage, then *you* must be the one to tell Jonathan and rescind all the arrangements.'

Lexi closed her eyes against the compelling sight of him, then slowly opened them again, aware of a primeval instinct for survival as she became trapped in the prison of his penetrating gaze.

'That amounts to emotional blackmail,' she said shakily.

'I'll use any tool I can.'

'*Why?*'

A faint, slightly cruel smile curved from the edge of his mouth. 'You think you have all the answers. Work it out for yourself.'

Without a further word he turned and walked to the door, opened it, then pulled it closed behind him.

Lexi lifted her hand in an involuntary gesture as her subconscious mind sought to call him back, then she shook her head and gazed sightlessly around the room.

Crossing her arms, she hugged them tightly against her breasts. Never before had she felt quite so frighteningly alone, bereft, and, with an aching sense of loss so acute it took every ounce of effort to walk to the door, she attached the safety chain, activated the alarm system, then made her way to bed.

CHAPTER ELEVEN

THE PORT DOUGLAS resort was aptly named Mirage, for that was how it appeared after an hour's drive from Cairns along a road that alternately hugged the coastal foreshore then swung inwards to weave its way through dense rainforest.

The heat hit Lexi the moment she stepped out from the air-conditioned limousine, the high humidity of a tropical wet season making the air seem heavy and stultifying, and tiny beads of sweat began to dew on her skin in the brief few minutes it took for her to pay the driver.

Her reserved suite was cool, decorated in pale muted shades that were visually restful, and as soon as she was alone she headed for the bathroom and stripped off her clothes.

A leisurely shower proved refreshing, and she selected shorts and a sleeveless top before extracting a bottle of pineapple juice from the refrigerator.

It was deliciously icy, and, sipping it slowly, she moved to the large sliding glass doors to view the lush sculptured grounds bounded by enormous palms, and, beyond, the wide expanse of ocean.

She should rest, she thought, have a quiet evening meal, and follow it with an early night, so that she would be ready to sparkle beneath the all-revealing eye of the camera first thing in the morning. Except that she felt impossibly restless, and she prowled round the suite, then crossed to the phone in a determined bid to ring Jonathan and tell him of her safe arrival.

Georg's name wasn't even mentioned, much to her relief, and after she'd replaced the receiver she stood staring at the telephone in brooding silence.

A discreet rap at the door provided an interruption, and she accepted the long slim cellophaned box from the delivery-man. As soon as she was alone she hurriedly tore open the accompanying envelope, only to discover that the flowers were from the management, welcoming her to the hotel.

A wry smile tugged at her mouth. Why shouldn't they make a token gesture? The publicity from this shoot would arouse tremendous interest in the resort.

And she desperately tried to ignore an inner voice taunting unmercifully that she should even dare hope Georg might have despatched a floral tribute.

Dear heaven, why was she so contrary? If the roses had come from Georg she probably would have given them to one of the staff. And why should he send her anything when she'd virtually walked out on him?

She clenched her hands, then winced as the stone from her engagement ring dug into her finger. And that was another thing, she thought wretchedly as she adjusted the ring so that it rested squarely. She should have taken the ring off and given it back to him before she left Sydney. Except that she hadn't, and she began to wonder why.

Damn. There were no easy answers, and she was darned if she was to embark on a fact-and-find soul-searching mission *now*.

She'd come here for a reason: to work, and to follow it with a few extra days of relaxation. And that was exactly what she intended to do. Georg, and every facet of her involvement with him, could be successfully put on hold.

But it wasn't that easy. At least *work* presented few difficulties. The cameraman was easy to work with, and the clothes were superb. It was afterwards, when she was alone, that the problems began, for with so much time on her hands she began to pursue a path of destructive introspection.

The days were bad enough, but the nights were worse, for then she lay awake, aware with each passing hour of a deep, aching sense of loss.

When she finally did manage to fall asleep her dreams were vivid and heart-rendingly graphic. Inevitably she came sharply awake to discover that Georg's presence was a figment of a fertile imagination, and reality was an empty bed.

To spend so much time alone was detrimental, Lexi decided, and in a desperate need to fill her days she embarked on every recommended tour available.

She made friends with a few fellow guests, joining them for dinner on two occasions, and she spoke to her father by phone every day.

However, the one call she wanted, more than any other, never came, and somehow she was unable to summon sufficient courage to make the call herself.

Why didn't Georg ring? she agonised at least a dozen times every day. Had he decided, after all, to believe all those hateful things she'd flung at him in temper? Perhaps he had used this last week for a bit of introspection of his own.

Oh, lord, it would be terribly ironic if *he* opted to

call the wedding off, just when extensive self-analysis of her emotions revealed she'd fallen irretrievably in love with him. For there could be no doubt it was *love*.

There was only one way to find out, and with new-found resolve she rang the airline, booked the next flight south, then packed her bag and checked out of the hotel.

Lexi arrived in Sydney, collected her holdall, then hired a taxi to take her to Darling Point, where she retrieved her mail and took the lift up to her apartment.

The answering-machine held a variety of messages, and she played the tape as she sifted through her mail.

One of the first things she must do was ring Jonathan, she thought, for she didn't want to cause him any anxiety should he phone the Port Douglas resort only to be told she'd already left.

'Come visit me this evening,' her father bade her after they'd exchanged a preliminary greeting. 'Bring Georg.' She almost heard the laughter in his voice as he teased, 'I won't expect you to stay long.'

Oh, heavens, how did she get of that? 'Georg doesn't know I'm back yet,' she responded lightly. 'Can I take a raincheck, and make it tomorrow night? I'll ring you in the morning.'

As soon as she'd concluded the call she depressed the reset button and dialled Georg's number before she had time to give the action any thought. If she hesitated she'd never summon the necessary courage.

But he wasn't at the restaurant, nor was he in his office.

'Would you care to leave a message?'

She hesitated for all of five seconds. 'No, I'll ring back.'

Fool, she accorded the instant she replaced the receiver. It would have been much simpler if she'd left her name. Except that then *she* would be the one waiting with bated breath for the phone to ring, and if he didn't call she'd be totally shattered. At least this way the ball was still in her court.

Or was it? Somehow she couldn't help thinking he was playing a very shrewd game, deliberately allowing her to think she had her freedom, while all the time aware she could never truly be free of him.

At five o'clock she emerged from the shower, and after completing her toilette she took painstaking care with her appearance, choosing the expensive lace-edged silk teddy Georg had bid impossibly highly for to wear beneath a cream silk ensemble of culottes, matching top and jacket.

Make-up was deliberately subtle, with emphasis on her eyes and mouth, and she caught her hair up in an elaborate chignon from which she teased free a few wispy tendrils for effect.

The end result was startling, as she had intended, and without pause for thought she collected a clutch-bag, her car-keys, then stepped out from the apartment without so much as a backward glance.

Halfway to Georg's apartment she decided she was quite mad. For all she knew, he could be at the restaurant, or dining with Alex and Samantha. He could be in any one of a dozen places, and least of all was he likely to be home.

Yet she had to start somewhere, she decided as she

parked the car and walked towards the elegantly designed foyer of his exclusive apartment block.

Depressing the appropriate intercom buzzer, she waited anxiously for a response.

'Carla. Who is there, please?'

'Lexi,' she relayed into the microphone. 'Lexi Harrison.'

'Mr Georg is not here. You want to come up?'

Relief washed over her. 'Please.'

The buzzer sounded, and the security door slid open. Three minutes later Lexi walked out from the lift into the penthouse lobby.

'Ah, there you are,' Carla greeted her in accented English within seconds of Lexi's pressing the doorbell. 'You are lucky I am still here. Tonight I am late in leaving.' A broad grin creased her attractive matronly features, and her eyes sparkled. 'You wait here for Mr Georg?'

'Yes.' Lexi preceded the housekeeper into the lounge and sank into one of the soft leather chairs. 'Is he going to be long?'

'I don't know.' An eloquent shrug lifted broad capable shoulders. 'He ring before and tell me he cook for himself tonight. You want I should get you something? A drink, maybe? I can fix you a snack.'

'No,' Lexi refused with a kindly smile. 'Thanks all the same; I'll be fine. You go.'

'You sure? It's no trouble.'

'Sure,' Lexi assured her, touched by the older woman's concern.

As soon as she was alone she rose to her feet and crossed to the huge glass window where she stood staring sightlessly out at the view.

The harbour glistened against a backdrop of city buildings and clear azure sky. A tugboat bustled importantly out to meet an incoming liner, and two ferries passed each other as they forged in opposite directions to their different destinations. Houses and apartment blocks dotted the foreshore, with trees and landscaped gardens covering numerous hills rising high from the sea.

In midsummer, with the advantage of daylight saving, there was still evidence of a heat haze lingering in the air, and it would be several hours before dusk would provide a gradually darkening shroud. Then the city would come alive with a galaxy of light, myriad pinpricks of electricity providing a veritable fairyland to complement the brilliantly flashing neon from city buildings.

It was a similar view to the one Lexi enjoyed from her own apartment, and she had become so accustomed to the visual beauty's being on constant display that it failed to register as she became lost in contemplation.

Would Georg be pleased to see her? Her features paled at the thought that he might not. Dear lord in heaven! How was she supposed to live without him? Oh, *why* did she have to suffer such a conflict of emotions? she cursed helplessly.

The faint sound of a key being turned in the lock momentarily froze her limbs, then she slowly swung round to face the door.

One glance at Georg's tall dark-suited frame was sufficient for the nerves in her stomach to begin a painful somersault, and she stood in mesmerised silence as he entered the room.

Her eyes flew to his face, seeing the dark set of his jaw, the broad chiselled cheekbones assembled into an unfathomable mask.

Everything she wanted to say remained locked in her throat, and she simply stood still as he carefully closed the door behind him.

Then he turned towards her, and she nearly died at the hard implacability evident.

'Lexi.'

His voice was a cynical world-weary drawl, and she drew a deep calming breath in defence against the agonising shaft of pain that ripped through her body.

'Hello, Georg,' she greeted him quietly, her eyes wide and clear as he moved further into the room. 'Carla let me in.'

He paused, surveying her with detached inscrutability for what seemed an age, then crossed to the drinks cabinet. 'Can I get you a drink?'

Lexi doubted she'd be able to lift the glass to her lips without spilling its contents, and if she so much as swallowed anything she'd choke! 'No—thanks,' she added with extreme politeness, watching as he selected a glass, added ice, a measure of whisky and a generous splash of soda before turning to face her.

'When did you get back?'

'This afternoon.'

He moved across to where she stood. 'You could have phoned.'

'I rang the office, but you weren't in.'

'A message would have reached me.'

The deep drawling voice sent goose-pimples scudding over the surface of her skin, and she had to steel herself against actually shivering. A spark of defiance lifted her chin and tilted it fractionally. 'You're not going to make this easy for me, are you?'

His eyes seared hers, hardening with frightening intensity. 'Can you give me any reason why I should?'

Lexi closed her eyes against the compelling sight of him, then slowly opened them again. The air between them seemed alive with latent emotion, and her heart gave a lurch as she glimpsed a muscle tensing along his jaw.

She was dangerously close to tears, and she looked at him, silently begging for his understanding. 'I spent every waking minute thinking about you while I was away, remembering, examining everything you said, all that had happened between us,' she began slowly. Her eyes unconsciously beseeched him to understand, but his expression remained an inscrutable mask. 'I even managed to persuade myself *before* Paul's revelation that marriage to you would have its compensations.' A hollow laugh rose in her throat to escape as a strangled sound, and she lifted her hands in a gesture of self-deprecation. 'Heaven knows, I'd rushed into my first marriage ignoring everything except my heart. There seemed to be some sense in using some caution with regard to a second attempt, and at least you had Jonathan's wholehearted approval. I even dared to think we might be happy together, and I began to relax, lulled into a state of contented acceptance. I felt I could trust you, and I became very—' she hesitated, hardly wanting to lay bare her heart '—fond of you.' Oh, dear lord, if only he knew just *how* fond!

She waited for him to say something, to give her some reassurance, but he remained silent.

'After Paul, I didn't want to trust any man again. I didn't even feel I could trust myself.' She swallowed painfully, and felt the ache of unshed tears as she gathered the strength to continue. 'I hated having to live a lie, even for Jonathan's sake, and I especially hated you for taking me through the threshold of pain and showing me what pleasure could be.' Her mouth trembled as it tried for a smile and lost miserably. 'Must you have it all?' she demanded shakily, and it seemed a lifetime before he spoke.

'Yes.'

It took an inordinate amount of courage to continue, but she managed—just.

'When I discovered there was a deliberate conspiracy I was so angry, so disillusioned, so incredibly—hurt,' Lexi admitted poignantly.

His eyes never left hers for a second. 'And now?'

This was no time to be faint-hearted, and with a sense of trepidation she took the greatest gamble of her life. She lifted a shaky hand, then let it fall helplessly down to her side, and her eyes shimmered with the force of her emotion. 'I discovered I can't live without you.' She attempted a faint smile and failed miserably as her lips trembled. 'Don't you understand? *I love you.*' The words were torn out of her in a flow of wretched emotion, and she looked at him blindly through a well of tears. 'What more do you want?'

Georg carefully placed his glass down on a nearby table, then he caught hold of her shoulders and pulled her close, lifting a hand to catch hold of her chin and tilting it so that she had no option but to look at him.

'*You,*' he accorded softly. 'As my wife, by my side, always.'

There was no way she could still the silent trickling flow of tears as they spilled and ran slowly down each cheek, and her mouth shook almost beyond control.

His eyes darkened until they were almost black. 'Don't,' he groaned, gathering her close. '*Cristos*, don't cry!'

His hands were gentle as they slid through her hair to hold fast her head, and his mouth lowered to nuzzle the sweet curve of her neck, his lips caressing the softly throbbing vein until he felt the faint tremor in her throat; then he began a tantalisingly slow path to her mouth. He kissed her gently at first, then with increasing hunger as he sought to remove every last vestige of doubt.

It seemed an age before he relinquished her lips, and she could only look at him in total bemusement as he trailed a finger down the slope of her nose, and traced the soft, swollen contours of her mouth.

She was unable to prevent the slight shiver that raked her slender body, and he slid his hands up to frame her face.

'You're beautiful,' he accorded gently. 'So generous and warm and giving. A joy only a fool would discard.' He smiled as her eyes widened, and his thumb gently probed the tremulous curves of her mouth, then began tracing their outline with tactile exploration. 'It was impossible for me not to be aware of your existence,' he owned huskily. 'You intrigued me, and I wanted to get to know you better. Under normal circumstances Jonathan would have arranged for us to be formally introduced over dinner at his home, but both he and David knew you would see it as a deliberate guise. As soon as I learned of Jonathan's ill-health it was *my* suggestion to involve you in attempt to halt Paul's meddling.' His mouth moved to form a wry smile. 'I knew within days of going public with our supposed romance that only the reality would suffice, and I used every weapon at my command.' He laughed softly at her expression of disbelief. 'I knew I had insufficient time to afford you a gentle seduction. My pursuit had to be swift and blatant.' He paused to bestow a brief hard kiss to her soft mouth, thereby preventing any response she might have made. 'In my arms your body was its own traitorous mistress, alive and gloriously vibrant beneath my touch, and every time we made love I was sure you must know the extent of my feelings.' His lips touched hers, light and as fleeting as a butterfly's wings.

'I was sufficiently naïve to think it was merely sexual expertise,' Lexi admitted with a faint smile.

'I wanted to kill Paul,' Georg went on to reveal, and his eyes hardened with latent anger. 'A few days ago I had to physically restrain myself from going after him and committing serious bodily harm,' he asserted bleakly, and there was an inflexible quality evident in those tautly chiselled features that she longed to ease.

'It doesn't matter. *He* doesn't matter,' Lexi assured him, conscious of his darkening gaze.

'He'll never have the opportunity to hurt you again.'

She looked at him, loving the strength, the sheer animal magnificence that set him apart from other men. Her heart swelled, and her lips parted to form a soft tremulous smile.

'You're determined to play the role of my guardian angel?' she couldn't resist teasing, and received a husky growl in response as he gathered her close against him.

'Husband; lover,' he corrected, his expression softening miraculously, and she felt herself begin to drown in the warmth of his eyes. 'Friend; confidant,' he added, moulding her slim curves against his hardened frame. '*Yours*, for a lifetime.'

Her eyes clung to his, and for a moment she was unable to speak, then any words she might have said were lost as he lowered his head and kissed her with such gentle evocativeness that she almost cried.

'I love you,' he accorded gently. 'So much. These past few days have been hell. When I arrived home tonight and found you here I was so desperately afraid you had come to demand your freedom.'

Lexi lifted a hand to his lips, and her eyes widened measurably as he caressed each finger in turn, drawing first one, then the other into his mouth and gently biting each tender tip. A shaft of exquisite pleasure unfurled deep inside her, slowly radiating throughout her whole body until she was filled with delicious expectant warmth.

'Will you do something for me?'

His smile held such a degree of latent passion that she melted into a thousand pieces.

'What is this thing you want me to do?' He leaned forward and brushed his lips against the corner of her mouth in an evocative, deliberately tantalising gesture. 'Tell me.'

For a moment she almost hesitated, wondering if it was really important any more. 'Would you *ask* me to marry you?' Her voice was serious, and as he lifted his head she looked into his eyes, begging him to understand. In a defensive, unbidden gesture she edged the tip of her tongue over the soft curve of her mouth.

He stood regarding her in silence, his expression unusually grave. 'It means that much to you?'

'Yes.'

He caught hold of her hand and placed it against his chest so that she could feel the strong beat of his heart. 'Dear, sweet Lexi. Will you marry me? Let me love you, treasure you for the rest of my life?'

Her mouth shook a little, and her eyes ached with the wealth of her own emotion. 'Yes. *Yes.*' She slid her arms up round his neck and pulled his head down to hers. Then she kissed him, glorying in taking the initiative for a few long minutes before he became caught up with the strength of his own passion, wreaking a devastating assault on her feelings, plundering until she clung to him, unashamedly as anxious as he for a complete satiation of the senses.

It seemed an age before he slowly broke the kiss, and she gave a murmur in protest as he disentangled her arms from around his neck.

'Carla said you were going to cook,' she voiced reluctantly, wanting only to be close to him.

With infinite care he slid the jacket from her shoulders, then set about loosening her top.

'We'll have a midnight snack, and wash it down

with champagne.' His hands slipped inside the waist-band of her silk trousers and pushed them gently down over the slight curve of her hips. 'But right now all I want to do is feast myself on you,' he husked emotively, and she almost died at the wealth of passion evident in those dark eyes so close to her own.

Lexi gave a soft delighted laugh, and an inner radiance was responsible for the twinkle of utter bewitchment in the depths of her beautiful eyes. 'Here, in the lounge?'

With an exultant chuckle he swept her into his arms and carried her effortlessly down the hall to the master suite where he let her slip to her feet mere inches from the large bed.

'In my bed, minx,' he chided gently, shrugging out of his jacket in one easy movement. Her fingers began undoing the buttons on his shirt, dealing deftly with the belt buckle, and as she reached for the zip fastening on his trousers a long shudder shook his powerful frame.

Unbidden, she traced a slow pattern through the dark springy hair whorling on his chest, beginning a tactile exploration that brought a strangled sound from the depths of his throat.

'Do you have any conception of what you're doing to me?'

A shaft of exquisite pleasure exploded deep within her, radiating through every nerve until she felt incredibly alive, for it was a heady experience to imagine she held any power over him.

'I think the feeling is mutual,' she managed shakily some minutes later as his lips trailed an evocative path to her breasts, and she cried out as his tongue savoured one taut roseate peak, then drew it gently between his teeth to suckle, creating such delicious torture that it was almost impossible not to cry out at the degree of ecstacy spiralling through her body.

Gently he pulled her down on to the bed, and their loving became a long slow pacing of each other's pleasure that surpassed anything they'd previously shared.

Afterwards they rose and shared a leisurely bath, delighting in creating new depths of sensual arousal, and it was a long time later, cradled close in the protective circle of Georg's arms, that Lexi lifted her head towards his to voice quietly, 'Thank you.'

His lips trailed gently across her forehead to settle at her temple. 'For what, specifically?'

'Loving me,' she accorded simply. She felt his mouth begin a slow caressing path down to her cheek until it reached the curve of her lips.

'You're so unbelievably beautiful that you take my breath away.'

She smiled beneath the witching touch of his mouth, and a delicious laugh bubbled to the surface. 'Do you think you can summon sufficient energy to sizzle two steaks while I toss a salad?'

'Sizzle?' He caught her lower lip between his teeth in subtle punishment, and growled softly, 'A gourmet chef creates magic with food.'

'Not merely with food,' she declared solemnly, slipping easily from his grasp, but only, she suspected, because he let her.

She walked unselfconsciously into the *en suite* bathroom and plucked a large bath-sheet to wrap sarong-style round her slim curves, then she emerged into the bedroom to see he'd risen from the bed and was in the process of donning a silk robe.

Georg held out his hand and she placed hers into that strong warm enveloping grasp, then together they walked out of the room.

All the self-doubts, the pain, were gone, and in its place was love—everlasting.

Michelle Reid grew up on the southern edges of Manchester, the youngest in a family of five lively children. But now she lives in the beautiful county of Cheshire with her busy executive husband and two grown-up daughters. She loves reading, the ballet, and playing tennis when she gets the chance. She hates cooking, cleaning, and despises ironing! Sleep she can do without and produces some of her best written work during the early hours of the morning.

PASSION BECOMES YOU
by
MICHELLE REID

CHAPTER ONE

JOSH was late in the office on Monday morning—a sure sign that his weekend had been a heavy one.

Jemma's smile was wry as she dealt efficiently with the morning's mail. She had to give it to Cassie Drake—the gorgeous brunette had certainly succeeded where countless before had failed, and managed to keep the equally gorgeous Josh Tanner on a nice rolling boil for three whole months!

A record for him. His women usually lasted only as long as it took him to bed them thoroughly. A low boredom threshold, Josh called it—and the added fact that he couldn't resist trying it on with just about any presentable woman who happened to catch his wandering eye.

Jemma should know—he had tried it on her once or twice. Not that it had worked. She wasn't into men—not men like Josh anyway. He looked at a woman and saw sex with a capital S, and nothing else. He was a rake. A handsome, conceited, feckless rake, and the last type of man she would ever let herself become mixed up with.

She'd already been there—via her father, witnessed what his overactive libido had done to her mother. And no way— no way would she ever let herself fall into that thankless trap.

Josh hadn't given up on her that easily, though, she recalled with a smile. It had taken him two months to accept defeat. Another month to stop sulking about it. And since then—nearly two years ago now—he had made her his best friend and confidante instead.

Which was why she knew all about Cassie, and what she

5

did to him. How just one look at her softly rounded, sensually luxurious figure and his temperature shot off the gauge.

'Why her?' he'd once demanded in sheer exasperated confusion. 'She isn't even my type! I like them tall and slender with legs that go up to their armpits like yours do. And long blonde hair like yours I can strangle myself with!'

'My hair is not blonde, it's sandy.'

'Blonde,' he'd insisted. 'Golden-blonde like honey—hot honey.' His eyes had begun to smoke. 'Makes me want to—'

'Lay one finger on me and I'll tell Cassie!'

It was enough to cool his ardour. 'What is that black-haired witch doing to me?' he'd muttered and slammed away to his own office to brood.

Jemma thought she had the answer to that question, but refused to offer it to him. It would be bad enough working with him once he discovered it for himself without her bringing forward the dreadful day. But, in her opinion, Josh Tanner, the sexy blond rake of London town, had met his Waterloo—and at the hands of a woman who made no secret of what she wanted from Josh.

'Marriage, children—the full works,' she'd told Jemma recently while sitting on the corner of her desk waiting for Josh to take her to lunch. 'I'm sick of playing the field. And anyway, I'm getting on.' It seemed that in this day and age twenty-seven was really getting on by the expression on Cassie's face when she said it. 'So I started looking around me for a suitable candidate.'

Which happened to be Josh, something Jemma found rather strange since she considered her boss the last man on earth a woman would actually want to settle down with. After all, a rake was a rake in her book. Good fun to be with, great in bed, so the tale went, but not—definitely not—husband material.

'I happened to meet Josh at a party I'd gone to with an old friend of mine,' she'd gone on. 'Fell for the self-obsessed jerk on the spot and would have had to be blind not to understand the lecherous look in Josh's eyes. The air fairly sizzled between us, highly amusing Leon, I can tell you—you know Leon Stephanades?' she'd asked, and at Jemma's blank look had added, 'Darling, you do not know what you're missing. If I'd dared to set my sights so high, I would have gone all out to catch him instead of Josh. But Leon is—special. Very Greek. Very wealthy. And very, very possessive of his freedom. His father has tried all ways—threats, bribes, you name it—to get his son to marry the nice Greek girl with the hefty dowry he has picked out for him, but Leon refuses to so much as consider it. Caused quite a family rift, so I gather.' Her beautifully sculptured brows had arched ruefully, the reason why coming in the next sentence. 'So what chance does a not-so-nice English girl with nothing to offer him but a great body have against all of that? None,' she'd answered her own question. 'So I decided to go all out to catch Josh instead. Leon and I are still good friends, though—which Josh hates,' she'd added with a grin that was all feminine guile. 'He's as jealous as sin of Leon because he thinks we had something going between us once, which is not true,' she had insisted, though her expression had implied that she maybe would have liked it to be true. 'But his jealousy is probably the only ray of hope he allows me in this crazy relationship we're having—that and the fact he can't get enough of me,' she'd tagged on ruefully. 'Leon says if I land Josh Tanner he'll buy us a twelve-inch solid gold flying pig for a wedding present, because that's how much of a chance he thinks I've got of pulling it off! But I'm working on it,' she had concluded determinedly.

Cassie must have told Josh more or less the same thing, because it was only a few days after that conversation with

Cassie that Josh had come striding into the office, growling, 'I'm not marrying any woman! Not even for a solid gold pig!'

The phone began to ring now. Jemma picked up the receiver to have the familiar impatient bark of Josh Tanner hit her eardrums. 'I'm late,' he stated the obvious. 'I've had one hell of a weekend. Only just woken up. You're going to have to hold the fort until I can get there.'

'What about your ten o'clock appointment with that big cheese from the Leonadis Corporation?' she reminded him, glancing at her watch only to confirm that it was already twenty to ten. There was no way Josh could make it here in time.

Some very unsavoury vocabulary came slashing down the line. He had obviously forgotten all about the appointment. Not like Josh, she acknowledged. It had to have been a hell of a weekend. 'Him of all people,' he muttered. 'That's all I need today. Look, you're going to have to try and put him off,' he added impatiently. 'See if you can catch him before he leaves his office. Make my excuses. And if that conniving bitch I've been seeing turns up—tell her I've died and gone to hell! And not to bother following me!'

'Who?' she asked, frowning. 'Cassie?'

But Jemma was already talking to fresh air. Josh had slammed down the phone. She sat staring at the contraption for the space of ten seconds while trying to make head or tail of that final scathing remark, then shrugged, replacing her own receiver. It seemed that when Josh had said he'd had a hell of a weekend he'd meant it.

The lovers' bed must have had thorns in it, she mused, and smiled to herself as she hunted out the number of the Leonadis Corporation.

It was only as she waited for someone to answer that she realised she had no idea what the managing director's name was. Josh had made the appointment himself on Friday. And all he had said was, 'I hate the damned man, but he's hunting for new outlets to get his design components from and I need the business. So I suppose I'll have to fanny round him.'

She grimaced, wondering what the man could have done to Josh to make him dislike him so much; her boss was not normally drawn to taking personal exception to potential clients. In fact, he was usually quite happy to 'fanny round' anyone so long as it brought him business.

'The Leonadis Corporation?'

Jemma blinked. 'Ah,' she began, wondering how to get around this one without sounding like a fool. She explained who she was and why she was ringing, then added, 'So I hoped to catch your managing director before he leaves the building,' she concluded, mentally crossing her fingers that the receptionist on the other end would provide the name and save her having to ask.

'Oh, I'm afraid you may be too late,' she was informed. 'But I'll put you through to his secretary.'

'Thank you.' Jemma held the line while she waited to be transferred, but a single glance at her watch told her she was running out of time. 'Damn you, Josh,' she muttered to herself.

'Mr Stephanades's secretary speaking. Can I help you?'

Stephanades—now where had she heard that name before? 'I do hope so,' she said, then quickly went into her explanation again. 'Mr Stephanades had an appointment with Mr Tanner for ten o'clock this morning, but I am afraid Mr Tanner has been delayed. Am I too late to save him a wasted journey?'

'When I am already standing right here, I would say yes, you are much too late,' a deep, smooth, beautifully accented and drily amused voice drawled at her from across the room.

Startled, Jemma glanced up—then felt everything vital inside her grind to a shuddering halt when she found herself staring at the most disturbingly attractive man she had ever seen in her life!

He was leaning in the open doorway, hands shoved into the pockets of his dark silk business suit trousers so that the side panels of his jacket had been shoved out of the way to expose the solid breadth of his chest beneath the crisp clean whiteness of his shirt. He was tall and dark, his black hair cut in a short, neat style which kept the hint of a wave contained to the silken top of his head. His bone-structure was square and strong, the skin stretched across it smooth and tanned. Black eyes were teasing her from between jet-black, sleepily curling lashes. And he was smiling at her with the most startlingly sensual mouth she had ever encountered.

Faultless, she decided hazily. He is absolutely faultless. He set her blood pumping in a way which left her in no doubt whatsoever as to what was happening to her. And the dark, coiling warmth she was experiencing in the pit of her stomach confirmed it.

This, she accepted, as she continued to stare breathlessly at him, was what it was all about.

Attraction. Dark and hot and rousing.

Her continued silence sent his sleek brows arching. Jemma heaved in a deep breath of air in an effort to pull herself together. The action lifted her breasts in a slow quivering motion beneath her white silky blouse then dropped them again in the same tremulous way, making those gorgeous lashes of his fall in two luxurious curves over his eyes as he followed the revealing motion. Her nipples stung painfully in response, and she blushed hotly with embarrassment, wishing for the first time ever that she possessed such a thing as a bra, because she didn't have to look down at herself to know what he was witnessing happening to her.

'Miss Davis?' a slightly puzzled voice prompted in her ear.

'I...' She ran the tip of her tongue around her suddenly parched lips. 'It—it doesn't matter,' she whispered breathlessly and replaced the receiver without really knowing she had done it, her eyes not leaving the man leaning in the doorway.

The smile widened on his lips, giving them a sensually knowing quality that annoyed her even as she accepted his right to display it. She knew who he was, of course. He had made that clear when he let her know he was there. But she could not for the life of her respond with anything like the light brisk, 'Good morning, Mr Stephanades!' Josh would expect of her. She wanted to know his first name, to feel it curl off her tongue like a caress. Her heart was bursting, her breasts tingling, her calves and thighs trembling with the full fermenting blast of his attraction.

'Shall we leave now, or do you need a few moments longer to compose yourself?'

'W-what?' She blinked, blue eyes filling with bewildered confusion. 'L-leave for where?'

'My apartment,' he explained, levering himself away from the door-frame to come further into the room, closing the door behind him. 'I must say,' he went on lightly before Jemma had a chance to digest the full import of his first remark, 'I have in my life been propositioned in many ways, but never with such open and—dare I say it?—helpless invitation before. I find it rather—enchanting.'

Stung, Jemma closed her eyes, feeling the heat of embarrassed colour grow hotter in her cheeks.

'I'm so sorry,' she murmured, pulling herself together with an effort that cost her her dignity as she stumbled shakily to her feet. 'You took me by surprise, Mr...' She'd forgotten his name. His secretary had only just informed her of it, and already in her stupidity she had forgotten it!

'Stephanades,' he supplied it for her, the mockery spiked and cruel. 'Leon Stephanades, at your service, Miss...?'

Leon, his first name was Leon. Jemma actually had to count to ten to stop herself repeating the name in the breathless little way she knew was hanging on the very end of her dry, quivering tongue.

On a jerky movement she straightened her body, 'Davis,' she supplied, lifting her chin to face him as coolly as she could, but she knew the hectic flush still colouring her cheeks said it all. 'I'm sorry you've had a wasted journey, sir.' That's better, Jemma, she told herself encouragingly, refusing to look anywhere but at the left tip of his well shaped ear in case the look in his eyes sent her crazy again. 'But Mr Tanner has been delayed and cannot make your appointment. I was hoping to catch you before you left your office, but as we both see—' she tried a wry smile and it just about worked '—I was too late.'

'How fortunate.'

Oh, good grief! She almost choked in appalled horror when his reply made her breasts tingle again. She closed her eyes, only opening them again when she was sure she was looking down at her desk and not at him. 'If you will just give me a moment,' she murmured a trifle hoarsely, feeling a fool—a damned fool, 'I'll find Mr Tanner's appointment book and we can arrange another—'

'I have a better idea,' he cut in. 'Meet me for lunch and we will discuss...arrangements over a light meal and a bottle of wine.'

Jemma almost died inside with shame, not in any way missing the double meaning. 'I'm sorry.' She stuck to the official meaning in his words with all the secretarial cool she could muster, but it wasn't easy when her body was responding wildly to the other. 'S-someone has to m-man the office when Mr Tanner isn't here.'

'Shame,' he murmured, so softly that her eyes flickered up to clash with his, and her cheeks went even hotter at the expression on his face. This was not all one-sided. He was attracted to her also. 'For I am flying to New York this afternoon and will not be back for at least a week. A long time to leave something like this—pending…'

Suddenly, the office door flew open again, and Jemma looked towards it in wild hope that it was Josh come to rescue her.

But it wasn't Josh. It was Cassie, looking as mad as hell. 'Where is that low-down, no-good son of a—?' She stopped mid-flow, her unusually pale face lighting up when she saw the man standing in the centre of Jemma's office. 'Leon!' she cried, and threw herself into his arms.

It was at that moment, and only that moment, that Jemma's addled brain made the connection it should have made long, humiliating minutes ago. Leon. Cassie's good friend, Leon.

And their mutual affection showed in the way he gathered Cassie into his arms then kissed her warmly on both cheeks before smiling indulgently down at her.

Jealousy whipped through Jemma like a flash fire, contracting her nerve-ends until she could barely breathe across the acid taste of it filling her mouth. If Josh had ever seen them together like this, it was no wonder he was so jealous.

At least Josh has the right to be jealous, a little voice taunted inside her burning head. You don't.

You don't even know the man!

God in heaven! She sat down heavily in her chair, trying desperately to throw off what was happening to her. She wanted to scratch Cassie's eyes out. She wanted to drag her away from him. Scratch his eyes out!

'How's your love-life?' he was saying teasingly to Cassie.

She pulled a wry face and wound her arms more tightly around his neck. 'Not so good that this isn't welcome,' she said very drily. 'More than welcome…'

'Tanner not treating you well?' The mocking brow lifted questioningly.

Cassie's beautiful mouth took a downward turn. 'He's a rat of the first order,' she scowled, her dark eyes flashing bitterly. 'And I hate him!'

Jemma started at the other woman's virulence. Leon Stephanades frowned. 'Trouble?' he asked.

'Big trouble,' Cassie said ominously, and pulled out of his arms to turn on Jemma. 'Where is he?' she demanded. 'Skulking in some dark hole somewhere, waiting for the bogy-man to go away?'

Jemma opened her mouth to answer, wondering curiously just what had happened this weekend to make both Josh and Cassie this mad.

'He's…' She was about to trot out the same excuse for Josh she had given to Leon Stephanades when the phone began to ring. Absently she picked up the receiver and chanted out the usual.

'Did you catch him before he left?' Josh's impatient bark made her jump, and she pressed the earpiece tighter to her ear in an attempt to block Josh's voice off.

'Er—no,' she answered carefully. 'Can—can I call you back?'

Josh had never been slow on the uptake, and he wasn't now. 'He's already there?'

'Yes.'

'Damn…' There was a pause, then Josh muttered something and grunted. 'You'd better put him on so I can apologise personally.'

'I—er don't think that would be a very good idea at the

moment,' she said, lowering her eyes and her voice from the two watchful people listening to her to add, 'We're not alone.'

She didn't hear Josh's answer to that, because Cassie had leapt at her desk, eyes flashing green fire—and something else that Jemma could not interpret but hinted oddly at terror. 'Is that Josh? Give me that!' she demanded, trying to snatch the phone from Jemma. 'I have a few things I want to—'

'I don't want to speak to her!' Josh grated into Jemma's ear.

'Give, Jemma!' Cassie insisted, her eyes fire-bright with anger. 'It's time that rat learned a few home truths!'

'Get her out of my office—now!' Josh barked.

'I can't!' she answered both of them, jumping to her feet in an effort to stop Cassie from wrenching the phone from her, and Josh hurled out a string of abuse aimed entirely at Cassie while Leon Stephanades viewed the whole scene with a look of lazy amusement sparking his eyes.

Jemma hated him at that moment. The whole thing was utterly ridiculous. She felt stupid being a part of it, and he thought it was funny!

He glanced up at her then, caught the look burning in her eyes, and suddenly the amusement left him to allow something so elemental to take its place that she gasped as everything inside her went haywire in answer to it, heart, lungs, pulses, even her skin—as if every minute hair follicle she possessed had been delivered an electric shock which set her whole body tingling.

Josh was growling, Cassie was shouting, but suddenly they might as well not have been there for all Jemma knew. She was lost in a seething hot raid on her senses, and what really threw her into hectic confusion was the fact that he was feeling the exact same way—and doing nothing whatsoever to hide it!

Then it all came crashing in. With the help of a sudden pained cry from Cassie, Jemma refocused her attention on the other woman just in time to hear her choke, 'Whatever I am, you bastard, I am still pregnant with your child!' Then she crumpled on to the floor.

In a state of stunned shock, Jemma watched the lightning-quick reactions of Leon Stephanades as he caught Cassie's weight before she hit the floor, listened to Josh cursing and swearing on the other end of the line, his voice so thick that it was obvious he was feeling the pressure of his emotions as much as Cassie was.

'The bitch trapped me, Jemma,' he was saying hoarsely. 'She deliberately laid a trap for me.'

Jemma did not know what to say. In the end, she just murmured, 'I'll call you back, Josh. I'll call you back,' and slowly replaced the receiver.

By the time she had collected a cool cloth and a glass of water, Cassie was beginning to show signs of life. Leon Stephanades had carried her into Josh's office and placed her on the leather sofa in there and was now squatting beside her, gently chafing at one of her hands.

Jemma knelt down beside him and offered him the cloth. He took it without speaking, his expression grim to say the least as he applied the cloth to Cassie's brow.

It was him Cassie saw when she eventually opened her eyes. 'Oh, God, Leon,' she whispered tragically. 'What am I going to do?'

'Nothing, until you feel well enough,' he answered calmingly. 'Then I will take you home.'

Tears blurred the wretched green of her eyes. 'I didn't do it on purpose,' she claimed fretfully.

'Didn't you?' he said. That was all, but even as Jemma stiffened in violent protest at what his tone was implying Cassie's eyes were going dark with guilt, and on a pained choke she hid her face in her hands and began to sob wretchedly.

Shocked, Jemma sat back on her heels, the fact that any woman would set out deliberately to trap a man that way just too awful for her to take in.

Leon Stephanades turned his head to look at her, then grimaced. 'Don't look so appalled, Miss Davis,' he drawled. 'Your sex use this ploy all the time. To them, it is the next best thing to a genuine proposal—especially when it is a man like your Mr Tanner who is involved. Or me,' he then tagged on cynically.

Feeling sick, Jemma got up and walked back into her own office. She felt ashamed of her sex, if what Leon Stephanades had said was true. Ashamed for Cassie whom she had liked and even admired for what she'd seen as her candid honesty about her intentions.

And Josh? She sat down behind her desk and wondered what she felt for Josh.

She felt sorry for him, she realised. For the first time in two years of witnessing the way he used women for his own purposes, she actually felt sorry for him.

Because, no matter how much he deserved his come-uppance in one way or another, he did not deserve this.

The phone rang. And for the next few minutes she had to turn her attention strictly to business as a spate of calls followed one on top of the other.

She was just replacing the receiver for the final time when Leon Stephanades came through to her office. 'She is calmer now,' he said. 'When she has tidied herself, I will take her home.'

Jemma nodded dumbly, refusing to look at him, shock and distaste at what Cassie had done still evident on her face. He studied her for a moment, then closed the connecting door between the two offices and walked over to her desk.

'Are you all right?' he asked.

'I just find it hard to believe she actually did it deliberately,' she confessed.

'Women are devious creatures, Miss Davis,' he said heavily. 'They will go to any lengths to achieve their own ends.'

'Thank you.' She smiled tightly. 'Generalisations like that keep the world turning, I suppose.'

'They do in my sphere,' he said cynically.

His sphere—who the hell did he think he was? Were all women supposed to be as unscrupulous as Cassie? 'Well,' she said, coming stiffly to her feet and making a play of gathering her telephone notes together, 'I shall try to remember that when I decide to go hunting, and make a wide berth of your—sphere.'

'Now that,' he murmured, 'would be a great pity.'

She glanced up, drawn by the husky message in his voice. Their eyes clashed, and she stopped breathing, drowning instead in the dark, deep promise burning in his eyes.

No, she told herself from some hazy distance in the back of her foggy mind. Don't let this happen. Think of Cassie weeping in the next room. Think of Josh, just another version from the same mould as this man. Ruthless, selfish women-eaters.

He reached across the desk and touched a thumb to her mouth, drawing it downwards to part her lips a little. The softly padded flesh beneath his touch grew hot as blood began pumping into it, swelling it, assailing her with the most erotically sensual experience of her life.

'No strings,' he murmured so softly that she barely caught the words above the sudden roaring inside her head. 'No commitments other than that while we are together we neither of us turn to anyone else. When it is over, we part honestly, as friends. I will be your only lover. And I will give myself exclusively to you.'

The hand moved, sliding beneath her hair to curve her nape, then he was leaning towards her, drawing her towards him across the width of the desk, and he replaced the caressing finger with his mouth. It was cool and firm, her own hot and excruciatingly sensitised flesh contracting in reaction so that she jumped, startled as if stung.

'Think about it,' he murmured as he drew away again. 'And I will call you soon. Now.' While she blinked, still lost in the sensual daze he had so easily wrapped around her, Leon Stephanades straightened up and became the cool businessman. 'I will take Cassandra home. Tell Tanner I will be out of the country for a about a week. If he wishes to deal with me then he had better be available when I get back.' He turned to go back to Josh's office, then spun back again, his expression darkening when he saw how thoroughly he had incapacitated her, but that was all; he gave no other indication that he had just made the most audacious proposition Jemma had ever heard. 'You can also tell him that, no matter what his decision will be about Cassandra's condition, as her good friend, I expect her to be treated with respect. She is only human, after all, and humans are by nature fallible.'

CHAPTER TWO

'FALLIBLE?' Josh snarled, prowling around his office like an angry bull. 'The bitch isn't fallible. She's like an armoured tank, equipped with the most modern killing devices known to man!'

He had been in the office ten minutes—arriving just ten minutes after Leon had taken a wilting Cassie away.

'She said to tell you she'd be in touch.' Jemma relayed that message too. But she did not inject the same amount of tight defiance into it that Cassie had done. She hadn't dared. As it was, he hit the roof.

'I don't wish to set eyes on the conniving bitch again!' he bit out, then swung on Jemma, his grey eyes as hard and as sharp as glass. 'Did she tell you she did it deliberately?'

Jemma nodded. 'Leon Stephanades got it out of her.'

'And how fortunate for her that he was around!' The jeer was bitter and cutting. 'For all I know, they probably planned it between them!'

'What, that man aiding and abetting in stitching up another of his kind?' She only heard her own contempt once the words had left her tongue. 'He would rather cut his own throat first!'

'And what do you know about him?' Josh challenged deridingly. 'As far as I am aware, you only met him for the first time today.'

And what a meeting, Jemma thought with a small shiver. 'It doesn't take much to recognise the type, Josh,' she murmured drily. 'I recognised it in you on first sighting, too.'

His eyes sharpened, something in her tone diverting his attention from his own problems for a moment. 'Proposition

20

you, did he?' he mocked. She blushed—enough of an answer in itself. 'Well, I hope you had the good sense to give him the same put-down you gave me,' he said grimly. 'Because that guy is big-league. He plays to different rules from the rest of us.'

'As far as I can see,' she retaliated, simply because she felt uncomfortable in knowing that, far from putting Leon Stephanades down, she had virtually thrown herself at him, 'you're both tarred with the same brush!'

'Only he's a darn sight more powerful than me,' Josh pointed out.

'How powerful?' Jemma asked curiously, beginning to tingle again, just talking about him.

'Among the top twenty richest families in the world—that powerful,' Josh answered, then ran his fingers through his straight blond hair in frustration. 'And God help any woman who tried to pull Cassie's dirty trick on him!' he grunted, slumping down in a chair.

'Josh…' Jemma put out a hand to touch his arm in appeal. 'Cassie loves you! I know she does! What she's done is stupid and wrong,' she acknowledged. 'But I am sure she did it out of love! Doesn't that count for anything?'

He shook his head. 'Does love deceive, Jemma?' he challenged. 'Does it betray trust, connive to trap? Is it selfish and greedy and bloody ruthless?'

'I don't know,' she replied, hurting for him because she could see the real hurt his anger was trying to hide. 'Because I've never been in love to know.'

'I feel betrayed,' he confessed. 'Bloody betrayed!'

They sat in dull silence for a while after that, Jemma completely sympathising with Josh even though she could partly understand Cassie's motives. The woman had not tried to hide her ultimate goal, after all. Marriage and children. The full works. But the really sad fact among all of it was that Jemma had a sneaking suspicion that Cassie would have got it all from Josh if she'd only been a bit more patient. He'd been crumbling, she was sure of it. But now…?

'What are you going to do?' she asked him huskily.

He sighed and got up. 'I don't know,' he answered flatly. 'All I do know is that she's had it as far as I—me personally—am concerned. She's pregnant; there isn't a damned thing I can do about that now. If she wants to keep it, then I'll support her and it. If she wants an abortion, then I'll pay for it. But if she wants me, she can go to hell before she'll get me again.'

Fagged to death by the time she let herself into her flat that night, Jemma just dropped her bag and sank into the nearest chair. They had managed to get some work done during the afternoon, but not much, and what there was had been achieved in a grim mutual silence that had eventually left its mark on her throbbing head.

Trina walked into the room, chewing on a banana. 'Bad day?' she enquired when she saw Jemma's drained face.

'Hmm,' was all she could manage.

'Want cheering up?' Trina, the sexiest Mrs Mop in the domestic cleaning game, tended to finish work several hours before Jemma, simply because most people liked their homes cleaned and vacated before three o'clock in the afternoon. She ran her own business from the flat with the help of a veritable army of part-timers who worked in teams, and not one of them wore a turban on her head or dared have a cigarette hanging out of the corner of her mouth. They wore uniforms which rivalled the smartest airline ones, and they travelled around in neat little vans with neat little smiles and a brisk friendly manner. They were all paid well, but then Trina's charges were high. You get what you pay for, was her motto, and London, especially up-market London, had accepted and acknowledged that long ago. Trina had a waiting-list of potential clients almost as long as her list of real ones. She'd wanted to expand at one time, but the current recession had put paid to that idea—that and her super-sharp accountant-cum-boyfriend Frew. Trina was a tall, slim, easygoing redhead, with green eyes, a sharp tongue and a nasty sense of humour.

Jemma opened her eyes long enough to scrutinise Trina's deadpan face, then closed them again and shook her head. 'Not tonight, thank you,' she refused the offer. 'I don't think I'm up to one of your nice surprises.'

'Shame,' Trina pouted. 'Because this one is rather a cut above the ordinary. Still...' Jemma sensed her friend's shrug as she turned to leave the sitting-room-cum-office again '...I suppose it will keep.'

Jemma sighed, remained exactly where she was and how she was for the space of thirty delicious seconds, then sighed again and hauled herself out of the chair. 'All right!' she called after Trina. 'You win! I can't stand not knowing. What's the nice—? My God!' she choked. 'Where did those come from?'

She had walked out of the sitting-room and down the hall to the kitchen while she was talking; now she just stood, rooted to the spot in the kitchen doorway, staring at the largest basket of out-of-season fruit and flowers she had ever seen.

'Looking at them,' Trina said sardonically, 'from all over the world, I'd say.'

It filled their small kitchen table. The basket, an exquisitely woven affair of rich golden cane with a tall rounded handle, simply spilled over with flowers. Pretty, star-shaped lilies, sensually scented pure white jasmine, blood-red hibiscus heads that were almost too heavy for their stems. Pink, purple and the palest lilac sprays of bougainvillaea clustered everywhere, and at the base were oranges with the dark green leaves still attached to their short stems. Peaches as big as grapefruits. Grapes, green and black, in huge, succulent bunches. And figs, fresh, plump, juicy figs that made the mouth water just to look at them.

There was a card. Trina plucked it from the centre and mockingly passed it over to Jemma. 'For you, ma'am,' she drawled, watching her face as she took the card then dragged her rounded eyes down to focus on it. 'Methinks you have a passionate admirer. The writing on the envelope is sexy, too,' she pointed out. 'All sharp strokes and dramatic curves. I wonder who it can be?'

Jemma wasn't listening. She was trembling instead, staring at the envelope and frightened to open it. She knew who it was from; there was a little voice inside her head repeating his name over and over again. How he had found out her address she had no idea, but that cynical part in her she hadn't known existed until today was telling her that for a man like him it wouldn't be that hard.

What had Josh said about him? From one of the richest families in the world, was what he had said. Powerful. A man not to mess around with.

And Cassie? What had she said about him? Sexy. Loyal. Invincible. Even his own father could not dictate to him.

And what have you learned about him yourself, Jemma? she asked herself shakily. Beautiful, she replied. Dangerous. Fair-minded but cocksure and arrogant with it. Determined, if this basket was a sign of determination to get his own way. Honest, if his proposition was serious. Deadly, if her own tangled feelings were anything to go by. He had succeeded in tying her in sensual knots within seconds of setting eyes on him.

She sucked in a shaky breath, her fingers trembling as she slowly broke the seal on the envelope and took out the gold-embossed card inside.

The words blurred then slowly cleared before her wary eyes.

Today was no way to meet someone who is destined to become the most important person in my life. It was a day of bad smells and acid tastes. So I send you these. Fruits to sweeten your mouth and the flowers of my homeland to freshen the air around you. Keep the flowers warm and moist or they will wither and die before I can see you again. Eat the fruit, enjoy the sensual tastes of my native land and think of me.
Leon.

The air left her lungs on a tremulous sigh as she looked back at the basket filling the table, only to find its beauty superimposed by his darkly attractive and smoulderingly sensual face.

God in heaven. She pulled out a chair and sat down, the hand holding the card going up to cover her eyes.

'Bad news, then—not good?' Trina prompted, curious at Jemma's reaction.

She held out the card for her friend to take. 'Beware of Greeks bearing gifts,' she murmured, and left Trina to make of that what she may.

'Who is this Leon?' she asked after smothering several muffled chokes as she read the blatantly evocative words. 'I've never heard you mention a Leon before.'

'That's because I hadn't met him before today,' Jemma explained, and sat back in the chair, grateful to find his face had disappeared from the basket. 'He is one Leon Stephanades. A—business colleague of Josh's.'

'Wow,' Trina gasped, and sank down in the other chair.

'You've already heard of him, I see,' Jemma mocked.

Trina nodded. 'But Jemma,' she exclaimed, searching her friend's face worriedly, 'he's way out of our league, love!'

'I know it.' A funny expression crossed Jemma's face; she didn't even recognise it herself, except that it felt as if it came somewhere close to desolation. 'But try telling my senses that, will you?' She grimaced self-deridingly. 'I made an utter fool of myself today, Tri,' she confessed. 'He walked into Josh's office and I felt the earth move beneath me! I couldn't stop staring at him!' Her expression was pained. 'I couldn't think! I couldn't breathe! I couldn't even focus! There were birds flying around in my head and puffy white clouds floating across my vision! He smiled and my heart did somersaults! And—God,' she choked, covering her face with her hands, 'he would have had to be blind not to know what was happening to me!'

'Well,' Trina murmured slowly, looking down at the card still in her hand, 'he must have experienced something similar to respond with this.'

'Did he?' Her expression was cynical to say the least. 'What he saw, Tri, was a peach ripe for the plucking!' She picked a peach from the basket and brandished it bitterly in front of her. 'And does a man like that turn an easy meal down? Does he hell!' she answered herself scathingly. 'And he's all man, Tri,' she added helplessly. 'Big, tough and lean. So damned attractive he knocks your eyes out, and so disgustingly sure of himself that he quite coolly propositioned me!' The contempt was back, but aimed at Leon instead of herself this time.

'How?' Trina's eyes were round like saucers and eager with interest.

'How does a man like that proposition a potential lover?' Jemma snapped. 'He laid down the ground rules. If you want to play in my league then this is how it's done—and so on. I wanted to slap his arrogant face, but all I did do was let him kiss me!' Self-disgust rattled in her throat. 'By the time he let me up for air again, I was so dizzy I couldn't think, never mind hit out!'

'So?' Trina prompted. 'How did it get to the point that he sends you something like this?' she wanted to know. 'And I don't mean the basket—I mean this card. It reads like a *fait accompli* to me—except the talk about smells and acid, of course,' she frowned, not able to work that bit out. 'He expects to see you, Jemma, when he gets back from wherever he's gone off to. A man doesn't make that assumption unless you've let him.'

'This one does,' she grunted. 'Especially when the girl in question gave him no encouragement to think otherwise.'

'You mean—you just let him get away with kissing you and propositioning you like that?'

'I would have let him take me on the office floor if he'd wanted to,' Jemma said drily. 'That was the level I'd sunk to!'

'My God!' Trina sat back and stared. 'I can't believe it! Wait till I tell Frew! He'll go bananas! He claims the man hasn't been born who can get through your thick shell!'

'Well, thanks very much, Frew!' Jemma cried. 'And what gives him the right to think he knows anything at all about me?'

'Come off it, Jemma!' Trina scoffed. 'You and me both know you're as picky as a worm in a barrel of apples! How many twenty-four-year-old virgins do you think Frew knows?'

'That's a horrible thing to say!' Jemma flared, jumping to her feet and dropping the lovely peach on to the table. The soft velvet skin split open, allowing the sweet, sensual scent of its juicy fruit to seep out. It assailed her nostrils, whetted her tastebuds, and she had to close her eyes because she was suddenly thrown into a storm of sensation that was all directed by one cleverly manipulative man.

'Your parents are entirely to blame for that!' Trina went on, unaware of the torment going on inside Jemma. 'If it wasn't your father having some torrid affair with another woman it was your mother paying him back by putting it about with some other man! What an example they set you! And now look at you!' she exclaimed. 'You're standing

there, trembling with indignation over Frew's impression of
you when you know damned well it's only the truth! You're
afraid of starting your sexual ball rolling, Jemma,' she
stated bluntly, 'just in case you discover that you've got
more of your parents in you than you can deal with!'

'Do you want me to bed the very next man who walks
in that door just to prove you wrong?' she flared, her eyes
snapping open to glare at her so-called best friend.

Trina's mouth twitched. 'Not if it's my Frew, you'd better not,' she warned. 'Or it will be your first and last experience.'

'Oh, go to hell, Tri,' Jemma sighed, deflated by her flatmate's unfailing sense of humour.

'Don't you see what's happened to you today, Jemma?'
Trina appealed on a more serious note. 'You've been so
determined to keep your emotions under a tight lid that
when a man like Leon Stephanades came along your senses
boiled up and the lid flew off so they all came shooting out
like steam under pressure! That's why you made such a
damned fool of yourself with him!'

'Thanks for the analysis,' Jemma grunted, and sat down
again. 'You've made me feel so much better!'

'I was not attempting to make you feel better,' Trina
sighed. 'Only understand why you responded to him as you
did! The man is a god among men. You've ambled along
quite nicely while only confronted with mere mortals, but
when it came to a godlike being you blew your emotional
top!'

'Josh would not take kindly to being classed as mere
mortal,' Jemma pointed out.

'Josh Tanner,' Trina stated deridingly, 'does not even get
a look-in compared to your Leon.'

'Tell that to Cassie,' Jemma grimaced. And she told
Trina the rest of what had happened today.

'Oh, my,' her friend drawled when she finished. 'Now I

see what your Leon means when he writes about nasty tastes and smells. The whole thing stinks and tastes bad.'

'He is not *my* Leon!' Jemma angrily pointed out.

'No?' Trina quizzed. 'Then what are you going to do about him?'

'Nothing,' she shrugged. 'Just ignore him until he goes away.'

But that was not as easy as it sounded. Mainly because Leon Stephanades refused to be ignored. Over the coming week, Jemma was barraged with reminders of his existence and his intentions.

First there was a long velvet case hand-delivered to her flat with the logo of a very exclusive jeweller embossed on its lid. It contained a fine gold bracelet, linked at its clasp by a single turquoise. 'The colour of your eyes, don't you agree?' the accompanying note said. Jemma closed the lid and put it away, determined to give it back to him at the first opportunity she got. The next day came the matching earrings. On Thursday the matching necklace. 'Wear them for me on our first night together,' the accompanying note said.

Her mouth tightened, the idea that he thought he could buy her like this filling her with an icy anger, and she discarded the necklace into her dressing-table drawer with the same contempt with which she had discarded the bracelet and earrings. On Friday there was nothing. No special delivery to come home to, no note, nothing. Trina studied her face sagely, and Jemma lifted her chin in a defiant refusal to utter a single word.

That night she accepted a date with a man who had just moved into the flat below. He was an architect, just finding his feet in the big London company he had recently joined. He was good-looking, pleasant and companionable, and by the time the evening was drawing to a close Jemma was beginning to feel at peace with herself for the first time in a week.

If it hadn't been bad enough having Leon obsess her every waking thought, then trying to work with Josh in the mood he was in had been just as bad. Not that she blamed him for it—he had every right to behave like a bear with a sore head. But Cassie's constant phone calls, pleading to speak with him, had taken their toll on Jemma's nerves. And when his persistent refusal to speak to her had only had Cassie pouring out her heart on Jemma's ears instead, the tension inside her had begun to hit an all-time high.

So she was quite happy to give herself up to the light, congenial company of Tom MacDonald. As his name suggested, he was a Scot, and eager to make new friends. They talked about anything and everything over a quiet dinner in a small Italian restaurant a short walk away from their flats. He told her about his life in a small Scottish village just outside Edinburgh where his rector father and forbearing mother had reared a family of six boisterous children in the big, rambling vicarage home, and where he had sometimes been willing to sell his soul for a bit of privacy. And she told him about her life as an only child who'd spent her childhood worrying which of her parents was going to walk out next—or, worse, whether they both would at the same time. It surprised her that she told him all of this since the only other person she had ever discussed her lonely uncertain childhood with had been Trina—or maybe, she decided later, it was because of what Trina had said to her the other night that had made her open up to Tom. Whatever. By the time they walked back home, she was feeling comfortable enough to make another date with him for the next night.

They parted at his flat door since it was on a lower landing than her own, and she let him kiss her, half relieved, half disappointed that fireworks had not gone off in her head as they had done when Leon had kissed her.

Trina was still up when she got in, reclining across Frew, who was stretched out on the sofa watching the end of a cops and robbers film.

'Guess who's been calling you all night?' Trina taunted lazily.

Jemma went cold inside. 'I've no idea,' she said, hoping to God that she was right, and she didn't know.

'Mr Macho Stephanades himself, no less.' Frew dashed Jemma's hopes in one sardonically uttered sentence. 'I answered the last time,' he told her drily. 'And received the kind of reply that had me running to the mirror to see if my throat had been cut.'

'Ha-ha, very funny,' Jemma jeered and turned a cool face on Trina. 'I hope you told him to get lost,' she said.

'Me?' her flatmate squeaked. 'Why should I tell him to get lost? He's not my problem! Although...' she added with a teasing glance at Frew '...hearing that gorgeous sexy voice purring down the line at me had me thinking it would be quite something to have him as a problem.'

'He'd eat you for breakfast and not even notice,' Frew scoffed, refusing to rise to the bait.

'If he could eat me, what do you think he could do to Jemma?'

'Excuse me if I leave you to discuss me while I go to bed,' Jemma put in sarcastically. 'But please do continue none the less.'

'He's back in London!' Trina called as Jemma turned to leave the room. Her spine began to tingle, as though just knowing he was in the same city was enough to make her flesh respond to him. 'And he was not happy when I told him you were out on a date!'

'When I answered the phone on his last call,' Frew tagged on, 'he mistook me for your date and actually threatened to come around here and eject me!'

'I do hope you put him right,' Jemma drawled, turning

to send Frew a deriding look. 'Only I would hate him to have the wrong impression about my taste!'

'Whoa there, tiger!' Trina warned. 'That's the love of my life you're insulting!'

'Well, tell the love of your damned life to keep his nose out of my business!' Jemma snapped, wondering helplessly where all that lovely relaxed contentment she had rediscovered tonight had gone.

The phone began to ring. She stiffened up like a board. So did the other two, watching her with curious eyes.

'Want me to answer it?' Trina offered gently.

Oh, yes! Jemma thought frantically. Please yes! Anyone but me! I just can't let myself be— 'No,' she heard herself mumble gruffly. 'I'll do it.'

She walked into the kitchen and stared at the wall set for all of ten seconds before slowly lifting off the receiver.

'Jemma?'

She closed her eyes, swallowing thickly because just the sound of her name on his lips sent her mouth dry. 'Yes,' she whispered.

There was a short, very telling silence, and it didn't take much to sense the anger simmering within it. 'I want to see you,' he said tightly.

'Well, I don't—'

'Now.' Arrogantly, he cut right through her attempted refusal. 'I shall be around to collect you in half an hour.'

'But it's eleven-thirty!' she protested. 'I don't—!'

'I will sound my car horn when I arrive,' he interrupted yet again. 'You have three minutes from that moment to get in the car or I shall come up—do you understand me, Jemma?' he persisted. 'I am a man who does not play games—any kind of game.'

The line went dead. Jemma stared at it. He had just threatened her. He had actually had the gall to threaten her!

CHAPTER THREE

LEON didn't need to sound his car horn. Jemma was already waiting outside, huddled in her pale blue wool duffel-coat and simmering with resentment when the sleek silver-grey Mercedes drew up beside her.

She had a brief glimpse of his dark, chiselled features when the lamplight caught his face as he leaned across the luxurious interior to open the door for her.

He was angry, tight with it.

Well, she thought indignantly, so am I! And refused to so much as look at him as she climbed into the car and stared coldly at the windscreen.

'Seatbelt,' he snapped.

She opened her mouth to tell him to get lost, then shut it again on an inward gasp as the car shot forward on an angry burst of power. Fumbling, she fastened the belt around her, having to drop her purse and the small plastic carrier bag she had brought with her on to the car floor to do it.

Pausing at the next junction, he turned his dark head to slash her with an icy look; she gave it back defiantly, but just allowing her eyes to clash with his was enough to set her trembling, and it was he who broke the hostile contact. She had not been able to, he affected her so badly.

This is crazy, she told herself as they joined the late rush of traffic crowding the London streets. How could she be so acutely aware of a man she barely knew?

Perhaps Trina was right after all, and she had been heading for this kind of emotional fall-out for years, bottling it

33

all up, refusing to acknowledge that she had the ability to feel this way.

Trying to smother a helpless sigh, she obviously wasn't very successful, because the black eyes raked her again. She felt their touch all the way down to her toes. Don't, she wanted to say. Don't look at me—don't do this to me! But she pressed her trembling lips together and stared fixedly ahead, and after a moment he returned his attention to the road while the tension surrounding them grew so tight she could barely breathe.

He turned into a quiet, salubrious square that she recognised instantly, and a wry smile touched her mouth. Big-league wasn't in it; this man existed on a higher plane altogether than she could ever aspire to.

Good, she thought. It only helped to shore up her resolve to get out of this situation before it became impossible. She didn't want this—it—him. She did not need it, nor could she cope with it.

The car stopped, the engine dying. Leon unclipped both seatbelts then opened his car door. She watched balefully as he climbed out and came around to open her door. When she hesitated, he said coolly, 'Don't make the mistake of challenging me, Jemma. I am tired and my temper is worn thin. I could get nasty.'

Could? If he thought he was making this a pleasure then she did not want to be around when he did get 'nasty'! Bending, she scooped up her purse and the small plastic carrier bag, then slid out of the car, scorning the outstretched hand he offered her in assistance.

He closed the car door, pressed a sensor pad on his keyring which activated the car central-locking system and the alarm at the same time, then turned without sparing her another glance to climb the steps to a black-painted front door.

By the time she had joined him, he was standing inside

an elegant hallway. The plain grey-carpeted floor and pale peach-painted walls blended superbly with the rich mahogany woodwork.

He glanced at a silver tray on the hall table where a stack of envelopes lay unopened. Long fingers flicked idly at them then dismissed them as unimportant. It was only then that it hit her that he must not have been here since his return to London.

So, where had he been? Working in his office? Eating dinner at some exclusive restaurant? With another woman?

Jealousy swirled up from the pit of her stomach and burned its way into her brain. Shocked and appalled by her own reaction, she stumbled as she tried to turn and walk out of the house again before he saw what was happening to her.

But Leon was too quick, and in one stride was at her side, his hand like a clamp around her arm as he turned her back again.

'Going somewhere?' he enquired silkily.

'I don't want to come in here with you,' she objected, having now to fight her response to his heated touch as well the crazy jealousy.

For an answer, he reached over her shoulder and gave the door a shove. Jemma quivered as she heard it click shut behind her. Without a single word, he took her purse and the silly plastic carrier bag from her, unbuttoned her coat and drew it off her shoulders while she just stood there in front of him, cheeks hot, eyes lowered, trembling from head to toe at his domineering closeness.

Then he just turned and walked off down the hall, arrogantly taking her possessions with him.

It's getting worse, she noted tremulously as she meekly followed. Ten minutes in his company last time and her senses had been so responsive to him that she could barely breathe or think. Another ten minutes and she was now so acutely conscious of him that she was actually afraid.

She paused on the threshold of a beautiful pale lemon and white sitting-room, seeing her coat casually discarded on the back of a chair. Leon was standing across the room, pouring a drink into a fine crystal glass, his dark business suit moulding his muscled body with little attempt at hiding the power beneath.

Her stillness had him glancing around at her. 'Come in,' he drawled. 'I am in no mood to jump on you if that is what is making you hover like a frightened bird.'

She still didn't move, her eyes too big in her face as she continued to stand there staring helplessly at him, her loose hair flowing like liquid toffee around her face and shoulders. His thick lashes lowered, half hiding his eyes while he let them travel slowly over her, lighting candles inside her wherever his gaze touched. She was still wearing the cool blue slinky stretch Lycra dress she had worn for her date with Tom. It lay off the shoulder and moulded her figure to halfway down her slender thighs. It wasn't a cheap dress, but neither was it of the expensive designer kind he was probably used to seeing his women in. And where with Tom she had only felt pretty, with Leon's eyes on her she felt vulnerable and self-conscious beneath his connoisseur's gaze.

'You dressed for him like this tonight?'

The question startled her, putting a wary light into her eyes, but it also served to remind her of why she was here at all, and Jemma lifted her chin, her mouth firming as she looked back at him.

'Yes,' she said, adding defiantly, 'not that it's any of your business.'

'No?' The smile on his lips held no humour, nor did the mocking tone. 'You have a lot to learn, if you truly believe what you say.'

He turned, gathering up another glass and bringing it with him as he walked towards her. Jemma held her ground, but only on the outside. Inside she was a broiling mass of panic. If he touched her—if he so much as laid a finger on her—she had a fear she would go up in flames.

'Here.' He held out the glass. 'Drink this.'

She looked down at the dark golden liquid gleaming in the glass. 'What is it?' she asked suspiciously.

'The national drink of Greece,' he replied. 'Come—' He gestured with the glass. 'I drink the same, so you can be assured it is not drugged. Try it. It is called metaxa—a carefully matured brandy that is kind to the palate.'

She took the glass reluctantly, lifting it to her lips to take a wary sip. Like brandy, it heated the sensitive tissues of her mouth as it flowed across it, but, unlike brandy, it did not burn. She swallowed. 'It's nice,' she allowed, sounding surprised.

He smiled, a brief smile that had gone as soon as it had arrived. Then he was staring at her again, the anger she had sensed simmering in him when he'd spoken on the phone still burning in his eyes.

'You—care for him?' he asked. 'You want this man you went out with tonight?'

'How can I say?' she cried, objecting to his proprietorial tone. 'It was our first date! Far too soon to make a decision like that!'

'Yet you knew you wanted me at the first clash of our eyes,' he pointed out.

She shrugged, unable to deny what had to be the biggest humiliation of her life. 'Which doesn't mean I have to jump right into bed with you,' she snapped. 'Wanting and having are two completely different things.'

'I am here.' He held out his arms, mocking her reply and inviting her at the same time. But she wasn't fooled; the anger was still there in his eyes. 'For the—having. Yet you decide to play this—little game with your fresh-faced young man with the winsome smile and thatch of light brown spiky hair.'

Shocked by his accurate description of Tom, she stared at him. 'How do you know what Tom looks like?' she gasped.

He took a sip at his drink, dark eyes thoughtful on her while he took his time swallowing. Her head began to spin, that awful track of uncontrollable attraction spiralling its way through her system. It was the eyes that did it, she acknowledged hazily, feeling her breath begin to shorten and her body begin to pulse to a rhythm that was strange to her yet unbearably exciting. Those deep, dark, beautiful eyes could hold her captive at a single look.

'Thomas MacDonald,' he said suddenly, bringing her sharply back into focus. 'Aged twenty-nine. Recently employed by Driver and Lowe, architects.' Jemma's mouth fell open. 'Moved into the flat below your own on Tuesday last week. Has a passion for Simply Red and never misses a concert if he can help it. His current bank account rests at one thousand and fifty-two pounds. He caught the bus to work with you on Wednesday. Borrowed teabags from your enchanting flatmate Trina Beaton on Thursday. Trina Beaton...' He moved on while Jemma could only stand there gaping. 'A delightfully enterprising creature with bright red hair and a—satirical disposition. You have shared a flat with her since you arrived in London four years ago. She runs an interesting little business called—Maids in Waiting.' He actually smiled with amusement at that. 'An idea which began during her college years in an effort to make some extra money to prop up her grant and grew into the flourishing business it is today because she had the courage and foresight to see its potential. Her accountant is also her lover—though they never use your flat for their—intimate activities—reputedly in respect of your...finer feelings. His name is Frew Landers and he's clever and sharp. Upwardly mobile, I think is the popular term. His favourite pastime is teasing you. Jemma Davis,' he continued levelly, never for one second taking his eyes from her stunned face. 'Parents dead, killed in an automobile accident four years ago. Attended secretarial college for two yours and graduated with distinctions at the age of nineteen. Has worked for three companies, TDC being the last and current one. Josh Tanner employed you—not particularly for your exemplary secretarial skills, but because he wanted to take you to bed. But—and I compliment you on your good sense—you made him see the error of his—judgement. Since then you have become his right-hand man, though he does not realise it himself. And his complicated love-life has hit the doldrums—how is Cassie, by the way?' he concluded lightly.

'I n-need to sit d-down,' Jemma said weakly.

'Of course,' he said, immediately the indulgent host and taking her arm to lead her over to one of the comfortable damask sofas set before the flower-filled grate of a beautiful mahogany fireplace.

She lowered herself carefully, aware that the slightest puff of wind was likely to toss her into a crumpled heap. He watched her sink into a corner, her face gone quite blank, then sat himself down beside her. She was still holding her glass, and he gently curled his own fingers around it and lifted it to her ice-cold lips.

'I'm sorry,' he murmured, watching the colour take its time returning to her face. 'But you made me very angry or I would not have said any of that.'

'Why?' she managed to enunciate, but only just. In truth, he had completely knocked the stuffing out of her.

'I want you,' he shrugged as if that explained everything. 'By necessity I have to be a careful man. Power makes you dangerous, and your enemies do not always wear intentions on their sleeves. Danger can come in many guises—hostile take-overs, industrial espionage—'

'And you suspect me of being some kind of Mata Hari trained to seduce you for all your powerful secrets?' she gasped, disbelief and scorn warring in her anger-bright eyes.

He smiled, unrepentant. 'Or just a lady,' he suggested, 'with the kind of past that could affect me?'

'My God! You arrogant swine!' she choked, not for one second missing his meaning. Furiously, she shot to her feet. 'Well, hear this, Mr Stephanades,' she flung at him. 'This lady with a past is just a bit choosy herself!'

'I know,' he confirmed, his lazy smile enough to shoot the lid right off her temper.

'Oh, go to hell,' she muttered, and turned, her trembling legs barely able to support her as she stalked angrily for the door.

'Virgin,' he chanted cruelly after her. 'And proud of it. Friends call you "one-date Jemma" and lay bets on who will be the first to crack the ice.' She stopped, her spine stiffening in horror. 'Speculation has it that you must have suffered a bad experience at some time to make you so unresponsive to men. But I know better, do I not?'

Jemma closed her eyes, appalled that his investigators could dig that deep!

'I am not a promiscuous man, *agape mou*,' he informed her smoothly. 'The days of passing from one woman to another long ago lost its appeal with the risks it brings with it. I value my good clean bill of health, and am therefore very careful whom I share my body with.'

'My God,' she whispered, turning to stare at him. 'I don't believe I'm really hearing this!'

'I want you, but not at any price—you understand?' he said, a slight hint of apology in his tone as he came to his feet. 'So I had to have you thoroughly checked out.'

'So virgins are all you allow yourself these days, are they?' Jemma threw scathingly at him.

His open-palmed shrug said it all. 'In general, these days, I steer clear of intimacy with any women,' he confessed. 'You, are the exception.'

'And I suppose you expect me to be honoured by that confession?'

'No,' he denied. 'But I thought you may gain some comfort in knowing that I can offer you the same risk-free pleasure you will be giving me.'

'Go to hell,' she said again, her contempt of him only slightly overshadowed by the severe sense of disgust she felt at herself for being so obvious with him that he felt he could do and say all of this to her. 'I would rather take my chances with Tom MacDonald's more dubious sexual history than with a cold-blooded, calculating devil like you!'

On that, she spun away again, grabbing up her belongings before storming out of the room, feeling angry enough just maybe to put her words into practice and offer herself to Tom, if only to get back at all of them—both her so-called friends and the man she had just left standing there—for daring to make her personal life their business!

She'd reached the front door before he caught up with her, his hands like manacles as they closed around her upper arms to swing her round to face him. Her coat went one way, her purse the other. She saw the fury leaping in his eyes, the threat of violence, then his mouth was landing punishingly on hers and all hell broke loose inside her.

Her shock, the anger and utter contempt she was feeling, all colluded with her hungry senses to send them wild. Her arms snapped up to push him away, fists thumping at his shoulders and chest while she wriggled and squirmed and kissed him back with a vengeance. Her lips parted, wantonly drawing his tongue into contest with her own, and he made a husky little groan deep in his throat which she an-

swered with an animal growl of her own, elated that she
had actually managed to shake him.

'You think I would let you give all of this to him?' he
grated, thrusting her to arm's length so that she fell heavily
against the hard wood panel of the door behind her.

'Good, was it?' she taunted thickly, her eyes spitting her
contempt at him, even while her swollen mouth invited
more of the same mind-blowing kisses. Breasts heaving,
hands shaking, she challenged the harsh rasping of his
breath. 'Want it all? Shame,' she jeered. 'Because I'd die
before I would let you have me!'

'Then die!' he decreed, dragging her back against him,
the desire in him flaring up like her own, full of angry
passion. 'For I am the only man who is going to have you!'

And his mouth took hers again, his arms moulding her
writhing throbbing body to his with no chance of escape.
And it went on and on—a battle that was a crazy one because they were both using the same angry weapons to
strike sparks from each other. Jemma's fingers found his
hair and gripped, but not to pull him away. Instead they
held his mouth down on hers while his own hands curved
into the flesh at the tops of her legs, pushing up the fabric
of her skirt and pressing her hard against him so that the
mad gyration of their bodies inflamed them to full, throbbing arousal.

It was terrible. Jemma saw in a brief flash of sanity how
they must look together like this, and she whimpered in
horror, hot tears burning into her eyes and running down
her cheeks.

He felt them, tasted them on his tongue, and groaned as
he dragged his mouth away from hers. 'God,' he choked,
'what are we doing here?'

Raping each other, Jemma thought wildly as he muttered
something in a harsh guttural Greek before burying his face

in her hair, holding her tightly against him while the wild storm raged on inside them both.

It was a long while before they began to calm. And by then Jemma was feeling so ashamed of herself that she did not know how she was going to lift her head and face him. She was glad of the solid wall of his pounding chest to hide against. His arms had relaxed their suffocating grip on her body and were gently stroking her now. He, like herself, made no attempt to move, but slowly, as the seconds ticked by, she became conscious that one of them was going to have to break the crazy deadlock.

He did it, as if reading her mind, taking on the responsibility and slowly dropping his arms. She didn't move, didn't think she had the strength left to try! He turned his back, a hand going up to grip the back of his neck while he stared grimly at the carpet. The silence was gnawing.

'I'll make some coffee,' he said suddenly and strode off down the hall.

Jemma watched him go with empty eyes. Empty because he had just managed to drain her of every emotion she possessed. It would be better if she just opened the door and sneaked quietly away, she told herself as she continued to stand there. She was sure she would be able to hail a cruising black cab. Ten minutes and she would be home, safe in her flat with Trina's mocking presence to keep her safe. A few determined steps, she told herself, and you could end all of this for good. He would not follow. Like herself, he couldn't want this violent kind of passion.

It wasn't good. It wasn't even enjoyable. Just a hostile, bitter slaking of an ugly lust, that was what it was. Lust.

She managed to turn, legs trembling as she made the vital manoeuvre which had her facing the door.

'Where are you going?'

Gentle as the question was, it froze her in terror.

'H-home,' she whispered tremulously. 'I w-want to go h-home.'

Silence. She didn't move and she was almost sure he didn't either. Then she heard his heavy sigh. 'All right,' he conceded. 'But I shall take you.'

He began walking towards her, and the closer he got, the more she trembled until she shook in violent spasms that brought the tears back to her eyes. It was stupid, but when his arms came gently around her to draw her back against him she sobbed with relief, turning to bury her face in his shirt-front. 'I've never felt so ashamed of myself!' she whispered thickly.

'You and me both, *agape mou*,' he murmured grimly. 'But I think my shame has to be worse than yours right now. Come.' He shifted until he held her beneath the crook of his arm. 'You are in no fit state to go home as yet, and my guilty conscience will not let you go like this.' Gently he led her back along the hall. 'We will talk, I think,' he decided. 'Of things other than ourselves and what we seem to want or not want.' His dry tone made her smile, and she glanced up to find him smiling ruefully too.

Then their eyes locked. And even as she felt the upward surge of all that awful tension again, she saw him heave in a harsh breath in an effort to control his own feelings.

Sighing, he leaned back heavily against the wall behind him, his grip loosening on her. 'This is not going to work, is it?' he sighed. 'Talking is the last thing we both need to do right now.'

She lowered her face, shaking her tumbled mass of hair. 'I don't even know you,' she whispered helplessly. That seemed to shame her as much as the emotions running wild inside her.

'Our bodies seem to know each other well enough.' Reaching out, he threaded gentle fingers through her hair. Her eyes closed, face lifting on a sigh of such helpless pleasure at his touch that he breathed once, fiercely. 'Upstairs,' he murmured, 'I have a bed. A warm and comfortable, very large bed where, with a bit of trust on your side and a lot of control on mine, I think I could manage to salvage some of our self-respect from this night if you would let me.'

Her stomach muscles contracted, sending a flutter of appeal winging out across her body. 'Violence is not my way, Jemma,' he said quietly. 'What took place here just now was a—a culmination of my bad temper and your angry retaliation to it. But it does not alter the most fundamental reason as to why we are here together like this. We want each other—*need* would be a better word. Please,' he murmured huskily, 'will you let me make love to you as gently and as beautifully as I know how?'

'No strings attached?' She heard the words leave her lips in the shape of a surrender, her kiss-swollen mouth twisting wryly as she acknowledged it. 'No other lovers? No other commitment other than a pledge of loyalty while this thing lasts?' she quoted his own words back at him drily.

'Do you want a deeper commitment from me?' he asked, his expression quite serious.

Jemma thought about it. Thought about the man he was and the power he wielded. She thought about the social circles he moved in and the nice little Greek girl at home somewhere in his own country waiting for him to give in to family pressure and marry well. And she shuddered. 'No,' she answered. 'I want nothing more from you than—this…'

She moved into his arms, unable to stay out of them for a moment longer. Their mouths met and her eyes closed over the helpless need radiating from her dark blue irises. Leon came away from the wall, folding her against him as he deepened the kiss.

The anger had gone, lost in the surrendering of the battle.

But what replaced it was far, far more intense. With the aid of his kiss he seemed to absorb her into him, her mind, her body, her every sense opening up and closing hungrily around him.

He whispered something, a stunned expletive, it sounded like, though she barely registered it because whatever it was was groaned against her burning mouth and she was more aware of him picking her up and cradling her in his arms then moving, carrying her in a floaty haze up the stairs.

The kiss broke when he lowered her feet to the ground again, and Jemma lifted heavy lids to find herself gazing into eyes flowing with passion. It startled her, the look of fierce arousal, and her mouth parted on a protest—never uttered because he stopped it with a small shake of his head.

'Trust me,' he said, brushing his lips across hers. 'This is no empty seduction. I am as much a slave to this as you are, *agape mou.*'

A statement he quickly proved when her fingers flexed in an instinctive response against his shoulders and he shuddered, the breath rushing shakily from his lungs.

Taking hold of her hand, he led her across the room—a room, she realised for the first time, that was a bedroom, big and gracious, its green and grey furnishings softly lit by a bedside lamp.

By the big double bed he turned her to face him, eyes still black with need but gentle now as they gravely explored her face. She blushed, feeling shy suddenly and awkward now that he had given her a moment to realise just what they were doing.

'No,' he murmured, lifting her chin with softly stroking fingers when she tried to hide her face from him. 'Passion becomes you, *agape mou.* Don't hide it all away from me.'

He lowered his head again, silk lashes brushing tantilisingly against her flushed cheeks as he kissed her nose then each corner of her mouth and ran his fingers in a feather-like caress down her throat and over naked shoulders before sliding them into her hair, pushing the long, thick fall back from her face and making her senses leap as he lowered his head to run his tongue around her exposed ear.

She closed her eyes, preening sensually as the sweetest sensation turned her muscles to liquid. Her fingers curled into the lean, tight flesh at his waist. His tongue slid lower, forcing the breath from her lungs in short, sharp gasps as he licked his way to the other ear to wreak the same havoc there.

Then his mouth closed over hers again, his hands sliding down the sides of her body from breast to hip and back again, sending her arching sensuously towards him as, slowly, he began peeling her dress downwards. It had no zip, was nothing more than a tube of stretch fabric and it went easily, exposing her breasts, high-domed and peaked by two tight buds. His hands explored, probed, excited, then pushed the dress further, over her slender ribcage, her narrow waist and the softly rounded curves of her hips. By the time it fell in a pool around her feet, her arms were curved languidly around his neck, all hint of shyness lost to the pleasure of his touch.

They were kissing so deeply now that she was barely aware of his quick movements as he divested himself of his shirt. It was only as he crushed her against the heat of his naked chest that she realised what he had done. And by then she was revelling in the feel of him, of the hard-packed muscle beneath heated flesh, his skin like stretched satin beneath her fingertips, of the rasping pleasure of chest hair moving against her breast. The scent of him was warm and clean and intoxicatingly musky, sensual, so sensual that it sent her dizzy, dizzy enough to sigh and sway, and groan something helpless in her throat which she didn't understand but he seemed to do because he turned and, with her

still held in his arms, lowered them both on to the cool
green cover on the bed.

It was a long night. A beautiful night. Tender and excruciatingly patient, Leon guided her down sweet, sweet paths
of sensual pleasure. He taught her with each new intimacy
what making love really meant. First of the flesh, bringing
her skin alive with the lightest, most tantalising caresses
until she seemed to quiver all over with a bright tingling
pleasure that had her arching and flexing in movements that
were so instinctively sensual that she had no idea what it
did to him to feel her like this.

But she thought she'd die a thousand deaths at the con-
fusing rush of feeling she felt when his touch became more
intimate.

'Shh,' he soothed as she tightened in shocked rejection
to something utterly alien to her, and he caught her shaky
protest with his mouth while his fingers stroked the moist,
silken core of her, drawing her—inexorably drawing her—
deeper into the chasms of desire.

It flowed and ebbed, like a lazy summer tide washing
over her until she thought she would drown in its sensual
flow, only to feel it fade away again as, skilfully, she realised hazily, he brought her to a boneless state where nothing
he could do would shock her now. She began to feel restless, her body pulsing to a rhythm that seemed to demand
something more from him.

'Leon,' she whispered threadily.

'Yes,' he murmured. 'I know…' And he took her mouth
in a long, languid kiss while gently urging her thighs wider,
then slid his body over hers.

No pain, just a short, sharp sting that had her eyes flying
open on a breathless, 'Oh,' to stare at him in surprise.

He was watching her, supporting his upper body on his
forearms as he gazed into her eyes, his own face wearing
the glaze of a fiercely reined-in passion. He was hot and

tight, his laboured breath rasping over her face as he waited, lean hips pressing into the cradle of her hips, letting her feel—know—the power of his possession before slowly, carefully he thrust himself deeper inside.

Then they were one, moving together, breathing together. Mouths locked, bodies locked, and the pounding drumbeat of their hearts paced the growing power of their pleasure. She could feel him inside her, exalted in his pulsing strength, the power of him, the need in him, each stroke, each beautiful silken stroke carrying them closer and closer to some potent place hovering just out of their grasp.

Then suddenly they reached it, and as if a volcano were erupting deep inside her she was tossed into a world of fire and force and hot, pulsing lava.

Afterwards she curled herself up into his arms, clinging to him as though life itself revolved around him in its entirety. The fact that he held her close, said nothing but just held her, told her that he too was in awe of what had just happened. She hadn't expected it; she wondered if he had.

Whatever. As far as she was concerned, Leon had just given her the most beautiful experience of her life, and at this moment she wanted to do nothing more than be held close to him while she savoured it. Because surely it could not be that good every time, could it?

CHAPTER FOUR

'ARE you going to move in with him?' Trina demanded. It was late Sunday night and Jemma had not returned until half an hour ago.

What had gone on in the interim would, Jemma thought dreamily, go down in her secret store of memories as the most precious forty-eight hours of her life. As he had promised, Leon had made that first time beautiful for her. His care and patience and mind-blowing sensuality had left her stunned and dazed.

And it could be as good the second and even the third time around, she acknowledged with a soft secret smile. In fact, their responses to each other became so exquisitely tuned that they could barely look at each other without experiencing the electric fizz of desire.

'No,' she answered Trina's question, then grimaced, remembering the one of several small skirmishes they'd had during the weekend. 'He wants me to, but I decided it was best if I remain here. I'll find it less—stressful that way. He goes away a lot, and that big empty house would drive me insane with no one to talk to.'

'No servants?'

She shook her head. 'A woman who comes in daily to clean for him, but nothing more. If he wishes to entertain, he employs a caterer. He is surprisingly self-sufficient for someone from his background,' she confided with a smile. 'And his tastes are simple.'

'A Greek trait,' he'd told her. 'At heart all Greeks are simple people. We make money by necessity—and because we find we possess a rather good knack for doing so,' he'd added with a grin. 'But I live in a world constantly filled with people. People who are in constant demand of my attention, my thoughts, my time. When I come home I want only to answer to myself. Servants fussing around me would spoil that.'

'And so would a lover,' she'd pointed out. 'So I am right to remain in my own flat.'

He'd frowned at her when she'd said that, as if he wanted to argue—then changed his mind, pulling her towards him and kissing the top of her head. 'Perhaps you are at that,' he'd agreed. 'Except the weekends,' he'd added firmly, 'when you will arrive here directly from work on Friday and remain until Sunday night. And I will buy you a wardrobe of exquisite clothes so you won't have to waste time packing and unpacking.'

Which had begun the next small skirmish—or maybe it wasn't so small, she mused as she sat there on the lumpy old sofa after enjoying a day of sinking into luxurious feather.

'No wardrobe,' she'd refused. 'And no more presents, Leon,' she'd added, going to dig out the reason she had actually decided to meet him the night before, and handing the plastic carrier bag to him. 'You take me as I am—nine-carat-gold jewellery, off-the-peg clothes and all—or not at all, but I don't want any more…gifts.'

He stared down at the plastic bag for a moment before silently opening it up. Out fell the velvet boxes.

'I don't want you to buy me things,' she explained huskily when he didn't say a single word. 'When you do, it makes me feel…' She paused, searching for the right word which wouldn't offend.

He provided it. 'Cheap?' he clipped.

'Inadequate,' she amended. 'I can't match your generosity, Leon, simply because I don't have the necessary

...nds to do it. When you buy me expensive things, it makes me feel...'

'Bought.'

'Will you stop putting words into my mouth?' she flared, irritated because really he was only stating the truth. 'You are deliberately misconstruing everything I say!'

'And you are not misconstruing my reason for buying you these things?' he countered, suddenly so contemptuous that it hit her that she had managed to offend him anyway. 'You call these expensive!' On an act of disgust he threw the boxes to one side. 'They were nothing but *cheap* little nothings I saw and bought for you because they pleased my eye and reminded me of you!'

She gasped at the interpretation he had put on her words. 'So your choice of word was right, and I do look cheap?' she retaliated, her own anger and hurt rising with his.

'If you looked cheap, my dear Jemma,' he decided, 'you would not be standing here in my home right now!'

'So, why are you offering to buy me an expensive wardrobe of clothes?' she challenged. 'Why the expensive—sorry, *cheap* gifts? If it offends your ego to be with a woman who wears high-street bargain clothes and gold-plated jewellery, Leon, then maybe we should just call it quits right now!'

'I never said that!' he sighed in exasperation. 'Or even implied it! You are a very beautiful woman, Jemma—sackcloth or silk, you would always look beautiful. Why is it so wrong for a man to want to buy his woman beautiful things?'

'Because this particular woman feels more comfortable without them,' she replied. 'I have nothing but myself to give to you and I want nothing but yourself in return. Is that so difficult to understand?' she appealed.

He sighed at that, and, in a way which brought tears to her eyes, reached out and drew her against him. 'You are wrong, you know,' he murmured into her hair. 'You have given me the most expensive and precious gift a woman can give a man, *agape mou*. And if I let it pass by unacknowledged, then I would certainly be playing you cheap.'

She blushed, knowing exactly what he was referring to. 'It was given freely, Leon,' she whispered softly.

'And cannot be handed back as my—paltry gifts to you can be,' he pointed out.

She lifted her head to look at him at that, her eyes suddenly alight with mischief. 'And do you want to give it back?' she enquired provocatively.

'Vixen,' he scolded. 'You know I do not! But,' he added, 'in all fairness, according to your rules, you must accept something back from me in return.'

'All right,' she reluctantly conceded. 'One gift I will accept graciously—but nothing else!' she warned him sternly. 'And something small! If I come here next Friday night to find a wardrobe stuffed with fine clothes, I'll throw them out of the window!'

'Jemma...?'

'Mmm?' she murmured hazily now, the tender smile softening her face taking its time to fade as she slowly refocused.

Trina was looking anxious. 'Are you absolutely sure you're doing the right thing?'

No, Jemma thought, but I know I can't do a thing about it. She got up, stretching tiredly. 'What's right or wrong for me doesn't seem to come into it,' she confessed as she let her body relax again. 'I want him,' she tagged on simply. It seemed to say it all to her.

'You love him, you mean,' Trina grimly corrected.

Did she? Jemma paused to ponder a concept she had until now refused to so much as peep at. Had she fallen head over heels in love with Leon Stephanades at the first moment she saw him?

'I know you, Jemma, and there's no way you would put yourself in this kind of no-hope situation unless your heart was involved. You love him,' she stated again. 'And that bastard most probably knows it, and couldn't give a hoot so long as he gets what he wants from you!'

'I'm going to bed,' Jemma said pointedly, turning towards the door. 'Goodnight, Tri.'

'He'll hurt you!' her friend warned, real concern darkening her rich green eyes. 'He's the kind of man who sees something he wants and goes after it and damns the consequences! It wouldn't enter his arrogant head to wonder whether it was the right and fair thing for you! Men like him exist on a different plane from us mere mortals. They're takers, Jemma!'

'And you think I'm not taking as much from him?' she challenged.

'It's not the same,' Trina sighed. 'You'll be the one left hurting in the end while he walks away sublimely unscathed! Oh,' she groaned in frustration when she saw Jemma's set face. 'Why couldn't you have put it around a bit like the rest of us more normal creatures? Gained some experience before taking on a man like him!'

'Goodnight, Trina,' Jemma sighed out wearily, announcing the end of the discussion.

'Goodnight,' her friend mumbled. Then, as Jemma reached the door, 'I hate him!' she yelled at the top of her voice.

'I'll be sure to tell him,' Jemma replied, smiling, because poor Trina was only behaving like this out of concern for her.

'You won't need to,' Trina snapped, 'because I'll damn well tell him myself!'

And she did.

It was Wednesday before Jemma saw Leon again. He was tied up with business until then, and in a way Jemma was glad of the respite. Not least because her body physically ached from the sensual onslaught it had been put through.

He called her at work, though. Usually around three each afternoon, his voice like warm honey on her senses, gliding sweetly over her. On Wednesday, she received a beautiful posy of freesias, their luxurious scent filling the whole office. 'Not a gift,' he'd sardonically written on the accompanying card, 'but a hello because I will not have time to call you today. And I wanted to remind you to keep tonight free. It belongs to me. L.'

She smiled at his sarcasm, grimaced at his arrogance and inhaled the lovely perfume of the flowers as if she were inhaling that subtle spicy scent of him.

'Who's L?'

She hadn't heard Josh come in the room, and jumped when she found him leaning over her, blatantly reading the card. 'An—admirer,' she said, and quickly shoved the card away. She didn't want Josh to know about Leon. Things between the two men were strained enough as it was.

Cassie, it seemed, had gone into hiding. And Josh, for all he tried, could not find out where she was and was therefore blaming Leon. 'The man's no fool, I'll give him that!' Josh had grated bitterly after spending hours trying to locate Cassie. 'If she's with him then he's managed to secure himself the safest lay in town!'

'Josh!' Jemma had gasped. 'That's a terrible thing to say!'

He'd muttered something beneath his breath, scraped an angry hand through his straight blond hair then stormed back into his own room.

When Leon picked her up on Wednesday night, her first question was, 'Have you seen Cassie?'

His frown was genuine enough. 'No,' he said. 'Why should I? Aren't you ready?' he then demanded impatiently, glancing at her white towelling robe than pointedly at his watch, poor Cassie firmly dismissed. 'The table is booked for eight. I dislike being late.'

Reassured about Cassie, Jemma then forgot all about her when another concern leapt into her mind. The one which meant leaving him alone with Trina while she finished getting ready.

By the time she joined them, you could have cut the air with a knife. Leon was standing by the window, his elegant back in its beautifully cut dark silk suit an arrogant wall of dismissal. Trina was seated hot-faced on the sofa, glaring fiery daggers at him. Jemma took one look at them both and bit down anxiously on her bottom lip. Leon was a sophisticated man of the world, and not the kind you gave moral lectures to. She didn't want Trina spoiling this for her.

'I'm ready,' she murmured nervously.

He turned, his eyes darkening as they ran over her. She was wearing black tonight, figure-hugging silk jacquard black with a halter-neck that left her shoulders bare and fastened like a dog-collar around her slender neck. It was fashionably short, revealing more than enough of her long, slender legs. And she'd put up her hair, tying it in a topknot then teasing down some wispy tendrils to soften the shape of her face.

She knew she looked good. But under his expert eye she was severely on the look-out for any hint of criticism. What she actually saw made her blush warmly as she turned away to collect her bag, only remembering what the back of the dress did when she heard his indrawn gasp.

In fact, the dress did not have a back. It hugged her breasts and skimmed down the sides of her ribcage to her waist, but other than that she was naked.

'Want to borrow my black wrap?' Trina offered in an odd tone of voice which had her glancing sharply at her. It was then she realised that the offer had not been made out of the goodness of her heart, but as a taunt to the man who was staring at Jemma in a way that increased her anxiety. Had she gone too far? Was the dress too revealing for his taste?

'Do you think I need one?' She put the question to Leon—and they all knew she was not referring to the unusually warm weather they were having for April.

'He thinks you need bedding,' Trina drawled. 'But that is beside the—'

'Shut up, you acid-tongued bitch,' Leon cut in levelly. He didn't even flash Trina a threatening glance when he said it, just relayed the words with a cool indifference that made Trina shrug and Jemma gasp. 'You'll do exactly as you are,' he then murmured to Jemma. And the tone alone showed the perfect example of what a voice could say without using the right words.

She was still trembling with reaction to it when he opened the sitting-room door and politely saw her through it.

'Wait a minute,' Leon stalled her as she went to walk down the narrow hall.

She turned, lifting a self-conscious hand to her hair when she found him studying her narrowly. 'What is it?' she asked worriedly.

'Come here,' he commanded, 'and I will show you.' She went to stand nervously in front of him.

His hands came to her waist, almost managing to span the slender width as he drew her against him. 'She's right, you know,' he murmured huskily. 'I do want to bed you.'

His mouth was warm and seeking, hungry, without attempting to fan the fires they both knew were being carefully banked down right now. His fingers played lightly on her naked back, setting her flesh tingling as they brushed tantalisingly over her, his thumbs finding their way inside the dress to caress the satin sides of her breasts. She arched against him in seductive pleasure, and he groaned against her mouth, their lips clinging protestingly as they slowly broke apart.

'Feel what you do to me?' he murmured.

'Mmm,' she smiled, and presented her mouth for another kiss. He was just lowering his head when the rattle of the sitting-room door broke them both apart.

'Ah,' he mocked. 'The wicked witch is about to appear.'

'She's not a witch,' Jemma protested as she put some distance between them. 'And she's not wicked. She's just concerned for me, that's all.'

'And I admire her for that,' Leon surprised her by saying as he guided her towards the flat door. 'But it does not alter the fact that she has a mind like a sewer and the tongue of an asp!'

'Does it bother you,' Jemma asked him anxiously as they reached the top of the stairs, 'that she doesn't mind saying what she thinks to your face?'

'Bother me?' An eyebrow arched sardonically. 'Of course not. She believes she has your best interests at heart.' His hand came to her nape, curving it caressingly. 'And for that reason she can snipe at me all she wants, so long as she does not succeed in convincing you that what she believes is in the truth.'

Bending his head, he kissed the tip of her nose, then smiled, and Trina was forgotten—like everything else as he set himself out to charm and amuse her throughout the long, leisurely taken dinner at the kind of restaurant Jemma had only read about in good magazines.

He drove her home to her flat afterwards.

Her body grew cold as they went way beyond the point where she could continue fooling herself that he was taking the long way back to his own home.

Was this it? she wondered achingly. Thanks for everything, Jemma, but I've decided you're not really what I want in my life?

By the time he stopped the car, she was like a statue frozen in ice in the seat beside him. She couldn't believe it—couldn't understand why, when he had been so openly warm and tender all evening. His eyes had never left her for a moment, his concentration on her alone, so intense that she'd begun to glow inside in anticipation of what was to come.

Slipping free both their seatbelts, he turned, making her jerk violently as his long-fingered hand curved around her nape again. 'Thank you,' he said. 'For a beautiful evening.'

She swallowed, unable to stand it, turning pain-glazed eyes up to his. 'Y-you don't want me tonight?' she whispered tremulously.

'Want you…?' he repeated, black eyes frowning down at her. Then he caught on and sighed heavily. 'I am not a married man, Jemma,' he derided, 'with a wife and two-point-five children at home to give me all the companionship I require.'

'I never said you were!' she protested.

'Yet you expected me to treat you as a married man treats his mistress? Seeing you—being with you—only when I need some sexual relief?'

She frowned in confusion. She'd thought that was exactly what all this was about.

Removing his hand, he sat back in his seat. 'This is supposed to be a relationship!' he snapped out impatiently. 'Not a convenience!'

'I'm sorry,' she mumbled, feeling a fool for reading the situation so terribly wrong.

'You insult me!' he claimed stiffly.

'Well!' she snapped back defensively. 'How am I supposed to know the way these things are played? It is my

first try at it after all! Perhaps you had better write down
the ground rules so I won't insult your sensibilities again!'

Huffily, she turned, searching for the door lock, feeling
a big enough fool to want to get away from him as soon
as she could.

'Come back here!' he growled, catching her by the arm
and pulling her around and against him. 'You crazy
woman.' His chest lifted and fell beneath her cheek on a
long-suffering sigh. 'You've been sweet and amusing and
downright seductive all evening.' She felt his mouth brush
against her hair. 'And if I've had to fight the urge to rush
you home to my bed, then I did so out of respect for you,
not because I did not want you. But come Friday…' he
growled, pushing her away a little so that he could burn her
with his eyes. 'Pack only a toothbrush, *agape mou*. It will
be all you will need for two days!'

He was right: her toothbrush was all she needed. Which
from then on set the pattern for Jemma's first real love-
affair. If he was in town, then Wednesday evenings they
spent simply enjoying each other's company. If he was
away, then each night he would ring her up and spend long
delicious minutes just talking to her via the phone.
Weekends he always managed to be in London, working
his tight and busy schedule around it, Jemma guessed when
sometimes he looked so tired when she arrived at his home
on Fridays that it filled her with warmth to know he would
go to such lengths just to be with her.

One Wednesday, almost a month into their relationship,
he looked tired when he picked her up, and Trina's acid
glances seemed to irritate him. 'I'll tell her to lay off you,
shall I?' Jemma suggested when they'd driven the distance
between her flat and a small but exclusive restaurant he
intended taking her to in total silence.

'She does not bother me unduly,' he dismissed. 'I have

been continent-hopping for the last two days, and I am just a trifle jet-lagged, that's all.'

She studied him, seeing the lines of weariness tugging at the corners of his eyes and mouth, and gently placed her hand on his thigh. 'We don't have to go anywhere if you don't feel like it, Leon,' she told him softly.

He glanced at her, mockery twisting his beautiful mouth. 'You wish me to stop here? And we'll just spend the rest of the evening in the car?'

'No.' She smiled at his sarcastic humour. 'But we could go back to your house,' she suggested. 'Spend the evening just—relaxing.'

The car slowed while he spent several seconds reading the message in her eyes before, without a word, he returned his attention to the road. He didn't say anything, but his hand came to cover hers where it rested on his thigh, and remained there until they concluded their journey to his home.

That night they made love, then she made them omelettes for supper, strolling casually about his modern kitchen wearing only one of his shirts. He sat at the kitchen table in his dark towelling robe, following her lazily with his eyes. The mood was lazy, beautifully so. After they'd eaten in front of the TV set in his sitting-room, he stretched out on the sofa and pulled her down to lie beside him. In ten minutes he was asleep.

She just lay there watching him for hours, loving the way all the toughness had left his face, how he slept with his lips slightly parted, breathing light and evenly. At twelve o'clock she crept out of the house and caught a taxi back to her flat. The next morning he rang her at work before she'd even taken off her coat.

'You left me to make your own way home,' he said. 'Don't do it again.'

'You were sleeping,' she explained. 'It wouldn't have

been fair to disturb you when a taxi could transport me door to door just as easily.'

'But without the pleasure it would have given me to do so,' he stated. 'Tonight I expect reparation. Wear something sexy—like that disgraceful black thing you wore for me the first time I took you out. We are going somewhere special. I will pick you up at eight.'

The phone went dead. Jemma grinned at it. 'Arrogant devil,' she murmured, and spent the rest of the day smiling like an idiot because he was breaking from routine and taking her out on a Thursday.

Cassie rang during the afternoon. 'Will he speak to me?' she enquired stiffly.

'I'm not sure...' Jemma gave the closed door between the two offices a dubious glance. 'But I shall certainly try for you. How are you, Cassie?' she then asked gently.

'I'm fine,' came the cool reply. 'He's offered to keep me and the child, did you know that?'

Jemma mumbled a denial, hurting for both of them. Josh had not been the same person since this thing with Cassie blew up in his face. He walked around the office like a man made of stone, hard-faced and unapproachable.

'I was informed of his proposal through his solicitor,' Cassie continued tightly. 'A quarterly allowance and the mortgage taken care of on my flat.'

Jemma winced. 'I'm so sorry it worked out this way,' she murmured inadequately. In all honesty, she didn't know which of them she felt more sorry for. The whole situation was hopeless and ugly. 'If you need anything,' she offered, 'a sympathetic ear or just someone to yell at, I'm available.'

'Thanks, but no, thanks,' Cassie refused, her tone softened slightly by the offer. 'I don't think that would be a good idea.'

She meant her closeness to Josh, of course, and Jemma sighed as she buzzed him to tell him who wanted to speak to him. Surprisingly, he took the call without the bitter anger that Cassie's calls before had aroused in him.

They talked for several minutes before her console told them they'd finished. And she began to hope that, at last, tempers had calmed enough for them to begin talking sensibly about what they were going to do.

Those hopes were dashed the moment she saw Josh's face a few minutes later. He was even more stone-like than he had been before.

That evening, Leon was in a much livelier frame of mind. He even took Trina on, provoking her with teasing little remarks that ended with her stalking from the room. 'She's all fire, that one,' he remarked admiringly as he watched her go.

'Keep your eyes off!' Jemma warned. 'She's taken and so are you!'

His eyebrows shot up at her heated tone. 'That wouldn't be a hint of green-eyed jealousy, would it?' he taunted.

You can bet you sweet life it was! Jemma thought angrily, and lifted her chin. 'Do I need to feel jealous?' she challenged right back.

'Maybe,' he murmured thoughtfully. 'Red-haired witch or not, she does tend to grow on one, does she not?'

Jemma spun her back on him to collect her bag, refusing to rise to the bait. He was riling her deliberately; she knew that even as she seethed inside. Stalking haughtily out of her flat, she vowed to get her own back, if only to cut the arrogant devil down to size!

She got her opportunity sooner than she could have hoped.

Tom MacDonald was just coming out of his flat as she came down the stairs.

His face lit up when he saw her. 'Where were you the other Saturday night?' he demanded. 'I thought we had a date, but when I knocked on your flat door nobody answered!'

'Oh, Tom—I'm so sorry!' she cried, genuinely contrite because she had forgotten all about him! Impulsively, she lifted her hands to his shoulders and kissed his cheek. 'How could it have slipped my mind like that?'

'Maybe because you had other, more important things to think about,' another voice coolly suggested, and Jemma flushed with embarrassment when Leon pointedly gripped her wrists and lifted her hands away from Tom. 'Shame on you, darling,' he added smoothly, 'standing one man up while you made love to another.'

'It didn't matter,' Tom put in awkwardly, seeing more than his match in Leon and not even trying to stand up to him. 'It was only a tentative arrangement.'

'Ah,' drawled Leon. 'Then thankfully her...memory lapse did not cause too much inconvenience.' He dropped one of Jemma's wrists but held on to the other one with a grip aimed to hurt. 'You are lucky, my darling,' he murmured smoothly to her. 'Your—friend is willing to forgive your—tardiness. Other people may not be so willing.'

Now there was a threat if Jemma had ever heard one. She glowered at him, and he gazed coolly back. 'Now, say goodnight to your—friend,' he chanted softly, but his teeth were clenched tightly together while he said it. 'We are late enough as it is.'

'You're hateful!' she whispered as he pushed her in front of him and out of the house, leaving Tom staring awkwardly after them. 'How dare you tell him we were making love?'

'We were, were we not?' he challenged, wearing his arrogance like a mask on his mocking face.

She tugged at her wrist. 'Let go of me,' she demanded. 'You're hurting!'

'And if I ever see you kissing another man like that—'

he turned angrily on her '—I shall hurt you a lot more!' His grip tightened for a short threatening second before he threw it away from him.

'Now who's green with jealousy?' she taunted, and gained real satisfaction from the way he stopped in the middle of opening the car door, his dark head shooting up as if her words had stabbed him in the back. Jemma stood watching him with her teeth pressing down on her bottom lip. She'd gone too far, she realised. Leon was not a man who liked his weaknesses thrown back in his face.

'Get in,' he said, and walked around to the other side of the car to climb in himself. It wasn't like him. If Leon possessed any endearing quality at all to offset his arrogance, then it had to be his impeccable manners. Always, he made sure she was inside the car and comfortable before closing the door for her.

'Where are we going?' she asked when the silence between them grew too tense for her to cope with.

'To a party,' he told her. 'It is time you met my friends.'

Oh, God, she thought heavily. That's all I need tonight—to meet his rich, sophisticated friends while he's in this mood and I feel like throttling him!

CHAPTER FIVE

THE party was in full swing when they got there, people spilling out of dimly lit rooms with glasses in their hands and false smiles on their faces. And most of them turned to stare as they walked in. She supposed Leon alone would get such a reaction, but with her by his side the interest honed in on her, and despite their mutual hostility she moved closer to him.

'I feel like a curiosity on show,' she muttered. 'This isn't Madame Tussaud's, is it?'

At least he smiled, even if she was being sarcastic. 'Too many famous faces for you?' he mocked.

'Too many something,' she agreed. 'That's Mike Williams over there, and I know for a fact that he's in Madame Tussaud's because I saw it on TV the other month!'

'Do you want me to introduce you to him?' he offered.

'No.' Jemma studied the attractive pop star from beneath her lashes. 'He isn't my type.'

'And just what is your type?' he enquired, that coolness returning to his voice.

Black-haired arrogant devils with sexy Greek accents! she thought angrily. And sighed, refusing to answer him.

'Leon, darling!' With a voice like thick syrup, the most exquisite creature Jemma had ever seen glided up to them. She was as dark as Jemma was fair and wearing white taffeta silk that shone like the five-string pearl choker she had clasped around her beautiful throat. 'You made it after all!'

Her arms went around his neck, and by the time they parted again Jemma had been effectively shoved to one side and the newcomer stood firmly in her place, her arm lovingly crooked through his. 'Carlos is here and dying to speak to you,' the woman informed him. 'That Pritchard deal you set up was an amazing coup for him! Come and…'

Jemma didn't hear any more, because the two of them had been casually swallowed up in the crowd, leaving her standing there feeling as redundant as a rag on a highly polished floor!

And that is exactly what you are! she told herself bitterly. Nothing but a rag among all these riches.

Well, 'all that glisters is not gold', she mused acidly as she let her hooded gaze scan the glittering crowd. For a start, she was sure that was Sonia Craven over there, locked in a heated clinch with a man who was most definitely not her husband.

'Been deserted?' a light male voice murmured from just behind her. She spun, and found a stranger—who was not quite a stranger because she had seen his face plastered on billboards all over the city advertising his latest film—offering her the same smile that knocked women dead all over the world. 'I saw you come in with Stephanades,' he explained his opening gambit. His incredibly piercing blue eyes slid down her then back again. 'I'll give it to him,' he mocked ruefully. 'That handsome Greek devil certainly knows how to pick them.'

Jemma stiffened instantly. 'Are you trying to be insulting?' she demanded.

His eyebrows shot up in surprise. 'Of course not!' he denied. 'It was actually supposed to be a compliment.'

'Your technique needs polishing, then,' she informed him, and turned away, searching the milling throng for a glimpse of Leon.

The man's soft laughter shivered down her naked back. Then suddenly he appeared in front of her and stuck out his hand. 'Jack Bridgeman,' he introduced himself.

Jemma glanced down at the hand then back into his amazing eyes. 'I know who you are,' she said drily. 'One would have to be blind and deaf not to—wouldn't one?'

The eyebrows shot up again. 'Now who's being insulting?' he challenged.

She sighed, accepting that he was right, and took the proffered hand. 'Jemma Davis,' she said. 'Most definitely not a name you will recognise!' She sent him a rueful glance.

He grinned. 'Let's go and find you a drink,' he offered, and took her arm.

She let him guide her away, out of one room and into another—just as crowded—but where a superbly stocked bar stood against one wall, manned by white-coated waiters.

She saw Leon then, standing in a group of laughing people, his arm draped across the shoulders of the woman in the white dress. Red-hot humiliation swam up from the pit of her stomach to encompass her whole being. He had forgotten all about her! In among this lot she was nothing, and she felt like a nothing.

I hate him! she thought and took a deep gulp at the contents in the glass that had arrived in her hand. The cocktail almost took her head off, whatever was in it burning like fire down the back of her throat. It took all her control not to fall into a fit of choking. Beside her, Jack Bridgeman watched her lazily.

'Whose is this party, anyway?' she asked him when she felt able to speak.

'Hers,' he informed her, nodding his head towards the woman who was draped all over Leon.

'Oh,' said Jemma, looking down to hide the jealous look in her eyes. Why had he bothered bringing her if he preferred his hostess's company?

'She looks like a fluffy black kitten when in actual fact she's a dangerous, money-eating panther,' he added with a small smile which didn't meet his eyes. 'Which is why you only see her with men who stink of the stuff—like your Mr Stephanades.'

'He is not *my* Mr Stephanades,' Jemma denied, and realised bleakly that that was probably the truest thing she'd allowed herself to say about her relationship with Leon since it began.

'Good,' Jack Bridgeman said. 'So let's you and me go and dance.'

He took her arm again, but Jemma hesitated, her eyes helplessly drawn to the other side of the room where Leon still stood talking with their hostess. Should she just boldly go over there and claim his attention? The urge to do just that was burning alongside the jealousy in her blood. But, even as the idea entered her head, she watched Leon draw the woman closer and lower his dark head to drop a kiss on her upturned cheek.

She looked away, her eyes glazed over with hurt. Then, on a mammoth gathering-together of all her pride, she smiled brightly at Jack Bridgeman. 'Dance, you said?' She took a final gulp at her drink and put down the glass. 'Just lead the way and I'll follow!'

He guided her on to the tiny dance-floor. 'Right,' he said as he drew her into his arms. 'Tell me about yourself, Jemma Davis!'

So she did, prattling on about anything so long as it kept her mind off Leon. By the time they had circled the room for two records, she was beginning to relax and enjoy herself, Jack's easy manner and needle-sharp sense of humour actually managing to make her laugh.

'Ah,' he sighed ages later when the music went even slower and he took it as a cue to pull her closer and slide his fingers lightly along her uncovered spine. 'You've no idea how much I've been aching to do this. You're the first woman, Jemma Davis, whose back view has managed to turn me on even before I took a good look at the front!'

'Charming!' she mocked. 'Was that supposed to be another one of your compliments?'

He grinned boyishly. 'Oh, don't worry, sweetheart,' he murmured huskily. 'The back view is a delightful appetiser but the front is positively lethal!'

'You aren't so bad on the eye yourself,' she told him, flirting deliberately. 'Despite the sex symbol image,' she tagged on teasingly.

'Or because of it, maybe?' he suggested drily.

Jemma studied his face for a moment, then shook her head. 'No,' she decided. 'Sex symbols tend to strut their wares for all to see. You don't strut, so I'll give you the benefit of the doubt and presume your ego is not as big as it's reputed to be.'

'You precocious little madam!' he choked, not slow on picking up on her hidden meaning. 'Give me five minutes alone with you and I may well just prove you wrong there!'

He stopped dancing, teasing her by grabbing hold of her wrist and turning towards the doorway. Still laughing, Jemma tugged against his grip—then saw Leon leaning against the open door a mere two feet away, his black eyes fixed on her, and she went still beside the other man.

'Ah,' said Jack, seeing the reason for her stillness. 'Do I see a royal summons written in those frightening eyes, ma'am?' he mocked.

'Yes, I think you do,' Jemma confirmed with a nervous little laugh.

Jack looked down at her, his expression suddenly serious. 'You don't have to go with him, you know,' he said quietly. 'All you have to do is turn your back on him and that will be the end of that. Stephanades is not a man who likes to make scenes. He won't come after you.'

Jemma knew that, even as she stood there, locked in

silent battle with those eyes; she knew that Leon was not going to make a single move towards her. That pride-shrivelling gesture was down to her.

'So?' Jack prompted, bringing her eyes flickering up to meet his sardonic ones. 'What are you going to do?'

'Goodnight, Jack,' she said a trifle ruefully. 'And—thanks.'

Reaching up, she kissed his lean cheek, her eyes full of a silent apology before she turned and walked slowly to Leon. 'I'm ready to leave if you are,' she told him stiffly.

He didn't answer or even acknowledge her for the space of ten turbulent seconds, his gaze fixed on something beyond her shoulder—which had to be Jack, she assumed, or Leon's eyes would not look so shiveringly steely. Then his dark lashes flickered, forming two perfect, sleepy arches over his eyes as he lowered them to her hot, defiant face.

'More than ready, *agape mou*,' he answered quietly, and to her utter confusion he smiled. Not a threatening smile nor even a deriding smile, but a warm, if slightly rueful smile, and his hand, when it reached out to curve around her waist, was surprisingly gentle. He drew her against him and kissed her softly on the lips. As he drew away again, his gaze slid over her shoulder and hardened fractionally. But when it returned to her it was warm again, revealing no hint of anger at all. 'Let's go,' he said.

She went willingly enough. But her confusion at his manner did not leave her, so nor did her own stiff manner. Whatever he was up to, she decided as he saw her indulgently into the car then came around to join her, she wasn't going to let down her guard to find out. If he was trying to soften her up before jumping on her for kissing Jack Bridgeman, then he was in for a disappointment! she decided huffily as they drove away. And she answered his light conversational remarks with monosyllables, her own mood becoming blacker the lighter his become.

'You are angry with me,' he decided after several attempts to draw her out failed.

'What could you have done to make me angry?' she drawled.

'All but dumping you as soon as we arrived there is a good enough reason,' he admitted. 'Business, I'm afraid,' he shrugged.

Funny business, Jemma derided bitchily on an upsurge of that evil jealousy she was beginning to feel so familiar with.

'At least you fond some light relief with Jack Bridgeman. You enjoyed your—dance?'

This is it, Jemma thought with a slight stiffening of her spine in readiness. 'I enjoyed his company very much!' she stated coolly. 'He was charming and attentive and a very good dancer, and without him I would have been bored to death!'

'Then I must thank him next time I bump into him,' was all Leon said to her outright provocation. And changed the subject.

To her surprise and confusion, he didn't refer to it again. And over the ensuing weeks she noticed that, wherever they went and whoever tried to make a pass at her, he never revealed any hint that it concerned him overmuch. He often left her alone while he went off to 'discuss business', as he called it, and, no matter whom he found her with when he eventually came looking for her, he was always aggravatingly at ease about it.

It was meeting Tom on the stairs a couple of days later that put the missing piece into the puzzle, when he asked if her boyfriend had got over his fit of jealousy. And it clicked suddenly that Leon had not liked revealing that hint of weakness in himself when he'd reacted jealously to her kissing Tom. Since then he had gone out of his way to show the opposite reaction, as if he was determined to quash any idea she might develop that he thought more of her than their relationship suggested.

Which was—what? she asked herself. Lovers. Nothing more, nothing less. Jealousy grew out of deeper feelings. Feelings that Leon just did not have for her. Or if he had, for one brief blinding moment when he'd seen her kissing Tom, he had firmly squashed them. And if he could do that so easily, then they couldn't have been very strong feelings.

The week after the party, he went off to New York for a week. She had come to realise that his business commitments seemed to flow equally between London and New York—with a trip to his head office in Athens thrown in only very occasionally. Friction with his father, she suspected—not that Leon had ever spoken about it. But his expression was tight-lipped whenever she broached the subject of his family and, remembering what Cassie had once said about a family rift, she drew her own conclusions.

While he was in New York, she missed her period. Jemma was not overly worried about it since her cycle had never been that reliable at the best of times, and she accepted that the physical and emotional stress she had taken on since Leon had probably helped to throw her out of sync.

For the next few weeks he remained in London. And they were barely out of each other's company. Josh had found out about them by then, and his disgust was unveiled. 'Are you crazy?' he cried. 'Of all the bloody men in London you have to fall for Leon Stephanades! I just don't bloody well believe it!'

'He's what I want,' she answered simply. 'And for as long as he wants me I'm happy.'

'And when he doesn't?' he challenged brutally.

Jemma shrugged to mask the ache his words evoked. 'I'll cross that bridge when I come to it,' she said.

Josh sighed heavily, but let the matter drop.

Late Friday afternoon, when she was just considering

packing up to leave for the weekend, the telephone rang. Leon sounded grim and irritable. 'Something has come up,' he said. 'I'm afraid this weekend is out.'

'Oh.' Her disappointment sounded clear in her voice. 'So when will I see you?'

'God knows,' he sighed. 'I have to be in New York on Monday and will be away the whole week. I'll call you,' he said, and rang off.

She went out with Trina and Frew on Saturday night, meeting up with all her old friends for the evening. But she felt restless and out of place among them. Leon occupied her whole mind these days and she couldn't seem to enjoy anything that did not include him.

On Monday, she woke up feeling dreadfully ill. 'Tummy bug,' she said to Trina, and took herself back to bed. By Wednesday she was beginning to feel a bit better, but only marginally. Still, it was enough to send her back to work.

Josh took one look at her and remarked, 'You look shocking.'

'Thanks,' she drawled. 'That does make me feel better.'

'Beginning to get to you, is it?' he drawled out cynically. 'Hanging on to a man like Stephanades wears a woman down, doesn't it? And I should know,' he added bitterly. 'I've had his leftovers, after all.'

Jemma winced at his cruelty, hating the ugly twist he had put on Leon's friendship with Cassie. And it made her realise that if there had ever been a seed of love growing inside him for the other woman, then it was well and truly dead now.

Leon noticed her poor state of health the moment he saw her. When she explained, he just continued frowning and said, 'Are you sure it isn't something worse than just a stomach virus? You look pale and you've lost weight.'

She just shrugged the question away. 'You know what it's like with these things. Once they get a hold of you they can take an age to go away again. I'm feeling a whole lot better, really.' So long as she didn't eat anything, she added grimly to herself.

He ran his eyes over her slender figure. 'Perhaps you need a break,' he murmured thoughtfully. 'When did you last have a holiday?'

'Christmas,' she told him, smiling wistfully. 'I spent it in Barbados with Trina. We had a great time.'

'Lots of men, I suppose,' Leon growled, pretending to sound jealous, but Jemma now knew better. Leon did not get jealous—and why? Because he did not care enough for her, that was why. Not with any emotions which really mattered, anyway. He fancied her like hell still, could still lose himself in her body with enough passion actually to shock her sometimes. But as for any deeper feelings, they just did not exist.

He was in London for a week. And they saw each other every night. But her continuing virus and all the late nights began to take their toll on her, and she was actually relieved when he went away again.

She only wished she could have a break from Josh, too. He had become a boor to work for, his bitterness with Cassie reflecting in his attitude to all women—including her now. He was brusque and impatient all the time. 'If you can't do your work to your usual standard, Jemma,' he snapped at her one day when she had somehow mislaid a file he wanted, 'then perhaps you should start thinking about either giving up Stephanades or giving up this job!'

'This thing with Cassie has really soured him,' she confided in Leon when Josh had been worse than nasty all day and she felt exhausted by the time she met Leon for dinner that night.

'What do you expect?' he countered coolly. 'To be tricked as Cassie tricked him is, in my opinion, the ultimate betrayal.'

Something in the way he said that hit her on the raw. It was if he was warning her—try that kind of trick on me and see what you get!

She shuddered and changed the subject. But that weekend her manner towards him cooled slightly. It wasn't that she wanted it to, it was just that, after over two months of living exclusively for him, she was beginning to realise how hopeless the relationship really was. After all, there was still the nice Greek girl with the dowry waiting somewhere for Leon to give in to family pressure and marry. And she could suddenly appreciate what Cassie had meant when she'd said, 'What chance does a not-so-nice English girl with nothing to offer him but a great body have against all of that?' None, Jemma acknowledged, and began to wonder if it was perhaps time to start weaning herself off Leon Stephanades.

If he noticed her coolness, he said nothing, not until Sunday evening, that was, when he was dropping her off at her flat, and he surprised her by saying, 'Before you go, Jemma, I have a proposition I want to put to you.'

'A proposition?' she repeated curiously.

He nodded, his expression unusually grim. 'Next week, I close a take-over deal I have spent the last year putting together in New York,' he informed her. 'When it is done, I will be hard put to come up for air during the following few months while I drag the company up to the standard the Leonadis Corporation requires of all its subsidiaries. The company is in a bad way, has been badly run, badly managed, and recklessly bled by its owners to the extent that nothing short of some ruthless tactics will give it a hope of surviving the next few months...' He paused, watching her face. 'I will not be able to come to London as often as I have been doing,' he explained. 'Maybe not at all, the way things are stacking up.'

'So...' Jemma kept her voice steady by sheer strength of

will '…this explanation is your way of saying goodbye?' she assumed, feeling the weight of knowledge bearing heavily down on her. She had been so busy trying to cool her own feelings for him that she had not noticed that Leon was going through a similar process for her!

But his reaction surprised her. 'No!' he denied, reaching out to haul her across the gap separating them so that he could issue a hard, angry kiss to her lips. 'What in hell gave you that idea?' He actually sounded shocked enough to bring weak tears floating into her eyes. 'Damn you, Jemma!' he muttered. 'I have never known such a difficult woman to read as you! You spend the whole weekend giving me the cold shoulder—then have the cheek to suggest it is me who is doing the cooling off!'

'I haven't been feeling well…' she offered as a very lame excuse for her behaviour.

He nodded curtly and kissed her again. 'And you think I have not noticed—or, worse, have not cared? I said I had a proposition for you, and it is with your poor state of health and my refusal to let you go out of my life that I offer it! Come with me,' he invited huskily. 'Next weekend will be the last I can promise to devote to you here in London. But if you will come with me to New York, I will promise to devote every moment of my spare time to you!'

'M-me—to New York?' she choked, hardly daring to believe he was offering it. 'But—my flat—m-my job!' She sat up and away from him, trying to make her whirling brain think.

'You said yourself that Tanner is becoming impossible,' he inserted. 'Losing that job will not come as any hardship—except financially, of course,' he added when she sent him a wry glance. 'But I am not just asking you to come to New York, Jemma,' he went on softly. 'I am asking you to move in with me, be my woman. Allow me to worry about all the practicalities of your life while you just worry about making yourself beautiful for me.' His hand slid beneath her hair to curve her nape. 'I want you—need you there with me, *agape mou*,' he murmured softly. 'Will you come?'

Well, will you? she asked herself for the hundredth time that same night. She lay alone in her small single bed, missing him, missing the warmth of his body curled up against hers, missing the scent of him, the soft sound of his breathing when he slept.

Will you—can you give up everything here for the man you love, knowing that he wants you to only because his desire for your body has not yet worn out?

Not that Leon saw any of that as a reasonable excuse not to give him an answer straight away. 'What is there to think about?' he'd demanded when she'd asked for time to do just that. 'Either you want to be with me or you do not. It really is as simple as that!'

'Is it?' she'd mocked, then sighed heavily. 'You're asking me to uproot my whole life for you, Leon!' she'd cried. 'I would have to be crazy not to think carefully before making that kind of decision!'

'Or not crazy enough about me to know instinctively that where I am is where you want to be!' he'd suggested, his pride touched.

'And for how long would I be welcome there?' she'd thrown back. 'I am to uproot while you simply exchange one of your many addresses for another. What happens to me when you grow tired of me and find someone to take my place?'

'That can work both ways, you know,' he'd countered. 'I am not so conceited that I don't see the way you can enjoy other men's company!'

'Nor am I so conceited that I don't see how you enjoy other women!' she had snapped.

'I am not promiscuous!' he'd stated haughtily.

'And neither am I!'

He had sighed. 'No, I know you are not,' he'd agreed, then sighed again, heavily this time. 'Look,' he'd said, 'I am not ready to lose you, my darling! Do you think I would be making a proposition like this one if I were?'

She'd thought about that, and had to decide that no, Leon was nothing if not scrupulously fair. He would not be asking her to change her whole life for him if he did not think the change worth her making it.

It had been her turn to sigh, to soften her manner. 'You're right,' she'd conceded. 'And I apologise for implying that you would. But you must see, Leon,' she'd gone on quickly before the triumph grew too bright in his black eyes, 'that I have to have time to think about this!'

A point he had conceded grudgingly. 'Next week,' had been his parting shot. 'I will be here next week and I will expect your answer then.' The kiss he had issued then had been so sweetly possessive that she had almost caved in and said yes there and then. But something held her back, she wasn't sure what.

Just as something held her back from telling Trina, she acknowledged with a frown, wondering if it was the same elusive 'thing'.

Sighing, she turned over and punched her pillow into a more comfortable shape. She didn't know what she was doing, lying here in the middle of the night wondering about what she was going to do when she already knew, if she was honest, how she was going to say, Yes, please, to him, because, from the first time she'd ever seen him, she had not been able to deny him anything.

Then, two things happened in quick succession during that week to change her mind irrevocably.

The first was on Wednesday morning, when Josh came striding into the office with all of his old energy back. Instead of stalking straight by her desk with a grunted 'hello' as had become his habit, he stopped in front of her, leaned down and banged the desk-top in exhilaration.

'She got rid of it!' he announced in gleaming triumph.

'Got rid of what?' she frowned. 'Who?'

'Cassie!' he cried. 'She got rid of it, and I suddenly feel so free it's like walking on air!'

She didn't know where it came from, but, on an acid surge of bitter, vile-tasting disgust, she shot to her feet, a dark red tide of anger swimming across her vision as she struck out with the flat of her hand.

'You bastard!' she breathed out contemptuously as he leapt back in stunned amazement. 'You nasty—selfish—evil bastard! How dare you come in here dancing with joy when you should be huddling in some dark corner somewhere cringing in shame? God, you make me feel sick!'

And she was, violently sick, only just making it to the bathroom before she threw up. When she went back to her office, Josh wasn't there, the door to his office firmly shut. She didn't even think twice about it. She just gathered her personal things together and walked out. She could not go on working for a man who could behave like that. It went against the grain of every moral code she believed in.

Trina was in the flat when she got in, working on her books at the kitchen table.

'I'm ill,' was all Jemma could manage to say. 'I'm going to bed...' She turned away, her senses still too sickened by Josh to want to talk even to Trina about it.

But Trina had other ideas. 'For God's sake, Jemma!' she snapped out impatiently. 'Don't you think it's about time you faced it? If you leave it much longer, the shock of it could do you some physical harm!'

'What shock?' she asked blankly. 'Face up to what, for goodness' sake?'

Trina stared at her, her expression almost comically tragic. 'Come on, sweetheart,' she sighed. 'You're not that

thick! He'll notice if you're not careful, and then where
will you be?'

Notice? she repeated in her head. Notice what?

But even as she was thinking it, she was beginning to
tremble, her body lowering itself carefully into a chair, eyes
going dark with horror.

'Oh, God!' she choked, and buried her face in her hands.

Pregnant. The elusive little thing which had held her back
from giving Leon an answer to his proposal. The same elusive little thing which had held her back from telling Trina
what he had offered. And the same elusive thing that had
made her react so violently to what Josh had said.

Pregnant. Her body had known for weeks, her mind probably for just as long! Only she'd blocked it out, refusing to
so much as think about it—not daring to think about it
because she knew exactly what it would mean to her relationship with Leon.

'Oh, God!' she whispered again and slipped into deep,
silent tears.

'Oh, Jemma!' Trina sighed, coming to squat down beside
her. Then, exasperatedly, as if she couldn't help herself,
'What did you think was happening to you when you've
gone two months without a period?'

'One,' Jemma choked.

'Two,' insisted Trina, then very gently, 'Darling, you
haven't had a period since you started going out with Leon!
Think about it—that's been over two months now!'

Two—two months? She stared unbelievingly into Trina's
anxious eyes, then burst into tears again. She was right—
so damned right! And she'd just thrust the knowledge away
as if doing so would make the situation go away! But it
hadn't—well, it couldn't!

Oh, what was she going to do?

'When will you tell him?' Trina asked quietly later when
the storm of shocked weeping had abated and she'd man-

aged to get Jemma undressed and into bed.

'I'm not going to,' Jemma said thickly. 'How can I, Tri?' she demanded at Trina's expression. 'After going through all of this with Josh and Cassie, he'll think I've done it to him deliberately!'

'But this is nothing like the situation which developed between those two fools!'

'Isn't it?' It looked exactly the same to Jemma.

'I just knew he was too much for you to have your first love-affair with—and I was proved right, wasn't I?' Trina said angrily. 'I mean, look at you!' she sighed, glaring down at the pathetic picture Jemma presented huddled beneath a mound of blankets with her face all swollen and pale. 'Heartbroken and pregnant. It couldn't be worse!'

'Call a spade a spade, why don't you?' Jemma muttered, then felt the rise of fresh tears again. 'I love him, Tri!' she whispered. 'I just couldn't do it to him!'

'All right—all right!' On another sigh, Trina sat down on the edge of the bed and stroked a soothing hand over Jemma's tumbled hair. 'So,' she murmured. 'What will you do?'

'I don't know yet.' Jemma made an effort to control herself, pulling herself up into a sitting position and wrapping her arms around her bent knees. 'I just can't think yet—how could I have been so stupid as to ignore what was happening to me?' she choked out contemptuously, lowering her head so that the curtain of hair tumbled about her face.

'Maybe it isn't what we think,' Trina suggested. 'Maybe I've jumped to the wrong conclusions about what's wrong with you.'

Jemma's face came up again, blue eyes stark with tears and mockery. 'Do you honestly believe that?' she drawled.

'No.' Trina shrugged, so did Jemma, and a silence fell around them for the space of a few dull minutes.

'How the heck did it happen, anyway?' Trina demanded suddenly. 'I thought you were being careful.'

'We were!' Jemma declared. 'But that first time, I— we—' She stopped and blushed, then went on huskily, 'After that he used something—'

'Do you mean to tell me that that—highly experienced rake took you without protection that first time?' Trina jumped in in disgust.

Several times, Jemma corrected silently, unable to keep the soft smile from her lips when she remembered that first earth-shaking night in his arms. They'd both been too lost in each other to give protection a single thought!

'But that alters everything, Jem!' Trina said eagerly. 'It means that he is as much to blame as you are! And even Leon himself can't deny that!'

Jemma stiffened, her vulnerable face closing up suddenly. 'I will not trap him into a situation he has no wish to be trapped into,' she said firmly.

'Marriage, you mean? It's what you deserve.'

'Any kind of situation!' Jemma declared. 'Marriage and babies are not what Leon wants from me,' she added dully.

'Yet he *has* invited you to go and live with him in New York!' Trina persisted. 'That has to mean he cares something for you, doesn't it?'

'Nothing alters the fact that I will not trap him with this baby,' she stated stubbornly. And was glad she had the rest of the week to come to terms with what she must do instead.

CHAPTER SIX

JOSH rang the next morning, asking stiffly if she was returning to work or not. Trina spoke to him. Jemma couldn't. And he took her resignation without argument, promising to send her what he owed her in the way of salary by post. Jemma suspected that after what she'd said and done yesterday he was probably as relieved to see her go as she was to leave.

Leon rang each evening as he always did. And Jemma used these calls to begin distancing herself from him. He noticed. He had to do. She was cool and polite and rather vague if he touched on anything too intimate—and cried herself to sleep every night.

By Thursday his voice was terse and aggressive. 'I will be arriving back about five tomorrow night,' he informed her. 'Shall I expect you at your usual time, or not?' His sarcasm cut, even though she knew it was well deserved.

'Of course,' she said, biting down on her bottom lip to keep the ever-ready tears out of her voice. 'I'll be there about six.'

She spent Friday reinforcing her resolve to finish this with as much style as she could manage. Luckily the dreaded sickness seemed to be leaving her alone today, so she felt and looked a lot better—physically, that was. Inside was a different matter. Inside she felt as if she was splitting slowly into two.

She took nothing with her to the house, simply because she was not intending staying long.

Leon opened the door to her knock. He looked deeply

into her sombre eyes and his own expression closed up tightly as he stepped to one side to let her go by him.

He barely gave her a chance to remove her coat before he got ruthlessly to the point. 'I presume by your manner all week that you have decided to remain here in London.'

She paused in sliding the cream raincoat from her shoulders, a pang so painful that it held her breathless for a moment, slicing right through her. He looked so wonderful to her hungry senses, so big and dark and achingly withdrawn. He had showered recently, and his hair lay in a sleek, damp gloss flat against his well shaped head. And gone were the business clothes he would have travelled home in and instead he was wearing a casual pale blue cotton shirt and grey trousers that hung loosely over his flat stomach from the fashionable pleating at the waist. His eyes were so dark that she couldn't see anything in them but a grim reflection of her paler self, his mouth a thin straight line that told her that, like herself, he had prepared himself for this meeting.

Despair suddenly drenched her, and she remained standing there, wanting to run to him, wrap her arms around him, soothe that closed expression from his face, make him smile, laugh, pick her up and hug her tightly while he gave her that first long satisfying kiss they usually shared at this moment.

But, 'Yes,' she answered him huskily, and followed him with her eyes as he simply grimaced and walked into the book-lined room to pour them both a stiff drink.

She shook her head in refusal when he offered her a glass, unable to hold his gaze when he remained standing in front of her, sipping out of his own glass while he studied her pale face narrowly.

'Have you found someone else?'

'No!' Her head shot up, sheer surprise at the question making her answer honestly, but later she realised it might have been easier on both of them if she'd had the foresight to lie and use another man as her excuse. As it was, things only got worse.

'Leon—you knew last week that I wasn't very—enthusiastic about the idea of leaving everything I know and feel safe with, to go to New York with you!' she reminded him with an appeal in her voice. 'And the more I've thought about it, the more sure I've become that it just isn't the right thing for me to do!'

'Why not?' Nothing else, just the blunt enquiry.

Jemma swallowed on her dry and tense throat. He was not going to make this easy. 'There's no future there for me,' she said dully.

He took his time absorbing that reply, his eyes so black they were impossible to read. Then his mouth tightened again and he said coolly, 'If you're angling for a marriage proposal, Jemma, then you're in for a disappointment. It is an institution I have no intention of joining, whoever I have to sacrifice to keep that vow.'

That brought the sparkle back into her eyes. She glared at him angrily. 'And I never for one moment so much as considered marriage as an option!' she snapped with an honesty he would never be able to appreciate. 'But neither am I prepared to become any man's mistress! At the moment we share a relationship,' she went on more calmly, 'in which I have a job and a home of my own and a level of independence which allows me to keep my pride and self-respect. But the word "mistress" is an ugly one, Leon. Yet that is exactly what I would become if I agreed to come and live with you in New York.'

Silence met that, and it came down around Jemma like a death-knell, sinking her into a helpless despair because she knew, as she watched Leon turn slowly and go over to pour himself another drink, that she had achieved exactly what she had set out to achieve.

The end to their relationship.

'So, this is it.' It was he who put it into words.

'Yes,' she answered huskily. 'You said no commitment, Leon,' she reminded him, seeming to need to hammer the point home for her own benefit as much as his. 'Honesty and loyalty, you said. Well…' She took in a deep breath, her voice beginning to tremble along with her body. Inside she was weeping just as she had wept every night this awful week. 'You've h-had my loyalty, and now I am giving you my honesty.' Liar, a small voice jeered inside her head. You're lying to him with every word you say! She flinched but ignored it. 'I c-care for you deeply, but…'

'Not enough to trust yourself to me,' he finished for her.

She shook her head, the tears managing to find a crack in her defences and creep into her eyes. He saw them and sighed, slamming down his glass to come striding over to her. 'No,' he muttered as he took her into his arms. 'Forget I said that. It was unfair and unworthy. In fact, when I have had time to come to terms with your decision—' he was deliberately instilling a lighter tone into his voice '—no doubt I shall even learn to admire you for it. But,' he sighed, lowering his head so that he could kiss the trail of salty tears away, 'at the moment I see only the end to a very special period in my life, and for that I hurt too, just as these tears tell me you are hurting.'

He hurts, she repeated achingly to herself, and wanted to hold him tightly to her until his hurt went away. Her arms went around his waist, revelling in the feel of warm, taut skin beneath her fingertips, her face burrowing into his throat on this one last surrender to this weakness she had which was him.

'Ah, Jemma,' he murmured heavily. 'Are you sure I cannot change your mind?'

She shook her head, but held him all the closer, and he

laughed softly. 'But maybe it would be enjoyable if I were at least to try?' he suggested.

He lifted her chin, his eyes dark and intent as they ran over her pale, unhappy face, then he sighed again, and his mouth came down to meet with hers. His hunger and her need met in a powerful kiss which verged on desperation.

Their tongues tangled, their bodies melting together as though they were drawn like that by some power beyond their understanding. It wasn't sexual, it was something else far more disturbing. With the prospect of a final parting and the emotion which came with such an end, it was as if each fine nerve-end was pushing its way up to the surface of her skin in an effort to absorb every last ounce of him into her.

A muffled sob broke in her, and Leon groaned, his mouth hot as it buried itself in her throat. 'Change your mind,' he murmured huskily. 'Neither of us is ready to give this up.'

Jemma came spiralling down from whatever heights she had been flung to, with a shiver that racked her whole frame. 'No.' She shook her head, having to force her fingers to break the anguished grip they had on him.

His own hands slid up her body to curve her ribcage then tightened painfully, stopping her from moving away from him. 'Then give us this weekend!' he urged. 'One last wild, beautiful weekend, Jemma, to lose ourselves in each other before we must part!'

Oh, she was tempted, so severely tempted. She wanted him and he wanted her. It was like manna from heaven to her aching heart. But she dared not give in to it. She knew even as she hovered on that fine dangerous line between self-delusion and sanity that just in this last week since she accepted her condition the changes in her body had been too obvious to dare take the risk of him noticing them— and ultimately drawing the right conclusions.

So, 'No,' she breathed, and took the last vital step which would separate them forever. 'I'm sorry, Leon, but I can't.'

'Cannot or will not?' he mocked, changing from sweet to bitter in response to her rejection.

'Can't, Leon—can't!' she choked out wretchedly, then whirled away from him, the tears blinding her eyes as she snatched up her coat, desperate to get away from him before her control snapped altogether.

'Jemma—!' She was at the door when his harsh voice brought her to a stumbling halt. She didn't turn, and there was a tension in the short silence which followed that sent violent shudders of reaction spurring through her body while she prayed that he would just let her go while she still had the strength to do it. 'Take care of yourself,' was all he said in the end, quietly and so gently that she almost crumpled in a heap of misery on the floor.

She nodded her downbent head. 'And you,' she whispered, then left quickly without looking back.

He didn't try to stop her again, and for that she was grateful. Her heart was breaking and if she'd stayed in his company a moment longer he would have seen it happen.

Jemma was sitting at the kitchen table, flicking through the morning newspaper while chewing desultorily on a slice of lightly toasted wholemeal bread when the doorbell rang.

'I'll get it!' Trina called from the hallway, and Jemma grimaced with relief, glad to be doing what most pregnant women did first thing in the morning and keeping as still as possible while she coaxed her stomach not to give up on the meagre amount of food and liquid she had managed to swallow.

Only most women lost this inconvenient malady three months into their condition. Jemma, on the other hand, was now well into her fifth month with no let-up in the sickness. Morning sickness, afternoon sickness, evening sickness— you name it, she suffered it.

It showed, too, she grimly acknowledged as she felt that

old familiar churning begin in her stomach. For an otherwise perfectly healthy pregnant woman, she looked hagged to death. The inability to hold down more than half of her daily intake of food had certainly taken its toll.

She weighed less now than she had at the beginning of her pregnancy. And, although her hair shone with a thick golden lustre that her doctor assured her was the clearest sign that she was doing fine, the rest of her looked thin and gaunt—except for the bulge forming in front of her, that was. She glanced at it. Her mound, she called it. 'The lump'. 'Leon's parting gift', since he had never quite managed to come up with anything for that one special gift he owed her.

But as for the rest of her—she wouldn't give it mirror-space if she could avoid it: bruised eyes, pale cheeks. And a distinct lack of energy which seemed to require every ounce of determination to get her through each day.

It really wasn't fair.

A bad dose of the flu just after she'd broken off with Leon hadn't helped. If she'd thought the virus she hadn't had had been bad enough, then the real thing had proved to be twice as awful. Trina blamed it on all the emotional stress she had been under. And Jemma could not really argue with her about that. It had seemed, that day she'd challenged misery to do its worst and told Leon that she was not prepared to uproot her whole life for him, that the emotional stress could not get any worse. She had been wrong. The constant sickness kept her in a permanent state of taut readiness for the next bout. Fear for the baby's health had her creeping about like an invalid, afraid that at any moment she would dislodge the poor thing with her constant retching. And if the doctor had not assured her that despite it all—the flu and the sickness—the baby was doing fine, she had a suspicion she might well have given up the ghost and taken to her bed to die languidly.

She felt so rough. And she missed Leon. It hurt most of the time even to think about him. Yet she thought about him constantly, a never-ending circle of self-inflicted misery which in no way helped her present condition.

On a brighter note, Leon's take-over of the huge American shipping company had made the headlines several times this week, the papers singing the praises of the Greek tycoon who had managed to turn the company's fortunes around with such devastating speed. This morning's article said:

> Leon Stephanades, the strong arm of the Leonadis Corporation, has worked a miracle on the old company. With heavy investment and a bomb up the backsides of all those who believed themselves to be on to a cushy number under the old regime, he has managed to secure contracts that have set all those mocking doubters in his own family by their ears. His father took time off from his second son's wedding celebrations to concede last night, 'Leon has a nose for a good risk', as their stock on the market hit an all-time high. What Dimitri Stephanades forbore to add was that this success came despite the way he had tied his son's hands over the last year by refusing to give him *carte blanche* on this venture. One must ask, though, if it is sensible to tie the hands of a man like Leon Stephanades. And whether maybe it is time the old man abdicated his power to his elder son.

Jemma had read and re-read the article, simply because it told her more about Leon than she had ever learned from the man himself. Namely the fact that there was someone above him who could tie his hands. Then there was the fact that he had a brother at all.

'Well, lump,' she murmured to her slowly steadying

stomach, 'your daddy is certainly a clever devil. No wonder I was worth dropping if this was what he was going after.' And she stared down at the two aerial photographs where the vast square acreage of part of New York's dockland was shown in 'before' and 'after' comparison. One photo showed its dry docks half deserted of both products and people, but in the other the whole place seemed to be a veritable hive of constructive activity.

'Jemma...' Trina's voice sounded tentative to say the least.

'What?' she asked, glancing up from the newspaper article.

'Trouble,' Trina bluntly announced and put an envelope down in front of her.

Jemma stared at it, a cold shiver of alarm skittering down her spine. Like Trina, she recognised the bold scrawl instantly. And, like Trina, she knew it could only mean trouble. 'Hell,' she muttered.

Trina pulled out the chair beside her and sat down. 'What can he want?'

'I don't know.' In all honesty, she had not expected to hear from Leon again. This had come as a shock.

'Hadn't you better open it and find out?'

I would much rather not, Jemma thought ruefully, but even as she was thinking it her fingers were working tremulously at the seal. Dry-mouthed, she stared at the few hastily scrawled lines before their meaning began to sink in. It said:

I am due in London Friday. I would like to see you. Have dinner with me? Shall call for you at eight. L.

Her heart gave a pathetic little leap, then began to palpitate so fast that she could barely breathe, her lips going as dry as her mouth. The mere idea of him being so close as in London made her want to weep with longing. Then she was instantly hardening herself. There was no room in her life for that kind of weakness now.

'What does it say?' Trina asked.

'Nothing,' she said, and handed the note to Trina.

Trina read it slowly, her usually open face studiedly impassive, then she looked at Jemma. 'I think you should go,' she elected quietly.

'Is that your idea of a joke?' Jemma derided, sitting back in her chair and pointedly placing her hands on the top of her rounded stomach.

'No.' Trina shook her head. 'I mean it. I think you should go and meet him…I think it's time, Jemma, for you to ask for his help.'

'Don't be stupid!' she snapped, going to get up from the table, but Trina stopped her by grabbing hold of one of her hands.

'You'll stay here and hear me out!' she insisted. 'Jem,' she appealed at the other girl's glowering hostility, 'carrying his baby has been harder than you anticipated! It's weakened your health! Left you without a job—'

'I quit working as a temp because I couldn't stand being shunted around all over the place!' she reminded Trina angrily. 'It had nothing to do with my condition!'

'It had everything to do with your condition!' Trina sighed. 'You were off sick so often they had to let you go—you know they did!'

'Which has nothing to do with my meeting Leon!'

'It does when you're only just managing to exist on social handouts,' Trina said bluntly.

'Thanks,' she muttered, thinking of all the things she had to go without so that she could pay her share for living here. 'Rub it in, why don't you?'

'I am not trying to rub anything in!' Trina cried. 'Jem—Leon has a responsibility to help you!'

'He does not!' she snapped, and walked away.

'When are you going to stop being so stubborn?' Trina demanded, following her with a determined look on her face. 'What right have you to decide what Leon may or may not want? It's no use you tripping off to the bathroom in the hopes I won't follow you because I will!' she warned as Jemma turned in that direction. 'You're on your last legs, love, and if Leon is holding out a hand towards you you've got to take it!'

She turned at that, blue eyes flashing in a way they had not done for months now. 'Since when has he become flavour of the month for you?' she gibed. 'I always got the impression that you thought him the worst thing to happen to me!'

'I did,' Trina conceded. 'And I still do. But it doesn't alter the fact that he did happen, and the results of that are staring me right in the face!'

'Hear that, lump?' Jemma said acidly to her stomach. 'Your aunty Trina is having a go at you!'

Despite herself, Trina had to laugh. 'I wish you would stop talking to that thing as if it were alive,' she protested drily.

'It is alive,' Jemma pointed out. 'And my problem.' Her hand possessively covered the lump. 'No one else's.'

'Wrong,' Trina disagreed. 'That lump has a father. Do you honestly have the right to deprive it of that?'

No answer—simply because Jemma did not have one, since it was one of the very things she had agonised over herself since she and Leon had split up.

'I'm still not going to meet him,' she said with a stubborn thrust of her full bottom lip. 'Leave it, Tri!' she cried when Trina opened her mouth to argue again. 'Just—leave it!' she whispered, and turned away, leaving Trina standing there staring helplessly after her as she locked herself in her bedroom.

By the time she reappeared, Trina had left the flat to go to work. In the spotlessly clean kitchen, lying like a pointed threat in the dead centre of the scrubbed table, was Leon's note. Jemma sat down, drawing the piece of paper towards her.

She read it slowly, wanting to read more warmth into the few short sentences than was actually there and knowing that it would be folly to try. Friends, she reminded herself. We parted friends—or at least we didn't part enemies, she corrected ruefully, remembering the way she had run out of the house. 'Take care of yourself,' he had said, as a friend would say to a friend. This note was just a friend wanting to look up a friend while he was in town.

He would be hurt when she turned him down. 'It hurts me to turn you down,' she whispered, a flush of hot tears blurring her eyes. But she folded the letter back into its envelope anyway. 'I'm sorry, lump,' she murmured as she stood up again. 'But it just can't be.'

When Trina returned late that afternoon, Jemma was tossing a light salad in the kitchen. 'I'm whacked,' the other girl said, throwing herself down into a chair. 'We've had to spring-clean a six-bedroomed town house from top to bottom today. You know what these old houses are like,' she sighed. 'All twelve-foot-high ceilings with intricate cornices specifically designed to gather dust.' She stretched tiredly then rotated her shoulders, wincing when the aching muscles protested. 'Tomorrow we re-hang the curtains— huge heavy things with swags and flounces—but at least when we've done that it'll be finished.' She picked up her mug and gulped thirstily at her tea.

'That's the house near Grosvenor Square, isn't it?' Jemma asked lightly. Since giving up her own job, Jemma had taken over Trina's office work for her and over the last month or two she had become quite familiar with Maids in Waiting's customer roll.

Trina had gone still, her face coming out of her mug to look narrowly at Jemma. She wasn't a fool; she knew exactly what Jemma was going to do. With a jerk, Jemma fished a letter from her pocket and placed it on the table. 'Tomorrow is Friday, and I want to be sure Leon will receive this or I would have sent it by post today,' she explained. 'Will you take it for me, Trina—please?'

Trina was a long time answering, her expression difficult to interpret as she looked from Jemma's pale, defensive face to the sealed envelope then back again. Feeling uncomfortable, Jemma shrugged her shoulders awkwardly. 'I would take it myself,' she murmured awkwardly. 'Only I have a hospital appointment tomorrow and…' She shrugged again; Trina knew how long and tiring those expeditions were.

'All right.' Trina picked up the letter. 'I'll take it,' she agreed, but the look of grim disappointment on her face made Jemma feel worse.

Was she becoming a heavy weight around Trina's neck? she wondered suddenly, and felt a new fear rip right through her. Without Trina, she just didn't know what she would do!

Trina went out with Frew that night. When they came back, Frew was unusually quiet, his responses terse when Jemma attempted to speak to him. She took herself off to bed in the end, presuming they'd had some kind of a row and deciding to leave them to it.

The next day Trina had left for work before Jemma had surfaced, and was still out when she trudged back home from the hospital late that afternoon. Trina had left a message on the answerphone, warning Jemma that she was going out with Frew directly from work and not to expect her back again tonight. It wasn't unusual. It was Friday, and Trina often stayed over at Frew's flat on the weekend—

much the same as she had done with Leon, she recalled bleakly.

It was warm outside, and unusually humid for September, with a distinct threat of a storm in the air. She wasn't hungry, but she made herself a jug of freshly squeezed though heavily diluted orange juice and drank thirstily at a glass of it before taking herself off for a long soak in the tub in the vague hope it might ease some of the tension out of her body. The hospital was pleased with her progress, but not with the continuing sickness that dogged her still. They had booked her in for another scan next week—just to check a few things out: nothing to worry about, they had assured her.

But she was worried. Anything out of the ordinary where her baby was concerned was a worry. All right, so her weight was still too low, but they were all pleasantly surprised by the size of the baby! And, despite the sickness, she made sure she ate good nourishing food. So, what else could go wrong?

Sighing, she pulled out the plug to let the bath-water escape, then levered herself into a standing position and turned on the shower, allowing the clean cool water to wash over her for long minutes before loading her palm with shampoo and washing her hair.

Six-thirty, she noted as she walked into her bedroom wrapped in a fluffy white towel. She had managed to waste a whole hour and a half in the bath without thinking of Leon once! All she had to do now was think of something which would fill her mind for the rest of the long empty evening.

She would go out! she decided impulsively. Take in a movie. Jack Bridgeman's latest was playing at the local. It was supposed to be good. And really, anything was better than sitting here mooning over a man who was even further beyond her scope than a great big movie star.

Hastily, she pulled on fresh underwear then hunted out a pair of white stretch leggings and a navy blue baggy T-shirt that adequately covered her lump. Clipping her hair into a tortoiseshell slide at her nape, she applied a bit of blue eyeshadow to her eyes and a pink gloss to her lips, then snatched up her bag. If she hurried, she would just make the first film, she decided, opening the flat door.

Then she froze.

CHAPTER SEVEN

'GOING somewhere?' a deep, soft, beautifully accented voice questioned. 'How fortunate I managed to catch you, then.'

Jemma couldn't move. One hand had a white-knuckled grip on the door while the other had stalled in the process of throwing the strap of her bag over her shoulder. She was shocked—horrified. Yet, despite it all, her wide, staring eyes drank him up, her senses stinging into bright startling life as they recognised their master. He was wearing white, a white summer shirt and white cotton trousers, the complete lack of colour in the outfit only helping to enhance the rich dark brown of his skin. He looked big and lean, essentially sexual and innately dangerous.

Dangerous. She picked up the word and tasted it warily. Dangerous he certainly was. Pulsing with danger, throbbing with it, standing there smiling at her while his eyes burned with it.

She blinked and swallowed, trying to pull herself together. 'W-what are you doing here?' she heard herself asking foolishly. 'D-didn't you get my note?'

'Note? Yes, I got your—note,' he confirmed, then, while she still stood there staring at him, she watched as the danger metamorphosed itself into blinding anger. 'Inside,' he snapped, taking hold of her wrist to twist her fingers off the door so that he could push her back into the flat in front of him.

The door slammed shut. Jemma stood there trembling while he maintained his grip on her wrist, then he was pulling her into the sitting-room, before spinning her to face him and grasping her by the shoulders. 'Were you ever going to tell me?' he demanded harshly.

She sucked in a short, fast, shaky breath then let it out again, her heartbeat beginning to race out of control. 'I d-don't know what you're talking about,' she stammered constrictedly.

'No?' It was so quietly spoken, so silkily produced that he made her shiver in real fear of him for the first time. He moved, lifting his hands from her shoulders to spread them over her swollen stomach. She gasped at the blatant intimacy of the action, and his eyes burned darker. 'Then to whom does this belong?' he demanded.

'I...' She tried to move away but he stopped her simply by snaking one hand around her back and sandwiching her between the two. 'M-mine,' she whispered threadily. 'This baby is mine.'

'No father?' he mocked. 'An immaculate conception, maybe?'

She flushed at his sarcasm, but stubbornly clamped her lips together and lowered her eyes from the burning threat in his. But he waited. Oh, how he waited, drawing out the silence between them until she thought she could actually hear their child's heartbeat throbbing beneath his resting hand. Perhaps he thought the same thing, because his hand moved, stroking in a light caressing gesture as if to soothe the agitated child. And in answer the baby kicked and with a sharp intake of breath Leon went still.

'You feel that?' he enquired huskily. She nodded, swallowing. 'He speaks to his papa, *agape mou*. Are we to waste any more time on your lies, or are you going to be honest with me for once?'

'Honesty!' she flashed, her chin coming up aggressively. 'You want honesty, Leon?' Angrily she pushed his hands away. 'Well, I honestly don't want you touching me!'

'I was not touching you, I was touching our child!'

'My child—mine!' she flashed. 'This child is my mistake. My responsibility. I didn't ask you to come here. And I don't know why you have! But if it is to tell me how wrong it is for me to have this baby, then you're too late!' The blue eyes were spitting challenge, the fierce, threatening challenge of a woman protecting her unborn child. 'They won't abort this baby without a damned good medical excuse!'

'Abortion?' he choked, his black brows drawing downwards over his eyes. 'What the hell are you talking about? I never mentioned the word!'

'No,' she agreed, feeling the monster nausea begin to claw at her insides. 'Because I never gave you the chance! I'm not Cassie,' she stated thickly. 'And no man is going to dance with joy at the loss of *my* child!'

'Cassie?' he said bewilderedly. 'What does she have to do with any of this?'

'N-nothing,' Jemma stammered, running a shaky hand through her hair. In all honesty she was so staggered at him turning up like this that she barely knew what she was saying. 'Sh-she let Josh off the hook in the most unequivocal way she could, that's all,' she told him bitterly. 'But I didn't put you on the hook, Leon!' she cried. 'So you have no right to come here throwing your weight about, telling me what I should—'

'Cassie aborted her baby?' Leon interrupted in a voice that said this was news to him.

'Yes,' she whispered, feeling decidedly shaky on her legs all of a sudden.

'And you think,' he persisted slowly, as if he was having trouble taking it in, 'that I would have expected you to do the same?'

No! Oh, God—no! she thought, and shuddered in horror at her own vile words. How could she accuse him of something like that? She knew—*knew* he was not that kind of man!

'I'm sorry,' she apologised huskily. 'Of course I never thought that of you.'

His chest moved harshly. 'Well, that is something, I suppose,' he muttered, yet still flaying her with a contemptuous look.

'I'm sorry,' she whispered again, feeling so guilty that she wanted to cringe.

'Oh—sit down!' he ground out, and it was only when he took hold of her arm and helped her into a nearby chair that she realised how badly she was trembling.

'Good God,' he muttered, 'you barely look fit enough to support yourself, never mind the child you carry! How the hell have you let yourself get into this state?'

'I've been ill,' she mumbled distractedly.

'Sick with your own deceit, I should imagine,' he muttered unsympathetically.

'Who—who told you about the baby?' She asked the question which had been burning at her brain since he had arrived, distinctly unsurprised by her pregnant state.

He was glaring at the floor, and for a moment Jemma thought he wasn't going to answer her, then he glanced up and grimaced. 'Your flatmate, who else?' he said, and watched what colour she had left leave her face at this ultimate betrayal.

'She was supposed to just deliver my note,' she whispered painfully.

'Which is exactly what she did do,' Leon nodded. 'Only fate happened to take a hand in things. I arrived home— early, since I had managed to catch an earlier flight—to find her at my door. What happened next is between myself and your friend,' he stated grimly. 'Except to add that she is more of a friend than you deserve. We will, of course, invite her to our wedding.'

That thoroughly shook her, bringing her head up sharply to stare at him. 'But I can't marry you, Leon!' she cried.

'And why not?' he demanded haughtily. 'You have other crimes to lay at my feet, maybe? Other sins I am to be found guilty of without trial?'

She flushed. 'No, of course not. But—'

'Then perhaps it is a sin of your own which makes you stare in horror at the idea of marrying me?' he suggested. 'Maybe there is more to this than even your best friend divulged to me? Something, perhaps, to do with the man you were on your way to meet tonight when I—surprised you with my arrival?'

Man—what man? She frowned, having no idea what he was talking about.

'The man your note spoke of,' he illuminated for her. 'The man you informed me you are heavily involved with.'

Oh. Jemma flushed and lowered her eyes as enlightenment dawned. She had forgotten all about the lie she had made up for not wanting to see him.

'Maybe,' he went on grimly, 'this man is the father of your child, hmm? Who is he?' he demanded. 'Anyone I know? Is he a better lover then I? Is that why you dropped me for him? Regarding your condition, I must also presume that you met him long before we parted!' He eyed her narrowly. 'Could it be that your flatmate and I have jumped to too many conclusions all round?'

'Stop it!' she choked, unable to bear any more. 'You know I'm not like that! When did I ever give you the impression that I could be?'

'Devious, you mean?' he asked. 'A liar and a cheat?'

She went white at his words, the sickness beginning to crawl up inside her. 'I w-want you to leave,' she whispered, coming shakily to her feet.

'You don't like these accusations?' he asked. 'They offend you as deeply as your accusations offended me?'

So that was it. He was simply getting his own back on her in the most insulting way he could think of. 'I s-said I was sorry,' she murmured. 'What else do you want me to say?'

'You can tell me whose child it is you are carrying.'

'Yours!' she choked out wretchedly. 'You know it's yours!' Then she turned and made a dash for the door.

At least he saved her the ultimate humiliation of watching her while she was wretchedly sick, caught off balance by the urgency with which she had thrust him out of her way so that she could run to the bathroom. By the time he had joined her there, she was already hanging weakly over the bowl, and after a moment's stillness he turned and walked away.

She was sitting limply on the edge of the bath when he returned. He said nothing, but there was a grimness about him as he reached behind her for the bath sponge then ran it under the wash-basin tap before squatting down to apply it to her hot, clammy face and neck.

'You've lost weight,' he observed. 'How the hell does a woman in your condition lose weight?'

She shook her head, unable to utter anything at the moment while she fought this never-ending battle with herself. It didn't help that he was so close, the warmth of his body and the familiar subtle scent of his aftershave making her head whirl all over again.

'Why did you do it, Jemma?' he gruffed out suddenly. 'What did I ever do to make you mistrust me so?'

'I didn't mistrust you,' she sighed. 'I just—mistrusted our relationship.'

He lifted her chin with his hand, his black eyes boring into her weary ones. 'Yet I offered you more than I have ever offered any woman. Did this count for nothing?'

'How arrogant,' she scoffed. 'You offered to make me your kept woman and went out of your way to make your opinions on marriage clear! Just as you were very clear about your opinions on women who set out to trap men by getting pregnant!' Impatiently she knocked his hand away, then picked up a towel to dry her face. 'You didn't leave me much choice, did you?' she muttered finally.

He didn't answer, but his expression revealed enough for her to know she had managed to make him think.

'Tell me why you look so pale and thin,' he demanded on a complete turn-about of subject.

Jemma grimaced to herself. What cannot be defended, must be ignored! she noted drily. 'I've been ill, I told you,' she said, 'with the flu.' She lifted an unsteady hand to her hollowed cheek. 'It—dragged on a bit, but I'm beginning to recover now.'

He ran his eyes over her. 'And the child?' he asked. 'Has he suffered through this—flu?'

She found her first smile for that, a rueful one that Leon could not begin to understand. 'No,' she said. 'He hasn't suffered.'

Something passed over his face, a look gone before she had a chance to interpret it, but it had a disturbingly relieved quality about it. He threw down the sponge and straightened, then seemed uncertain as to what he should do next.

'Are you all right now?' He ended up referring to her for advice. 'Should you lie down for a while or something…?'

'I'm fine now,' she assured him flatly. 'Thank you.'

He frowned. 'Then why are you still sitting there,' he wanted to know, 'as if you have decided to take root?'

Jemma glanced impatiently at him. 'Because my legs are not quite ready to support me yet, that's why!'

'Then why didn't you say?' Instantly he was gathering her up in his arms and walking out of the bathroom. 'Where?' he enquired, stopping in the hallway.

'The kitchen,' she said, feeling the bitterness of helplessness bite at her nerves. 'I need a cool drink.'

He nodded, moving smoothly through the kitchen door to deposit her carefully on a chair. 'Stay there, I'll get it.' He went to the fridge, bending to peer inside then coming out with the jug of orange. 'Will this do?' He looked at her questioningly.

She nodded and he busied himself then, finding a glass. He put it down in front of her then poured out the orange.

'It looks disgustingly weak to me,' he said, eyeing the mixture dubiously.

'It's how I like it.' She didn't add it was the only way she could take it.

'Do you mind if I refrain from joining you and make myself a coffee instead?' he requested.

'Help yourself,' she invited, adding drily, 'So long as you don't place it under my nose, that is.'

'Your stomach is that sensitive?' He had moved over to the kettle and was checking the level of water inside.

'Only when I laugh,' she joked, feeling at least some of the tension ease out of her overwrought muscles.

He turned and grinned at her. 'That bad, eh?'

'It depends on your definition of bad.' She grimaced. 'Trina thinks it horrifying. Watching me has put her off having children for life, I think!'

'Ah, Trina,' he murmured, loading his mug with two heaped teaspoonfuls of instant, no less. 'A very good friend you have there, Jemma. One of the best, I would say.'

Jemma sat back in her chair, eyeing him narrowly. 'Quite a mutual-admiration society you two have set up together, isn't it?' she drawled, recalling the way Trina had spent every available moment the day before singing Leon's praises. 'I remember a time when you could do nothing but bite each other's head off!'

'We share a mutual interest,' he defended mildly. 'That kind of thing can draw the most unlikely people together.'

'Enough to make one betray another friend?' she suggested succinctly.

'Betrayal?' He glanced thoughtfully at her, then returned his attention to pouring hot water on his coffee. 'Trina did not betray you.' He did not even try to misunderstand. 'If anything, she betrayed herself in her efforts to maintain her loyalty as your closest friend.' Bringing his drink with him to the table, he sat down then looked levelly at her. 'Did you know she has turned down an offer of marriage from her accountant because she is so concerned about what will happen to you if she did marry him?'

The easier mood shattered, sprinkling around her like a million and one shards of sharp, piercing glass.

Leon watched her for a few minutes, sipping calmly at his coffee while the full impact of what he had just said sunk indelibly in. Then he set down his cup and said smoothly, 'Now we talk weddings, Jemma.' And her eyelashes flickered as she focused on his grimly determined face. 'Ours, not your friend's. She has taken enough interference from us.'

The 'us' was a mere sop. But it stated its point well enough. Trina must have been feeling as if she was being pulled in two, what with her sick, pregnant and alone friend tugging her heartstrings on one side, and the man who wanted to marry her tugging frustratedly on the other!

It was no wonder she'd gone to Leon. She must have seen him as her only salvation!

She swallowed, seeing herself as Trina must see her, and felt the rise of nausea bite into her stomach again. A weight. She had become that weight around her best friend's neck.

Slowly, she lifted her eyes to Leon's. 'What do you want me to do?' she asked, and Leon nodded once firmly, as if her reply moved her up a couple of notches in his estimation.

'I want you to pack your things and be ready to move out of here by tomorrow lunchtime,' he said, giving his instructions in much the same way he would give them to anyone under his power—with a level but an unchallengeable tone. 'By the time I come to collect you, you will have left a long letter for your friend, convincing her not only that she did the right thing in confiding in me, but that you also can't thank her enough for it. You will tell her how ecstatic you are. How much in love!' He slid the words out mockingly. 'Then you will thank her nicely for being the good friend she has been to you, and wish her good luck and goodbye. But at no point will you so much as hint that you know anything of her own frustrated wedding plans,' he warned. 'Because she is no fool, that one, and she will guess that I have used my knowledge of it to coerce you, which will in turn only make her feel wretched and guilty—which we do not want, do we, Jemma?'

She shook her head, too full up with aching tears to speak.

'Good,' he said, and got up. 'Now we go out and eat,' he announced as if the rest just hadn't happened.

'I can't,' she whispered thickly, the idea of food appalling her delicate stomach.

'You can.' His hand, firm on her arm, lifted her out of the chair. 'And you will.' He looked determinedly into her defeated blue eyes. 'If I have to carry you there with a bucket stuck beneath your nose, you will come—and eat. Understand?'

Understand? she echoed dully. She understood everything. She had just become one of Leon's possessions, to do and be whatever he demanded of her.

Surprisingly, the nausea subsided again. It hovered for a little while longer, threatening to send her running, but after a couple of deep controlling breaths of the warm humid air it left her, and she climbed into his silver Mercedes feeling more settled inside than she had for days.

Weeks—months? a little voice inside her head quizzed. Now there was a loaded concept, she mocked it. But not one she wished to dwell on right now.

He had her back at the flat by ten-thirty. 'I won't come in,' he informed her as the car engine died. 'Get some sleep,' he instructed, lifting a hand to comb a stray lock of hair lightly from her cheek. 'And try not to dwell too deeply on your lot, *agape mou*. I am not such a bad catch, surely?'

She glanced at him, her blue eyes clashing with his in the darkness of the car. 'The point is,' she posed, 'would the catch be caught if it weren't for a heavily baited hook?'

'You are referring to my lot?'

'I just don't understand why you're doing this,' she explained, then sighed heavily. 'I never asked for marriage from you, Leon, and still don't expect it from you!'

'You would prefer I set you up in a nice little semi-detached house somewhere in London suburbia?' he suggested. 'With a nice little allowance with which to live on while you rear my child?'

'I would rather you just leave me alone to get on with my life in my own way!' she snapped, retaliating to his disparaging tone.

'Your life?' he snapped out angrily. 'What has your life got to do with this? Or my life come to that?' He turned on her, his hand once again making the possessive statement by coming to lie over her stomach. 'This is the only life that counts now, Jemma!' His eyes flashed in the late summer darkness, naked with a stunning sincerity. 'What you or I want for ourselves from now on can take only second place to this! And this needs both a mother and a father! Which is exactly what he will get, if I have to drag you screaming to the altar by the roots of your beautiful hair!'

He moved jerkily, throwing himself away from her and back into his seat to sit glaring out of the car window as though the world beyond it had suddenly become his enemy while the space inside the car hung with the echo of his passionate vow.

And it had been a vow, she acknowledged as she sat there and shook in reaction. A vow which put all her high-minded principles about leaving Leon his freedom while she struggled to bring their child up alone to shame.

As if he could read her thoughts, Leon twisted his dark head to look at her, his voice calm now but grim when he spoke. 'We will not speak of this again,' he decreed. 'The deed is done, our futures set.' He paused, levelling one final implacable look at her, then leaned across her to open her door. 'I shall be back here by noon tomorrow. Be ready.'

The next day, she was packed and waiting when his knock sounded at the flat door. He stepped inside, his gaze running briefly over the loose pale blue cotton sundress she was wearing without revealing his thoughts.

She wondered what he was seeing when he looked at her like that—the desirable woman he had once taken in his arms so passionately? Or did he see the pale shadow of that woman she felt she had become?

'Ready?' he asked, glancing at the neatly stacked suitcases standing against the wall.

She nodded mutely.

'Nothing else?' He seemed surprised, and Jemma forced her dilatory tongue to move.

'I've left a few boxes of things in my room. Nothing important,' she told him. 'They can be picked up—whenever.' Her accompanying shrug said she didn't care.

'Then they come now,' he said decisively. 'You won't be coming back here again, Jemma.'

She shivered, the words having a much more final ring to them than just thinking them all night long had.

CHAPTER EIGHT

'No,' JEMMA refused outright, staring in horror at the room he was in the process of placing her suitcases in. 'I won't sleep with you, Leon!'

Turning, she stalked back down the stairs and into the sitting-room, where she stood staring angrily out of the window. How dared he? If it wasn't bad enough him taking her straight from her flat to a private clinic where he proceeded calmly to stand right beside her while a top London gynaecologist put her through just about every embarrassing examination a woman could be subjected to, he was now just as calmly expecting her to share his bed!

'I hate you!' she whispered without turning when she heard him come into the room. 'How could you be so bloody insensitive?'

'Are we about to discuss our sleeping arrangements or the fact that I insisted on being present throughout your examination?' By contrast he sounded smooth and beautifully cool!

'Both!' she snapped. 'I find both intrusions on my privacy utterly distasteful!'

'It is not the fact that I intrude on your privacy that you find so distasteful, Jemma,' he argued drily. 'It is the fact that I intrude at all!'

She went to deny it, then snapped her lips tight shut over the words. She did see him as an intruder, so much so that she was still trembling from the indignity of it all. She felt trapped, wrung out and trampled on. In less than twenty-four hours, Leon had completely taken over her right even to think for herself! And she was just beginning to understand what it was like to become a Leon Stephanades business take-over. The iron hand in the velvet glove! she called it helplessly, because he was doing it all with the kind of quiet authority she found impossible to fight against.

'You could at least have shown some—taste and allowed me to lose my dignity in private!' she threw tensely at him.

'And what about my rights as a prospective father to be interested and concerned for you and the child?' he countered. 'You think it did not move me as deeply as it moved you to see the actual evidence of our child moving—living inside your womb? Yes...' he taunted softly when his words surprised her enough to turn and stare at him. 'I saw your expression when the scanner showed our perfectly formed child, *agape mou*. I saw the glow of pride and the more obvious feelings of relief when the good doctor assured us that everything is well. You think I did not experience the same emotions, should not be allowed to experience the same things?'

'That isn't what I meant!'

'Isn't it?' He walked towards her, his expression grim suddenly as he made his usual statement by placing both hands on her swollen body. 'We are a unit,' he declared. 'Three parts of one whole, joined by the irrefutable existence of our child—ours!' he repeated with soft ferocity. 'And the quicker you come to terms with that, the more comfortable we can all become with it!'

Comfortable? He honestly believed she would learn to be comfortable being with a man who could turn his back on the woman, yet was prepared to put up with her because she was suddenly the mother of his unborn child? 'Which does not include my having to sleep with you!' she declared stubbornly.

'It does if we are to have any hope of making a success of this marriage,' he said grimly.

'We are not married yet!'

'But we will be in two days' time!' Another shock announcement that set her poor head reeling. 'And wherever you decide to sleep tonight, Jemma,' he warned, 'you will sleep with me from then on!'

He meant it. The hard flash of his eyes said he meant it, the possessive grip of his hands said he meant it, and the dark, angry sense of frustration she felt burning inside told her she just did not have a single say in it. But she had one last try. 'Can't you at least give me a little time to get used to the idea of us being together like this before I have to—?'

He was already shaking his head, grim-faced and immovable. Jemma sighed, feeling the threat of tears block her throat. 'Then I repeat,' she whispered thickly, 'you are an insensitive brute!'

'Perhaps,' he conceded, coming down from anger to a rueful kind of self-mockery when he sensed her defeat. His hand moved from her body to her shoulders, then slid gently to her throat, his long fingers burrowing into her thick, shining hair to cup her nape and his thumbs gently pressing beneath her chin to bring her face up to meet the smile softening his eyes. Her heart flipped over, her senses beginning to buzz as the look awakened all those weaknesses she had always harboured for him. 'Surely, *agape mou*,' he murmured, 'it is not so long ago that we slept together that you could have forgotten how good it was for both of us?'

'I don't remember sleeping much!' she snapped, trying to fight both him and her own wayward feelings.

Leon laughed softly. 'But this time will be different,' he promised, adding ruefully, 'If only because the good doctor prescribed rest and no excitement!' Taking her by surprise, he kissed the top of her nose, then released her. 'Now,' he said on a complete change of subject, 'I want to know your opinion of boats.'

'Boats?' She just stared blankly at him. 'What have boats got to do with anything?' she demanded bewilderedly.

'A lot if you like them,' he replied. 'Nothing if you are prone to seasickness. Your body has enough to contend with from that particular malady without my wanting to worsen it.'

Jemma lowered her eyes, refusing to tell him that she had not felt sick once since he arrived back in her life. The doctor had hinted at worry and stress as being the culprit. And she was beginning to believe he was right.

Heart sickness, not morning sickness? that small voice inside her head suggested.

'Are you?'

'What?' She glanced up at him, having lost the thread of the conversation in the tangle of her own troublesome thoughts.

'Prone to seasickness.' He sighed out patiently as if he were talking to a child.

'No,' she answered. 'I used to belong to a sailing club when I was a teenager. And I did a bit of sailing with Trina last Christmas when we were in Barbados without feeling any ill effects. But I don't see—'

'Good,' he cut in. 'Because I have one—or,' he then amended wryly, 'I have a yacht. The doctor prescribed rest, good food and no excitement for the next few weeks while we bring you back into decent health, and I cannot think of a better place to ensure all three than cruising the Greek islands on my yacht with the most exquisite chef your taste-buds have ever encountered. What do you think?'

What did she think? For the first time since he had walked back into her life, she felt the stirring of pleasure. 'I think it sounds lovely, but…'

'No buts,' he dismissed arrogantly. 'We will pick the yacht up in Corfu on Tuesday, and work our way south through the Ionian islands—a good idea for a honeymoon, eh?'

Honeymoon? Jemma couldn't help it, she shuddered, the whole idea sounding utterly hypocritical to her. 'You don't have to put the rest of your life on hold for me, Leon,' she told him huskily. 'I am quite aware that I must have messed up your...schedule enough as it is!'

'Have you?' he murmured thoughtfully. Then, 'Yes, I suppose you have,' he agreed. 'Still,' he added with a careless shrug, 'that is what we will do. Now,' he went on before she had a chance to make up her mind whether to be hurt or not by his answer, 'I'm hungry. Let's go and see what there is to eat.'

They ate in the kitchen with no formality, just as they used to do before. And Jemma was rather surprised at how easily they slipped back into their old easy ways. By the time they had cleared away, her long day had thoroughly caught up with her, and she couldn't stifle a weary yawn.

'Bed,' Leon commanded, turning her towards the stairs. 'There are five bedrooms up there, *agape mou*. Take your pick.' It was a reassurance and the allowance of one small victory for her. Jemma accepted it with a tired smile and a contrary sense of disappointment inside. 'Take what you need for the night, but leave your cases where they are until the morning. I have several hours of work to get through before I can retire,' he added. 'So I will say goodnight now.' He bent to press a light kiss against her lips.

She responded—couldn't stop herself even as she damned her own weakness for it. As Leon drew away, it was her lips that clung, her soft sigh which whispered between them filled with helpless longing. Opening her heavy eyes, she then wished she hadn't when she found herself staring into his, so dark with knowledge that it made her want to weep at her own pathetic vulnerability.

'I wish I could really hate you,' she whispered helplessly.

'Do you?' He smiled strangely, as though the idea that she could hate him was not that impossible to imagine. 'Well,' he murmured, his gaze roaming over her pale, wan face, 'I will be giving you no reason to hate me tonight, so go to your bed. And be at peace.'

And she was, totally, utterly at peace, Jemma decided two weeks later as she lay in the depths of a sublime laziness on the sun-drenched deck of Leon's disgustingly luxurious yacht, shading the sun from her eyes with one hand while the other held up a letter she had just received, via the speed launch that came skimming across the water from the mainland to pull alongside them every morning, bringing Leon any business papers that might need his attention.

It had surprised her that he had not shown the least inclination to get back to the cut-throat excitement of a powerful tycoon's life. But, if there was one new thing she had learned about him during these weeks—and there had been several—then his ability to play the sloth had been the most surprising. Oh, he worked, certainly. A man with his responsibilities could not simply close shop and forget about it completely. But he restricted his time spent shut up in his fully equipped stateroom to a few hours every morning and the same in the afternoon while she took her enforced rest. Between times, he became a lazy, good-natured, intoxicatedly charming companion, willing to indulge her in anything from lying next to her here on the sun-deck for hours on end without bothering to move, or taking her out in the on-board speedboat to the nearest island where she could enjoy her newly acquired skills at snorkelling around the rocks.

The improvement in her health had been remarkable, even to Jemma herself. The sickness had gone, she had acquired a very carefully nurtured but rather attractive golden tan to her skin, and a bloom to her features which was a one hundred per cent improvement on the hollow-eyed pregnant wraith she had been threatening to become.

She had stopped being self-conscious of her new maternal shape within hours of arriving on the yacht, forced to dismiss how she looked by the sheer heat of the sun and the utter arrogance with which Leon had walked up to her while she stood on the sun-deck in one of her long, baggy T-shirts, boiling hot and wondering if she dared slip away to the delicious coolness of her cabin—which was more like a luxury hotel suite with its *en-suite* bathroom and delicious air-conditioning—so that she could hide away from yet another day of fierce Greek sunshine. But Leon had had other ideas. He had simply reached out and coolly stripped the T-shirt right off over her head! Then, while she'd stood there red-faced and struck dumb with mortification because she was left wearing only the briefest pair of cotton panties, he'd taken his time exploring every inch of her and even gone as far as to grip her wrists and wrench them apart when she had attempted to cover herself.

'Now we have got that embarrassing little moment out of the way,' he had drawled eventually, 'perhaps we can begin to relax and enjoy this cruise as it was meant to be enjoyed?'

Since then she had lived in one of the bikinis Leon had provided for her—sometimes topless, sometimes not—or in a light cotton shirt when it was sensible to cover herself from the sun for a while.

They lived, ate and slept on the yacht, and her feet had only touched dry land on the few rare occasions Leon had let them visit a secluded bay for the odd picnic. And in general she was more than at peace with herself, she was happy. At least, she amended ruefully, she was happy within the confines of the contented little bubble she was living in just now.

Which was probably why she was looking at Trina's let-

ter without reading a single word of it. She was afraid her
friend might say something that could burst the bubble.
Remind her, perhaps, of the realities she had so successfully
thrust aside.

'Read,' she told herself firmly, and forced her eyes to
focus on the tightly crushed and very rushed lines of words.
Trina began:

> Guess what! I'm married! And if you think yours was
> a disgustingly rushed affair, well, wait till you hear about
> mine!

Jemma grinned, settling herself back to enjoy a good
read. Frew, it seemed, had taken Trina off to Barbados and
married her on a beach! They had been away a week, and
been back in London a week. Trina was now madly trying
to find a house for them.

> Frew's flat is just too small for us both, what with all
> my office stuff littering up the place and the work he
> brings home piled everywhere. We should have thought
> more about it before deciding to live at his place. It may
> be nearer to his office than our flat was, but at least ours
> had your bedroom free to turn into an office. Still, it's
> too late now. I closed the lease on our old place, so now
> we've just got to find something bigger.

The flat was gone. Jemma felt the tiniest bit of distur-
bance within her bubble—as if some of the air was trying
to escape. No home, she realised. Nothing in London to go
back to if she ever felt she needed to. It felt a bit strange,
realising just how totally she was now dependent on Leon.

The sound of approaching footsteps almost had her falling off her lounger in an effort to snatch her straw sunhat
up off the deck and quickly stuff it on her head. Leon ap-

peared, just as she had settled herself back on her lounger looking as though she hadn't moved in hours.

He came to stand beside her, silently offering her a tall glass of iced water and two small pills. Making heavy weather of it, she pulled herself into a sitting position, exchanged the glass and pills with him for the letter, then found herself studying him covertly from beneath the shadowed brim of her hat.

He was wearing nothing more than a faded old pair of dark grey shorts—his usual attire when aboard the yacht—and he looked big and lean and brown, the dark cluster of crisp black hair on his broad chest curling downwards over the flat planes of his stomach to disappear beneath the elasticated waist of his shorts.

Her senses leapt and she looked quickly down and away. It never had done her any good to feed her weak love of simply looking at him, she noted drily. Her senses always ended up spoiling it.

And her senses were not allowed to ignite, she drily reminded herself. Because this was a 'no sex' marriage. Ironic really, when before it had been a 'no marriage' sexual relationship! He had kissed her only once since the day they married when he'd turned her into his arms and placed his cool lips against her own in what she could only describe as a civil seal to their civil marriage!

Since then—well, the matter of sharing a bed had never arisen again. And, other than the fact that she sunbathed in next to nothing, for most of the time they were both scrupulously respectful of the other's privacy.

Quite a change from those long lazy weekends they'd used to spend invading each other's privacy as if it were their right!

Still, she mused, it had its benefits. Without the added ingredient of sex to complicate their relationship, she and Leon had actually become quite good friends. And although she sometimes awoke in the middle of the night, her body tight and hot with a need which could sometimes hold her tense in desperation, she had never so much as considered giving in to the feelings and creeping into the room next door and Leon's bed. Mainly, she acknowledged ruefully, because Leon had not shown any inclination that he still wanted her physically. He flirted and teased in that light-hearted way friends did with each other, but she had never glimpsed, even once, any hint that he could still desire her as a lover.

Not that she blamed him. With a small grimace, she glanced down her reclining body where their child thumped rhythmically against the tightly drawn walls of its home. She had to be about as undesirable as she could get!

'This is from Trina?' he asked, breaking into her thoughts to wave the letter at her.

'Oh, yes,' she confirmed. 'You can read it if you want,' she invited, popping the pills into her mouth and swallowing them down with the water. She did it all without really thinking about it now. It had become a ritual she had grown used to over the weeks. If it wasn't Leon following her around making sure she took her daily dose of iron, it was one of his stewards.

'You do not mind?'

Jemma just shrugged. 'There's nothing in it I wouldn't want you to read. Just Trina going on about weddings and flats that are too small...' She fell into contemplative silence, unaware that Leon studied her clouded face for a few moments before hitching his hips on to the nearby table and bending his dark head to read.

'Your friend sounds happy, *agape mou*,' Leon muttered quietly after reading the letter.

'Mmm,' Jemma replied absently, sitting up to hug her arms around her bent knees.

'So, what has she said to—upset you?'

'Upset?' she echoed. 'I'm not upset,' she denied. 'Just…'
A sigh broke from her and she went silent.

Leon frowned, his dark eyes fixed thoughtfully on her.
'You wished you had attended her wedding?' he persisted
despite her denial.

Jemma shook her head. 'It wasn't that kind of wedding,
was it?' A romantic beach wedding in the Caribbean was
not the kind you invited all your friends to!

Leon glanced at the hurriedly written sheet of paper in
his hand, his puzzled frown darkening his face as he quickly
scanned the chatty but pretty innocuous sentences searching
for a clue to what had put that gloomy expression on her
face.

'She closed the lease on our flat,' Jemma murmured suddenly. 'I spent four of the happiest years of my life there.
It was my home, and I know it sounds silly, but it's suddenly hit me that I no longer have one. No home. No place
in England I can actually call my own.'

'But we have a home in London,' Leon pointed out. 'I
don't see the problem.'

'Your home.' She glanced at him over the top of her
knees. 'Yes, I know. But it isn't—' The same, she had been
going to say, but could see from his expression that he
didn't understand. Couldn't understand what it felt like to
be made suddenly aware that you had nothing—nothing
you could call your absolute own, even if it was only a silly
little flat on the cheap side of London with draughty windows and a bath-tap that leaked. She didn't even have a
best friend any more. Trina belonged to Frew now, just, she
supposed heavily, as she belonged to Leon.

Glancing thoughtfully at him, she wondered if he would
understand if she tried to explain, then decided it was at
least worth a try. 'I spent most of my younger years moving
from house to house, town to town with two parents who
were constantly unfaithful to each other. One would find

him or herself a lover and go off for a month or two then they would come back and the other would be off.' She shrugged, knowing that really did not explain anything more than that she had two faithless parents. 'I never knew from one week to the next which one of them I would be living with. And I never got a chance to develop long-term friendships with any children of my own age because I was constantly being shunted around. Fresh starts, they called it,' she mocked. 'Which meant different towns, different schools, different parents—different homes.' She shrugged again, her blue eyes bleak. 'When they died and I moved to London to work I answered an advert in the paper for a flatmate, which was how I met Trina. She, and that little flat, gave me the first taste of real stability I had ever known. Four years,' she murmured softly. 'Belonging to someone and somewhere. And now it's gone again.'

'And you do not believe that I can give you all of that and for much longer?'

'I don't know, do I?' she shrugged, twisting to put her feet to the sun-heated deck. 'We married because of our baby, not because it was what either of us particularly wanted to do—not the best of foundations to build a stable relationship on. Still,' she concluded as she came to her feet, 'that was not the point I was actually trying to make. I was trying to explain to you why the flat and Trina had been so important to me, and why therefore I was suddenly feeling their loss.'

She went to turn away, but Leon stopped her by catching her hand. 'They have not been taken from you, Jemma,' he said quietly. 'They have just been replaced, that's all.'

With what? she wondered, and gained no comfort at all from his words. 'It's time for my rest,' she said, and sent him a small hollow smile before slipping her hand out of his and walking away.

When she awoke again, it was to the sound of the yacht's engines throbbing steadily beneath her.

She got up, dressed quickly in a simple pair of white calf-length baggy trousers made of a lightweight cotton, and a pale blue cotton over-shirt, then went in search of Leon, eager to find out where they were going.

She found him sitting at the table beneath the shaded awning on the sun-deck, reading business papers over a tall pot of Greek coffee. Like her, he had changed into lightweight trousers and had pulled a short-sleeved white shirt on to cover his darkly tanned chest.

He looked up and smiled as she approached, getting up to pull out a chair for her and seeing her seated.

'Where are we going?' she asked curiously.

'One moment and I will answer,' he said, striding off to order her some refreshment. It was a task he had made a habit of while they'd been on the yacht. The boat might need a sizeable complement of crew to keep it running as smoothly and efficiently as it did, but Jemma rarely ever saw any of them. As with his home in London, Leon liked to be alone to relax. Servants, staff, crew—call them what you like, they irritated him. And she had a suspicion that, if it were possible, he would have sailed this yacht single-handed just to maintain his desire for privacy.

He came back carrying a tray bearing her usual jug of freshly squeezed orange juice and a tall frosted glass, but by then Jemma was over at the rail, gazing out at the scenery going by them.

'I thought you might enjoy a change,' he answered her question as he came to lean beside her. 'So, we are making for a small fishing village called Fiskárdho on the northern tip of Kefallinía—the largest island in the Ionian group,' he explained informatively, 'where I think we will spend what is left of the day doing what any normal tourist would do and browse around the shops, maybe eat dinner in one of the local tavernas—would you like that, *agape mou*?'

'Sounds great!' She lifted smiling eyes to him.

'Good,' he nodded, and drew her attention to the view.

They were moving smoothly through a narrow stretch of deep blue water between two huge misted blocks of land.

'What are they?' she asked, curious because, other than that rushed journey from Corfu airport to pick up the yacht three weeks ago, they had steered well clear of the bigger islands in the group, calling only at the smallest mainly uninhabited islands where tourists rarely went.

'Kefallinía on the left and Ithaki—you might know it as Ithaca—to our right,' he informed her.

'Ithaca?' she cried. 'The island of Homer and the *Odyssey*. How wonderful!' She turned a wistful gaze on the man beside her. 'You're so lucky to be a part of all of this! The legends, the sheer romance of it! I'm jealous,' she confessed.

'Then dare I make another admission?' Leon mused out loud. 'This is my homeland,' he announced. 'I was born here.'

'On Ithaca?' she gasped out enviously.

'No.' Ruefully he shook his dark head. 'I am afraid I cannot make that particularly romantic claim. I am Kefallinían,' he explained. 'And remember how I said that,' he warned. 'Because when we land there Kefalliníans do not like to be called Greek!'

'But the island belongs to Greece!' she protested.

He nodded in agreement. 'But the Irish are Irish, the Scots are Scots and the Welsh are Welsh,' he made the comparison. 'I am Kefallinían.'

'Not Greek,' she said mock-solemnly but her eyes were twinkling.

'Not Greek,' he confirmed with equal mock-solemnity.

'So I didn't marry a Greek tycoon.'

'You married a Kefallinían tycoon,' he corrected.

'Leon Stephanades, the Kefallinían tycoon,' she said frowningly, trying the words out for taste. 'It doesn't have quite as good a ring to it, does it?'

He was trying not to smile. 'Wondering if you'd made a bad mistake marrying me?'

'Well…' Jemma turned to lean her elbows against the rail behind her, totally unconscious of the curving grace of her swollen body '…a girl has to consider her social standing, doesn't she? How much is a Kefallinían tycoon worth?' she quizzed.

'This one is worth—enough,' he answered with a smile.

'Enough for what?' she enquired provocatively.

He laughed, the sound warm and huskily alive. He lifted his hand so that he could take hold of her chin, giving it a playful shake. 'Enough to keep you in luxury for the rest of your beautiful life,' he said, and kissed her.

It was a surprise—enough of a surprise to keep her own mouth still beneath his, her eyes wide and startled when he drew away to look into them. 'You are happier now?' he asked. 'The feelings of homesickness have faded?'

'Yes,' she assured him, smiling apologetically. 'It was a few moments' silliness, that's all, gone before I woke up from my rest.'

His eyes glinted darkly in the sunlight while he explored her face for a few moments longer, then he said quietly, 'You must trust me, Jemma, to do what is right for us. I am both your home and your family now. I do not intend to desert you or play you false.'

'I do trust you,' she said, and surprised herself because she meant it. 'And I'm sorry if my mood upset you.'

'Not upset exactly, but concerned me rather.' He lifted a hand to her hair, gently touching the silky roots at her temple. 'We may have embarked on this marriage because of the coming child, but I never stopped caring for you, Jemma; you must also remember that.'

His words warmed a special place inside her, and she smiled up at him. 'I remember,' she confirmed.

And he had cared, cared enough to ask her to go live with him in New York. Cared enough to marry her when he came back to find her pregnant with his child. And he had cared enough to spend the last few weeks personally supervising her recovery to good health in the most luxurious and pleasurable way he could think of. But—

But what? she asked herself impatiently as she turned her attention back to the view slipping lazily by them.

But caring wasn't enough, she answered herself bleakly. Not any more—not ever, probably. But perhaps more so now because she had become so wholly dependent on him for everything.

CHAPTER NINE

FISKÁRDHO sat at the end of a narrow inlet, its rich blue waters protected by mountains on either side. Because of the size of the yacht, they had to anchor just outside the tiny harbour itself, and within minutes the crew had launched the small speed-boat, Leon had helped her climb down into it and they were speeding across the water towards a pretty hamlet of whitewashed buildings with red-tiled roofs.

It was a busy little place; sailing yachts of all shapes and sizes floated side by side along the two-sided harbour wall. Leon nudged them in between a tall-masted sailing yacht and an expensive-looking motor cruiser, then called out to a small white-haired man who came ambling across to catch the rope Leon threw to him. The two men chatted amiably in Greek while they made the boat safe, then, with an ease that surprised her, Leon picked her up and placed her neatly on the quay before making the two-foot leap to the quayside himself.

Jemma pushed her sunhat off her head so that it hung down her back on its strings and she could look interestedly around her. The little Greek man looked at her hair and said something to Leon who grinned and answered and the man gave a nod of approval and shook Leon's hand.

'What did he say?' she asked curiously.

'He was complimenting me on my taste,' Leon replied.

'And what did you say to him?'

'I told him I was Kefallinían,' he shrugged. 'Of course I had good taste.'

'Conceited devil,' she said.

He just grinned carelessly. 'What would you like to do first?' he asked.

'Stop my body from floating,' she said ruefully. 'I feel as if I'm still on water!'

'It will take a while to get your balance,' he warned. 'Would you rather we sit down and have a drink or something, while you get your land legs back?'

'No.' Jemma's eyes were already darting eagerly around her. 'I haven't seen a shop in weeks, and I want to browse.'

'I thought you might say that,' he sighed. 'Come on, we will begin at one end and work our way to the other. Oh,' he added belatedly, 'this is for you.' He pulled a thick roll of banknotes from his pocket and handed them to her. 'Drachmas,' he explained. 'You will need them if you want to buy anything.'

Jemma bit pensively down on her bottom lip, her reluctance to take the money showing in the expression she could not keep off her face.

'Good grief!' Leon sighed, reading the expression for exactly what it was. 'I have never known a woman like you who will not even accept the simplest offering from her own husband! Take it—take it!' he insisted impatiently, thrusting it into her hands.

'But how much is here?' she demanded suspiciously. It looked an awful lot of money to her.

'The equivalent of a few English pounds only,' he dismissed, watching her grudgingly push the roll into the pocket of her baggy white trousers. 'Now can we go?' he mocked.

She let him lead the way through the crush of people packing the quayside towards the little shops lined up on the other side of the quay, where she soon forgot to be uncomfortable about him giving her money as her eyes began to feast on the array of interesting touristy goods for sale.

They explored the tiny hamlet together, moving in and out of shops which were little more than the front rooms of private houses that had been converted for the season and would, Leon told her, revert back to their original use for the winter months. It was an enchantingly pretty place, and, Jemma realised, rather an up-market one, going by the quality of the produce on show. She went into raptures when they happened to stroll through the narrow door of one shop and she found herself literally tented in the most beautiful hand-made lacework, crochetwork, and exquisite embroidery. She lost Leon almost immediately, becoming immersed in a veritable maze of hung linen. When he eventually found her, she was standing fingering a beautifully crocheted baby shawl. He recognised what it was immediately and she blushed because, although they had married because of the child she carried, other than discussing her own health they rarely mentioned the child itself.

'You want it?' Leon asked her softly.

Jemma nodded, her eyes unknowingly vulnerable when she lifted them to him. 'Do I have enough drachmas to buy it?' she asked uncertainly. 'Only it's hand-made and looks very expensive...'

But Leon was already reaching for the delicate garment, his hands appearing big and dark against the soft white lacework as he unhooked it from its hanger then gravely presented it to her, draping it over her arms—carefully, as though their baby were already wrapped inside it, then stood back, something so intense about the look in his eyes that it caught at Jemma's breath and made their child kick out in protest at the flurry of emotion that rippled through her.

'You are beautiful, do you know that?' he murmured huskily, and bent to kiss her.

He paid for the shawl with his Visa card and had it wrapped in tissue paper and placed in a plastic carrier bag which he then solemnly presented to Jemma. She took it blushingly, feeling unaccountably shy all of a sudden.

A new intimacy seemed to grow between them after that. Leon rarely let go of her hand as they continued to wander from shop to shop, and Jemma felt a dire need always to have her body within brushing distance with his. Her senses began to buzz, and she knew by the new darkened look in his eyes when he looked at her that Leon was feeling the same thing too.

Darkness came around eight o'clock and they decided to make for one of the busy harbourside tavernas, sitting at a rickety old table on severely uncomfortable chairs. And Jemma found herself studying him curiously as he ordered some freshly caught snapper fish and the usual Greek salad to share. He couldn't often put himself into situations like this one, mingling, eating with tourists, yet, despite the unmistakable air of class about him, he blended in quite comfortably.

The meal came with a basket of fresh crusty bread and a large bowl of salad topped with rich feta cheese anointed with oil and herbs from which Leon broke off bits with his fingers and fed them to her as if it was the most natural thing in the world for him to do. They shared a bottle of wine—well, Jemma was allowed one glass; Leon had the rest. They talked quietly, she asking questions about the island, he answering them with a quiet depth of pride that held her more fascinated than the knowledgeable words he spoke. They watched the endless passage of holidaymakers taking an evening stroll along the harbour wall, and the way the lights danced on the silk dark waters in the harbour. They listened in to other people's conversations, smiling with them when someone made a joke, and Leon translating if the language was strange to her, his knowledge of French, Italian, and even a smattering of Danish both surprising and impressing her.

People talked sailing mostly because Fiskárdho, it seemed, was predominantly a sailing resort. And most remarked at some point or other during the evening on the big luxury yacht anchored just outside the bay, making Jemma blush and Leon grin as they speculated on who owned it, their suggestions ranging from Arab sheikhs to the Italian Mafia.

And through it all Leon was unusually attentive towards her, his fingers hardly ever out of contact with her own where they lay on the table, and his eyes warm and slumbrous on her face.

By the time they'd finished their long, leisurely meal, it was getting late. Leon suggested they return to the yacht, the look in his eyes promising that this new intimacy they were sharing was not going to end on their return. Trembling a little in anticipation, she let him help her to her feet. Their eyes met, and they kissed gently, then his arm was about her shoulders and her hand slid around his waist as they strolled silently back to where they had left the small boat.

The little white-haired man was there to hold the boat steady on its rope while Leon jumped in then reached up to lift her down to join him. Their bodies brushed, sending a sprinkle of awareness skittering through her, and on a soft gasp she looked down and away from his knowing gaze, hiding the sudden heat that rushed into her cheeks.

She trembled all the way back to the yacht where two crew members waited to make safe the little boat and help them board. Leon broke their usual routine by escorting her down to her cabin when usually he stayed on the sun-deck when she came to bed.

A *frisson* of heat tingled through her at the sound of the door closing quietly behind them. She turned to look at him. 'Thank you f-for a lovely...' Evening, she had been about to say, but the look in his eyes dried up her mouth, and she had to look away, her agitated gaze darting around the room in search of something, anything she could pretend interest in so long as she didn't have to look at him. Her eyes alighted on her nightdress laid out on the bed and she snatched it up, crushing the soft cotton to her breasts only to gasp when Leon captured her wrist and pulled her around to face him.

'Not tonight, *agape mou*,' he murmured softly, taking the nightdress from her and tossing it aside. 'Not tonight.'

Then he was cupping her face, his fingers threading into the silky thickness of her hair as he urged her to look at him. His eyes were dark and disturbingly alive, transmitting his next intention even before he lowered his head. And it was no passive kiss. It was a hot, hunting kiss that demanded an answering response from her and got it hungrily, her hands snaking up to grasp the sides of his face, holding him, urging him on, her mouth warm and seeking, telling him that she wanted this too.

It had been building up all evening. She had known it even while she'd tried hard to pretend it wasn't there. But now, as his arms slid around her to draw her fully against him, there was no pretending any longer.

Leon wanted to make love to her. Why he had chosen today to change the status quo she had no idea, but it certainly had changed, and she could feel the power of his desire pulsing urgently against her.

He undressed her slowly, his fingers loosening buttons and sliding sensually over her throat, the satin slopes of her breasts, the rounded firmness of her stomach, smothering her soft responding gasps with the passionate crush of his mouth. His hands slid inside the elastic waist of her trousers, drawing the thin fabric downwards with an agonising slowness. She shuddered when he touched her intimately, a crescendo of tight curling pleasure arching her back so that their child pressed against him and her mouth left his so that she could let her head fall backwards on a soft, pleasurable sigh.

His mouth found her breasts, making them sting into tight, painful life and she inhaled on a sharp gasp of air.

'I hurt you?' His head came up, burning black eyes shot through with concern.

'No,' she denied. 'I'm just—sensitive, that's all.' Then on a driven groan, 'Oh, God, Leon. Do it again!'

Her breathless plea seemed to rock him, his own breath crashing from his lungs as he caught her mouth. Her shirt slid from her shoulders to land in a pool at their feet, followed by his shirt, then their naked torsos were together, hot and throbbing. He drew her down to lie on the bed, hands hurriedly removing the rest of their clothes before he joined her, and Jemma was already reaching for him, one arm hooking around his neck while the other hand went for the muscled tightness of his hip, pulling him against her, legs tangling, bodies moving in that hot, sensual rhythm of urgent need.

It had been a long time—too long for both of them if their responses were a measure. His mouth was moist and searching on her breasts, his caresses urgent as he aroused her.

'Will I hurt you?' he asked tensely when it was obvious neither of them could stand much more of it without full, exquisite possession.

'No,' she whispered, and was sure of it. She was ready, her body so supple that it felt boneless in its need. He came over her, his forearms keeping most of his weight from her, but as he carefully thrust himself inside her Jemma let out a frustrated groan and pulled him down on top of her. It wasn't enough just to join. She needed to feel him—all of him, bearing down on her with all the heat and passion she had missed for so long.

Relief came like the slow-motion shattering of glass,

bursting out from a central point where the nub of her desire had coiled itself tightly in readiness for this final devastating blast. He went with her; she felt him, heard him, cried out as he cried out, and their bodies blended in a hot fusion of moist flesh and trembling limbs.

Afterwards, he just held her, held her curled closely into the curve of his own body. And when she tried to move he stopped her, hands tightening, mouth brushing a silent plea across her heated cheek. They didn't speak, he didn't seem to want that either, her only attempt cut off with a husky, 'Shh. You belong, *agape mou*. You must feel it now. You belong here with me.' And again the tightening of the arms to stop her when she tried to answer him.

It was a mark, she realised, of how deeply her melancholy earlier had affected him that he needed to keep referring to it. Oh, not just with words, but with the way he had been with her since she woke up this afternoon. More attentive, physically more responsive, in the way he had constantly kept her close to him, touching her—with the caress of his eyes as well as his hands. As if he had realised that the kind of easy friendship they had developed over the last few weeks was not enough for her to feel secure with him, and he wanted her to feel secure. Was that also why he had made love to her just now? she wondered. As a statement of possession, for both of them, because she would have to be stupid not to know that Leon had gained as much from their loving as she had.

Then another thought trickled insidiously into her mind, one which filled her with a purring warmth she had never dared allow herself before. He had already reminded her once today that he cared for her. But then to go to the lengths he had done just to reassure her again? It had to hint at more than caring, more than just a reluctant husband wanting to make the best of his lot.

Could it even be that he was falling just a little bit in love with her?

Jemma sighed wistfully, and burrowed deeper into the circle of his arms, feeling a new level of contentment settle softly over her, and she fell asleep like that, coiled against him, he wrapped around her.

It was very early in the morning when something woke them. A sound that impinged on their subconsciousness and brought Leon alert with a jerk before he was suddenly leaping naked out of the bed. He glanced out of the window, swore, then turned angrily towards the bathroom.

'What is it?' Jemma asked sleepily.

'Nothing,' he muttered. 'Go back to sleep.'

He disappeared through the bathroom door, leaving her lying there frowning in puzzlement at his odd behaviour. Then the noise became louder, and she recognised it as the whirling sound of a helicopter's blades. She listened sleepily as it swooped low over the top of the yacht then whirled away across the surface of the water before coming to a hovering stop somewhere not far away.

Leon came back showered, with a towel draped around his hips. He didn't look at her but bent to recover his clothes still lying where he had tossed them on the floor the night before.

'Is that helicopter bringing someone to see you?' she asked.

'Yes.' The answer was tight and angry.

'But who?' she persisted. Other than the launch which brought him papers daily to the yacht, no one else had tried to see him.

'I cannot tell as yet,' he said. But his angry expression alone said he had a damned good idea. He looked at her at last, that anger flicking at her, until he realised whom he was looking at and he sighed shortly, and came over to sit down on the bed.

'You look beautiful in the morning, do you know that?'

'Flattery will not get you anywhere,' she pouted. 'I want to know what's going on.'

'And you will,' he assured her. 'When I know.' He covered her mouth with his, tasting cleanly of toothpaste and smelling freshly of soap.

Then he was up again, and shrugging into his creased trousers and crumpled shirt. 'Stay there,' he commanded over his shoulder. 'It is still early. Try to get some more sleep if you can. If you cannot, then ring for your breakfast to be served in here.' He turned back to her at that, his expression firm when he added commandingly, 'I want you to remain in here, *agape mou*, until I have got rid of—whoever it is.'

'But why?' she said, puzzled by the command.

'Because your husband asks you to, of course,' he answered arrogantly.

'That is not a good enough reason,' she responded, watching the economical way he made himself look reasonably decent. 'And anyway, how do you know that helicopter was bringing someone to see you? You can't be the only important man on this island. Perhaps it's come to…'

Her voice trailed off, made to by the sound of the speedboat being lowered into the water. Leon glanced wryly at her, as if that sound said it all. Then he was coming to lean over her and placing another clinging kiss on her lips. 'Do as I ask, please,' he requested. 'It is important to me that you stay in here.'

'All right,' she agreed, but she didn't like the feeling she got that he was hiding her away like some dark and dirty secret.

'Thank you,' he smiled, then kissed the top of her nose and was gone, striding out of the room and firmly closing the door behind him, leaving Jemma feeling hurt and confused.

Surprisingly, she did sleep. She hadn't intended to—but, after lying there for several long minutes listening to the familiar roar of the speed-boat and the scuffling sounds of people boarding the boat, she felt her eyes drooping sleepily, and the next thing she knew she was being disturbed once again by the swishing sound of the helicopter blades swooping low over the yacht as it sped away.

She sat up, struggling to bring her fuzzy mind into focus. Then she remembered, and climbed quickly off the bed to dress and go in search of Leon.

She found him in the main salon, standing with a cup of coffee in his hand staring out of the window. 'I presume I can come out now,' she drawled sarcastically.

He didn't answer or even turn to greet her, and Jemma paused on the threshold of the room, a cold sense of alarm dispersing her sense of injury.

'Leon?' she questioned anxiously. 'Is something wrong?'

He made an effort to pull himself together. 'Of course not,' he said, turning to smile at her. 'Actually,' he added, 'we have been invited to a party tonight.'

'A party?' She blinked, not understanding the mixed vibrations she was receiving from him. One set warned her he was furiously angry about something, and the other set were saying he was as relaxed as any man could be.

'Yes. A birthday party to be exact. Have you had breakfast?' he enquired suddenly. She shook her head. 'Then I will order you something.' Smoothly he walked over to the telephone and punched in the number which would connect him with the galley. 'Inside or on the sun-deck?' he asked.

She blinked, shaking her head in confusion. 'I... Here, I think,' she decided absently, wishing she could work out what was going on here, because she was sure that something was. 'Whose birthday party is it?' she asked him frowningly.

There was a distinct pause before he answered though he tried to cover it up by making the most of replacing the telephone receiver and straightening the twisted cord. Then, 'My father's,' he informed her.

His father's? A sudden thought hit her. 'Leon, y-your father does know about me, doesn't he? Th-that we're married and I am—pregnant?'

Another pause. Then, 'No,' he told her, 'he doesn't know about you—or the child.' That stiff smile touched his mouth again. 'So you will both come as a—pleasant surprise to him tonight, won't you?'

Will we? Jemma sank heavily into a chair, that feeling of dread emulsifying. She was remembering the Greek girl from the wealthy family Cassie had once mentioned, and knew without a doubt that, far from being a pleasant surprise for his father, she was going to be the complete opposite.

'I don't want to go,' she said dully.

'And why not? I thought you wanted to know about my family,' he reminded her, adding drily, 'Well, tonight you will get your chance.'

But Jemma shook her head. 'No,' she repeated. 'Not like this. Not just dumped on them with no prior warning. It wouldn't be fair, not on them, not on me. I won't do it.' She shook her head. 'Go on your own, if you like, Leon, but I shall remain here on the yacht, if you don't mind.'

'But I do mind,' he drawled, and suddenly that hard, cool core in him that he rarely ever turned on her was very evident in the air. She looked up, saw the intractable expression on his face, and her heart sank. He was standing across the room, leaning against the window-frame, but he might as well have been sitting behind his desk in an office somewhere on the other side of the world for the distance she suddenly felt between them. 'You are my wife now, Jemma,' he reminded her. 'And as my wife you will accompany me to my father's house tonight and be presented to him as such.'

'And the woman your father had already picked out for you to marry?' she cried. 'Will she be there, also?'

Surprise flickered in his eyes, followed by almost instant comprehension. 'Cassie, I presume,' he drawled. Then, on a sigh, 'All right,' he conceded. 'So, it is not going to be a—pleasant evening. But whatever happens there tonight, *agape mou*, none of it is going to change a single thing for us.'

'You're sure about that?' Her voice sounded uncertain and pleaded for reassurance. 'What if your father throws you out on your ear for marrying yourself to the likes of me?'

Leon actually laughed at that, albeit harshly. 'I can positively assure you, my darling, that on meeting you, throwing me out will be the last thing on my father's mind!'

CHAPTER TEN

THEN why do I feel a bit as the lamb must feel when being led off for the slaughter? Jemma wondered miserably hours later as she stood in her bathrobe, staring at the several beautiful evening gowns Leon had provided for her, hating every one of them. 'Or worse,' she muttered, 'as if I'm about to attend my own wake?'

'Did you say something?'

Leon appeared at the half-open door, already dressed in an exquisitely cut taupe linen suit and a loose-fitting cream shirt left open at the throat to reveal the rich brown skin. He looked sleek and expensive and so darned attractive that her mouth went dry, her senses, just like the first time she'd ever set eyes on him, veering madly off course.

'You're not dressed!' he proclaimed the absolute obvious.

'Nothing fits!' she snapped, her eyes sparkling the threat of war if he wasn't careful. 'What use is all this—couture elegance to me—' she waved a scornful hand at the outfits which had been delivered to the yacht barely an hour ago '—when I'm six months pregnant and blown up like a stupid balloon?'

'Have you tried any of them on?' His voice sounded velvet-smooth in contrast to her shrill onslaught.

'Why bother?' she derided, moving to sit down on the dressing-stool. She stretched her bare feet out in front of her and stared mulishly at them. 'I just know they won't fit.'

Leon studied her in silence for a moment, seeing what to him what must look like a silly pregnant woman having

140

a temperamental fit! When really she was just plain frightened. She did not want to go. She had, in fact, turned so chicken inside that she was actually shaking like a leaf.

'*Agape mou*—' he walked further into the room '—I had these clothes flown in specially from Athens—'

'I know that!' she responded scornfully.

Couture dresses from couture houses with couture labels stitched inside, transported from Athens to Argostólion by special courier on one of the Stephanades private planes! She hadn't even known they owned their own planes until she'd discovered how the dresses arrived. Just as she hadn't realised—thick, stupid fool that she was—just how wealthy a family she had married herself into until she'd seen the stir they caused when they sailed into the island's capital of Argostólion this afternoon.

'It doesn't mean they will fit,' she reiterated glumly.

'Maternity clothes,' Leon said quietly.

'What?' Her chin came off her chest so that she could stare at him.

He sighed impatiently. 'I may be a mere man,' he mocked, 'but I do have some sense. These are garments specially designed for a woman in your condition.'

He was not mere anything, Jemma thought peevishly as she slid her eyes back to the four dresses hanging on the outside of the wardrobe. They didn't look like maternity wear. One was a slinky blue thing that looked from here as if it poured itself down to the ground. The next was short straight and black, and she knew, because she'd looked, that it had no back in it whatsoever. The red one was pure Ginger Rogers with a gathered layer of fine georgette over a satin underdress. And the last one was white, short and strapless, made in an unusual fabric that was soft and stretchy and as light as air—and looked as though it would fit her rather like an elastic tube would—hiding nothing.

None of them was suitable. 'Specially designed or not,'

she grunted, 'I would rather wear one of your shirts than any of them.'

'Fine,' Leon said, deliberately, she suspected, taking the wind out of her bad-tempered sails. 'If that is what you will feel most comfortable in, then wear one.' He shrugged as if he didn't care less. 'But make up your mind quickly because the car will be here in ten minutes to pick us up.'

'Chauffeur-driven, I presume,' she jeered.

'Jemma!' He sighed. 'What is the matter with you?' He glanced at his watch, solid gold and glinting against his dark brown wrist. 'You have done nothing but mock me since we arrived here this afternoon! What have I done to deserve it?'

'Nothing,' she mumbled, and he hadn't—not really. If anything, Leon had been as pleasant and attentive as a man could be since he'd told her about tonight. Soothing her into a false sense of security, that bitchy voice in her head taunted. She let out a short sigh of defeat, and looked uncertainly back at the dresses. 'You choose,' she told him. 'I'm just too nervous to make up my mind.'

He looked about to argue, his good mood ruined by her peevish manner. Then he saw the honest anxiety in her deep blue eyes and sighed heavily. 'Jemma, you have to trust me. I won't let them lay a single finger on you.'

'Maybe not,' she agreed. 'But you can't stop them looking at me as though I were a rogue cow who's just run off with their prize bull!'

'Prize bull, am I?' He grinned, sharp even teeth gleaming white between his attractive lips. 'Then you had better wear the red,' he decided ruefully.

Jemma looked at the red, then shook her head. 'It's long and it must be thirty degrees out there. I'll be too hot in it.'

'Which therefore cuts out the blue, also,' he said, 'which leaves only the black or the white.'

'I don't want to wear black.' She would really feel as if

she was going to a wake in black. 'And the white one is too—clingy-looking. They'll know at a glance why you married me if I wore that!'

Silence. Jemma wasn't sure what she had just said to make him react like that, but Leon was suddenly very still and very grim-faced. She soon found out. 'Are you ashamed, by any chance, of the fact that you carry our child?' he questioned silkily.

'No!' she denied. 'Of course I'm not!'

'Ashamed of me, then?' he suggested.

'Don't be stupid, Leon!' she scoffed. 'Why should I be ashamed of you?'

'Then it has to be yourself you are ashamed of,' he decided, walking towards her with a mood about him that had her jumping warily to her feet.

'I'm not ashamed of anything!' she snapped as he reached out and took hold of her upper arms.

'Good,' he said. 'Because no wife of mine has anything to be ashamed of, do you hear?' He gave her a small shake. 'And neither does she have to hide the evidence of our lovemaking as if it were some dirty secret!'

She winced visibly at his cutting words, but found she could not deny there was a hint of truth in them.

Letting go of her, he moved away, his back stiff with anger. 'Be ready to leave in ten minutes or be sure, Jemma,' he threatened, 'I shall come and dress you myself!'

She wore the white, and was surprised to discover that, far from clinging to every generous curve of her, it had a clever cut to it that made it skim rather flatteringly. She left her hair down, mainly because it gave her greater confidence to feel the long, twisting waves brushing against the sun-kissed skin of her shoulders. And, on impulse, she added a second protection, with a large white silk-fringed shawl which she draped around her shoulders.

Leon was standing by the salon window frowning out at

the pitch-black night, but he turned when he heard her come in, then went still, his eyes dark and appraising as they ran slowly over her from her white strappy mules to the free-flowing richness of her sun-streaked hair.

'Beautiful,' he said simply, and held out his hands in a 'what else can I say?' kind of compliment that warmed her all the way through. Then he was coming towards her, a sudden sober expression on his face.

'I have something I want you to wear for me,' he murmured, producing a flat velvet box from his pocket. 'They will expect to see it,' he explained, and flicked open the lid.

Jemma stared down at it, and felt an odd chill clutch at her heart. It was a necklace. Big and conspicuous, almost gaudy with its huge sparkling diamonds surrounded by rich dark rubies. Priceless it had to be; she did not even think of questioning its authenticity. But it was ugly to the point that she actually shuddered, and was relieved when Leon said drily, 'I know, it's awful. But it was my mother's and they will expect to see it on you—even though it was a well known fact that she hated it too.'

His mother's. Somehow hearing that changed her whole impression of the necklace. 'Did your father give it to her?' she asked with sudden insight.

'Yes.' Leon's smile was wry. 'Says a lot for his taste, doesn't it? It was his first big social mistake and he's going to hate being reminded of it when he sees it on you—if you'll wear it for me, that is.'

'You like riling him, don't you?' Jemma noted drily.

'Love it,' he admitted. 'You see, he married my mother simply to get his hands on the Leonadis fortune, then proceeded to make her life hell until the day she died.'

Oh, my, Jemma thought as suddenly lots of missing pieces from the puzzle began to slot neatly into place. So, the Leonadis Corporation had belonged to his mother's family and not his father. It had never occurred to her to question the reason for the two different names.

'And your brother?' she asked. 'Where does he fit into all of this?'

'Half-brother,' he corrected. 'Nico was born just eight months after my father remarried, which was six months after my mother died.'

'How old were you?' she questioned gently.

'Eight.' He paused, a sudden flash of pain hitting his features. 'Anthia was my father's mistress before and during his marriage to my mother,' he said, then added flatly, 'She wanted everything my mother had—even this necklace.'

'I'll wear it,' Jemma said, and accepted the kiss he pressed to her forehead for what it was—a thank-you for her understanding.

'Turn around and hold up your hair.'

She did so reluctantly, shivering as the cold, heavy necklace came to rest against her warm skin. She looked down at it, seeing the way the jewels flashed in the overhead light. 'I feel as gaudy as a Christmas tree,' she complained.

Leon kissed her exposed nape. 'I promise to replace it with something more tasteful at the first opportunity I get,' he vowed, settling her hair back about her sun-kissed shoulders. 'In fact,' he added as he turned her to face him again, 'I never did get you that special gift in return for the one you gave to me.' His mouth went ruefully awry, as though he did not like himself much for the omission. 'I owe you, *agape mou*. I—'

'But you did give me my gift, Leon,' she inserted softly. 'A beautiful gift. One I wouldn't change for the world.' Taking hold of his hand, she laid it tenderly on their child.

His eyes went black, emotion burning up from somewhere deep inside him, then he was pulling her into his arms. He didn't kiss her, but just held her very close for a moment, and Jemma felt tears sting at the back of her eyes because she knew she had just unwittingly reached in and touched a very vulnerable part of him.

'I do not deserve you,' he murmured as he drew away.

'Mmm,' she agreed, teasing him with the gentle humour in her eyes.

Yet, rather than making him smile with her, if anything he looked suddenly angry. His hands tightened on her shoulders. 'Jemma,' he said impulsively. 'I—' Then he stopped himself, impatience straightening the softer line of his mouth. 'Let's go,' he muttered instead, his mood dark with purpose as he led the way off the yacht to where a dark limousine was waiting at the bottom of the companionway.

A white-uniformed chauffeur jumped to open the rear door for them. Leon saw Jemma inside then joined her, the mask of cool sophistication she only ever saw him wear when they were in others' company slipping smoothly into place now.

They didn't speak, and Jemma fixed her attention on what was going on beyond the car window as they flashed smoothly by invitingly lit tavernas and bars with their tables packed with scantily dressed holidaymakers who looked tanned and happy and relaxed.

As they must have looked last night, she thought wistfully, wishing they were back in Fiskárdho wearing the casual clothes of the tourist and enjoying a simple meal in congenial company.

Last night had been one of the sweetest she'd ever spent—mainly because Leon had made it that way. Tonight promised to be the opposite in every way.

Leaving the main part of the town behind them, they began to climb through residential suburbs then out into a starlit countryside. To their right, the sea shone like billowing black silk with the silvered light of the moon on it. And she could just make out the dark bulk of land on the other side of the water curving like an elephant's trunk around the Gulf of Argostólion.

'Lassi,' Leon murmured when her face lit with interest as they dropped into sudden bright, busy life again. 'It is the main holiday resort on the island, because of the good sandy beaches here.'

'It looks very lively,' she remarked, her voice unknowingly wistful.

'Hmm,' was all he said to that. 'My father's villa is not far from here,' he told her instead.

That brought back her tension, and she sat quietly beside him as they turned off the main road, taking a narrow lane that went beneath a canopy of trees which made it difficult to see much after that, with no street-lights to ease the darkness, until they slowed suddenly and turned in through a stone-arched gateway. And she felt her tension increase when she saw the rows of expensive cars lining the wide driveway where the two-storey building at the end of it looked more like a medium-sized hotel than a private home.

The car came to a stop at the bottom of a set of shallow steps which led up to the wide arched doorway where two white-shirted servants stood waiting to receive the guests.

The chauffeur jumped out of the car to open the rear door for them. But when Jemma went to alight, Leon laid a hand on her arm and shook his head. 'Wait,' he said, and climbed out on the other side, coming around to help her alight himself.

It was an oddly courteous gesture and one which warmed her even if it did nothing to ease the nervous tension from her stiffened limbs as she walked beside him.

The two doormen jerked to attention as they walked in, by the respectful looks on their faces, recognising Leon instantly. He ignored them with that arrogance which used to annoy her, but she was beginning to read it better now, and see it for the defence mechanism it was to him.

Leon was not at all comfortable being here in his father's house. Not that it would show to anyone else, she noted as she kept pace with his smooth, easy stride with his arm comfortingly warm around her waist.

The entrance hall was big and luxurious, with a pure white marble floor and modern black furniture set against white walls. It led right through from the front to the back of the house, and by the emptiness of the rooms either side of them Jemma had to assume that the party was taking place elsewhere, which proved to be outside, as she realised when Leon led her down the marble hallway towards the growing hum of chatter coming from the garden beyond the open rear doors.

They were late. It took Jemma just ten seconds to realise it as they paused on the threshold to look out on the subtly lit garden where—at a quick and frightening guess—about one hundred people sat around the tables set upon a large paved area in front of a circular swimming-pool.

Not just late, but rudely late, she realised, when she noticed the coffee-cups and liqueur glasses on the table. And deliberately so if she was reading Leon accurately.

As if picking up on her thoughts, he murmured softly, 'It looks as though we have timed it just right.'

But before she had time to ponder on this last cryptic remark someone noticed them, and the woman's surprised gasp brought all heads turning in their direction.

It was amazing how total silence could deafen, Jemma thought as she felt her body go heavy with dread. She slipped her hand beneath Leon's jacket and clutched at a fistful of his soft linen shirt.

'Easy,' he soothed her quietly. But Jemma could feel the tension in him. He was as uptight as she was.

'So, you deign to arrive at last.'

Two things hit her at that moment: one, that the voice which spoke was harsh and angry, and the other that it spoke in English, which surprised her. The anger did not.

Leon's father, it had to be, she assumed, because the man just rising to his feet was simply an older version of the man standing beside her. On his right sat the most exquisitely beautiful woman with the coldest pair of black eyes Jemma had ever seen, and on her right reclined a young man who could only be Leon's half-brother because, again, he looked so incredibly like him—except for the thinness of his mouth. That had a slightly peevish look about it, and cold, like the woman he sat beside.

It was then she saw the two empty places on the other side of Leon's father, and felt a wave of embarrassment wash over her. Those had to have been their places for dinner.

'Father.' Beside her, Leon acknowledged the other man with a smooth nod. 'Many happy returns for your birthday.'

His father's mouth tightened angrily. 'Is that all you are going to say?' he demanded.

'No.' Leon nudged Jemma into movement. She didn't want to go, so he had to exert pressure to her shoulders to make her, and she found herself walking on shaking legs towards the clutch of tables. 'I wish you many more of them,' he added politely.

There was one small comfort, she noted tensely as she felt the prickling sting of one hundred pairs of eyes pierce her. No one had noticed her condition yet, simply because their eyes were locked on the awful necklace gleaming between the fringed folds of her otherwise concealing shawl.

A great diversion, she acknowledged half hysterically, her fingers taking an even tighter grip on that precious piece of shirt she was clinging to as a whisper of gasps and murmurs skittered around the garden. The woman seated beside Leon's father was staring at Jemma's throat in something close to horror, his half-brother stiffening in his seat. Yet no one spoke—no one seemed daring enough—as Leon guided them between their tables and chairs until he came to a stop beside his father, his arm resting across her trembling shoulders.

The older man had been staring at the necklace too, but now his glance flicked up to clash with his son's. There was a question in his eyes—and a strange touch of excitement that Jemma did not understand. He seemed to swallow rather thickly. 'Is this—?'

He was interrupted, not by Leon, but by the woman sitting to his father's right. 'We expected you at seven, Leon,' she censured, coming stiffly to her feet. She was tall and incredibly slender—and with an aristocratic manner about her that put Jemma in awe. She flashed the necklace a hard look, but other than that honed her cold eyes exclusively on Leon. 'It is now gone nine o'clock!'

There was another moment's short, sharp silence while Leon continued to hold his father's gaze, strange messages, Jemma sensed, flashing from one man to the other, then he flicked his eyes to the other woman. 'Anthia,' he acknowledged. 'As beautiful as ever, I see.'

She did not take the remark as a compliment, her cold face stiffening. And it was only then, and at such close quarters to her, that Jemma realised that she had to be in her late fifties. It was just that she had cared for her body and face through the years, and it had paid off, because there was hardly an age-line on her.

'Were you deliberately trying to ruin your father's birthday?' she demanded. 'Does he not even get an apology from you for your rudeness?'

Leon leaned forward a little, the eye-to-eye contact between the two of them a formidable force in itself. 'Does my companion get an apology for the way you are deliberately ignoring her?' he threw back softly.

Jemma stiffened up like a board, even her chin going rigid on a complete overload of stress.

Again, the woman's eyes flicked to the necklace, and something close to panic spoiled their soulless expression before she was coolly back in control again. 'Since it is you who are so rudely late,' she drawled, 'I therefore think your…companion will understand why your introductions will have to wait until after we have finished here.' She made a gesture towards their listening audience with a long, languidly graceful white hand. 'As you very well know,' she went on tightly, 'your father is about to make an important announcement, and we would appreciate it if you would at least show some manners, and let him get on with it.'

Another moment's taut silence while Leon held the other woman's angry gaze. Then, 'But of course, Anthia, you are quite right,' he conceded with a sudden back-down from the confrontation that everyone, even Jemma, had felt brewing. 'Father must be allowed to continue—no matter what,' he agreed. 'But first I am afraid I really must show my poor manners yet again, and insist on making my own small announcement. *Agape mou*,' he murmured, drawing Jemma closer to his side, 'I would like you to meet my father, Dimitri Stephanades. Father,' he continued softly, 'my beautiful wife, Jemma.'

Stunned silence. It drummed in her ears. Dry-mouthed—terrified how she would be received—Jemma lifted her eyes to Dimitri Stephanades's, the tension so fraught inside her that she could feel her blood-pressure rising perilously. Leon's hand tightened on her shoulder as if to give her courage, and she swallowed nervously, her dry tongue sweeping around her parched lips as she forced a trembling hand upwards to offer it tentatively to the older version of Leon.

How it happened she was never sure, whether by accident

or design. But as she lifted her arm, Leon shifted his resting
arm, catching her shawl so that the fine silk slithered from
her shoulders and fell in a whisper to the floor.

An audible gasp shot around the garden, the necklace
losing its impact as all eyes honed in on her obvious state
of pregnancy. Someone knocked over a drink, the glass
splintering noisily as it smashed against a wine bottle.
Someone else giggled, a nervous sound that was cut off as
acutely as it had begun. And Jemma stood, paralysed and
feeling utterly exposed, as Leon's father went perfectly
white, his eyes fixed unblinkingly on her body.

Then Leon was saying in a tight commanding whisper,
'Take her hand, Father. Welcome your new daughter into
the family.'

Dimitri Stephanades jerked his eyes back to his son's.
There was definite shock written there and something else
Jemma could not interpret but knew that, whatever it was,
it went very deep. Then he swallowed, and said something
hoarsely in Greek. Leon nodded. 'Most definitely mine!' he
said with a fierce driving possessiveness. 'My child. My
son!' he added triumphantly. 'I have seen him living and
moving with my own eyes!'

Shock hit her broadside, closing her eyes and draining
her face of the last vestige of colour, sending her outstretched hand dropping to her side where it clenched into
a tight, trembling fist. A son. Leon knew their child was a
boy, and her mind flicked back to the day they had visited
the doctor and Leon had slipped away to speak to him pri-
vately while Jemma got dressed again. The doctor had
asked while they watched the scan of their child whether
they wished to know its sex, and Jemma had said no, firmly,
because she wanted to enjoy the element of surprise.

Now Leon had spoiled that forever, and in front of one
hundred witnesses. Ruthless she knew him to be, or he
would not be the formidable force he was to the business

world. Angry with his father she had known. But this angry—this ruthless, that he would use her as some kind of weapon that was at this very moment causing some great chain reaction among the murmuring crowd, and that he had destroyed forever her trust in him?

She wanted to turn and run, get out of here and away from all these people and their little power games—because she was in no doubt that it was a struggle for power that was taking place right now—but her legs would not allow her to move. They were stiff and tingling with the imminent threat of completely collapsing beneath her and she knew the only thing that was holding her upright was Leon's arm—treacherous though it was—clamped about her thickened waist.

Someone tried to say something, her voice sharp with shock. But Leon's father waved her into silence. It was Leon's stepmother, her black eyes glazed with horror as she sank heavily back into her chair. Then Dimitri Stephanades was looking pleadingly at his eldest son.

Leon did not move, neither physically nor emotionally. 'You have an announcement to make,' he reminded him. 'I suggest you do it—then we talk, I think.'

It was so obviously the conditional terms of a victor to the defeated that it seemed decidedly odd, even to Jemma's totally stunned mind, that his father's eyes should suddenly look fire-bright with what she could only describe as elation.

'Of course,' he agreed, and almost dutifully turned to face the silenced party.

'As you all no doubt know,' he began smoothly enough, 'today I reached my sixty-fifth year, and the doctors, wise men that they are, have advised me it is time to abdicate my throne and go tend my vines.' A ripple of nervous laughter skittered around the garden. 'Let no one think it is an easy thing to accept that I am getting too old to maintain control of what has been my life's work, for it is not,' he confessed. 'But, for my own health's sake—and the sake of the Leonadis Corporation—I have decided to hand over the reins of power into more—capable hands.' His tone alone said he was doing so reluctantly. 'I have two sons,' he continued flatly, 'both of whom I am undoubtedly proud of, both equally capable of reigning supreme in my place. I therefore had a choice,' he explained. 'To split the company into two and give them one half each, or do what any wise businessman should do and keep the company strong in unity. I chose unity,' he informed the listening throng. 'Consequently, several weeks ago I had drawn up a legal document, laying down the grounds on which either son could ascend into my place. It involved several points I considered necessary before I would hand my life's work over to their care, the most important of these being, of course, the continuance of the Stephanades line. I therefore made this proviso…' He paused and took in a breath of air. 'The first of them to provide me with the grandson I so much desire will take my place as chairman of the Leonadis Corporation. This, of course, was to be the nucleus of my announcement tonight but—' the twisted smile appeared again '—as you can all see, my son Leonadis has pre-empted me. So…' he lifted his eyes, sending them on a cool scan of his rapt audience, then picked up the half-filled champagne glass standing in front of him '…please stand and raise your glasses to Leon and his wife—Jemma…' The name fell stiltedly off his tongue. 'And, because Leon informs me it is so and I have never had any reason to doubt his word, my as yet unborn grandson. I therefore announce Leon as my immediate successor. *Yássas*!' he concluded, and drank.

Silence—it was both spectacular and nullifying. Then the place seemed to erupt as a hundred people came to their feet, and while Jemma stood, numbed through to the very core of her being by the depth of Leon's usage of her, they raised their glasses and said, '*Yássas!*' just as she sank into a deep, dark faint.

CHAPTER ELEVEN

JEMMA came around slowly, the sound of voices raised in anger and the blurred impression that she was not going to like what she was coming back to keeping her sunk in a semi-conscious haze. She vaguely recalled Leon carrying her inside the house and laying her gently on something smooth and soft, but other than that she did not remember—and did not want to.

'But this is madness, Dimitri!' a shrill voice suddenly cried, high-pitched and impossible to ignore. 'We know nothing about this woman—or the child she carries! It could well not even be Leon's child!'

'Are you suggesting I am a fool, Anthia?' From much, much closer, Leon's voice was quiet but deadly grim.

'No. But I am suggesting that you would sink to anything to grab full power!'

'Including claiming another man's child as my own, it seems.'

'And why not?' the cold voice challenged. 'It is all a little too convenient, is it not? After all, who is she? What is she? Why is it that we knew nothing of her existence until tonight?'

'She is my wife,' Leon stated harshly. 'The rest is none of your business!'

'It is if this is just a deliberate ploy to disinherit your brother!'

'Half-brother,' Leon corrected. 'There is a subtle but fundamental difference. The Leonadis Corporation belonged to my mother, not his.'

'Enough,' another deep voice commanded. 'This has

gone far enough! Leon, you will remember, please, that the Leonadis company is mine, regardless of its origin. And you, Anthia, will not imply that Leon is a cheat. He is my son, and his loyalty to me has always been unimpeachable.'

'Until tonight,' Dimitri's wife could not resist adding.

God, thought Jemma, she could taste the bitterness and hostility. It sickened her, turned her stomach and made her wonder just what she had been thrust into here.

She moved, struggling to push herself into a sitting position, and brought an icy hand up to cover her clammy brow.

'Jemma.' Leon was beside her in an instant, squatting down to bring his face at a level with her own. He looked grim and anxious, his eyes raking over her colourless face. Behind him Jemma could see the small clutch of stiff and angry people eyeing her grimly from the other side of the room. 'How do you feel?' he murmured concernedly. 'Any pain, discomfort? I grabbed you quite roughly when you fainted. And you have been out a long time.' Frowning, he reached out to brush a stray lock of hair from her ice-cold cheek. 'It concerned me enough to call the doctor,' he informed her. 'He will be here soon.'

'Safeguarding your interests, Leon?' she jeered, shrugging his hand away.

His mouth tightened, but he did not retaliate, studying her frowningly instead, calculating the extent of her physical distress, the emotional one already self-evident.

A glass of water appeared in front of her and she went to wave it away, but a soft female voice urged, 'Drink; it will help.' And she looked up to find herself staring into the kindest face she had seen here tonight. Older than herself, the woman was smiling encouragingly. Jemma took the glass, but her fingers were shaking so badly that she couldn't drink from it, and the woman closed her own warmer fingers around Jemma's and gently helped the glass to her lips. She was glad she was there, glad because her elegant figure effectively blocked Jemma off from the rest of the room, and glad because it meant she did not have to concentrate on the man squatting in front of her.

A few tentative sips at the cool water, and Jemma felt her rocked senses begin to settle. She smiled her thanks at the woman and let her take the glass from her.

'Jemma—'

'Don't speak to me!' she flashed.

The woman looked surprised as though she couldn't believe anyone would dare speak to Leon Stephanades in that tone. 'You have found your ideal match, I see,' she drawled mockingly to Leon.

'More than my match,' he said with a tight forced smile. 'She beats me with her broomstick twice a week.'

'Be careful I don't decide to turn you into a snake!' Jemma snapped.

The woman laughed, and so did Leon, but there was a moment's angry flash in his eyes that said he had more than understood her acid meaning. Then he sighed heavily and lowered his gaze to where he had his hands clenched between his bent knees.

'You bastard,' she whispered threadily.

'I know,' he acknowledged quietly.

The doctor arrived just then, slicing through the tension in the room by briskly ordering everyone out—except for Leon, who straightened to shake his hand then moved stiffly to stand behind the long sofa Jemma was sitting on. He was a short, stocky man, Greek to the marrow in his bones, but his grasp of English was superb, and it was only as he flashed a series of comprehensive questions at her that Jemma realised hardly anyone present tonight had spoken in Greek.

Maybe it would have been kinder for her if they had, she concluded as she suffered the usual physical examination with Leon's sharp eyes on her looking for the smallest sign of discomfort. Understanding nothing would have left her sublimely ignorant to what was going on.

Instead, she had heard all, and now knew all. Leon had married her for one reason only. She conveniently suited his urgent requirements.

And it hurt, hurt so much that she couldn't even look at him without feeling ravaged.

'Right,' the doctor said firmly, removing his stethoscope and shoving it into his little black bag. 'You will be pleased to know that there is nothing drastically wrong with either of you!' He smiled briefly at his own joke.

For the life of her, Jemma couldn't smile with him, so she took diversionary tactics, by straightening her dress and levering herself back into a sitting position. She saw Leon's hand snake out to help her, but ignored it. She didn't want him touching her. She didn't want to look at him ever again.

'But,' the doctor continued, 'we are in the middle of a heatwave—even by Greek standards—and partying in your condition, Mrs Stephanades, is perhaps asking for trouble. I suggest you take it easy for a few days. Enjoy making your husband dance attendance on you.' Another joke and another smile he expected to be returned. Leon might have done, but Jemma just lowered her head. 'Then come to my surgery—perhaps Friday?—and we will check you over more thoroughly then.'

Leon saw him out, leaving her alone in the elegant room of his father's house where the beautiful cream and grey décor looked as vapid as she felt. Then her baby kicked, and Jemma smiled sadly to herself. Perhaps not quite that vapid, she allowed, stroking a tender hand over the shifting mound.

The door opened, and she looked up sharply, a fizz of defensive rebelliousness stiffening her spine—only to sag again when she saw not Leon coming back into the room, but the woman who had brought her the glass of water.

'The party goes on, and Leon is grilling the doctor,' she said ruefully. 'So I thought I would come and keep you company.' As gentle in movement as her manner was, she walked across the soft grey-carpeted floor and sat herself down next to Jemma. 'How do you feel?' she asked.

'As well as can be expected, I suppose,' Jemma mocked, not even trying to paper over what had really caused her faint tonight. It would be a waste of time anyway, since this woman had been a party to the row which had followed it in here.

'This is a strong family,' the other woman remarked, 'with each and every one of them a force to be reckoned with. They fight each other as ruthlessly as they fight any battle in business.'

'English,' Jemma murmured irrelevantly. 'They all speak in English.'

'Oh, did you not know? Dimitri is English! Or at least,' she amended, 'he was born in England to Greek parents. They emigrated there after a—series of misfortunes left them with little else to do but start afresh somewhere new.' She was choosing her words carefully. 'He thinks in English—though his Greek is good. But around him, whatever nationality you are, people tend to speak English. He expects it.'

'You seem to know an awful lot about them,' Jemma observed guardedly. 'Does that make you one of them?'

'Ah!' For some reason, she was thoroughly amused. 'No, I am not,' she assured Jemma, 'but I think perhaps it is time we formally introduced ourselves, since manners this evening seem to have been sadly lacking.' She held out her hand. 'I am Melva Markopoulou, a—very old friend of Leon's.'

There was a look in the woman's smiling eyes that

Jemma could not interpret—a hint of mockery spiced with something else too intricate to catch. Jemma took the hand and returned shyly, 'Jemma Dav—'

'Stephanades,' a cool voice from the doorway corrected.

'Ah.' Melva's eyes lifted to their intruder. 'Leon, your wife and I were getting to know each other.'

'So I see,' he said, coming further into the room. He was looking at Jemma, but her eyes were blank and staring, focusing on nothing. 'You are feeling more yourself, *agape mou*?'

The endearment made her shudder. But, 'Yes,' she answered, and forced her eyes to focus on a point somewhere between the rigid set of his jaw and the dark brown skin at his throat. 'May we leave now?'

'Of course,' he concurred. 'The car is being brought round now.'

'Good,' she said, and made to get up. Leon reached out to help her and once again Jemma pulled violently away from his touch. 'No,' she rasped, and he stepped back jerkily.

She sensed the other two exchanging glances and knew she had to get away from here before she split wide apart. Her legs were barely supporting her and a hot sense of agitation was disrupting her insides. 'M-my shawl,' she murmured, glancing distractedly around her. 'I c-can't see my shawl—'

'Jemma—'

'Go and collect your wife's shawl, Leon!' Melva inserted quickly. She was on her feet and gently taking Jemma by the arm. 'I shall walk Jemma to the door and we will meet you there.'

There was a short tense moment when Leon thought to argue, then more glances passed between the other two and he sighed impatiently and walked away.

'Please, Jemma!' Melva appealed urgently as soon as he

had gone. 'Try not to condemn him out of hand for what took place tonight! It was more his father's fault than anyone's—and of course that avaricious bitch, Anthia's. She has been planning towards the evening—with a different result, of course—for twenty-eight years! She is shrewd and clever and totally without scruple. Leon had to use his weapons carefully or she would have twisted things to suit herself!'

As Leon had twisted things to suit himself, Jemma likened. 'Just what is Leon to you,' she demanded, 'that you come down so completely on his side?'

'She is the woman my father picked out for me to marry.' Once again, Leon had come upon them without their realising it. 'But I obliged Melva by refusing to accede to his threats—did I not, *agape mou*?'

'Don't tease the poor girl, Leon!' Melva scolded. 'Neither of us had any wish to be married to the other, and it really was as simple as that!'

Laughing up at him, she moved the few steps away from Jemma to kiss Leon on both cheeks. What she did next was so deftly done that Jemma wondered afterwards if she would have noticed if she had not been so hypersensitive to everything happening around her, but somehow, by the time Melva moved away from Leon again, Jemma's shawl was in her hands and she turned—still smiling—to settle carefully the fine white silk around Jemma's shoulders.

The thoughtful gesture brought a brief wash of tears to her eyes. She knew she didn't want him to touch her, and she was saving both of them from any more discomfort.

'I am well known on the island,' she informed Jemma gravely. 'If you ever find yourself in need of a friend, then just ask and you will be directed to my home.'

'I... Thank you,' Jemma whispered, but she knew she wouldn't take her up on it. She was Leon's friend, and therefore could not be Jemma's as well.

They drove back to the yacht in complete silence, the presence of the chauffeur making conversation impossible—of the kind they would have, anyway. And Jemma was glad. She had no wish to speak to Leon— or, worse, listen to him while he tried to justify what he had done.

There could be no justification. He had used her. From the moment he had walked back into her life, he had cold-bloodedly planned, calculated and manipulated—everything, from the ruthless way he'd played on her reliance on Trina, to the way he had spent the last three weeks personally supervising her return to good health with his aim focused entirely on this evening. Even the beauty of yesterday had been a coolly thought-out calculation! she realised as hot tears of hurt sped across her eyes. He must have seen her moment of unhappiness as a sign of discontent and the last thing he needed so close to his ultimate aim was an unhappy wife standing by his side! So he'd set out to woo her—woo her into the soft, contented woman he wanted her to be in front of his family, and she, fool that she was, had fallen for it all like a lemming walking blindly towards its own destruction.

And, all the time, he'd known something else that she did not know. He'd known the sex of the child she carried for him. A boy child. More tears burned and she blinked them angrily away. His ultimate weapon in a power game so despicable that it filled her with a bilious disgust of all of them—Leon *and* his family.

The car turned in through the security gates and came to a stop at the yacht. She was trying to open the door even as the engine died.

'Jemma—' Leon's hand on her arm sent a shudder of revulsion through her and she struck it away, not even looking at him as she got out of the car and walked quickly up the steps of the yacht.

She did not stop until she was in their stateroom with the

door locked firmly behind her. Then she walked into the bathroom, switched on the shower, stripped off her clothes and stepped beneath the stinging hot spray.

Arriving back in the bedroom, wrapped into her long white towelling robe, she stopped dead, surprised to find Leon standing by the darkened window.

He must have sensed what she was thinking because he murmured, 'I have a pass key to all the locks on board,' without turning to look at her.

Of course, she thought wryly. He would have, wouldn't he? It belonged to him, after all—which by his philosophy meant he had the right to open any door he chose to and damn the invasion of someone else's privacy! Just as he had been damning his invasion of her privacy since he'd decided to make her one of his precious possessions!

Well, never again. 'I'm tired,' she informed him stonily. 'Would you please leave?'

He turned to face her at that, his eyes dark and carefully guarded. 'We have to talk,' he said quietly.

Talk—? Her mouth tightened, losing all of its natural sensual softness. 'The way I read it, it has all already been said.'

'No,' he denied. 'There is a lot you haven't heard. A lot you need to know if you are to understand why I had to do what I did tonight.'

'Used me?' she mocked him bitterly. 'Used our child— and its sex!—as a means to an end, you mean?'

'You have to understand,' he persisted grimly, studiedly ignoring her pained remark. 'I was playing for high stakes tonight. I needed you on my side! Not bristling with indignation and openly despising me as you surely would have been if I had warned you what I was about to do!'

'And that excuses you, does it?' she demanded, blue eyes hot and bitter.

'No,' he conceded. 'It simply explains why I didn't tell

you. Look,' he sighed when she continued to wither him with her eyes, 'the company is mine by right! And there is not a person connected with the Leonadis name who does not know that it belonged to *my* mother, and her father and grandfather before that! I was even named Leonadis in anticipation of the day I take over! Of course I am not going to let anyone cheat me out of what is mine by right!'

'So you sacrificed my rights for your own.' She nodded in bitter understanding. 'How honourable!' she added scathingly.

He winced, but didn't try to defend himself from that attack. 'I had to do what I had to do!' he insisted instead. 'You heard my father tonight,' he went on harshly. 'His health is failing him. He has known for several months now that he is no longer fit to run a company the size of ours with the success he used to enjoy. But you also heard him say that accepting that point has not been easy for him. As he feels himself grow weaker he has to watch me grow stronger! He resents that, naturally! And, in a last-ditch attempt to prove his power over me—the *only* person worthy of taking over from him,' he said with angry conceit, 'he dredged up an old grievance of his—the one where he made the ultimate coup by marrying me off to Melva Markopoulou and so uniting two of the most powerful families on this island! He wanted to bow out on a high note. But, as always when he tries to bully me, I refused to comply! So he had that stupid document drawn up and proceeded to threaten me with it. It was a bluff!' he muttered on an angry shrug. 'Just a bluff! He plays these games with me all the time!' From nowhere, the memory of the newspaper article saying how his father had tied Leon's hands over the New York deal popped into Jemma's mind. 'But eventually he tires of the game, sees sense, gives in, if you like.' Another shrug. 'He's not a fool; he knows the company needs me! That I am its strength and its future! And, left to his own devices, he would eventually have withdrawn the threat. Except that Anthia got to hear of it.' His grim mouth tightened. 'And suddenly Nico is announcing his intention to marry and the damned document is mysteriously made public! Which means my father cannot withdraw it without looking a complete fool. So he begs me again. ''Marry Melva—marry anyone and get yourself a child before Nico beats you to it''!'

'So I was your father's scapegoat,' Jemma concluded, hurting in so many ways that she didn't know which one was the worst. 'How convenient it was to you both that you happened to find me like this!' she mocked. 'The ideal solution to your problem, in fact!'

He looked at her through hard, impatient eyes. 'If I attempted to deny that, you would not believe me, so I will not!' he snapped. 'But I will insist that you believe me when I say that even without the threat hanging over my head the consequences of my discovering you were pregnant with my child would not have changed. I would still have married you, Jemma. I—care for you. I always have.'

'Oh, yes,' she jeered. 'You cared enough to bring me on board this yacht and spend the last two weeks personally supervising my return to robust health so I wouldn't look so pathetic when you made your move tonight!'

He sighed, seeing no way past her bitterness. 'That is not true, Jemma,' he said grimly. 'And when you have calmed down a little, you will see that.'

'All I see,' she retaliated, 'is that everything you have done since you walked back into my life has been one huge deception. Everything,' she repeated thickly, bright tears of hurt and humiliation filling her eyes when she remembered the beauty of the day before. 'You used me,' she whispered tremulously.

'Yes,' he sighed, not even trying to deny it. 'I'm sorry

if that hurts you, but—yes—' He sighed again '—I used you.'

And it did hurt, hurt so deeply that she had to turn her back on him so that he would not see the tears burning in her eyes. It was as she turned that she saw it, glittering luridly among her tears, and in an act of sudden violence she snatched up the necklace from where she had tossed it angrily on her dressing-table top earlier, and threw it contemptuously at his chest.

'There,' she said as Leon caught it instinctively. 'One of your props returned to you. But I am afraid you will have to wait several months more for the other, more important one to arrive to complete your victory!'

'Dammit, Jemma!' he exploded, his rough voice shaking as he took a step towards her. 'You are blowing this up larger than—'

'Don't you dare touch me!' she choked, spinning away so that she didn't have to see the look of pained appeal in his eyes.

He muttered something in angry frustration, sending her spine stiff in rejection as he took another step towards her.

'Just leave me alone,' she whispered, pressing her clenched fist against her quivering mouth again.

There was another tense pause, when he seemed to hesitate. She couldn't look at him. If she had done she would have seen the anxiety pulling at his face, and the underlying burn of anger aimed entirely at himself.

Then he sighed heavily. 'All right,' he said. 'If that is what you want.' Then she heard him quietly let himself out of the cabin.

It was then the tears came, hot and pained and scalding. She let them flow, let her hurt and anger and miserable sense of disillusionment pour out with them.

When eventually the storm of weeping subsided, she

crawled into the bed and went to sleep still huddled in her robe.

The next morning she got up, dressed herself, plucked the bankroll of drachmas out of the drawer she had put it in and walked outside and right off the yacht. She did not stop to tell anyone where she was going, nor did she even attempt to look for Leon. She needed time, time to be herself again—to learn to be herself again and not the person Leon had been turning her into. So she walked across the quay and out of the security gates enclosing their private moorings, across the busy quayside road and turned down the first street leading away from the harbour, putting herself right out of sight of the yacht as quickly as she could, unaware that Leon stood against the boat's rail, watching her every step of the way, and unaware of the way he snapped out instructions to one of the crew who quickly scuttled after her.

She eventually found herself in what could only be the town square—a big place, flanked by brightly adorned tourist shops and cafés.

She picked a café at random and ordered herself fresh-orange juice and a bottle of chilled water, then sat back simply to let the world go by, her mind swept ruthlessly blank of anything even vaguely contentious.

It felt good, being just a simple tourist enjoying a simple breakfast in a simple café. And slowly, whatever had driven her to walk away as she had eased, until she began to feel a semblance of peace within herself.

After that, she spent the whole morning just wandering around the town, browsing through its narrow busy streets all tightly packed with interesting shops, and, in an absent, purely superficial kind of way, enjoying herself. The Kefallinían people were friendly, warm, and instinctively caring when they noticed her condition, going out of their way to find her a chair if she happened to walk into their shop, asking after her health, the baby's health. Nice people. Genuine people who made her want to weep because they reminded her so much of the man she had married—or the man she'd thought she had married.

Wretchedly, she swung her mind away from that. She didn't want to think of Leon—didn't think she could cope. It wasn't as if he'd told her lies! she reminded herself painfully. He'd just been so cleverly economical with the truth.

And even accepting all of that, accepting that he had married her for very specific reasons of his own did not hurt her as much as the way he had betrayed her with the sex of their baby.

The tears returned, burning at the back of her eyes and forcing her to swallow them down. To think, she scoffed cruelly at herself, I had actually let myself consider that he may love me!

What a fool!

Play with him and you're playing in the big league, someone had warned her once. Well, she'd played, and got burned—not once but twice.

You utter fool!

Could she go on living with a man like that? Did she want to?

It was then she saw it, and she stopped dead, her brain burning with a combination of horror and excitement at the sudden idea which popped unexpectedly into her head.

It was only a tiny place, its windows cluttered with posters advertising the services it sold. But it was the instantly recognisable logo of one of Britain's biggest airline companies that had caught her attention.

With the sun beating down on her uncovered head, she lifted a hand to shade her eyes. Her fingers were trembling. She wasn't surprised. The idea was so incredible that she could barely believe she was actually considering it!

Yet it was tempting—so very tempting—tempting enough to send her feet uncertainly into the shop...

Hot, tired, and ready for a nice cool shower followed by a long rest, Jemma stepped back on to the yacht, hoping Leon was not around to waylay her. Two crewmen watched her come aboard, but other than that she managed to slip quietly back to her own room, the coolness of the air-conditioning a relief after the fierce heat outside.

Walking over to her dressing-table, she dropped down wearily on the stool. She was clutching an envelope in her hand, and she gazed dully at it.

This was it. Her means of escape. Her heart shook, making her sigh heavily.

The price they'd quoted her was in drachmas, yet, even as she'd dug out her roll of notes and begun carefully counting them out, she hadn't really believed she would have enough. She had been wrong. Leon's idea of a few pounds turned out to be the equivalent of a few hundred pounds. Enough—more than enough to buy her a seat on a plane home to England.

It had been so easy—so damned simple that she had to believe it was fate that had sent her into the shop.

Saturday. The day after tomorrow. The envelope held her ticket to freedom. The day after tomorrow she would be flying home and away from Leon. She did not know what she was going to do when she got there, what she was going to live on or even where she was going to stay, but suddenly she knew it was the right thing to do. The only thing to do. She just couldn't stay with a man who could use her so carelessly. It hurt too much.

A sudden knock at the door had her jerking upright, and she spun around, eyes wide, face pale, heart palpitating so badly that she actually felt dizzy with it.

Leon. It had to be Leon. Only he would dare knock in that peremptory way.

'Jemma.' Not a question but a quietly issued command. It was him, and on a sudden spurt of panic she opened her dressing-table drawer and pushed the envelope in it, what was left of her money following it before she turned back to stare at the door.

'Jemma!' His voice was not so quiet this time, and the knock was sharp with impatience. Pulling herself together, she schooled her face into a cool mask and went to open the door.

He looked just the same as always, she noted bitterly. A little tired maybe, but no sign of guilt spoiling his handsome face, no hint of remorse. She stared coldly at him, hating the wretched ache she felt stir inside her, and turned back into the room. He followed, closing the door behind him.

'Where have you been?' he asked quietly enough.

Still she bristled. 'Out,' she said, moving jerkily to close the dressing table drawer when she saw she had left it open. 'Why?' she challenged, fingers curling around the smooth cedarwood as she turned back to face him. 'Do you have a problem with that?'

His eyes had narrowed on her hands, making her heart thump agitatedly in her breast. Did he know what she'd done? Could he have found out?

'No,' he answered. 'But it would have been—kinder if you had warned someone about what you intended to do.'

'Like you do, you mean?' Her chin came up, her meaning excruciatingly clear.

Still, he ignored it. 'The doctor said you should rest. Yet you've been gone for hours. Didn't it occur to you I may be worried?'

'For whom?' she goaded. 'Me or the child?'

'Both,' he said. Then, with a hint of impatience at last, 'Listen, I did not come here to argue with you, Jemma. I am not a fool; I am quite aware that you consider me beneath your contempt at the moment. But, despite what you prefer to think or believe, I am concerned for your health. I have to attend a meeting this afternoon,' he went on grimly. 'But I would rather go to it without worrying whether your desire to punish me could make you foolish enough to go out again and thoroughly exhaust yourself.'

'Then go to your meeting.' She shrugged indifferently. 'Despite what *you* seem to think, I care for this baby's health too. I shall not be leaving the yacht again today.'

'Good,' he murmured. 'And thank you. Your reassurance eases my mind.'

'You trust me to keep my word?' Surprise at his instant acquiescence coloured her tone.

Leon looked steadily at her. 'I have always trusted you, *agape mou*,' he said softly. 'I am the deceiver here, not you, remember?'

On a bleak self-mocking smile he let himself out of her room, leaving her to deal with the sudden rush of guilt she was troubled with. He trusted her. And she was already planning to break that trust.

CHAPTER TWELVE

JEMMA didn't see Leon again that day—thankfully, she told herself firmly when she found her solitary meal that evening an interminable affair where a white-coated steward served small, tempting dishes to her in a concerned effort to inspire her lost appetite.

She had eaten little lunch, had found her usual ability to fall into an undisturbed sleep for a few hours in the afternoon had deserted her, and had in the end wandered restlessly around the yacht, not quite knowing what to do with herself.

You miss him, that little voice inside her head informed her bluntly. And if you can miss him now, when you're riddled with hurt and anger at his deception, then how will you feel when all this hurt fades and you're back in England, having completely cut yourself free of him?

The hurt will never fade, she told that voice when, by ten o'clock, Leon had still not appeared and she took herself off to bed, exhausted by the see-sawing stress of her ravaged emotions. How can it when I only have to feel our son move inside me to remember how cruelly he used us?

Our son. Every time she let herself think the words, her eyes filled with the aching tears of that cruel betrayal. No daughter with blue eyes and her mother's soft mouth. No sweet little girl with golden hair or even her father's dark exotic looks.

But a son, with Leon's bottomless black eyes and charm enough to captivate anyone who came into contact with him. A boy with a sturdy build and an independent mind. Would he have any of her softer genes in him? Or would

173

he be all Greek—all Stephanades—big and strong and heart-rendingly ruthless?

She shuddered, feeling sick but not really understanding why. It wasn't as if she minded whether her baby was a boy or a girl so long as it was whole and healthy. But—

Rape, she realised. It felt like rape. As if someone had come along and coolly robbed her of the most precious part of motherhood.

And it was that which hurt her above everything else, and why she was determined to leave him. He had taken something else from her he could never give back, only this time she minded, minded so much that she could not forgive.

Sleep came suddenly, like the throwing of a switch, as if her brain had taken the decision to shut her off from the stresses of the last two days.

She slept long and deeply, waking in the morning feeling decidedly sluggish and with a banging head. Remembering she was to see the doctor this morning, she dragged herself out of bed and into the bathroom, grimacing when she caught sight of her pale, listless face. The last twenty-four hours had effectively wiped out two weeks' convalescence.

Which only helped to confirm one thing—it was the man who was her weakness, not her health.

She took her time in the shower, letting the tepid water gush over her hair and down her body for ages in the hope that the refreshing spray would disperse her headache.

It was only as she walked back into her bedroom fifteen minutes later wrapped in a towel and with her hair slicked to her skull that something about the movement of the yacht caught at her attention, and she frowned, moving to the window to glance out.

Nothing. Her body jarred on shock. She should be looking across the clear waters of the bay of Argostólion towards the misted green hills above Lixoúrion. But there was nothing in front of her but a bright, glinting stretch of water for as far as she could see.

'No,' she murmured, beginning to tremble all over. 'No!' They couldn't have moved during the night—she would have heard the engines! Been awoken by the movement! She had an appointment with the doctor! Leon could not have moved them!

Turning, she ran to her wardrobe and grabbed at the first thing that came to hand—a baggy white cotton T-shirt that finished halfway down her thighs—only belatedly remembering to add a pair of cotton briefs before she was rushing through the door.

She ran up on to the deck then stopped, her eyes gone slightly wild as she searched the far horizon for a glimpse of land. There was none. She turned, heart pumping, and ran back inside, only to skid to a halt at the open door to the main salon.

Leon was there, sitting on one of the elegant sofas, bent forward so that he could rest his elbows on his spread knees. He was wearing his grey shorts and nothing else, she noted pensively—as if the casualness of his attire was making a statement in itself.

'W-where are we?' she gasped out breathlessly.

He looked up, his eyes full of dark shadows in his grim face. 'Nowhere,' he said, looking away from her and back at his hands. 'Anywhere.' He shrugged as if he couldn't care less.

It was then she saw them spread out on the low table beside him, and her heart leapt to her throat, eyes spiralling out of focus then back in again on the items lying there. Her passport. Her wallet containing her bit of English money. Her thin roll of drachmas and, most damning of all, the envelope containing her ticket away from him.

'You went through my drawer!' she accused him hoarsely.

'I could not let you do it, Jemma. No matter how much you hate me, you need me right now. I could not let you do it,' he repeated grimly.

Her legs lost their ability to support her, and she had to feel her way to the nearest chair and drop heavily into it.

'How—how did you find out?'

'I had a man follow you yesterday, but he could not go in the travel agents and enquire which flight you had booked without drawing attention to us.' He grimaced. 'The Stephanades name is too well known on this island,' he explained. 'It could have caused quite a sensation if it had come out that my wife was trying to run away from me.'

'So you waited until I was asleep,' she whispered, 'then quietly rifled through my private things to get your information.' Her contempt showed at this latest invasion of her privacy.

Leon just shrugged. 'And what did I find?' he mocked, lancing her with a sardonic look. 'I found that my unending patience in waiting until you were asleep before trying to discover just what you were up to was a complete waste of time, because you didn't book your flight under the Stephanades name, did you? You didn't need to while your passport still bears your maiden name. You really should learn to come to terms with who you are now, *agape mou*,' he added cynically, 'for in this case just the simple mention of who you really are would have got you on the first flight off the island, instead of having to wait two whole days to do it.'

'Except that it is a name I have no wish to be associated with!' she threw bitterly at him.

'Too late,' he drawled. 'It is already yours and will remain so for the rest of your life.'

'Not if I decide otherwise.' She jumped up, disturbed by the deadly serious look in his eyes. 'There's such a thing as divorce, you know.'

'Not with me, there isn't,' he stated.

'Not until I have safely delivered your son, you mean!' Moving jerkily, she went over to the fridge to get herself a bottle of chilled water. 'After all, he is the only reason I'm here at all!'

'Not true,' he denied.

She spun on him. 'Of course it's true,' she declared, her fingers working agitatedly at the stubborn bottle-top. 'It was always true from the moment you asked the doctor back in London what the sex of our baby was! Dammit!' she sobbed out wretchedly. 'I can't do this!'

Tears of angry frustration blurring her eyes, she held the bottle out to him. Leon came to his feet and took it from her, easily twisting the cap open and pouring the water into a glass before handing it to her.

He stood, watching her gulp thirstily at the drink, then said quietly, 'I did not ask the doctor anything about the child. I only asked him about your health.'

Her angry blue eyes scoffed at him. 'Then how else would you learn the sex of our child?'

'I don't know it,' he said. 'I lied.'

Jemma went still, staring at him in stunned disbelief. Then, 'What?' she gasped.

'I lied,' he repeated flatly, taking the empty glass from her and putting it aside. 'I needed to leave Anthia and Nico with no leg to stand on, so—' he shrugged '—I lied about knowing the child's sex. It was only when I saw the effect the lie had on you that I realised how unforgivably cruel I had been by using it.'

Jemma began to shake. 'I don't believe you,' she breathed.

'I didn't think you would.' His smile was brief and rueful. 'Which is why I have not tried to tell you before now. After all, why should you believe me after the way I set you up for all of that?'

She stared into his face, looking—searching for the truth in those impossibly black eyes, then shook her head. 'You're lying now—not then,' she said, wrapping her arms about her body as if she needed their protection. 'You wouldn't dare make such a claim without being sure it was the truth because there is a fifty-fifty chance that I will give birth to a girl, and then it would be you left without a leg to stand on, looking the fool. No company, nothing.'

He had to gall to laugh, then shake his head ruefully. 'You are quite wrong, you know,' he attested. 'Personally, I couldn't give a damn what sex our child is so long as it is healthy. You see, the Leonadis Corporation is already mine. My father officially signed it over to me yesterday— with relief, I might add, because I managed to get him out of such a sticky situation without making him look like the fool. Seeing Nico taking his place was enough to give him nightmares. But Nico is his son, too. He had no wish to hurt his feelings by being forced to tell him he was not fit for the job.'

'So my feelings were sacrificed instead!'

'Now that I have no excuse for,' he quietly acknowledged.

'You hurt me!'

'Yes.' He acknowledged that also.

'You deliberately set out to use me!'

'Yes,' quietly again. 'Forgive me. Please?'

'How can I?' she cried. 'If this baby is a boy, I will never be sure when you told the truth!' Her blue eyes filled with wretched tears. 'I can never trust you again, Leon!'

Sighing, he reached for her, but she shrugged him away. 'No,' she protested. 'Don't touch me.'

When he touched her, she weakened. Hadn't she always been weak with him?

'Then at least listen to me,' he asked. 'Please, Jemma,' he begged when she went to turn away. 'Listen—just listen?

And when I have finished, if you still want to leave me I'll—arrange it.' Even Jemma in her wretchedness heard that hesitation in his voice for what it was.

She lifted her eyes to look at him. 'Another lie, Leon?' she challenged.

'No,' he denied. Then on a grimace, 'Perhaps,' he conceded. 'Letting you go is not what I want to do and, selfish swine that I am, I am not sure that I can do it just like that.' Grimly, he raked frustrated fingers through his hair. His face was pale, and she could see the strain of sleepless nights pulling at his features.

Her heart began to ache—for herself or for him she wasn't sure, but it made her want to weep. Shakily, she put up a hand to cover her eyes. 'I feel so wretched!' she choked.

'Come and sit down.' His voice sounded gruff, and the hand he curled around her arm was trembling a little. She let him lead her over to one of the soft cushioned sofas and guide her into it. Then he pulled up a matching chair and sat down in front of her, bending to place his forearms on his knees while he waited for her to get a hold of herself.

Then, 'Jemma,' he said quietly, 'I love you.'

She stiffened in instant rejection. 'You don't know the meaning of the word!' she denounced, bitterly denouncing, too, that weak flutter of joy her heart responded with.

'I thought I didn't,' he agreed. 'I thought I never wanted to know, until I met you.' His smile was heavy with irony, then was gone as he looked into her tear-washed eyes. 'But I missed you when I was in New York,' he murmured softly. 'Nothing seemed worth breaking my neck for when I did not have you to rush back to.'

'You seemed to do well enough,' she remarked, remembering the article in the newspaper that had so sung his praises.

'That is because I hardly ever went home,' he explained.

'I just bit people's heads off and made the kind of reckless decisions that should have been the finish of me.'

'Then it was lucky for you that it went the other way,' she mocked that explanation acidly.

'Yes.' He deliberately ignored her scorn. 'Then all this stuff with Nico blew up, and my father was on the phone panicking because Nico has announced his intention to marry and that stupid document he had drawn up to make me toe his line was suddenly backfiring on him because Anthia knew about it, and, although he loves her—almost to distraction—he also knows of her insane need to possess, if not for herself then for her son, anything that was once my mother's. It is not entirely greed that drives her,' he admitted. 'She was my father's first love—his only love! But he sold her out for a big purse, and if she ever forgave him for it she never forgave my mother—or me for that matter.'

Another grimace, and Jemma found herself wondering painfully what kind of childhood he must have had, with a stepmother who resented the very sight of him.

'Being well aware of this,' he went on, 'through the years, my father had been very careful never to give her the slightest hope that Nico will ever inherit anything that belongs to the Leonadis family. There are other things,' he explained. 'Other ventures which are kept entirely separate from the main corporation. Ventures my father set up and built on his own merit. Those are Nico's for the taking. He knows it—I know it! Nico was, until recently, content with what he knew was to be his. But Anthia wasn't. This chance appeared and she took it with both hands by quickly marrying Nico off and making that document known to anyone who mattered.'

For a moment, angry frustration roughened his voice. 'My father was now facing the prospect of having to make the biggest climb-down of his life by withdrawing that document. I couldn't let him do it!' he muttered. 'He is old and he is ill, and, though we may not always see eye to eye, I love him and I am proud of all he has achieved with his life. I could not let him go out on such a low light.' He took in a deep breath then let it out again. '"Marry Melva", he begged. "Marry anyone but get me out of this mess"! And I realised that there was only one woman I could think of marrying—only one woman I wanted to marry! You!' he stated huskily. 'You and only you.'

He was looking at her, willing her to lift her eyes to his, but she didn't, keeping them lowered on her twisting hands.

He sighed heavily, then went on. 'So I came back to London to see you. I meant to explain all of this to you then ask for your help—keep it all as honest as I could. But—you know how I found you, Jemma!' he declared. 'Pregnant with my child! Weakened by sickness and so obviously struggling to survive that suddenly my priorities changed! Or maybe they were only excuses in the first place, I don't know.' He shrugged. 'But from the moment I set eyes on you again it was you I was concerned about. Your health, your happiness and well-being! Blow my father, I thought to myself. He can stew for a while; Jemma needs me—and it felt so good to be needed by you,' he chanted huskily, 'that I proceeded to put the rest of it to the back of my mind because I was enjoying myself too much making up for all those miserable months in New York when I missed you so badly. I'll explain the rest of it to her tomorrow, I kept telling myself. And the tomorrow became another tomorrow and another and another because we were happy and I didn't want to spoil it with what had really become such an insignificant part of why I married you at all! Then suddenly I had run out of tomorrows!' he bit out angrily. 'And it hit me hard the morning my father came to the yacht that I had left it too late; that whatever

I said now was going to hurt you because it looked so damned calculated!'

He ran a hand over his eyes, eyes that had been alight with a burning sincerity all the way through his long explanation.

'Jemma,' he pleaded, 'you have to believe me when I say that I never wanted to hurt you. It just—reached a point where there was no other way out without hurting you! But, if you will let me, I will try my best to make it up to you.'

He didn't know it, but he had already gone a long way to doing just that. Yet—

Confused by the wrangle of emotions churning inside her, she got up and walked over to gaze out of the window.

'I lied, Jemma, about knowing the sex of our child,' he said quietly. 'My father knows I lied. I told him before I would let him sign anything over to me.'

Surprised, she glanced at him. 'And he didn't mind you lying to him in public like that?'

He shook his head. 'He only wanted to save his own face. If we have a daughter it will be my credibility placed in question, not his.'

'Which could happen if we do have a daughter,' she pointed out.

Oddly, Leon smiled. 'Actually,' he murmured rather ruefully, 'you quoted fifty-fifty odds at me on that event happening. But,' he confessed, 'I feel it only fair to warn you that there has not been a female born into the Stephanades line for five generations, which must widen the odds considerably.'

'In your favour.'

He nodded. 'Which does not help me in convincing you that I lied—does it?'

'No, it doesn't,' Jemma agreed, turning to stare at the rich blue Ionian Sea sparkling in the morning sun. Yet she was beginning to believe him. Why she was not quite sure except, perhaps, because she wanted to believe him, needed to if she was going to be able to forgive him and put all of this aside, try to pick up the pieces of their relationship from here, but...

But what? she asked herself bleakly. What exactly is it you're so upset about? A lie that, since you've been told it is a lie, has lost its power to wound? Or the fact that you trusted him so utterly that when he let you down you couldn't take it?

What has changed? What has really changed over the last twenty-four hours other than you've witnessed a more ruthless side to his character and have been made painfully aware that he is capable of going to any lengths to win?

And what else would you expect of a man like him? He's strong. So strong that even his father leans on him. *You* lean on him! You barely exist when he isn't near you—last night proved that, when you sat here on this yacht, pining for him even while you were hating him.

As she turned back to look at him, her heart gave a painful squeeze when she saw he was sitting there with his wide shoulders hunched, dark head lowered in grim contemplation of his hands again. He looked oddly vulnerable sitting there like that—cut off and alone, as perhaps, she realised, strong men had to be if they were to maintain that air of strength.

Yet she didn't like it. It hurt something precious inside her to see him like that. It wasn't the man she had come to know so well, that other warm, caring and crushingly gentle man he had always been when alone with her.

The man who claimed he loved her.

Dared she believe him? Dared she take the ultimate risk and let herself trust in that love?

She swallowed thickly, her heart beginning to drum with need and fear and a host of other emotions she could not begin to separate as, warily, she let her defences come tumbling down.

'Leon?' she asked, her tense throat working as she watched his head come up, expression carefully guarded as it focused on her. Lips dry and unsteady, she ran her tongue over them then whispered thickly, 'If I tell you I love you, will you break my heart?'

His eyes closed—on what she didn't know, but she felt the power of it wash right over her. Then he was on his feet and coming towards her. 'They say beauty is only skin-deep,' he responded huskily as he reached for her. 'But with you it glows from every living cell. Thank you. And no,' he answered her question, 'I will never break your beautiful heart. How can I, when it is so precious to me?'

'Then just hold me,' she begged. 'I need to feel you holding me.'

His body became the rock she clung to as he drew her into his arms. She wound her arms around his body, fingers splaying across the muscled blades of his shoulders, and, sighing shakily, she lifted her mouth for his kiss. He took it passionately, stirring her into bright, vibrant life as no other man had ever managed to do.

And there it was, she acknowledged from somewhere within the deep abiding warmth of his embrace. The reason why she was here at all. This man, his touch. Her catalyst. She could deny him nothing.

'It frightens me, what you do to me,' she told him breathlessly when at last he eased the hungry pressure. 'You tear my senses to shreds. I can't resist you!'

'You think it is any different for me? *Feel* me!' he commanded. 'I am trembling.' And as he pressed himself against her she could feel the tremors shaking him—even his hands as he ran them beneath her shirt, up over her hips then caressingly across the child before cupping her breasts.

'I love you, Jemma,' he declared. 'Please, whatever else you doubt about me, do not doubt my love.'

She looked up at him, blue eyes searching impassioned black ones for a hint—the slightest sign—that he was being anything but sincere. But it was all there. The man she had come to admire and respect for the strong, powerful personality he was. The man she had come to love deeply and depend upon so totally that she knew she couldn't live without him now, even if she wanted to, which she didn't. And the man she knew—had always known, no matter what else got in their way—cared for her. A care he was now insisting had turned to love. A love she did not have the strength to turn her back on, especially now when she could see it glowing warmly in his eyes.

'I do believe you,' she said at last. And she did. At last she dared to let herself believe.

'And forgive?' he asked. 'Can you do that too?'

'Oh, yes.' She smiled a wryly rueful smile. 'I can forgive you anything when you hold me like this!' she confessed.

'Then I have a better idea,' he said. 'Bed,' he decided, black eyes gleaming as he bent to swing her into his arms. 'There I can hold you much closer and for much longer and therefore receive a deeper forgiveness!'

'But—what about my appointment with the doctor?' she protested as he began striding towards the door.

'Blow the doctor!' he grunted. 'I need you right now more than you need him!'

'But—!'

He kissed her, his mouth covering her own to muffle out any other protest she might have been considering. And the next time she came up for air he was lowering her on to her own bed, still rumpled from last night's sleep.

He left her to go and close and lock the cabin door. When he back back she was smiling ruefully. 'Who has the pass key?' she asked.

'I do, of course,' he grinned, and came to lie beside her.

Strangely, the fever of passion had passed, leaving them without its raging flame to hide behind. A silence settled around them. Leon seemed suddenly extraordinarily concerned in smoothing her long hair out behind her. And she found a similar interest in the absent combing of the silk dark hair at his chest.

'Where would you like to live?' he asked suddenly. 'London? Athens? New York?'

She glanced at him from beneath her lashes. 'You choose,' she offered. 'I have no personal preference so long as we are together.'

'Mmm, my sentiments exactly,' he agreed, brushing a kiss across her cheek. 'But we have to make our base somewhere, if only until the baby is born. After that, you both travel with me wherever I go,' he decreed, adding grimly, 'I do not ever want to go through another separation like the age I spent in New York without you.'

Jemma bit down lightly on her bottom lip, then said softly, 'I missed you too. A million times I wanted to call you up and tell you how frightened and alone I felt. But—' She sighed, unable to explain.

'But you could not because you did not think I cared enough,' he finished for her.

She shook her head. 'No,' she denied. 'I knew you cared, Leon. I never, ever doubted that you cared for me. But caring was not enough—not with a baby coming and you being so very against marriage. It wouldn't have been fair on you, would it?'

'And was it fair on you,' he posed, 'that you should have to cope alone?'

She shrugged. 'That business with Cassie and Josh obsessed me. I just couldn't see you reacting any differently than he had.'

'Did you do it deliberately?' he asked.

'No!' she denied, her eyes jerking up to clash angrily with his. 'How could you think I would do such a thing?'

'I did not,' he denied. 'I just asked the question, that's all. And you answered it.' He gave a 'that's the end of that' shrug.

'You believe me—just like that?' she choked.

His eyes, sombre beneath their lazy lids, held on to hers. 'Did you not know?' he mocked her gently. 'I would believe you if you told me the world was square. You are the most honest person I know, *agape mou*.'

'Oh,' she said, and for some stupid reason felt tears press at her eyes again.

'Don't.' Sighing, he pulled her to him, curving his body protectively around her. 'Don't cry,' he commanded. 'God, you have no idea what it does to me to see you unhappy! Of course I know you did not deliberately set me up!' he scolded. 'I can do simple arithmetic too, you know! And, even if you had done it deliberately,' he then added wryly, 'I would not have cared less. My life is incomplete without you, my darling,' he murmured softly, coming to lean over her so that she could see the sincerity burning in his eyes. 'I learned that in New York.' He kissed her gently. 'Here I am complete.' He kissed her again. 'With you—anywhere with you.' Another kiss, soft and lingering. 'You,' he murmured. 'You—you—you.'

Modern Romance™
...seduction and
passion guaranteed

Tender Romance™
...love affairs that
last a lifetime

Medical Romance™
...medical drama
on the pulse

Historical Romance™
...rich, vivid and
passionate

Sensual Romance™
...sassy, sexy and
seductive

Blaze Romance™
...the temperature's
rising

30 new titles every month.

Live the emotion

Sensual Romance™
4 brand new titles each month
...sassy, sexy and seductive.
Available on subscription every month from the Reader Service™
GEN/21/RS2

Medical Romance™
6 brand new titles each month
...medical drama
on the pulse.
Available on subscription every month
from the Reader Service™
GEN/03/RS2

Tender Romance™
6 brand new titles each month
...love affairs
that last a lifetime
Available on subscription every month
from the Reader Service™
GEN/02/RS2